UnHoly

Ghost

A Dr. Kel McKelvey Novel

Thomas Holland

For TPH and DSH

Other Books in the Kel McKelvey Series:

One Drop of Blood

KIA

What others are saying about the Kel McKelvey Series

"Block out some time—you won't want to put it down. Engaging characters, high-octane suspense, and Holland's remarkable storytelling skills combine . . . to provide a terrific read."

—Jan Burke, author of *Bloodlines* and *Bones*

"An exciting new series that looks at cold cases with lightning heat and speed—a fascinating read."

—Linda Fairstein, author of *Death Dance*

"A riveting read . . . This is an engrossing thriller that immerses the reader in an historical injustice that only *One Drop of Blood* can resolve."

—Dr. Michael Baden and Linda Kenney, authors of *Remains Silent*

A BRIEF HISTORICAL NOTE

The German POW camps at Tonkawa, Oklahoma, and Fort Chaffee, Arkansas, were real. The German POWs held there were real. The *Heilige Geist* that dwelt among them was real.

Real German POWs died at the hands of their real fellow soldiers at those camps. Their names were Johannes Kunze and Hans Geller. There were others as well. The real killers, some of them anyhow, were identified, tried, and convicted. A real Leon Jaworski saw to that. Some of them really were hanged in an elevator shaft at Fort Leavenworth; they are buried today at the Fort Leavenworth Military Prison Cemetery in Kansas. Really.

The U.S. Army really made a conscientious and thorough effort to recover and identify this country's war dead in Europe after World War Two. It did the same in the Pacific, and after the Korean War, and following the Vietnam War. The effort was real, but the characters and their actions depicted in this story are not.

The U.S. Department of Defense continues to make a conscientious and thorough effort to recover and identify its war dead from all past military conflicts. The U.S. Army Central Identification Laboratory also really did exist, but it is no more. This is not a story of the CILHI's past staff or their actions and shouldn't be construed as such. A vestige, or version, of the lab exists today as part of the Defense POW/MIA Accounting Agency. This story also has nothing to do with the current lab, its staff, or the Department of Defense.

"History repeats itself, but in such cunning disguise that we never detect the resemblance until the damage is done."

Sydney J. Harris, American Journalist, 1986

PROLOGUE

Metz, France
Friday, October 4, 1946

Second Lieutenant Trevor Smith figured he had no room to complain. Not really.

It was his twenty-second birthday, and while there were a good thousand other places he'd rather be spending the day than in the bombed-out rubble of Metz, he also knew that the trade-off was well worth it. He'd missed the shooting; he'd missed the bombing; he'd missed the maim and the malice and the killing. All he had to do in return was spend two years in postwar Europe, traveling around with a graves registration team digging up skeletons. Ghoulish, certainly, but it sure beat the six-ounce piece of red-hot shrapnel that his cousin Riley caught in Okinawa.

"L T," Technical Sergeant Jeff Ludlow called out as he stepped over some rubble and approached the officer, "Lieutenant Smith. Sir."

Smith visibly snapped out of his thoughts with a shudder and looked up at his young sergeant. "What is it, Sarge? You got us something?" They'd spent the previous three days running down various leads in an attempt to find the remains of two soldiers last seen in early 1945 near the north end of the cathedral. They'd interviewed a dozen people including a priest, the burgermeister, and the town's former police chief. None of them had any information on missing Americans that was proving very useful, and Smith was ready to call it a day. If they left now, he could be back to what passed for his office before dark, and he could have his report typed up in time to get an early dinner and treat his twenty-two-year-old body to a glass or two of wine and maybe even an early bedtime.

"Yes, sir. Sure do, sir," Sergeant Ludlow called out. The enormous smile on his face validated his belief that he was the bearer of good news. "I think we got our guys. Both of them by the looks of it."

"Is that right, Sergeant? And what makes you think that?" Smith liked Ludlow, but he also knew that the kid was quick to believe whatever an informant told him, especially if the informant was young and female and possessed of the right fleshy topography. "What's her name this time? Maria? Greta? Haven't had a Simone in a while."

"Now, L T, you know that ain't fair."

"It's not, huh? Okay, in that case, tell me what leads you to think you've found our guys?"

"Work, hard work, and more hard work, sir," Ludlow replied, tapping his right temple with his index finger and exposing more than the usual allocation of dirt under the nail. "Not to mention the superior intelligence and uncanny intuition possessed by all of the Ludlow men."

"It's almost legendary, Jeff. Almost," Trevor Smith smiled. He leaned back into the thin sheet-metal back of the passenger seat of his jeep and canted his head slightly to the side. "Why don't you humor me and tell me about all this hard work of yours?"

"I can do better than that, Lieutenant. If you'd be so good as to follow me, I'll show you."

The young lieutenant paused and then swung his legs over the side of the jeep. As he stood up, he reached behind him and grabbed his steel pot; more than once it had protected him from falling debris while searching amid the crumbling rubble that was postwar France and Germany. He put the helmet on and adjusted his web belt, making sure that the flap of his holster was buttoned-down and secure. Having no reason to ever draw his .45, Smith lived in fear of losing it somewhere and having to fill out all of the paperwork that would be required. He'd actually taped the pistol into the holster when he first arrived in country, until he discovered that in the seeping dampness of wintertime France, the tape was a recipe for impossible-to-explain rust and corrosion. So instead, he simply checked it frequently—and worried. "Move out and draw fire, Sergeant. The show's all yours."

Tech Sergeant Jeff Ludlow almost sprinted around the side of the cathedral, jumping from mound of rubble to mound of rubble, slowing only to verify that his lieutenant was still in tow. Ludlow had been in what he liked to call the *Ghoul Corps* for almost two years and had personally located and recovered the earthly remains of over a 150 missing men, and while everyone else in his Army Graves Registration company had quickly developed malignant cases of the postwar Who-Gives-A-Shits, Ludlow fed off the work to a point where his exuberance and dedication were at times almost annoying.

As Trevor Smith rounded the corner of the cathedral, he saw Ludlow talking animatedly with the two privates that made up the muscle part of their team. Both were standing knee-deep in a freshly dug hole, leaning on the idiot ends of their shovels, looking blank-eyed and somewhat slack-jawed at their sergeant. The hole they were digging was located in what had probably once been a flat, grassy area in the shadow of the massive rear wall of the cathedral. Smith couldn't help but think that it must have once been a good place for a picnic, a lazy afternoon with a pretty girl with winsome eyes and a sugary voice, but which now was little more than a bare patch of ground best suited for stockpiling brick and rubble and the odd length of rusty plumbing.

As Lieutenant Smith closed the distance, he could take in the full-bodied flavor of Ludlow's words. Belying the boyish freckles, his sergeant had a tongue like a jagged strip of corrugated roofing tin, and now, interlaced with the predictable obscenities necessary to motivate the two privates, Sergeant Ludlow was trying to convey the commonsense utility—if not decorum—of not standing on top of the corpses being disinterred. Neither private seemed to comprehend why this should be a topic of discussion, and Ludlow was forced to take one of them by the back of his shirt collar and physically pull him out of the hole as if he were landing a hundred-and-fifty-pound catfish into his Jon boat.

The smell creeping out of the grave gained Smith's respect as he got closer. It wasn't overpowering the way it sometimes was, but it certainly was attention getting in the late-afternoon stillness. It had his attention, anyway. Smith had done enough of these to know what to expect even before getting close enough to see past the lip of the hole; waxy, moist, vaguely recognizable human remains shrouded with the muddy remnants of a military uniform.

He wasn't surprised.

"Sir," Sergeant Ludlow said as he pulled an elderly man to the forefront. The man had been standing a few steps away, watching quietly, and Smith hadn't noticed him as he approached. He was bone-thin, with a translucent complexion that looked almost like sculpted tallow, and his clothes were too large and showed signs of repeated darning. "Sir, this is Herr Belke. A despicable little sieg-heil of a Nazi if ever there was one—*ain't that right, Adolph*?" Ludlow said, directing the question at the uncomprehending little man. Among his other skills, Ludlow spoke passable beer-hall German and assisted in all the interrogations, but he'd developed the habit of calling all adult German men *Adolph*.

Herr Belke smiled unknowingly and nodded in a way calculated to win favor.

"My compliments to the company you keep, Sergeant. I assume your buddy here has some information for us, or is he simply a bystander?" Smith asked.

"Yes, sir, he does, sir. He's the one who pointed out this spot here. Fact, Jonesy says—"

"Where is Corporal Jones, anyway?" the lieutenant interrupted.

"Ahh," Ludlow said, reluctantly nodding in the general direction of what had once been downtown, "Well, sir . . . ahhh, he's off taking down some more statements . . . from some informants we met. I told him we could finish up here."

Smith nodded his head slowly. "I'll tell you, the two of you about wear me out. Let's hope they're prettier than the last ones he got statements from. Go on."

"Well, sir, according to my buddy Adolph here, he and a couple of other brave homeland heroes found the remains of a couple of our Joes after one of our recon teams got whacked by a machine gun hidden in the cathedral. They buried them in a bomb crater here in the churchyard. Of course, they couldn't be bothered to mark the grave— ain't that right?" Ludlow smiled and nodded at the old man. "Right? *Nicht wahr?*"

Herr Belke smiled and returned the nod.

"I don't suppose he wrote down their names; got their ranks; anything like that?" Smith phrased his question as a statement.

"He didn't get any names. He says some German officers took the dog tags, but he's sure they're American GIs, and he says this is the same bomb crater where they were buried."

"And you believe him?"

"Affirmative, L T. And if you look close," Sergeant Ludlow pointed toward the open pit, "you can see enough of the uniform to confirm that—at least you could until the Chucklehead Twins here walked all over the bodies." He flashed the two privates a look that promised them trouble later. He adjusted his belt and looked at his lieutenant. "Adolph also says that one of the two was a medic. Big red cross painted on his steel pot and all, though apparently not big enough to keep one of their fine *Volkssturmers* from shooting his ass—*Jawohl*, right Herr Belke? Piss on that old Geneva Convention, right? Understand? *Verstehen Sie* piss?"

"*Ja, Ja*," the old man nodded agreeably. "*Jawohl.*"

Lieutenant Smith kneeled down on the hummock formed by the back dirt from the grave, and peered closer into the hole. He cracked his lips and tried to breathe inconspicuously through his mouth to avoid the ripening smell. "Two of them?"

"Yes, sir." Tech Sergeant Ludlow knelt down beside his lieutenant, and if he knew that Smith was trying to avoid the smell, he had a good NCO's diplomatic skill to let it pass without comment. "Kinda in a sixty-nine position; one on top of the other. There's the feet of one of them," he replied as he used his hand to outline the body in the air. "See it? Legs, hips, you can see his web belt poking out of the dirt. Arms there and there. He's face down."

"Yeah. I can see that one. How do you know there're two?"

"Well, before these two made such a mess of it, you could see another arm down there. He's face down, too, I think. Could be more, I guess, but my good buddy Adolph here says there's only two." Ludlow looked up at the old man. "And you wouldn't lie to me would you, Adolph? No, of course not." The sergeant shook his head slowly. "*Nein?*"

The old man hesitated, unsure of what was expected. Slowly he began shaking his head, synchronizing his movements with that of the American. "*Nein,*" he replied in concert.

Trevor Smith looked up at the old man and then back into the pit. He spit off to the side as he pressed a dirt clod between his fingers and let it crumble while he thought about what to do next. "Face down. Some honor for a warrior." He picked up another dirt clod and began crumbling it. "Only two, huh? You think there might be more in this area?"

"Dunno L T. You want to keep searching?"

"No. We came looking for two, and we found two," Trevor Smith said as he closed his eyes and sighed. When he opened them, he stood up and dusted his hands on his thighs and verified that his sidearm was still in its holster. He looked up. There was a front moving in, and the temperature would be dropping soon. "Let's get these men dug up and out of this goddamn shithole of a country, Sergeant. It's time they go home."

"Yes, sir, Lieutenant. I thought you'd say that."

CHAPTER 1

Fort Chaffee Reservation, Sebastian County, Arkansas

Friday, October 24

Byno Pruitt had been a big man once; not a giant, but big, and corked together with sinew and braided gristle. He was still tall, but now had the odd shape that comes from muscle gone soft and tired of resisting gravity. His broad forehead was cracked and creased from too many days staring across the glare of a bulldozer's throbbing hood, and his eyes had a perk and spark to them that spoke more to some long-lost good breeding and not from any residual root intelligence.

He pulled up the sleeve of his insulated overalls and looked at the scratched crystal of his Timex watch. In the forty-five minutes he'd been shut down, the temperature had continued to drop like spit off a sunny balcony. The Channel Ten AccuDoppler weatherman last night had predicted the season's first freezing rain by Saturday night, unusual for Arkansas this early, very unusual, and the jagged, leading edge of the cold front was already blowing through in seeming validation. The sun would set in another hour, and then it'd really be cold as a wedge. He couldn't remember an October like this in a long time.

Byno Pruitt had half a mind to fire up the big Caterpillar D-9, level the rest of humped-up rock and spoil, and get out of the cold. The longer he sat, the more he regretted ever calling the straw boss on the radio and reporting the find. He could almost predict the tangle-footed outcome. First, he'd spend an hour sitting on a ball-numbing-cold piece of machinery waiting for the boss to drive out to the site from his meeting with the sub-contractor in Fort Smith—which wasn't a meeting as much as it was an excuse to sit in some place warm, drink coffee, and smart-tongue some large breasted waitress while the worker bees—working Joes like Byno—froze their tails off. Second, when the boss did show up, he'd cuss a well-digger's blue streak and somehow contrive a way to blame it all on Byno. And third, in the end, everyone would turn a blind eye and let the big Cat's shiny steel blade eliminate the problem anyway—something Byno could take care of by himself without the delay and without frosting his jewels any longer than need be.

He was reaching for the switch to re-start the bulldozer and resolve his problem when he saw the big, red Dodge King Cab come bumping over the hummocks and ruts. He waited and watched as it pulled up alongside him. Byno would have clubbed his minister with a stick to have a truck that shiny.

"Aw, goddammit to all hell, Byno," Frank Kenner was already yelling as his door exploded open, and he sprang out like a white dove from a magician's hat. "Bones? Bones! What is it you don't un'erstand, son? What is it you just don't un'erstand? We're already four good godly damn weeks behind schedule, and the big boss is 'bout ready to chew me a new one as is, and now you go and find this . . . these . . . aw, goddammit, Byno, goddammit. You're out here by yourself, son. Ain't nobody around. What was you thinkin' callin' me on the walkie-talkie and mentionin' bones?"

"Don't blame me, Frank. I don't do no thinkin', now you know that, but this here Cat don't always understand company policy the way me and you do." The words hung in fat clouds of foggy breath.

"You know what this means, don't you? You know what this means? I had this happen once on a highway project over by Lavaca. The shit got wound around the axle so bad that we had to shut the whole goddamn project down for three months while a bunch of damn college kids spent the summer diggin' the place all the hell up with friggin' toothpicks and little-bitty mascara brushes."

Byno Pruitt climbed down from the deck of his bulldozer. He wiped the glisten from his nose with the back of his jersey glove and then crossed his arms and snugged his hands under his armpits for warmth as he walked over to Kenner. "I hear ya, Frank, I hear ya, but don't be jumpin' the gun here. There ain't no guarantee that it'll come to that, is there? Maybe we're mistaken. You with me, Frank? You're right, I was alone, and I could have figured this out, but I'm also not takin' this shit on all by myself."

"What you sayin'?"

"I ain't sayin' nothin', but I am pointin' out that it sure is hard to see from up there on the deck of that D-9—you with me here?" He smiled and smacked his lips as if his tongue were coated with butter. "I mean, the light's startin' to fade and all. Just gimme the word . . ."

Frank Kenner paused while he searched Pruitt's broad, pie-pan-shaped face. They formed an unspoken understanding. "I'm with you, Byno," he said slowly. "I'm with you, but I can't form'ly tell you that, un'erstand? I'm tellin' you we're behind schedule, and we need this field leveled out. That's all I'm tellin' you. Now, how some crazy-ass dozer operator like you interprets that when I drive off is clean outta my control. We might have us a misunderstandin'; those things happen. That'd be all it was, just an honest miscommunication. No harm intended; assumin' anyone ever found out and all. We fishin' with the same set of hip waders here, Byno?"

Byno Pruitt smiled. He gave a quick nod of his head and knocked a wallop of mud off one of his boots before he climbed back on board the track of his dozer. "That's all I needed to hear. Light's fadin', boss man, and I got to smooth this here field out," he said as he settled into the seat, worked the levers clear of the cold, and started the engine. "Like you told me, I still need to level some of them ruts and all. Hope I understood properly." There was a belch of diesel exhaust as he canted the blade edge to take a deeper bite into the soil. That's when Byno Pruitt saw his foreman kneel down by the last cut.

Frank Kenner tugged off the glove on his right hand and poked at the clumped dirt and shattered rock and broken bone fragments with one of his stubby pink fingers.

"Don't pay none to be lookin' so damn close, Frank," Byno Pruitt yelled down over the top of the dozer blade. "You just go and let it be, now. This whole field will be slick as a gut in an hour."

Frank Kenner didn't answer immediately. He slowly stood up and backed away a step, a strange look on his face as he turned what appeared to be a clump of dirt over in his hands.

"Frank?" Pruitt yelled again. The big engine throbbed and the ground shook in patient anticipation.

Frank Kenner looked up at the big yellow Caterpillar dozer and its operator. "Shut it off, Byno," he yelled. "Shut the dang thing off."

CHAPTER 2

Fort Chaffee Reservation, Sebastian County, Arkansas

Tuesday, October 28

Frank Kenner sat in his truck drinking coffee from a dented aluminum thermos and chain-eating small donuts from a cardboard box as he watched. The front of his brown, insulated coveralls was blanketed with a snowfall of white powdered sugar that he made no attempt to disturb or even rearrange. The pickup's engine was running, for warmth, and from time to time he cracked the side window long enough to vent the stale air and unfog the sweating windows. He had a Porter Wagoner CD playing; a homemade compilation that was more scratches than guitar licks. Porter was singing, "The Farmer and the Lord."

It was almost ten o'clock, and the kid from the university had promised him they'd be finished before noon today. Of course he'd also promised they'd be finished before dark yesterday, and now he was back with two of his students, laying on their bellies, scratching away with their little trowels and what looked to Kenner like sharpened Popsicle sticks; occasionally sitting up to write something down on a clipboard or drop something into a brown paper bag or snap off some flash pictures. Still, all things considered, Frank Kenner couldn't complain. The truck was warm, the donuts good, the music inspirational, and, best of all, one of the students had a butt on her that Kenner wouldn't have let out in public if it had been attached to his daughter. When Byno's bulldozer had turned up the skeleton last Friday, Kenner could do little more than envision a whole month's shutdown of a project already soggy with red ink, but what with the weather turning and the holidays coming on and all, a day-and-a-half delay wasn't much to complain about given the goat rope it might have been. He'd seen these things drag on for months sometimes. Instead, the Sebastian County coroner apparently had enough juice with somebody that he'd arranged to get these three archeology kids down from the university up in Fayetteville. If everything went as planned, they'd be finished by noon and Frank Kenner could have his boys back to work by early afternoon; tomorrow at the latest. He couldn't complain.

Kenner took another noisy slurp of coffee and swallowed another miniature donut whole as he watched the kid who was the leader of the archeologists stand up and bow a kink out of his back. The leader gave the student with the nice ass a few words of instruction and adjusted the frayed bill of his New England Patriots ball cap before he turned and walked toward Kenner's pickup and opened the door.

"Cold enough for ya?" Frank Kenner said with a spray of powdered sugar that cascaded down the front of his coveralls and collected into tiny drifts amid the folds and creases of cloth. "Ain't never seen it this cold in Arkansas in October. Course it'll be eighty degrees by next week—you just watch. If you don't like the weather in Arkansas, you just wait and it'll change. Surely will. So tell me, y'all 'bout fixin' to be finished out there, I hope? I'm way behind schedule as is, and this sure ain't helpin' me none." He popped another donut. Porter and Tammy Wynette had begun a crackling duet of "Two Story House."

"About," Pat Trader answered as he climbed into the passenger side of Kenner's truck and quickly shut the door. He was red-haired and raw-boned, with a complexion that freshened angrily in the cold and the popping wind. He was forty-two but looked half of that, and when he'd accepted an assistant professorship at the University of Arkansas three years earlier, he became the first male in his family for four generations that had failed to find a permanent calling in law enforcement, and the first to sojourn out of Boston for more than an extended weekend of camping in the Berkshires. Now he settled into the cold vinyl seat of Kenner's truck and held his hands against the warm air blasting from the heater vent before responding. "We got the skeleton out of the ground and bagged up. They need to finish up some of their notes, and make sure they get all the photographs we need." He bobbed and weaved his head to better locate a clear spot in the fogged windshield from which he could watch his two graduate students finish their digging.

"Coffee?" Kenner offered. He nodded his head at the thermos lying on the seat between them. "I don't got an extra cup, but I'm about finished with this here one. Ain't the best, but it'll warm up the business, if you know what I mean."

"No thanks."

"Tiny donut?"

"That either. Thanks anyhow."

"They're good."

"No. Thanks, though."

"You can eat 'em with one bite. I do."

"That's the best kind. No thanks, though."

Kenner shrugged. "So, what's the verdict out there? Is it *Po-co-hantas* or *Gee-ronnie-mo?*"

"Verdict? The verdict's neither. The verdict is that I think you were right all along, and the coroner was wrong. That isn't a Native American skeleton, Mr. Kenner, and I don't think it's an early unmarked historical grave either. In fact, I'm sure of it." He rubbed his hands together and blew on them before stuffing them into the waist pockets of his jacket. His gaze was fixed on the spot where his students were finishing up the last of their notes and collecting their gear.

"Yeah?" Kenner said slowly, visions of more delays and down-days beginning to dance anew in his head. He popped another powdered donut into his mouth and chewed it deliberately as he smeared a circular opening in the foggy windshield in front of him and peered out, matching the angle of his gaze to that of the archaeologist seated next to him. "So . . . what exactly would you be sayin'?"

Pat Trader paused and weighed his response before replying. He shrugged slightly, maybe as a comment on the situation or maybe a shudder from the cold. "I guess what I'm saying, Mr. Kenner," he finally responded, "is that the coroner here was doing some very wishful thinking when he contacted us."

Frank Kenner peered out his windshield again and then looked back at the archaeologist. He swallowed his donut. "How come you figure that?"

"I think you were right to contact the police last week. I think you made the right call all along." Pat Trader turned his look from the windshield and engaged the older man's eyes. "I guess what I'm saying is, this is no case for a college professor."

CHAPTER 3

Sarajevo, Bosnia

Wednesday, October 29

"Well, Dr. McKelvey, I heard a rumor you were here, but I was startin' to think it wasn't true."

Dr. Robert Dean McKelvey was sitting in an unpadded wooden chair, about to give in to the effects of jet lag, when he heard the voice behind him. He recognized the soft-edged Virginia drawl of Thomas Pierce, director of the Armed Forces DNA Lab and one of his favorite people, and roused from his stupor. "Hey yourself," he replied as he stood up and shook hands. He couldn't help noticing that Pierce was smartly dressed and creased like a brand-new road map—the imprint of twenty-five years in the military that even three years of civilian life couldn't erase. In contrast, McKelvey looked as if he'd just taken a long nap in a rented cement mixer. His khaki pants were creased in long diagonals and his blue shirt and blazer had an unappetizing patina that made him resemble an antique chair in need of refinishing.

Pierce nodded his thanks to the man who'd led him into the room—an ingot of Slavic pig iron wearing a chocolate-brown suit and a bright purple tie. The man nodded back and then left, closing the door behind him.

"See you met Igor," McKelvey said, nodding at the door as if the man were still standing there for reference.

"Is that really his name?"

"Nope, but I couldn't pronounce his real name on a dare." The man's name had clusters of *z*'s and *v*'s that McKelvey's thick Arkansas tongue couldn't even start to wrap itself around.

Pierce pulled up a chair next to McKelvey's and sat down. He slapped him on the knee. "We missed you during the lab visits. Where've you been?" Pierce asked. Both men were part of a scientific advisory group asked by the U.S. State Department to review the work being done in the former Yugoslavia to identify the victims of ethnic cleansing. Dr. Pierce and two other DNA experts had spent the week traveling to the several labs recently set up in the area, while Kel—only impatient school teachers and even less-patient policemen holding small notebooks ever called him Robert—had been asked to evaluate the field recoveries. Now Pierce and he were scheduled for a close-out protocol meeting with the Bosnian Minister of Justice to discuss their observations.

"Yeah, where haven't I been is a better question," Kel replied. "They figure I don't even know how to spell DNA, so I've been makin' the grand tour of mass graves. Bosnia, Serbia, Croatia, Kosovo. If there's a dead body, I think I've seen it this week."

Pierce nodded. "And I bet some of them look better than you. No offense, but you look like hell."

"Don't start," Kel laughed. "Took me forty-nine hours to get here from Hawaii."

"That was a week ago. Besides, I'd think you'd be used to that sort of thing by now. That's almost a commuter flight for you, isn't it?"

"Just about. The problem is that it took my luggage fifty hours to get here, and it's been followin' me around for over a week. It's managed to stay one town behind me the whole time. They tell me that I'm supposed to finally get it tonight, just in time to go home."

Pierce nodded again and looked at McKelvey's clothes. "Wasn't goin' to say anythin'."

"Don't have to. I know. Believe me. After dinner each night I go to my room and wash everythin' in the sink and then sit around buck naked all night hopin' it'll all dry by mornin'."

"Wow. Thanks for that image," Pierce responded and slapped McKelvey on the knee again.

"You're welcome, and for the record, cotton doesn't dry in this country this time of year. It just sort of . . . malts."

"The imagery only gets better." Pierce looked back at the door as if to determine how much time they had before their meeting with the Minister. "So, tell me, is this another avoid-Colonel-Boschet trip again? Didn't you volunteer for that mission to Iraq last year?"

"Yeah, I did, but no." Kel smiled. "I promised the wife no more axis-of-evil trips for a while. Hell, I've made peace with my demons. Demon. Botch-it and I are like that," he said as he held up two crossed fingers. Botch-it was the nickname given to Kel's commander at the U.S. Army Central Identification Laboratory in Hawaii—the CILHI—Colonel Peter Boschet. Kel's relationship with him had started out badly and soured steadily over the last several years; so much so that Kel had taken to assigning himself to almost any mission that would put miles between him and Hawaii. "We're tight."

"Bullshit."

"You don't cuss."

"That's not cussin'. That's being descriptive."

"No, really. We've developed a good workin' relationship. In fact, I so impressed him with the unit's Diversity Plan that he forced me to write a while ago, that he tasked me to develop the command's Balanced Workforce Strategy for him."

Pierce burst out laughing. "I know. I won't say who, but somebody in the lab sent us a bootleg copy a couple of weeks ago. It's a joke, right?"

"Nope."

"C'mon, you didn't really get the personnel office to advertise for trained monkeys?"

"*Ateles paniscus*, actually. Spider Monkeys preferred. No prosimians need apply."

"No way."

"Way."

"How?"

"Shit. Like anyone in the personnel office reads Latin. They thought it was some sort of college degree. Like *magna cum gorilla*."

"But Colonel Boschet?"

"Shit, like he can even read English. All I had to do was go in all hang-dog like and tell him that I couldn't make the deadline he'd given me; told him I needed more time. He felt so magnanimous grantin' me an extension, that he never even read the damn thing."

"I thought you said you'd made peace with your demons?"

"Peace takes many forms, my friend," Kel replied.

The door to the room opened.

"Gentlemen," Igor in the brown suit said. "If you please. The Minister will see you now."

CHAPTER 4

Clayton, Missouri

Monday, March 20, 1944

"Look at you," Alice Porter said, flicking at some imagined lint on his sleeve. "Don't you look so handsome in your uniform? All the young ladies must want to eat you up with a shiny spoon."

Bill Porter blinked slowly and sighed patiently, dropping his suitcase to his side as he hugged his mother. It was his first day of a two-week leave, and he was reasonably sure it would seem more like six weeks before it was over. "Why else would I have signed up in the army if not to attract a prospective wife?" he responded.

His mother pushed back from him, holding on to his shoulders. She smelled of lilac, and talcum, and pumpkin-pie spice. "Now you. Don't you tease me."

"Me? Tease you? Never," he said, taking her head in his hands and kissing her on the forehead. He was a spare man, just a half-head taller than his mother, but solid and honestly formed. His hair was the color of candle soot, shiny and thick, and he was constantly battling a five o'clock shadow. His grey eyes had the tendency to reflect the color in the room, causing them to shift and shimmer and to give people the impression that his mood was mercurial when in fact he was remarkably even tempered. "My getting married is definitely not a teasing matter. At least not as long as you and Mrs. Grant continue to scheme."

"Oh, quiet. We do no such thing." Her face flushed red. "Now come along to the kitchen and have something to eat. You've gone and gotten yourself so skinny I hardly recognize you."

"And here I thought I looked handsome."

"Your uniform looks handsome," Alice Porter responded as she pinched a fold in her son's sleeve and led him into the kitchen. "You, you look skinny."

"Too skinny for little Mary Grant?" His eyes reflected the sunny yellow of his mother's apron.

"Too skinny for anyone. And she's not so little anymore, by the way. And her mother will tell you the same thing. Now sit."

"Now I'm worried. I don't want Mrs. Grant thinking I'm too skinny for her daughter." He draped his uniform jacket over the back of a chair, loosened his tie, sat down at the kitchen table, and rolled his shirt sleeves before pulling a large plate of biscuits over in front of him.

"Miriam Grant should feel blessed if my son even took the time to look in the general direction of her daughter, and that's the Lord's truth," Alice Porter said over her shoulder as she poured a glass of buttermilk. She returned the milk bottle back to the ice box and placed the glass on the table. "But you eat up just the same."

"Don't worry about that, Mrs. Porter," he replied as he mortared up a biscuit half with a thick slather of pale oleo. "By the time I report back for duty in two weeks, I'm sure I won't be able to even button up my handsome uniform. Even Mary Grant and her mother—"

"Oh, mercy, my old head is getting so that I can't keep a thought in it long enough to make it worth putting there," Alice Porter said as she hurried down the short hallway to the front door. She returned quickly, carrying a cream-colored envelope with a small, oval window in the front. She held it out ahead of her like a relay baton while she walked. "Mercy, mercy, mercy. I was so excited about seeing your pretty face that I completely forgot. This arrived for you about an hour ago. It looks very official."

Bill Porter took it from his mother and smiled. "It looks very Western Union to me, mother."

"You don't think they want to send you to Guadalcanal, or one of those awful places, do you? I see those places on the newsreels. They look so awful. Just dreadful. I won't let them send my little boy to one of those places."

"I might be wrong, but I don't think Western Union much cares to send me anywhere."

"Hush. You know what I mean. The War Department, that's who I mean."

"I seriously doubt they do either, mother," he laughed. "From what I read in the newspapers, the War Department actually aims to win the war. I'd only be lethal to the Japs if I happened to be wearing one of their handsome uniforms." He wiped a spit of jelly off of a butter knife and used it to slit the end of the envelope. He smiled and winked at his mother as he extracted and unfolded the telegraph. "More than likely, they just realized that someone was crazy enough to grant me a commission and they want to try and pull it back before Mr. Roosevelt finds out and heads begin to roll."

"Or just maybe Mr. Roosevelt came to the realization that my son would make a good general." She smiled at her response until her eyes registered the strange look on his face as he read. "Oh, Lord," she said. "It's so, isn't it? You're going to one of those awful places, aren't you?"

Bill Porter screwed his eyes into a squint as he reread the telegraph for the second time. He nodded at her, though hardly perceptively, and dug into the strips of words a third time.

"Is it that Guadalcanal place? Lord have mercy."

"Maybe worse," he responded quietly, his nodding growing in amplitude as he read. "Maybe worse than that."

"Worse than Guadalcanal? Mercy, Lord. Where could that be?"

Captain Bill Porter looked up into his mother's soft, powder-blue eyes. "Camp Chaffee, Arkansas," he said.

CHAPTER 5

U.S. Army Central Identification Laboratory, Hawaii

Friday, October 31

"This time—for once—I'm going to talk and you're going to listen. You copy that?" Colonel Peter Boschet enunciated slowly in a manner that he thought would pass for grit. He had his face screwed up into a pointed knot, an involuntary gesture that seemed to accompany any attempts at thinking, but had the unfortunate side effect of making him resemble a large rat getting up the courage to gnaw through a concrete block. Colonel Boschet, or *Botch-It* as he was known to most of the staff, had been the commander of the U.S. Army's Central Identification Laboratory for three very long years, and, thanks to branch assignment officers at the Pentagon, who knew a good joke when they saw it, and who also were happy to keep him assigned to an island in the middle of the Pacific, he would remain the commander for at least another twelve months. "You understand?" he repeated. "I'm talking; you're listening. I'm in send mode, and you're in receive mode. Copy that?" He sat up straight in his chair and looked at the scientist facing him.

Kel stared back.

"I said, d'you read me?" Boschet repeated. This time his eyes flicked to Les Neep, his civilian deputy, sitting next to McKelvey, and then back to the scientist. Boschet often used Neep as a translator when talking to McKelvey.

Les Neep cleared his throat and wagged his head back and forth in an attempt to get McKelvey's attention. He cleared his throat louder. When it failed to attract McKelvey's attention, he spoke up. "Ah, Kel, the commander is . . . ah . . . I think he's waiting for you to respond."

Kel's attention had drifted up to a flat-screen television mounted in the corner of the room. A fat man was behind a counter with a hot plate, stir frying what looked to be asparagus, and a woman with enormous teeth was very excited about what the man was doing. Botch-It had the sound muted.

Neep cleared his throat again. "Ahh, Kel . . ."

Kel looked at Neep and smiled. "He told me not to speak."

Boschet's face screwed even tighter. "What? You'll speak when I want you to, and right now, I want you to respond. I want it. I want it. You read me? You will say something." He thumped his index finger on his desk for emphasis. The desk was devoid of anything resembling work. His staff tried to keep it that way so that he wouldn't injure himself while trying to think.

"Kel?" Neep prompted. "Kellllll."

Kel looked back at Boschet and shrugged. "You said you wanted a balanced work force. We're on target."

"Monkeys? Like I wanted *monkeys*?" Boschet almost spit.

"You can be the alpha male. Show your teeth and Les here will groom you."

"Kellll," Neep pleaded.

"Monkeys. What? What? You think I wouldn't find out? Is that what you thought? That I wouldn't find out?" Boschet looked at Les Neep for clarification. "Is that what this prick thought?"

"That would be Dr. Prick," Kel interjected, glancing up again at the TV screen.

Les Neep had a pretty good sense of when shit was about to hit the fan blades. He sensed it was close and leaned forward in his chair in hopes of still heading it off.

"What?" Boschet frothed a response. "Who the fu——. This a joke to you? Huh, Dr. *Prick*? A joke? Or maybe you think I'm a joke? Is that it? I'm a joke?"

Les reacted quickly and threw his body in front of McKelvey's as if he were taking a bullet for the president. "Ahh, sir, let's not go there, shall we. Dr. McKelvey here . . . he didn't . . . I mean, this is probably just some administrative SNAFU. You know the personnel office.

They screw things up right and left. Right Kel? Just a SNAFU. You didn't really want to advertise for monkeys—"

"SNAFU my ass," Boschet shouted. "He's made me look like an idiot. I look like an organ grinder to you? That's what the Adjutant General asked me. He calls me at home—calls me from Washington—middle of the night—wants to know if I'm an organ grinder. Says he wants to know why I'm advertising to hire goddamn spider monkeys to work in the lab and this overeducated prima donna wiseass thinks I won't figure out who's behind it. Isn't that right? You assume that because I don't have a P-H-fucking-D that I won't figure it out?"

"Sir . . ." Les Neep bobbed and head feinted like a rodeo clown trying to attract the bull's attention. "Sir—"

"I'm sure," Kel spoke quietly, "that when you saw their tails stickin' out of their little lab coats, you'd have had your suspicions."

"Oh, crap," Les mumbled as he sank back into his chair.

CHAPTER 6

U.S. Army Central Identification Laboratory, Hawaii

Friday, October 31

"Good morning, Kel," Davis Smart said.   The CILHI's deputy scientific director was typing on his computer and didn't take his eyes off the screen. He'd misplaced his glasses again, and his eyesight had gotten to the point where he had to hover his nose an inch from the monitor to see clearly without them. "How'd your meeting go with Botch-it?"

"Credit where it's due. The man's smarter than I thought," Kel responded as he looked past the doorframe into his deputy's office. His face was long and tired and sagging like old window putty in the afternoon sun. It wasn't the early hour, or the jet lag from the fifty-two-hour flight back from Bosnia the day before, or even the early morning encounter with Botch-it. From the time he'd taken the job as scientific director almost twenty years earlier, Kel had been vitally committed to the laboratory's mission of recovering and identifying America's unaccounted-for war dead. And he was good at it; the lab was identifying a missing man every two-and-a-half days—one hundred a year. But lately the politics and the government's inherent need to reinvent the wheel on a regular basis was starting to erode his spirit.

"Did you just use *Botch-it* and *smart* in the same sentence? Man, maybe I need to play today's lottery."

"What I said was that he's smarter than I gave him credit for, which is not sayin' much. He's wise to the spider monkeys."

"Damn. They would have lightened up the Christmas party."

"I know. I was lookin' forward to havin' them attend the commander's staff meetings for me," Kel replied as he dropped a pile of reports onto the floor in front of his locked door. The stack of folders made a plopping sound as if it were waterlogged. Kel took a deep breath and blew it out before continuing. "I'm supposed to write myself up for insubordination."

"You going to suspend yourself again?"

"Haven't decided. May fire myself this time. Speakin' of which, you got a minute? I need to talk with you, and not about balancin' the workforce. It's really not talk as much as I need to tell you somethin'."

"Sure. Let me finish this email." Unlike McKelvey, who stabbed at each key like a trained crow pecking on a piano, Davis Smart's fingers flew across the keyboard, and to Kel's ongoing amazement, D.S. could type and carry on a conversation at the same time. Sometimes neither the conversation nor what he was typing made any sense whatsoever, but he could still do it. "I've been trying to answer this one email for a week and keep getting interrupted."

"Hear ya." Kel verbally shrugged. As the director of the world's largest skeletal identification laboratory, Kel found himself doing less and less forensic anthropology and more and more administrative paperwork each year. And where he'd once led recovery missions to far-flung exotic locales, he now just as frequently built up his frequent flyer miles with trips to the Pentagon—at least until recently when he'd started sending himself to any remote corner of the world where Botch-it wasn't. He sighed and leaned against the door frame.

"Don't take this the wrong way, but you look like a corpse I once dissected. You need a vacation," D.S. pronounced. He accentuated his comment by hitting the enter key with his index finger, punching it as if he were launching a nuclear missile strike against the Evil Empire. He swung around in his chair so that he was facing McKelvey. "Okay, what's up?"

Kel stood quietly. Stalling. Unsure how to start.

"Your place or mine?" D.S. asked, nudging the conversation forward. He motioned to a vacant chair against the wall beside his door.

"Here's good," Kel responded. He slung his backpack to the floor next to the pile of reports and took the seat in his deputy's office. He looked at D.S. for a moment without speaking. The two men had known each other for twenty years and had grown close, despite having virtually nothing in common. "Ahh, I'm not sure what the best way to say this is."

"You sound like someone who wants a divorce?"

"Do I?"

"Been there; done that. A man can always tell, you know. Is it my gray hair? I can dye it."

"You're not too far off with the divorce, partner. I've been asked to interview for another job, D.S."

"Holy shit. You serious? Who?"

"Afraid I am; serious anyhow. ATF is looking for a director for their lab near Atlanta. They called me right before I left for Bosnia."

"You going to take it?" D.S. stood and closed his door. It was early but the staff was starting to filter in and most would pop their heads into his office to say good morning. D.S. sensed the need to keep this conversation confidential.

Kel closed his eyes and sighed. He let his head tilt back against the wall behind him. "No offer yet. Got to go to Atlanta for an interview. Not a done deal."

"C'mon, Kel. You say they asked you to interview. They're head-hunting. They wouldn't have contacted you if they weren't serious. They must not have called Botch-it for a reference."

"Or maybe they did," Kel laughed. "Five minutes on the phone with him and maybe they felt sorry for me. Threw me a life vest."

"So, let's say they do offer, you going to take it? I'll bet they wouldn't let you hire monkeys."

Kel kept his eyes closed and slowly tapped his head against the wall behind him. "Don't know. I'm torn, sure enough. At least I was until I walked in the door this mornin' and Colonel numb-nuts in the tree suit caught me first thing. That makes the decision easier. Nothin' like a dose of Inspector Botch-it to turn a sunny day suicidal." He tapped his head harder. "*Botch-it.*" Either through a subconscious slip or through a vagary of his Arkansas accent, Kel's pronunciation often made it sound a lot like *Bull-shit.*

"Or homicidal."

"You got that about right."

"But Kel, c'mon, he'll be gone soon. You can't leave us like that. Hell, you recruited this staff. Built this place. Half of them are here because you personally convinced them to come here. You did that. You, Dr. Robert McKelvey."

Kel slowly shook his head; his eyes still closed. "Nice try, bubba, but they're here because this is a hell of a job—or used to be. Some will miss me, but half of them will be measurin' my office within ten minutes of gettin' the news."

"Like hell they will. They know I got dibs on it."

"Thanks, Tonto. Loyalty has always been one of your stronger values."

"But what about anthropology?" D.S. continued. "The last time I checked, the *A* in ATF doesn't stand for anthropology."

Kel opened his eyes and laughed again. "Last time I checked, partner, I push paper for a livin', and that ain't anthropology either. Fact is, paper's just paper. The letterhead doesn't matter, and I reckon I can push paper just as well in Atlanta. And as for Botch-it bein' gone soon—I think we've been sayin' that for—what?—three years now, remember? I've tried. Goddamn I've tried, but I can't keep it up. He's like the damn undead."

"Actually, zombies might be smarter."

"This carpet's smarter on most days. I suspect that's why the monkeys threaten him so. But, that's kinda the point, isn't it? He's bringin' this place to its knees and nobody seems to be able to stop him; least of all me. It's like watchin' a train wreck, and I don't know that I can stand to watch it happen any longer."

"So you stop him. Fight it. You're the only one who can."

Kel leaned forward with his elbows on his knees and rubbed his eyes. He didn't respond.

"He's an idiot, Kel," D.S. continued. "A short, pear-shaped idiot and everybody knows it. You know it. The army knows it. We all know it. Hell, I'll bet he knows it."

"Yeah, I do know it. I do. That's the problem, isn't it?" Kel sat up and arched his back. "Not just that. I'm flat exhausted. I'm so tired of spendin' my life—my family's life—in places where no one has ever seen a flush toilet and they eat shit like . . . like fried monkey scrotums." He looked D.S. in the eye. "What's scary is that I'm afraid I might start likin' fried monkey scrotums."

"Not too bad with fish sauce."

"There you go. Spoken like a man who's been there. Maybe it's fine for you, but I don't want to be watchin' the Super Bowl one day and catch myself thinkin', damn if I couldn't go for a platter of monkey scrotums. I gotta punch out before then. I'm afraid I didn't leave enough breadcrumbs. I got go before I'm too far gone to find my way back."

Davis Smart stared at his boss quietly for a moment before speaking again. "When's your interview?" he asked.

Kel shrugged. His gaze stayed fixed on the carpet. "Don't have a firm date yet, but I'm sure that sooner is better for them. Couple-three weeks, I reckon. I need a little time; so a month or so, maybe, if I stretch it. They need to fill the position soon, but I figure I can stall them a little while. Even if they offer . . . family needs to talk it over. I'm not sure how the boys will react. They're at that age when they don't want to leave their school; their friends."

"How about Mary Louise?"

Kel shrugged again. "She knows how miserable I've been for the last three years; even worse, she knows what this job is turnin' me into, and she doesn't like what she sees. We haven't talked about it too much—the possibility of movin' that is. Need to now, I guess. And soon." He stood slowly and took a deep breath and then rearranged the putty of his face into a smile. "I guess we'll just see, but I wanted you to know. I owe you that."

"You don't owe me a thing."

"Like hell."

Davis Smart watched McKelvey turn and start to walk out of the office. "Hey, Kel," he called out.

Kel stopped in the doorway and turned. He didn't respond but he arched his eyebrows as if to ask, *What?*

"You see that story on CNN this morning? About that skeleton the FBI found in Arkansas?"

CHAPTER 7

Prisoner of War Compound, Camp Chaffee

Sebastian County, Arkansas

Wednesday, March 29, 1944

"Captain William Porter. Reporting. Sir."

"At ease, Captain. At ease," Colonel M. Fritz Wiggins, Jr., responded, looking up from a file that he was reading and returning the young captain's salute with a snap of his left hand. He smiled, almost imperceptibly, as he saw the flicker of confusion that crossed the younger officer's face. He was used to it by now. Soldiers are conditioned to give and receive right-hand salutes, and the mirror image of a left hand always took them aback. "I know, son, looks strange, doesn't it?" the colonel said.

"Sir. No, sir. I just—"

"It's okay, Captain. I'd want to stare too. Believe me, it's not nearly as strange as it'd be if I tried to salute with this old tree trunk," he laughed as he raised the shortened stub of his right arm. It had been amputated in midforearm, just above where a watchband would have gone, and the cuff of the colonel's tailored uniform shirt was carefully stitched shut like the toe end of a sock. "About all this is good for now is cracking nuts and smashing bugs." He laughed and brought the stump down on the desk with a force that rattled his pencil box.

Bill Porter had, of course, heard of Wiggins. As a lieutenant colonel with the Thirty-sixth Infantry Division in Salerno, he'd lost his arm, and almost his life, partially smothering a German hand grenade. Five men were alive because of it—or had been. Two of the five bought the farm four weeks later; of the other three, two were in southern England waiting on the invasion of France that everyone knew was sure to come, and the third was mending an injury stateside before being sent back into Harm's Way again. For his part, Morris "Fist" Wiggins came home to a hero's welcome; receiving the Medal of Honor in front of a packed football stadium at the University of Kansas where, only a couple of decades before, he'd been an All-America tight end. At times when Wiggins allowed himself to think of such matters, he often thought how ironic it would be if he ended up being the only one of the six to survive the war.

"Sit down, Captain. Sit down," Wiggins said. He motioned to the chair in front of his desk. "Did you just get in?"

"Yes, sir. About half-hour or so ago. I stopped at the B-O-Q long enough to drop off my things; then here to report for duty," Bill Porter responded as he took a seat. He had that odd St. Louis accent that made *or* come out as *are* and *for* sound like *far*.

Wiggins took a deep breath, and he nodded as he looked down at the folder on his desk. He used his stump to anchor the edge of the paper as he flipped a couple of pages with his left hand. "Good timing; I was reading through your file just now, Captain Porter. Most impressive. Very impressive credentials."

"Sir?" Porter replied with a question in his voice.

The colonel laughed as he looked up, "Oh, hell, son; that's bullshit, and we both know it. This is a pretty piss-poor record actually—but then you know that better than I do. Don't you?"

"Yes, sir. I've never pretended that—"

Wiggins waved his stump heavily; dismissively. "No need. I said the *record* was piss poor, I never said that the man was piss poor. This pile of paper doesn't even start to tell the whole story; isn't that correct?"

"Sir?"

"I may be an old crippled-up soldier, but—"

"No, sir. I don't think that, I was just—"

"Now hold on, Captain. I am a crippled-up soldier. Gimped-up quite properly. And old. No use arguing that one to the jury, but that doesn't mean I'm a lazy one. I've done my homework on you."

"Homework, sir?"

Colonel Wiggins leaned back in his chair and clasped the stump of his arm in his good hand. "William Calloway Porter. Only son of Thomas and Alice Porter. Born in Creve Coeur, Missouri. Father died when you were six. Raised by your mother and grandparents in Clayton, Missouri, outside St. Louis. Worked your way through the University of Missouri School of Law by working nights at the AB Chance factory in Centralia. Also tutored English and economics. Sent all your money home to your mother. Finished in the lower third of your class—well below all of your professors' expectations for you. Commissioned in the Judge Advocate General Corps last . . ." he leaned forward and looked briefly at the file in front of him. "November." He paused and took in Porter's eyes before continuing. "That about sum it up?"

"Yes, sir. Afraid so."

"No, sir, would be more like it. No, sir, that doesn't even start to sum it up." Wiggins leaned forward. "You go by William or Bill?"

"Bill works fine, sir."

"Good. You know why you're here, Bill?"

"I believe so, Colonel. I read over the file on the train coming down from St. Louis. A German prisoner, a private—name of Hans Geller—was killed—murdered, most likely—by fellow prisoners. There's—"

"He wasn't *likely* murdered," Colonel Wiggins corrected, sternly. "No *likely* to it; he was murdered, by God. Brutally murdered, and by his own brothers-in-arms."

"Yes, sir. Ahh, well, he was assaulted by fellow prisoners and left to die," Porter picked up his recitation of the case. "He was found by the guards, but too late, and now we need to prosecute a murder trial."

Colonel Wiggins smiled but the look in his eyes belied any humor. "Yes, yes, you've read the case, good, but *why are you here*? You in particular, Captain Porter?"

Now it was Bill Porter's turn to smile; almost laugh. "I've been asking myself the same question, Colonel, and for the life of me, I don't have an answer. I've been reading about the trial of the prisoners over in Tonkawa, Oklahoma. This case here seems like a job best suited for someone else; somebody with more trial experience—maybe the same JAG officer that handled the case over there." He paused and looked down as he slowly shook his head. "I guess I don't know the answer to your question, sir. I guess I'm here because the army told me to be here."

"That's close. The army ordered you here, Captain, but the army ordered you here because I personally requested you." Colonel Wiggins waited for Porter to look up and engage his eye before continuing. "Surprised?"

"Yes, sir. You requested me, Colonel?"

Wiggins pushed his chair back and slowly stood up. He was a tall man, almost six three; solid and well built, with long muscular limbs. His once-thick auburn hair had started to thin and shade silver, notably at the temples, and his brown eyes were so dark as to hide the pupils. Most people found it hard to maintain eye contact with him for more than a split second. He stretched and quietly inflated his lungs before turning and walking to the window. With his back turned, he spoke, "I went to law school myself, Captain. Did you know that?" He turned his head and looked over his shoulder momentarily before returning his eyes to the activity of the base outside his window.

"No, sir. I didn't. That's surprising."

"And why's that?"

"It's just that . . . well, sir, you're in the infantry and . . ."

"And too dumb to be a lawyer?"

"No, sir. It's just . . ."

"I know, I know," Wiggins said good humoredly. "Maybe I'm too dumb because I went to the University of Kansas?" He held up his good hand in mock surrender. "Don't hold that against me, you being from ol' Mizzou and all. Yup. *Rock Chalk Jayhawk.* Class of 1928. I had a pretty good law practice going in Overland Park when the war broke out. Not big, but comfortable. I plan on returning to it—maybe sooner than intended. In fact, if things work out, my son and son-in-law may join me." He paused while his thoughts spooled before his eyes. "But that was before the shit hit the fan. Somebody had to sign up to fight—we can't all be army lawyers, can we?" He paused as he realized how his comment might have been misconstrued, and he turned to face Bill Porter. "Now it's my turn to apologize, son. I didn't mean that the way it came out. Didn't mean to make it sound like you're some sort of pussy. Hell, Captain Porter . . . *Bill*, the shooting will be over soon enough, and then the hard part will really begin—the lawyers' part; your part. We're going to have to rebuild that shittin' continent. Japan too. From the goddamn ground up—and that's going to take lawyers and politicians, not old broken-down soldiers. Your time's coming, and God almighty I don't envy you one bit."

"Yes, sir."

Wiggins sighed and smiled and retook his seat. He leaned back again until the chair squeaked. "You know, you're not the only man to ever put himself through law school. I worked summers on the MKT railroad. I used to deadhead back and forth between St. Louis and Kansas City."

"Really, sir? My father was an engineer on the Katy."

"I know." Wiggins paused. "In fact, I knew your father, Bill. He was a damned good man."

"You knew my father, sir? I don't understand."

"I did. I did indeed. Not well, mind you, but I knew him. It was a sad day when he died."

"Yes, sir. I was pretty young at the time . . ."

"I know." Colonel Wiggins paused as he looked out the window again, as if refilling his thoughts from a trough. "A great many people are alive today thanks to him. You know that, don't you? If he hadn't derailed his locomotive when he did, a lot of people would have died." He smiled and looked at the young captain. "Me included."

"You, sir?" Bill Porter asked. He shook his head slowly to indicate his confusion.

"Yes, me. I was on the other train that day; headed back to Kansas City for the weekend. We'd blown a main line seal and stalled out on the tracks near Warrenton. If your father hadn't derailed that big old engine of his, we'd all . . . well . . . he was a good man."

"Thank you, sir. I like to think so. My mother certainly does."

Wiggins smiled. "He'd be proud of what you've accomplished."

"I don't know that I've accomplished much," Porter said quietly. "Especially compared to men like you, sir." His eyes involuntarily flicked to the colonel's stumped right arm.

"Oh, but you have, and more importantly, you will. You will. As I said, your time is coming. In fact, perhaps your time begins right now."

CHAPTER 8

Prisoner of War Compound, Camp Chaffee

Sebastian County, Arkansas

Wednesday, March 29, 1944

What had started out as a warm day grew chill as the sun disappeared behind a bank of on-coming grey. Captain Bill Porter had left his trench coat in the Bachelor Officers Quarters and now had to wedge his worn leather briefcase under his arm and dig his hands deep into his pockets to keep warm as he crossed the POW compound to Building T58.

"Shut the damn door," Captain James Jordan ordered. He didn't know who had opened the door, nor did he care. He didn't look up, but kept reading a newspaper—the *Southwest American*. He was built like a six-foot iron wedge set on its point; the shoulders displaying the width of a varsity sculler. His blue eyes sighted down a long narrow nose. His thin hair was the color of broom straw, and an odor of moneyed smug clung to him like brightly colored cologne.

"Sorry," Bill Porter apologized reflexively and closed the door. He stood for a moment and looked around the room, waiting for the other captain, the one who'd barked at him, to look up and acknowledge his presence. When he didn't, Porter spoke again. "I'm looking for Captain Jordan. That be you?"

"Who's asking?" Jordan replied, his eyes still on the paper.

"Name's Bill Porter. Colonel Wiggins sent me over."

James Jordan looked up from his paper. A smile broke across his narrow lips. "Did he now?" he said as he stood up and walked over to meet the visitor. He was a toe walker, always walking on the balls of his feet and never wearing out the heels of his shoes; it made him appear even taller than he was. He stuck out his hand. "What was that name again?"

Bill Porter smiled and shook hands. "Bill Porter," he repeated. "And if you're Captain Jordan, we're going to be working together."

"That right?"

"So, are you Jordan?"

"Your lucky day."

"Mind?" Bill Porter nodded at a desk near the door. It didn't appear to be in use.

Jordan followed the nod and processed the question. "Sure. Help yourself. Tech Sergeant Elliott's been using that one, and Sergeant David sits there," he smiled and pointed to another desk by the window. He nodded at Porter's collar and said, "But, rank has its privilege."

Bill Porter put his briefcase on the desk, looked around, and sat down on the corner edge. He crossed his arms and tucked his fingers under his armpits for warmth. "The colonel say anything to you? About why I'm here."

"Jim Jordan, Captain, United States Army Mushroom Corps," Jordan responded with a deep stage voice. He relished the confusion on Porter's face before continuing. "As they say, kept in the dark and fed shit."

Bill Porter studied the captain's eyes. The man didn't have the look of someone who enjoyed bad jokes and clichés. Porter took a deep breath and began, "I'm the new Trial Judge Advocate. They brought me here to prosecute a murder case; the German POW that was killed."

Jordan walked back to his desk and sat down. He flipped a metal trashcan over, propped his feet on it, and put his hands behind his head. "Private Hans Geller. Yes, sir. Didn't know we were ready to proceed with a trial though. Who you going to prosecute, counselor?"

"You tell me, Captain. My—"

"James or Jim. If we're going to be working together."

"Okay, Jim. I'm Bill. Anyhow, my understanding from Colonel Wiggins is that you've been heading up the investigation, at least up to this point. I was led to understand that you'd made some headway."

"Your understanding is wrong, Cap— *Bill*. No offense, but Colonel Wiggins gets a little . . . let's just say that he gets a little ahead of himself at times. Bird colonels do that with some frequency, I've come to learn."

"You don't have a suspect?"

"You might say that. Not even any leads really; certainly nothing definite."

"But you're running the investigation? You a cop?"

Jordan laughed. "Now what did I do to deserve that? A cop? Shit no. I'm MI."

"Military Intelligence?" Bill Porter got up from the edge of his new desk and walked around to his chair. He put his hands behind his head, realized that he was mirroring Jordan, and put them in his lap. "Isn't that a bit unusual? Why aren't the MPs handling this? Or the provost marshal? They might be PWs, but this is still a criminal case."

Jordan laughed again. His skin was pink and without a mark or blemish. His teeth, which he flashed to great effect when it suited him, were even and white. "Let me guess, you haven't been in the army long, have you, Bill? I assume you haven't dealt much with MPs. They're fine rounding up drunks and rousting some AWOL kids who have been dipping their dicks in the local merchandise, but believe me, you don't want them handling anything important."

"Maybe. But why MI?"

"Beats the living shit outta me. Who else, I guess. Besides, I work with these Nazi bastards regularly. Routine MI stuff. Interrogations and shit. Unit strength. Troop locations. Eva Braun's bra size. I *sprechen* the language a little. I've got some MPs working for me on the investigation, though. Tech Sergeant Elliott for one. That's whose desk you just commandeered. Sergeant David is the other one. They'll both be back soon."

Bill Porter looked at the desk as if he were seeing it for the first time. He nodded slowly. "That's more or less what the colonel said. That's why he's assigned you to work for . . . with me. You're to be my interpreter."

"*Jawohl*," Jordan answered. His face was smiling, but his eyes were noncommittal.

"But I'm still confused. You say you don't have a suspect in this Geller murder."

"That's right. Nothing definite."

Bill Porter opened his briefcase and removed a folder. He began reading it as he continued speaking. "Nothing? No idea who might have had the means? How about motive?"

Jordan shrugged and crossed his arms. "Who knows? Shit happens in prison. Maybe this Geller stole somebody's cigarettes. Maybe he was queer. Came on to the wrong *Übermensch* in the shower. Maybe both."

"You don't think it's linked to the incident at Tonkawa?"

"Tonkawa?" Jordan frowned at the strange name. "You mean that PW camp over in Oklahoma?"

Porter nodded and looked up from his file. "You're familiar with it?"

Jordan shrugged. "I prefer the sports page, but I may've heard about it."

"So are they connected? What's your MI opinion?"

"I doubt it. But you never know. I don't know this for a fact, but I suspect they may have cigarette-stealing queers over in Oklahoma as well. Some of them might even be Germans."

"Ummm," Bill Porter resumed reading. He flipped through several pages before tossing the papers on to the desk and leaning back further in his chair. "You might be right. What I'd like someone to explain to me is how I'm expected to prosecute a case if we don't have any suspects. It seems like we're way out ahead of the horse."

"Slept through that class in law school, did you, Captain?"

"I slept through a lot, believe me, but I think I must have missed that one entirely." The lawyer closed his eyes, pinched the bridge of his nose, and sighed. "I want to start interviewing prisoners tomorrow. I'll need your help. We'll start with the officers."

James Jordan had resumed reading his newspaper. Without looking up, he responded, "Already interviewed everyone, counselor. That's my job, remember?"

"Yeah, yeah. But maybe you missed someone."

CHAPTER 9

Prisoner of War Compound, Camp Chaffee

Sebastian County, Arkansas

Thursday, March 30, 1944

As the ranking German non-commissioned officer among the POWs, *Hauptfeldwebel* August Guttmann was used to being roused at odd hours, especially lately, especially since the body of that slack-mouthed *Soldat* Geller had been found. Hours of questioning and late-night musters had been interspersed with even longer hours of barrack's lockdowns and suppressed threats. And now another summons. In fact, he'd been expecting it tonight, which was partially why he hadn't bothered to undress. He was stretched out on his bunk, arms crossed behind his head, starting to doze when the order came.

"You have trouble hearing me, boy? I said, *now*," the young American private repeated. His backbone was considerably strengthened by the oversized pistol strapped to his undersized waist.

Hauptfeldwebel Guttmann cracked a mottled blue eye and looked up at the soft, pale, foul-complexioned American private standing over him. He closed his eyes again and sighed, but before the private could repeat himself a third time, he swung his legs over the side of his cot, forcing the guard to take an involuntary step back. "*Ich komme*," he muttered; his voice did little to disguise his utter contempt for the young American. He was seven years a soldier; a veteran of the Russian front and of Rommel's Afrika Korps; he had blood on his hands and had lost count of his decorations and commendations—one pinned on him by the Field Marshal himself. He was a warrior, and now he was forced to answer a midnight summons delivered by a soft young boy with a raw-complexion, who couldn't even locate Stalingrad or Tunis on a map let alone imagine the sights and the sounds and the stench of the dying. "*Ich komme, Soldat, Ich komme.*"

"Yeah? Well you better *itch comma*, buddy, and pretty damn fast. *Mack schnel.* PDQ. I don't give a rat's ass if you are a first sergeant, you're still a damn lousy Kraut as far as I'm concerned, and Captain Jordan wants to see you in his office five minutes ago. You hear me, boy? *Rause.*"

It was a short walk; short enough that Hauptfeldwebel Guttmann didn't even bother tying his short, ankle-high boots. He made it a point of walking quickly so that the American private had to hurry to keep up. He crossed the open compound to Building T58 and knocked on the door to Jordan's office and waited. The cool, wet night air fogged his breath.

"Come," said a voice behind the door. Guttmann recognized it as Captain Jordan's. This was not their first meeting.

Guttmann pushed open the door, not waiting for the private to initiate a move or giving him an opportunity to issue any further instructions, and walked in. The room was small and roughly finished and lit by a single, goose-necked lamp on one of the desks. In the shadows to the side, Tech Sergeant Elliott sat at another desk. Sergeant David was perched on the corner of it. Both were quiet and neither moved.

Guttmann stepped up to the front of the desk with the lamp, clicked his heels together, and assumed an exaggerated position of attention. It was designed to irritate, not to show respect. "Hauptfeldwebel August Guttmann," he announced, his eyes focused blankly on a spot on the wall.

Captain James Jordan looked about as happy to have called the meeting as Guttmann did for being called out of his bunk to attend it. He looked past Guttmann to the young soldier still hovering by the door. "That'll be all, Private. Thank you. You're dismissed. I'll see to it that the prisoner gets tucked back in for the night."

"Sir," the young American private saluted. "Yes, sir." He waited for Jordan to acknowledge his salute, and then he opened the door. He cast a sharp look at the German POW, to reassert the pecking order, but as the German was still focused on the wall, the effect was lost.   He nodded with satisfaction, as if his point had been made anyhow, and exited, closing the door behind him.

"Sit, Sergeant Guttmann," Jordan nodded at a chair to the side of his desk. Simultaneously, he flicked his eyes into the shadows. Elliott and David took their cue and stood up and stepped quietly outside.

August Guttmann paused long enough to emphasize his own sense of the pecking order and then took a seat.

"Cigarette?" Jordan tossed an open pack of unfiltered Lucky Strikes in the German's direction. Jordan was blonde and scrubbed and more Nordic looking than most of the German prisoners, the result of an undiluted Anglo bloodline that he could trace back to Hastings Bridge. Only his eyes belied wholesomeness.

"*Nein, danke.*"

"Let's cut the *nein danke* bullshit, shall we? We both know your English is better than half the men on this base. You taught it at the Gymnasium in Freiburg, didn't you? Before you answered the dear old Führer's call to world domination?"

Guttmann smiled and reached for the pack of cigarettes. He took one and put the pack in his shirt pocket.

Jordan watched him, but said nothing. Early on he'd secured a crate of pre-war smokes that he used with great success when questioning German prisoners. His store was growing smaller daily, but now was not the time to make an issue of it. He tossed his silver-colored lighter to the German and then leaned back in his chair and put his feet up onto the corner of the desk.

The prisoner clicked the metal arm on the lighter and struck a flame, watching it dance momentarily in an unfelt draft before he lit the end of his cigarette. The tobacco crackled and sputtered as it caught fire. Guttmann relaxed his thumb and extinguished the flame, and then, with a jut of his jaw he projected a thin blue plume of smoke at the ceiling.   He smiled again and said, "You cannot sleep, Herr Captain? Or do you just wish for my company tonight?"

"Maybe a little of both. Maybe I like our late-night talks so much that I can't sleep without a good dose. Then again, with everything that's been happening, maybe we both ought to be losing some sleep."

"Perhaps," Guttmann replied. He took another long drag on his cigarette and held the smoke deep in his lungs before answering. "The men, they are talking much."

Jordan nodded. He tapped his fraternity ring rhythmically on the desk top as he calculated his response. "I'll bet. That's what concerns me First Sergeant. There's been too much talk. That's why I summoned you; so we can talk. So you can listen. Private Geller's tragic death is an isolated event. Do we understand each other? Tragic and isolated. No reason for unrest; no reason for any trouble; no reason for the men to talk. Things work here because we let you people police yourselves. Things work here because we rely on professional soldiers—like you—to keep the friggin' lid on this place. Things work here because we don't have to get involved. I don't want to get involved, and believe me, you don't want me involved. What happened to Geller was tragic and isolated."

"Indeed, Herr Captain, I believe that we have . . . policed . . . ourselves, not true? Is that not why I am here? Yes? Because we have dealt with *Soldat* Geller. Yes, I think this is so. You do not have to get involved. This matter, it is *fertig* . . . ahh . . . finished."

Jordan sat forward quickly, his hands flat on the desk. "Bullshit, *mein gutes* Hauptfeldwebel Guttmann. Keeping a lid on the shit doesn't mean beating a man's brains out and leaving him in his bunk to die. You and your friggin' ghosts were way out of line this time. Went too damn far. Jumped the gun, and now we have a mess on our hands."

Guttmann shrugged.

"I mean it; you were way outta line. And because of it," Jordan continued, "now we're going to have all sorts of brass crawling around this camp like a bunch of damn cockroaches. I had to deal with one of them today, and there'll be more before this is over, and they aren't going to leave until there's some resolution here. Everyone's worried about some sort of nationwide unrest; some sort of PW uprising that might spread. You know what happened to your comrades over in Oklahoma, don't you? The ones convicted of killing that Kraut prisoner over in Tonkawa? Those five German comrades of yours are going to hang—you understand that? Hang, Sergeant, by their goddamn Nazi necks. You understand me? Washington is damn serious about this shit."

Guttmann took another drag on the cigarette and flicked some ash onto the floor. He looked at the lighter in his hand and rubbed his thumb over the fancy design on the face as if it were written in Braille. After a moment, he flipped the lighter onto Jordan's green felt desk blotter, but didn't respond.

The captain eyed the prisoner as if he were an old acquaintance whose name he couldn't quite recall. When he was sure the German wasn't going to respond, he continued. "You just don't get it do you, Fritz? Those boys in Oklahoma are going to hang, and someone is going to hang here as well. You can take that to the bank. Now, how many ropes get used—well, now, that's up to you and your ghosts. Like I said, the system we have here works. It's in your interest as well as mine that we get things back to status quo as soon as possible, but it's about to unspool pretty damn quickly, and we have a short time to screw the cap down tight and get a hold on things again. *Verstehen?*"

Guttmann nodded an affirmation. "*Ja,* understood. Yes, I understand the situation. You don't wish another Tonkawa. What I do not understand is that which you would have me to do."

Captain James Jordan pushed a small scrap of paper across the desk at the German POW. "For starters, there's one man in particular that it would be best if the investigator didn't talk to. You understand what I'm saying? I can't control who this investigator talks to, but he's a loose thread that if they start pulling, he might just unravel the whole sweater."

Hauptfeldwebel August Guttmann took the slip of paper and looked at the name written on it, and then he reached over the desk and took Jordan's lighter again, flicked it and struck a flame. "And what would you have me do, Herr Captain?" he asked as he lit the paper. He held it upside down as it began to burn. "You seem to disapprove of our . . . of our method of handling with these matters."

"That was before, First Sergeant, that was before. Desperate times call for desperate measures—and this is a desperate time; understand? *Verstehen Sie?* You just take care of the . . . matter, and do it discreetly this time. You do that, and I'll handle the administrative end of things. We do it right this time and maybe things will return to as close to normal as possible around here."

August Guttmann dropped the burning curl of paper to the floor and rubbed it into a black smudge with the toe of his boot. He knotted his brow in mock bewilderment and looked directly into Jordan's eyes. "Normal, Herr Captain? I believe this is a word for which I no longer understand the meaning."

CHAPTER 10

Memphis, Tennessee

Friday, October 31

He didn't use to daydream, but over the last year he found himself doing it with greater and greater regularity. He was doing it now. It had now been a little more than three years since Michael Levine had first been detailed to the FBI's Memphis Field Office in the Bureau's vain, but determined, hope that they could squeeze an early retirement out of him. Levine had always had the career-smudging habit of shaking the wrong tree, but three years earlier he'd definitely picked the wrong one, and when the nuts started to fall, he hadn't had the good sense to find cover. In the end, an influential senator was toppled, and Levine could look at himself in the mirror, but it came at the price of a one-way ticket to the land of Delta clay and overly large mosquitoes. He'd left his wife and two teenaged daughters in Maryland in anticipation of a short assignment and instead packed only a few clothes, some books, and a good-sized block of wood to balance on his shoulder. He'd arrived three years earlier, in the middle of a blister-hot summer. His supervisor then upped the pressure by assigning him to a forty-year-old unsolvable cold case in a small Arkansas backwater, which only served to distill his level of distain for what he viewed as gape-jawed southern crackers who seemed to have even fewer brain cells than teeth. The Bureau may have intended the assignment to help dry the ink on Levine's resignation papers, but instead it had brought about the opposite effect. He'd dug in. That was three long years ago, and now he was within sight of retirement. Perhaps in spite of himself, maybe he'd learned to be patient.

And to daydream.

His office was buried in the interior of the third floor of the sprawling brick-and-glass FBI headquarters building on North

Humphreys Boulevard, away from any sunlight or other redeeming feature, aside from an unblemished beige wall that served as a suitable canvas for his imagination. He'd been sitting, feet propped on his wastebasket, staring at it for half an hour or more, mentally Xing out days on the calendar until he boarded the airplane for a couple weeks of leave back in Maryland with his family.

"Agent Michael Levine, working hard as always, I see." Special Agent in Charge Lawrence Frank stood in the doorway, hands in his pockets, shirt buttons straining against too much fast food and too little exercise. He was Levine's boss, though their interaction was limited to a single cellophane-wrapped shit sandwich that Frank would hand deliver to Levine every month or so.

"As always, Larry. As always," Levine replied, not taking his eyes off the wall. Frank hated being called Larry, and so Levine loved calling him that. "You're a long way from the big office, aren't you? Hope you left a trail of bread crumbs back to the elevator. Wouldn't want to get lost."

"I think I can manage."

"I'm sure you can, Larry. Rats do well in mazes. By the way, I saw you on television this morning." Levine dropped his feet to the floor and swung his chair around to face his boss. "Today Show, CNN, Fox News. You've been busy. Too bad we don't have a public affairs office to handle that sort of thing." He snapped his fingers. "You know, on second thought, I think maybe we do have a public affairs office. But why involve them when you can get your own handsome face in front of the camera."

"Screw you, Levine. Maybe if you hadn't spent your whole fucking life flushing your career down the toilet, we could get you some face time. As it is, we have to keep you here," he looked around the small confines of the office, "with the dust mites and mold."

"Right, Larry. We all know that's what I want; some face time on television." Levine began picking up and putting down stacks of papers as if he were organizing the work on his desk. He'd actually cleared his workload in anticipation of taking some time off, but he didn't plan on sharing that with Frank. "So, what can I do for you? Or are you just making the rounds with some early Christmas bonus checks?"

"*Christmas?* I didn't know your people celebrated Christmas, Levine."

Levine shrugged. "Maybe I celebrate bonuses. You know how my people are."

Frank laughed. "Well, don't make plans to spend yours just yet. In fact, I think maybe I'll hold on to your check until you complete an assignment I have for you."

Levine leaned back in his chair and eyed Frank. "What kind of assignment?"

"A special one . . . for a special agent."

"Kiss my ass. What kind of assignment?"

"Well, since you've been watching television, you know about the body that was found over in Arkansas—"

"Skeleton. It wasn't a body."

"You're right. This skeleton; we need someone to go over to Fort Smith and investigate it."

"Gimme a break, Larry. Besides, the boys in Little Rock have that end of the stick."

"They're tied up investigating some bank irregularities, so I volunteered us. They were more than happy to transfer the jurisdiction."

"I'll bet they were. What's our interest? Check that—*your* interest?"

"That's my business."

"Glad to hear it. I guess that means you'll take the case yourself."

Lawrence Frank crossed his stubby arms and squared his stance. "Here's the way it works. I call the shots. I'm the SAC. You seem to forget that."

"Not at all, Larry. I always think of you as a sack."

"You're a funny man. But you want to hear something really funny? When I said I volunteered us, that was sort of like the royal *we*; what I really meant to say was, I volunteered you."

"Screw you. What the piss is there to investigate anyway? It's a goddamn Indian skeleton or something. Isn't that what I heard you tell the cameras this morning? Don't tell me the Bureau really gives a shit about this."

"If you'd really been watching television like you say you have, then you'd know that the medical examiner over there has—"

"Coroner."

Frank's face registered either disdain or confusion. Or both. "What?"

"Arkansas is a coroner state," Levine corrected. "Get it right, Larry."

"Whatever. The coroner over there says it may not be Native American. He seems to believe that it's a forensic case."

"So? Believe me, I've been there. Arkansas has police officers. Some can even tie their shoes."

"For your information, I've been there, too," Frank said.

"Well then you should know they have cops. You still haven't told me why you're getting us involved?"

Lawrence Frank sighed at the thought of having to take time to explain anything to Levine. He sighed at the thought of Levine in general. He was counting the days to Levine's retirement as much as Levine was. "Like I told them on CNN last night, maybe it's Native North American or maybe not, but the remains still were found on what used to be Fort Chaffee, and that means it's former federal property. If it turns out to be a forensic case, and we assume so until we determine otherwise, then that makes it our jurisdiction. And that means we need an agent with your vast experience to head over there and take charge."

"Bullshit, Larry. Remains like that turn up every friggin' day, and we don't send agents riding off to each and every one of them—

especially agents *of my vast experience.* And we sure as shit don't have the SAC giving press conferences about them. What's the real story?"

"Slow news day I guess. Doesn't matter why. All I know is that the damn thing has caught the media's attention for the next fifteen minutes. All I know is that we're going to investigate it because Washington says we're going to investigate it; check that, we're going to investigate it because I say we're going to." He smiled. "I said we again; I keep doing that, don't I? No, the janitor's busy, and all the college interns are working on much more important things, so I'm afraid that leaves you. You're going to investigate. I expect you to be on the job first thing Monday morning."

Levine sat forward. "Monday?" He shook his head. "No way."

"Excuse me?"

"You heard me."

"And I think you heard me." Frank looked at his watch and sighed. "You were officially assigned to this case twenty minutes ago. Your ass will be in Fort Smith, Arkansas, ready to begin your investigation at eight o'clock Monday morning, or your ass will be in the unemployment line by eight fifteen on Monday. It's really not that complicated; even for you."

Levine shook his head more emphatically. "C'mon, Larry. You know that I'm scheduled to take leave next week. I'm going back to Maryland. I haven't seen my family in four months. Don't pull this shit on me now."

"Well, as I see it, Mikey, you've got four choices." He held up four fingers and began counting off. "One, you can go to Arkansas like you've been directed to. Check that; ordered to. Two, you can be fired for insubordination and refusing a direct assignment from your superior." He paused and smiled, "Or, three, you can resign. Effective immediately."

Levine nodded at the remaining finger standing in Frank's hand. Against his better judgment, he said, "Four. You said four."

"Right. Four. Four would be, you could do us all a favor and shoot yourself. We did issue you a weapon. Pity really. So close to retirement. But don't let me stop you."

The two men stared at each other momentarily; then Levine began moving piles of paper again. "I'd really like to spend the day talking with you, Larry, but I've got work to do."

"So, which is it? I hope that if you decide to shoot yourself, you'll remember to put some plastic down over the carpet first," Frank asked optimistically.

Levine held up his middle finger. "How about we go with option one. You can expect a postcard. From Arkansas."

CHAPTER 11

Fort Chaffee Reservation, Sebastian County, Arkansas

Monday, November 3

"What used to be here? You have any idea? Trooper, ahh . . ." Levine asked.

"Geren," the tall Arkansas State Trooper replied. He'd been assigned to meet the FBI agent and show him where the remains had been found.

Special Agent Levine closed his eyes and took a deep breath. "Right. Geren." He was standing on a small hummock of loose earth, his hands snugged down deeply into the pockets of his blue, North Face parka shell. It was midmorning and the air was moist, and a light breeze made it chilly if you weren't moving much. He used his chin to gesture in a small semi-circle to indicate the immediate area. "Right. So, Trooper Geren, any idea what was here?"

"Ahh, yes, sir, this here used to be Fort Chaffee Army base," Trooper Ricky Geren said. He screwed his brow into a tight knot that resembled a clenched fist and spit a slobbery, brown string of tobacco juice between his boots as he worked up a fuller response. "A long time ago now it was Camp Chaffee, then it became Fort Chaffee. I don't know what the difference is between a fort and a camp, but it's been given back to the state now—at least six thousand or so acres. They call it a reservation now. The city of Fort Smith's gone and claimed itself a big slice of it; town of Barling's gettin' themselves a piece; Sebastian County got a good-sized chunk as well. The plan is to develop the whole area. Commerce, industry. Big plans. So they say." Trooper Geren paused and then smiled. He adjusted his Smokey Bear hat so that the tips of both ears touched the flat brim. "Bet you didn't know it, but this here's where Elvis got hisself inducted into the army. The barber shop where they cut his hair's over yonder. Buildin' eight-oh-three. It's still there, though it ain't a barber shop anymore. It's a haircut museum. You ought to go by there; they've got his photo on the wall and everythin'."

Levine smiled patiently and fished a handkerchief from his hip pocket to wipe his runny nose. Even after ten years, days like this—or maybe it was assignments like this—still made him want a cigarette. Instead, he settled for a cherry-flavored cough drop, which he tucked neatly into his cheek. "Is that right?" Levine indulged the young trooper. His sight was fixed on the line of leafless red and pin oaks. "You'd be right, trooper, I didn't know that. I guess that was some pretty famous hair." He paused politely and then gestured with his chin again. "No, what I meant was, more specifically, what was this area? Where we're standing. I know this used to be Fort Chaffee. There's a big-ass sign at the gate. Maybe you saw it when we drove in. No, what I was wondering about is this part of it. Specifically. Any idea what this area was used for?"

Trooper Geren smiled patiently back at Levine. He was junior enough in his job that he didn't need an adverse report from an FBI agent going across his sergeant's desk. "Barracks, I think. Probably, anyhow." He replied. "Whole dadgum place went up in smoke about a year ago. Biggest damn fire anyone around here has ever seen."

Levine kicked at some charred wood at his feet and looked around again as if some external clue would provide the answer that Trooper Geren couldn't. "Barracks? Right here? That doesn't very well explain a skeleton, does it? Any chance there could be an unmarked cemetery here? It'd have to be an old one, of course. How old is Fort Chaffee? Fifty years? Hundred years? Older?"

"No, sir. Not that old. I'm not sure when, but it was started up about the time of World War Two; maybe a little before. It was Camp Chaffee back then; like I said. It didn't become a fort until later, like during the Korean War or somethin'. I'm not sure what the difference is between a camp and a fort," the trooper repeated.

Levine kicked again at some more debris and turned slowly in a circle. The cold air smelled good and reminded him of weekend mornings at home in Maryland with his family. He watched his breath fog out of his nostrils as he thought. "And it was deactivated when? Pretty recently, I'd guess? Parts of it still look well maintained."

Geren nodded. "Yes, sir. Guard and Reserves have been usin' it off and on for a while, you know, for trainin' and all, but it wasn't given back to the state until just a few years ago. Big plans to develop it. Commerce, industry, big—"

"So," Levine cut the trooper off, talking more to himself than his new companion, "if that college professor is right and this isn't the gravesite of some Indian or some early settler, then how do you explain the skeleton being here? His report estimated it had been in the ground for at least twenty years, but you say that this was an active base until recently."

"Yes, sir, it wasn't what I'd call active, but it was used regularly until just recent," Trooper Geren decided to respond, even if Agent Levine didn't seem to be talking directly to him. "That's why you're here, ain't it? Twenty years ago, all this belonged to the federal government. Anythin' that happened that long ago is out of Troop H's jurisdiction." He clenched his face again. "You mind me askin' why Army CID isn't investigatin' this?"

"If this were still an active military post, they'd be here instead of me," Levine replied absently, his attention still focused on surveying the vicinity. "But since this is now city and state land, the army's out." Levine looked quickly at Trooper Geren to see if he was actually interested in an answer. "On the other hand, since it used to be federal property, the Bureau's got some interest in it; at least for now. To tell you the truth, the bottom line is that no one wants it, but somebody's got to grab the short end, and I happened to be in the wrong place at the wrong time. You can file that away as a piece of career advice; be careful where you are in line when they start handing out the plates of shit."

Trooper Geren laughed. "It may be too late for that."

Levine didn't respond, but he turned and looked at the line of bare trees again before reengaging the trooper's eye. "But you say you don't know what this part of the post was used for, specifically? Maybe barracks, you think, but you're not sure. Any idea who would know?"

Trooper Geren smiled and shrugged again. He kicked a stone as his eyes focused on something over Levine's shoulder. "No, sir. I know this though; my old lady's goin' to get a real hoot out of this tonight."

Levine looked up at the trooper and then followed the young man's gaze back over his shoulder. He saw a white van bouncing over the rutted field headed directly for them. The side panel was painted with an enormous cherry-red Channel 10 and below it was the slogan, *The Pulse of the River Valley*. "Oh, crap," Levine said.

CHAPTER 12

Fort Chaffee Reservation, Sebastian County, Arkansas

Monday, November 3

Levine had served with an infantry unit in Vietnam; he'd seen two companies of men deploy from Hueys into waist-high elephant grass in less than five minutes. Early in his FBI career he'd been on scene to watch the Bureau's Hostage Rescue Team seize and control a three-story inner city walk-up in less than two minutes. It had been a false alarm, but it had been impressive to watch nonetheless. Neither could compare to the efficiency that he'd just watched.

In less than thirty seconds after the news van stopped, five people boiled out of the side door, set up a bracket of lights, screwed the lens of a shoulder-held camera into focus, and sound-tested the mic. The reporter, a young woman with cat-like eyes and magazine-ad makeup, adjusted the cling of her blouse, flicked her auburn bangs with a polished nail, and ran her tongue over her flat even teeth to moisten them so they wouldn't stick to her lips. She quickly checked her reflection in the passenger window of the van, and then stepped forward and with a burst of energy thrust the microphone under Levine's chin.

"Agent Levine, Diana Jones, Channel Ten Eyewitness News, any developments to report?" she said. As she spoke, she looked over her shoulder at the camera and then back at Levine.

Levine didn't recognize Diana Jones. She obviously knew who he was, which wasn't necessarily surprising; someone at the hotel had tipped off the local news, and there'd been a camera crew waiting at his hotel when he'd arrived the night before. In fact, though he didn't recognize the young woman holding the mic in his face, he'd seen the camera man and two of the other men working the lights and toting the equipment camped out there.

"Agent Levine?" the woman repeated. She tossed her head to adjust her bangs and gave a tug to her blouse to make sure it caught the right contour.

Levine tried to avoid a scowl. That was a tall order under the conditions and feeling ambushed like this wasn't helping. "No," he said.

"No?" the woman repeated. "Is the FBI treating this as a homicide investigation? Isn't that why you were assigned? Care to elaborate?"

"No."

"No? Agent Levine. Isn't it true—?"

Levine saw this was headed nowhere. He also knew that he was standing in the middle of a field over a hundred feet from Trooper Geren's car and there was no way to turn and walk away without being filmed and made to look like a total ass. He tried to tie it off. "The cause and manner of death will be determined by the Sebastian County coroner. The Bureau's involvement is peripheral and routine in a case such as this. I'm here largely in a support function at this time." He took a step back to break contact with the microphone. "Thank you."

The reporter took a step forward. "Agent Levine, as you're aware, Fort Chaffee was used to house Vietnamese refugees in the seventies and with the Cubans in 1980. Any reason to believe your murder victim is connected to either of those groups?"

"What?" Levine asked in spite of himself. *Cubans?* "I'm sorry. I have no comment on that."

"In light of recent developments at Abu Ghraibe and Guantanamo, could these remains represent a Cuban victim? Is there a cover-up? How far up does this go?"

Levine looked at Trooper Geren for help and got none. The state trooper appeared preoccupied with fantasies of frisking Diana Jones for concealed weapons. Levine turned back to find the microphone even closer to his face. He'd given up on trying to contain a scowl. "I'm afraid I'm not following your logic," he said; *how goddamn stupid are you?* he thought.

The woman looked at the camera, flicked her bangs to the side with a snap, as if she were fly fishing for lake trout, and turned back to Levine. "The *Marielitos*. The Cuban refugees that fled by boat. They were sent here for holding, and it was rumored that some of them were criminals released by Castro. You're aware that in June 1980 they rioted for better living conditions, and there were allegations of brutality and even torture. In fact, five guards were indicted on charges of beating the refugees. Were you aware of that?"

Levine shook his head. "As I said, I'm not following this line of questions, and I have nothing else to say. Now, if you'll excuse—"

"In light of recent revelations about the treatment of prisoners at Guantanamo Bay, could the remains found here represent a victim of the 1980 riot? Is that why the FBI is involved? Is that why the FBI sent a senior investigator? What's being covered up?"

Shit, Levine thought.

CHAPTER 13

U.S. Army Central Identification Laboratory, Hawaii

Monday, November 3

Kel stood in his office, a black marker squeaking in his hand, adding to the growing list. A large sheet of butcher paper was taped to his wall and contained almost fifty words—beginning with the word *bistro* and ending with the latest entry, *empower*. He'd started it almost six months earlier as a warning to the staff to curtail the use of certain words in his presence. *Bistro, leverage, veggie, dialogue.* He was recapping the marker when the phone rang. Kel flinched and then looked at his watch and noted the time, surprised that it was almost ten and the telephone hadn't rung all morning. He wasn't sorry, just surprised.

In his fifty some years of living, Robert Dean McKelvey had developed a strong dislike for relatively very few things. While he disapproved of much, he actually had a strong dislike for relatively few things: Baseball caps turned backwards were a capital offense of course, so were grown men wearing flip-flops in public, air guitar, chewing gum, the words *veggie* and *bistro*, but on the top line of the stone tablet—telephone calls. Telephone calls were the most disliked thing of all. After what had seemed like a promising career as a young anthropologist, Kel had emerged from a prolonged coma one day to find that he'd become, not a swashbuckling Indiana Jones, but rather, an aging, paper-crumpling Administrator consigned to fielding phone calls all day. And the telephone seldom brought good news—no magazine publisher sweepstakes or mysterious, sultry voiced wrong numbers full of the promise of carnal intrigue—instead it was almost always a fire bell clanging; notification of some managerial brush fire that needed stomping out. Like a maze rat conditioned by repeated electric shocks, Kel had learned to flinch when the phone rang.

"Central Identification Lab," he answered on the third ring. His voice was professional but non-committal. Before he'd gotten up to update the word list, he'd been forcing his way through a mandated supervisor's refresher course—which would be useful only if he were subject to prolonged blackouts and completely forgot everything he'd learned about supervising people for the previous twenty years—and now he moved the spiral bound course booklet—aggravatingly entitled, *Empowering Human Assets*—onto the thick pile of papers that perennially blanketed his desk like an autumn leaf fall. With luck the booklet would quickly get covered and forgotten.

"I'm trying to reach Dr. McKelvey. Is this the right extension?" came the response. It was a male, middle aged or older by the honed patina of the voice, there was an undercurrent of big city, perhaps a hint of cigarettes, and a tone that suggested a don't-bother-me-just-get-to-the-point personality.

"Well, ahh, in that case, then I guess one of us got lucky. This is he . . . Him . . . He. I. Me. What can we all do for you, sir?" The knot in his gut cinched up another fraction. He closed his eyes and waited for the electric shock.

"Doc? I should have known. This is Mike Levine. FBI. We worked—"

"Mike Levine," Kel answered quickly. "I remember. Believe me, I remember."

"How you doing?"

"Fair to middlin'. You? What are you up to? Retired yet?"

"Shit no. I wish. I'm still in Memphis. Sort of. Actually I'm currently back in Arkansas, if you can believe that." Like a lot of native easterners still uncomfortable with the concept that the Atlantic seaboard and the Pacific coast couldn't be directly joined up without the need for what seemed like some meaningless acreage in between, he pronounced it Ar-*Kansas*.

"Oh yeah? That anywhere near Ar-Kan-Saw?"

"Pretty close," Levine responded without a wisp of humor lacing his voice.

"Liked it so much you had to return, huh? Where at? Not back in Split Tree, I hope." The reference was to a small town where they'd first met a few years earlier while working a case of mutual interest.

"No," Levine said, "Fort Smith."

"Oh yeah? That's my—"

"I remember," Levine nipped him short. "That's one of the reasons I'm calling. I need some help, and you popped into my mind."

"That right? Should I feel flattered? This have anythin' to do with that case over on Chaffee?"

"You know about that?"

"I caught the tail end of a CNN story that said the FBI was involved, but I didn't connect the dots to you. I figured the Tulsa or Little Rock offices would take that. Why Memphis? Who'd you piss off this time?"

"Who the hell knows? Actually, I do know. It's a schmuck named Frank. He's the SAC in the Memphis field office, and I'm at the top of his shit list. He volunteered me."

"I think you're always on the top of that list, aren't you? But aren't you gettin' close to retirement?"

"Yeah, but not close enough, not with college-age kids and the stock market in the tank," Levine said. "Listen Doc, I know how much you hate talking on the telephone so I won't prolong your agony. It's just that . . . I need a favor?"

Kel paused, wiggling his antennas to better gauge the depth of what he was about to step into. The last time he'd worked with Levine, it hadn't ended well. "Favor?"

"Yeah. I'll owe you."

"Don't you already?"

Levine finally laughed. "That's open to debate. The way I remember it, I'm running a tab on you. I was thinking this might even the score."

"We can argue that in a minute. What's the favor?"

Levine cleared his throat. "I have that skeleton you saw on TV. People can't figure out if it's in fed jurisdiction or not, and that's the problem. I need someone who can tell estimate the time-since-death."

"Tell me about it." Kel had started to warm up.

"If you saw the CNN interview, then you know almost as much as I do. Couple of construction workers with a bulldozer turned it up over at Fort Chaffee. Can I assume you know where that is?"

"I know it well, bubba. It's where the King got his hair cut off when he joined the army."

"So I hear. Must have been an historical highpoint."

"One of many. One of many."

"So I'm learning. I assume you also know they kept some Cubans here."

"Yup. Around 1980, I think. Vietnamese before that. But Cubans? Is that why you're involved?"

"I doubt it."

"But you don't know? I'm not followin'. The base has been turned over to the city of Fort Smith, hasn't it? Part of all the military base closures."

"That's correct."

"So, you still haven't explained why the FBI's involved? It's not federal property anymore. What kind of skeleton do you think you have that'd be in y'all's jurisdiction?"

"I believe that's why I called you. We're involved because the degree of skeletonization—is that the right term?—skeletonization—the condition of the remains suggests that they are at least a few years old, and a few years would put it before the closure of the base, and that means it occurred while it was still federal property."

"Wouldn't it be CID then? It'd be an army base."

"Fuck-if-I-know. I wish. I tried making that argument. All I know is I'm here, and I want to get out of here, and to do that, I need someone who can say how old the bones are."

Kel nodded as though Levine could see him. "Well, if it's any help, I'll bet you're right about it bein' a few years old. From what little

I heard on the TV, I suspect that it's probably on the order of a thousand years or so. Lots of Indian remains around there—as in prehistoric Indians. Lots of neat archaeology around that part of Arkansas and Oklahoma. My brothers and I used to deer hunt on some of the Chaffee property when we were growin' up; we'd find lots of arrowheads and pottery. Some real neat stuff. Kinda the reason I got involved in archaeology in the first place."

"I hope you're right about it being real old, but the archaeologist that dug these remains up thinks they're modern. The local coroner seems to agree."

"Hmm. What's he got to say?"

"Don't know any details yet. I haven't received the coronor's report. He's been out of town, and no one at his office will let me see the remains until he gets back. In the meantime, a local reporter is trying to connect the dots to Gitmo."

"Gitmo?"

"Don't ask. Scratch that for now. That's a red herring."

"The TV said an archaeologist from U of A dug them up. You know his name?"

"All I know is that it was some professor from the university over in Fayetteville. Trader, I think. Professor Trader. Something like that. I got it written down. Hold a minute." Levine paused. "Ahhh, yeah, Dr. Pat Trader, with a *d*. He's an assistant professor of anthropology at the university in Fayetteville."

"Name doesn't ring any bells."

Levine paused. "Look, I have no way of knowing whether this professor knows his shit or not. That's why I called you. Don't ask me why, but I trust you."

"I'm touched. Really. I may cry yet."

"Screw you, Doc. All I know is this schmuck says that the skeleton is probably recent and therefore it's fallen into my lap. I'd be more than happy if you tell me it's some poor Alley Oop who wandered away from his cave looking for Oona, or whatever the hell her name was."

"We'll see," Kel laughed. He'd learned that Levine's bark was worse than his bite, and despite his better judgement, Levine's problem was starting to interest him. "Did this Professor Schmuck give you any reasons why he thinks the skeleton's not prehistoric?"

"Like I told you, I haven't seen shit yet, but from what I've heard, it's got blunt-force trauma to the skull."

Kel laughed again. "Hate to be politically non-correct here, Mr. G-man, but American Indians were whackin' the livin' shit out of each other long before Christopher Columbus stepped ashore to schedule any anger-management workshops. Blunt force doesn't mean recent; just means human."

"The trauma's just one reason, Doc. There's also was some material evidence found at the scene. That much I've seen."

"That so? What kind? And stop callin' me *Doc*."

"Not the sort of trace that we deal with. Not the hairs and fibers and crap that I'm used to. That's sort of why I'm calling you; this is more like, well—more in your area, and the Bureau was hoping you could take a look at it."

Kel's shifted the phone to the other ear. "Bullshit. C'mon, Mike, let me get this straight. The FBI wants the CIL to do their trace evidence work? Try again. And make it believable if you want my help."

"Crap. I just want you to tell me how old this shit is."

"So send it to Quantico. What's the real reason?"

Levine paused. "Look, Doc . . . *Kel* . . . I've been put in this freakin' gulag here. Again. You can figure that out. And the local press here doesn't have any pig princess contest or any other breaking news happening this week so they're eating me alive. I just want out of here, and I can't leave until I resolve this case."

"Or find someone else to pawn it off on. Nice try, Tom Sawyer, but I'm not in the mood to paint that fence."

"All I need is a quick consult. This may surprise you, but this is not priority-one with the Bureau. If I send it to Quantico, it'll be six months before I get an answer—six months easy."

"So? Send it in and go home while you wait on the results."

"It's not that simple. They're looking to force me out. No results gives them more ammunition."

Kel thought for a moment, and then asked, "Assumin' I agree, can you send the remains to me? Do you know what kind of shape they're in? Are they bigger than a breadbox?"

"The material evidence is all I need you to look at, not the bones."

"If we're goin' to do this, might as well do it right from the beginnin'. Can you send it all or not?"

"I'm not sure the coroner will release the remains until we establish it's a fed case—which is the whole point. I'm hoping to avoid that, you understand? Look, I've got some digital images of the material evidence. I can email them if you're agreeable."

"I'm always agreeable. It's just . . ." He sighed and looked at the supervisor's course book on his desk—it hadn't managed to get covered up and lost in the last five minutes. "Sure. Why not? When can I expect them?"

"How about now? I'm in the business office at my hotel, and I'm ready to hit send. I assume you still have the same email."

"Pretty sure I'd agree, weren't you?"

"Pretty sure." There were sounds of keyboard clicks. "You should have them."

"Wait a minute. My computer's locked." Kel shifted his weight and hit the speaker button on his phone. He balanced the receiver on a pile of papers mounded at the corner of his desk and took his military identification card from the lanyard around his neck and inserted it into a slot in the top of his computer keyboard. In an attempt to improve security, the Department of Defense had reconfigured all of its employees' computers to require a military Common Access Card to operate. Since the Chinese military was successfully hacking into the U.S. computers without the benefit of a CAC, Kel reasoned the real security benefit was to ensure that the U.S. computers crashed so frequently that the Chinese would give up in frustration and hack the Brits instead. The theory seemed to have some merit because Kel's computer instantly crashed when the card was inserted. "Shit," he mumbled.

"What's the matter?" Levine asked.

"Nothin'. Goddamn government computer." He mumbled some more as he removed his card and rebooted his system. It took removing and reinserting the CAC three times before his computer came on line again. Kel cussed and mumbled the whole time and thumped the machine with the heel of his palm to make sure it understood that he meant business. It was still early in the day, and he'd intentionally not logged on to the network in order to devote some time to other things, and, so, when it finally came on line, he wasn't surprised to see 217 new unread emails spooling up on the screen. "Okay. Ahh . . ." He scrolled the curser up and down. "Ahh, I don't see anythin' from you . . . you sure you have the right address? It's my first name, R-O-B-E, wait, what's this? You wouldn't be— don't tell me you're Sassygrl25?"

"Don't ask."

"Sassygrl? Twenty-five?"

"Screw you, Doc. Just open the friggin' thing, will you?"

"Ahh, I don't know," Kel replied. "This one of those FBI stings I've read about? What kind of photos are you sendin' me, Sassy Girl? How old are you anyway?"

"Cut the crap. It's my daughter's account, okay? It's not like I have access to an FBI computer here at the hotel. Just open the damn thing up."

Kel continued laughing while he clicked open the email. "Roger that, sassy man, but if any of these are pictures of you in a push-up bra, I'm claimin' entrapment." It took several mouse clicks before four small rectangular icons tiled into place. They were labeled ChafBod1.jpg through ChafBod4.jpg. "Do I need to open these in any special order?"

"No," Levine replied. There was a growing impatience in his voice.

Kel heard it and backed off a notch. He knew when to stop pushing his luck. "Okay, photo one. Looks like," he blew out a long breath, "Looks like a rusty hinge or somethin'. Can't really tell from the angle. Probably not goin' to help you much unless your killer was disguised as a door." He minimized the image and clicked on the next one. It opened. "Number two. Well, now this is a bit more interestin'. It's a cigarette lighter, but I reckon you knew that already. Ahh . . ." he paused while he enlarged the image and rotated it clockwise. "Looks to be a Ronson, maybe. Lever arm. I don't work many material evidence cases anymore, but we've got a guy here who knows lighters in a way that a person shouldn't know lighters. I'd say it's a Ronson, though. This could be useful."

"You've seen ones like that before?" Levine asked. "So it's common?"

"Couple-three over the last few years."

"You said it might help," Levine said impatiently. "Tell me it's recent?"

"Hmm, don't think so," Kel leaned closer to the computer screen. "In fact, we had a similar one in the lab just a couple of months ago. Year maybe. Not identical but close; that's why I recognize it. We found it at a B-24 crash site in New Guinea. The corrosion is pretty mild on this one. Was it found like that or has it been cleaned?"

"I'm not really sure what condition it was found in. The local Gomers might have cleaned it when they found it. I suspect the college professor may also have cleaned it some. That's how it looked when the state police signed it over to me, that's all I know. My guess is that any trace evidence that was associated with it was lost when they cleaned it, but you never know. I guess you can't expect college professors to know about evidence collection."

"As a former college professor, I'll try and not read anythin' negative into that pronouncement."

"You know what I mean."

Kel laughed. "I'm afraid I do, Mike. But if it's any consolation, given the age on this thing, I'd bet that any trace biological evidence that might have been associated with it would be long gone by now."

Levine paused as he thought about what McKelvey had just said. It had looked like a regular cigarette lighter to him, except for the green color covering most of the surface. "So, what do you mean when you say *given its age*? You think this thing's old? How old?" he asked.

Kel minimized the image and clicked on the third photo. "You've asked that already. My guess is it's probably late thirties or so. Around then."

"Shit. So the skeleton dates to before the war?"

"You mean the Second World War? Not necessarily. Problem is, things like this get curated. It could have been kept around for decades. I carry around a pocketknife that belonged to my grandfather. In fact, these are big collector's items. Sassy girl could probably find one like it on eBay right now." Kel clicked on the third photo—a detail of the front of the lighter. "Hmm. Can't tell from this image, but is that engravin' on the barrel? If we get the real thing we can probably clarify that." He squinted at the computer screen. "Looks like initials in a little rectangular space. Sort of Art Deco maybe."

"But what about an age?"

"Yup. It's initials," Kel said without responding. He opened up the fourth photo. "Like I said, we've got a guy that can tell you when that lighter was manufactured. Be easier if it was a Zippo. Those are a piece of cake." He paused and studied the last photo. "Context good with these? I mean, were they found with the remains or just in the general vicinity?"

"The professor says they were in *association*. I assume that has some special archaeological meaning."

"Hmm, well, yes. If the context is good, then this—photo four—will help."

Levine was looking at the same image on the hotel's computer screen. "You shitting me? I figured that was the least useful. Looks like trash. An old cigarette pack. Paper. It can't be too old."

"One man's trash, like they say. Trash is actually a very good way to date things. Don't let the condition fool you. Lot of clay in the soil around Chaffee. Under the right conditions, you might get very good preservation. That looks like what you have here." Kel leaned back in his chair and rubbed his eyes. "You used to smoke, right? What's the brand?"

Levine looked at the image of the muddy paper wrapper on the screen in front of him. "Looks like Lucky Strike."

"It is. Except? What color is the background? Outside the circle?"

"Shit. I don't know. It's so dirty. Brown. Could be green."

Kel smiled. "The good news for you, Special Agent Levine, is that it is green. Lucky Strike switched from a green package to white, supposedly to aid the war effort. The story was that it had somethin' to do with the green ink and savin' copper and chromium, but I think it was really just a marketin' angle."

Levine looked at the cigarette wrapper with renewed interest. "And when was the change made?"

"Nineteen hundred and forty-two."

CHAPTER 14

U.S. Army Central Identification Laboratory, Hawaii

Monday, November 3

"Nineteen forty-two?" Levine said it more than asked it. "And you say the lighter is from around then as well?"

"No, I didn't," Kel replied. "I said, it could be."

"That dates it to when this was an active military base."

"Appears so. And that would make it a fed case."

"You got that wrong, Doc," Levine's voice took on a tone of excitement. "I was just thinking. As you said, active military base. It's probably a missing soldier. It's now your case."

Kel laughed. "Hold on there, Elliott Ness, that's not how it works. Let me explain: We have jurisdiction for men lost in past military conflicts. Underline the part about military conflicts. No conflicts like that in Arkansas since the War of Northern Aggression. You say this fella had blunt force trauma. That means a likely crime."

"Maybe not."

"Well, if it were a legal death, or an accident, it'd be in a marked grave; in a cemetery. Given where you say it was found, if it's not an Indian, then it's probably a clandestine grave and that means a possible homicide on federal property. That's your tar baby. Any missin' Cubans?"

Levine's tone changed. "Cut the crap. C'mon, Doc—Kel. I need some help. You could take this one on and not even break a sweat. You're the friggin' pro from Dover. I've seen you work. They don't get any better than you. Help me out, here."

"Nice try, but try strokin' someone whose ego is bigger than their dick. I can give you the name of an army CID agent I know, you could try to pawn it off on them, but my guess is he'll tell you to pound sand as well. No, I'm afraid this one's yours, Mike."

"But how about you owing me?"

"I think who owes who is still up for discussion. Besides, I did just help you. Be glad I don't bill your office for a photo consultation."

The phone went so silent that Kel thought the FBI agent had hung up.

Finally, Levine asked, "Doc . . . Kel, I could use some help."

Kel looked again at the administrative talus slope blanketing his desk and thought about Colonel Botch-it. He thought for a moment. Finally, he answered. "You'll owe me, right?"

"If you say so. Yeah, I'll owe you. Big time."

"Okay. I'll help you out but only because my momma told me to pity stray FBI agents and three-legged dogs."

Levine laughed. "Hold on, last time we met, you said your father told you to pity crippled dogs, or some such cracker barrel shit as that."

"No. My father said lame yellow dogs. My mother says three-legged dogs. You should learn the difference. Doesn't pay to mix those two up."

"So, you'll help me?"

"Only because you happen to fall into one of those categories. How quickly can you get the evidence to us?"

"I can get the lighter and cigarette package out as soon as I find the closest FedEx office. I assume they have one here in Dog Patch."

"Probably do. I hear they even have plans to install a flush toilet in the mayor's house by New Year's. Ask nice and I can probably get you an invitation to the ribbon cuttin'."

Levine sighed. "Don't get so defensive, Doc. I'm the one stuck here, not you."

"Right. I almost forgot." Kel decided to let the comment slide for fear of invoking another reference to Li'l Abner. "Anyhow, get the stuff to me however you can. And how about the remains?"

"Ahh, like I said, I may get some interference from the coroner on that score. Maybe you could talk to him when he gets back to town. You know, spit some tobacco juice on each other's shoes. Bond. I was thinking you could fly here. You have family here, right? Besides, you can probably write the trip off your taxes somehow."

"If you were an IRS agent who knew anythin' about tax law, that might sound intriguin'. As it is, you're barely even an FBI agent."

"So, how about it?"

Kel looked at the calendar on his wall and thought for a moment. "Hmm. This official? Like a consult?" he asked.

"Does it need it to be? Yeah, I guess. It can be if that's what it takes."

"Got your word that no one points a gun at me this time. No one abducts my ass. Too old for that shit."

"My hand to God."

"And no one blows their brains out in my lap. Like last time. I'm gettin' too old for that sort of shit as well."

"No brains. Hey, Doc, remember, it's Arkansas. Who down here has got any to blow out?"

"Bubba, you certainly know how to close a deal."

Levine laughed. "Just a joke between good friends. The sort of friends who help each other out."

"Friends my ass. Where are the remains now?"

"Still here. In Fort Smith, but they're planning on shipping them over to the state medical examiner's office in Little Rock in a couple of days."

Kel looked at his calendar again. He closed his eyes, not believing what was coming out of his mouth. "I might be able to squeeze you in," he said.

CHAPTER 15

Prisoner of War Compound, Camp Chaffee

Sebastian County, Arkansas

Thursday, March 30, 1944

The bat cracked and the ball seemed to leap up and clear the tar-papered roof of the German dining hall in a single blink.

The tall rangy American captain turned and grinned. He had no love lost for Germans in general, but he took his position as captor seriously. These men, like it or not, had fought bravely for their country and were now entrusted to his care. He held the bat up by the knob end and let it swing slowly back and forth like a clock pendulum in front of August Guttmann. "Now that, *Mein guter* Herr, is what you call spankin' the tater. Any questions?"

The German first sergeant took the wooden bat and felt its mass and its balance. It was heavy and solid. He smiled and nodded. When the young American had first approached him about teaching the prisoners the basics of baseball, August Guttmann had resisted. His men may be prisoners, but they were still German soldiers.

That had been almost six weeks ago and as the days had begun to lengthen and the temperatures warmed, so had his feelings toward learning the game.

Fraternization had its advantages.

"You are good, Captain Mac," Guttmann said. He motioned to one of his men to retrieve the ball before turning to face the American. "You have been spanking your . . . tater for long time, not true?"

"That I have, that I have. And I've been whackin' the holy blue shit out of baseballs for almost as long." The captain grinned and popped the German first sergeant on the shoulder with the back of his hand to ensure that his humor took.

Hauptfeldwebel Guttmann nodded in response. He generally was comfortable enough with most idiomatic speech but Captain Mac's slow, soft, almost sticky way of speaking seemed sloppy to his ear and some of the last exchange had eluded him. He was careful that his face didn't betray his confusion.

"Now, we all might as well make the best of what is decidedly a bad situation," the American officer said. He brushed a thick lock of hair back from his forehead and his grey eyes smiled openly. "Bad for y'all anyhow. Don't be scannin' the horizon for the cavalry. Y'all here for the duration, bubba; however damn long that turns out to be. And after that, your whole damn country has got a lot of apologizing to do to the rest of the world. But, after that . . . well, you need to be doin' some serious thinkin' about your future."

August Guttmann nodded as he translated the words; stringing them together like laundry on a line. "And you are a prophet, Captain Mac? This is a talent that I did not know of. What for future do you see for my men and me?"

"You mean *what kind*—not *what for*—what kind of future do I see? For you? Well now, that's easy. It's the one that you make." His eyes smiled again as the lock of hair tumbled back over his forehead. "But I tell you what, from where I look into the crystal ball, the future is spelled A-M-E-R-I-C-A."

The German squinted at the tall, American officer. "Ah, yes. And this is how you spell the future?"

"You bet, with a big sequin-covered capital *A*," he replied as one of Hauptfeldwebel Guttmann's men came trotting up with the retrieved baseball.

The captain clapped his hands together and motioned for the German to toss him the ball. The confused German prisoner looked at Guttmann for permission. Guttmann gave a quick, almost imperceptible nod of approval as he refocused his eyes on the American—the handsome young man who understood so little about the world.

"Perhaps you are correct, Herr Captain.   I should think of the future," August Guttmann said after a pause; then he lifted the wooden bat to his shoulder and swung it.

CHAPTER 16

Prisoner of War Compound, Camp Chaffee

Sebastian County, Arkansas

Thursday, March 30, 1944

First Sergeant August Guttmann directed a quick nod of his head toward the door. Sergeant Horst Klemp didn't need to be told; the thick, meaty Alsatian had already applied a wide shoulder to a spot on the door about two feet above the handle. It wouldn't move until Klemp moved, and Klemp wouldn't move until his first sergeant told him to, and until then they had the privacy they needed to conduct business.

A plan of action had been percolating through the coarser grains of Guttmann's brain for the last twenty hours. The rich-boy captain, Jordan, had been very clear—Corporal Dieter Ketel must die. And not just die, he must disappear. The body could not be found the way Geller's had. The why was understood—Ketel was a painful hangnail and there could be no hangnail this time. It was the how that had required planning. Private Geller's death had been handled poorly, Guttmann could admit that in hindsight, and now they had to snip off too many loose threads because of it. They couldn't make that mistake again. It couldn't be traced back to him or his men.

Guttmann nodded once more and Feldwebel Klemp snapped his heels sharply and bellowed. "*Achtung!*" Eight of the eleven men in the room shot to attention in unison, their voices hushing as if controlled by a single volume control—which in fact they were. Only August Guttmann and Dieter Ketel remained seated.

"You are not a soldier, Obergefreiter Ketel?" Guttmann said quietly. The tone was pedagogical, honed sharp on the bruised knuckles of hundreds of his students. "You are no longer a corporal of the Fatherland's Afrika Korps?"

Dieter Ketel swallowed loudly and cast a quick look at the men around him, fearful to take his attention off of Guttmann for more than a fleeting moment. "Jarwohl, Mein Hauptfeldwebel," he replied awkwardly. His mouth was dry and his lips had glued themselves together. "I am a German soldier."

"Then I suggest you stand to attention when ordered," Guttmann said. His voice dropped to almost a whisper. He rhythmically tapped the first two fingers of his right hand on the table top.

The German corporal stood, clicking his heels and coming to rigid attention. Behind him he could feel a closeness as if the others were silently shifting their positions. The wooden planks in the floor creaked from their movement, but Dieter Ketel didn't dare to take his eyes off of Guttmann's.

"Obergefreiter Ketel," Guttmann said. He was sitting rigidly at one of the wooden mess tables, his hands now in front of him, his fingers now interlocked. His voice was louder now, even and flat; the voice of a high school teacher forced to deal with an unruly teenager. "Do you know why you are here?" He unlocked his hands long enough to gesture vaguely around the room. "Why we are here?"

Dieter Ketel responded with a series of short, uncertain head shakes.

August Guttmann let out an exasperated sigh, his nostrils flaring with impatience. "You were held at the *stalag* in Oklahoma. You have been here a short time."

"Jawohl."

"You also were friends with Private Geller, not true? You were childhood friends—is this not so?"

"Jawohl. We knew each other since school. Yes. But I . . ."

"Yes. Yes. You were friends. You shared things. You had . . . conversations, not true?"

"Yes. We talked. He was my friend," Ketel replied. "As I have said . . ."

"And what sort of things did you talk of, Obergefreiter Ketel?"

The young corporal shrugged and smiled in a vain attempt to soften the hardening mood. "Of . . . of . . . of many things, Herr Hauptfeldwebel. Home. Naturally. Yes. Our girlfriends. Yes. What we would eat when we got home. Strudel and dumplings and fat, greasy sausages. Good beer. Many things. Friend things."

"Of Oklahoma? You spoke of this?"

"Yes. Yes, of course. And of the war, yes. That too. Naturally."

"And of other things, yes? You were often seen speaking with Private Geller."

"I . . . yes . . . I . . . I . . ."

"And you are sorry about his death?" Guttmann's eyes shifted momentarily to the men standing behind Ketel.

"Of course, he was my friend. He was a German soldier. A comrade . . ."

"Did you know that Private Geller also talked with the Americans? Frequently. You knew this, not true?"

Dieter Ketel shrugged nervously and shook his head, unsure of how to answer.

"What did Private Geller say to you about these . . . talks . . . these conversations that he had with the Americans?"

"Nothing, Herr Hauptfeldwebel," Dieter Ketel replied. He shot a quick, backward glance at the men shifting their weight behind him. "Of these things we spoke not at all."

"And you, Herr Ketel? Have you also been speaking with the Americans?"

"Nein. I do not understand . . ."

August Guttmann sat quietly for a moment. His eyes didn't leave the nervous young man in front of him. "You have seen the American Captain Jordan before? You recognize him, not true?"

Ketel slowly shook his head. "I don't understand."

"And do you know who we are, Obergefreiter Ketel?" Guttmann asked finally. His voice was barely audible, as if the question was more of a personal musing.

"Naturally. Yes. You are the first sergeant."

"I was speaking of this, this . . ." Guttmann's eyes took in the men standing about the room, "this group."

Dieter Ketel didn't answer. There was no need to answer.

The German first sergeant stared at the man before him. He took out a package of Lucky Strike cigarettes and removed one. He held the package up, indicating an offer to Ketel.

Ketel declined.

Guttmann offered again, and Ketel took the package. "Keep them," Guttmann instructed. He lit his own cigarette and fingered the silvery lighter, rubbing his thumb against the decorated surface; smudging his fingerprints. He tossed the lighter to Ketel. As Ketel was lighting his own, Guttmann made a small motion with his right hand; a small movement of two fingers. From behind Dieter Ketel a German soldier stepped forward, holding a green, canvas American duffle bag. Guttmann stood and took the bag and reached inside, withdrawing the object within. He held it up, turning it over slowly in his hands and reading the label branded into it. "Lou-*ess*-wille Slugger," he said the syllables slowly as he raised his eyes to again look at Dieter Ketel.

No loose ends, August Guttmann thought.

CHAPTER 17

Fort Smith, Arkansas

Wednesday, November 5

Kel looked at the clock on the dashboard of his rental car as he turned across two lanes of traffic into the parking lot—it was almost three o'clock. His flight had taken sixteen-and-a-half hours, connecting through Los Angeles to Denver to Tulsa, and the drive from Tulsa to Fort Smith via the Muskogee Turnpike and Interstate 40 had added another two hours and forty-five minutes to the trip. He'd agreed to meet Levine at a McDonalds on Rogers Avenue between two and two thirty. Now he was thirty minutes late thanks to a drunken rodeo clown who'd managed to take his spurs through the metal detector in Denver only to be stopped at the gate. The whole airport was shut down for almost ninety minutes while the TSA screeners figured out which one of them was the most expendable.

Michael Levine was sitting in a booth, sipping coffee and staring out the window at the ceaseless string of automobiles inching their way toward the Wal-Mart Supercenter. Aside from a little added weight, most notable in the formation of slight undulations of loose skin along what used to be a sharp jaw line, he looked the way Kel remembered him. Maybe a few more grey bristles at his temple. Maybe a slight deepening of the furrows on his forehead—brought on by a relentless scowl. It had been slightly over three years since they'd worked together, but in many ways it had been a stressful three years—for both of them.

Kel stopped at the counter to order a Diet Coke, paying for it with a pocketful of noisy loose coins that he'd accumulated in the airport in Denver during his layover. He smiled at the gap-toothed young girl behind the counter whose name tag identified her as *JayMe T*—the T suggesting that management had several JayMe's running around behind the counter and needed a way to distinguish them—and nodded his thanks as he took his drink. He paused and took a slurp of carbonated caffeine before approaching the federal agent.

"So Special Agent Levine, welcome back to God's country," Kel said as he slid into the booth, his back to the large plate-glass window facing the traffic. He wiped his lips with a pinch of his thumb and index finger. "Glad you get to see this side of the state for a change. Now you know it's not all treeless, rice and cotton fields like Split Tree."

Levine took a long sip of coffee, looking at McKelvey over the rim of the cup, before answering. "Doc." He nodded in acknowledgment. "Long trip?"

Kel shrugged dismissively and waited for Levine to continue. Neither man particularly liked small talk if it wasn't necessary, and in this case it wasn't.

"So, how you been?" Levine asked.

"Fair to middlin'. You?"

"I guess I should thank you for coming."

Kel shrugged. "I was able to tie this into a trip to Atlanta." A moment of silence followed. "But you can still thank me if you want."

"Atlanta?"

"Yeah, I, ahh," Kel paused, "Technically I'm on leave. I'm goin' for a job interview with ATF. I've been puttin' it off, but when you called and—"

"Shit. Take my advice; avoid any government body that calls itself a bureau."

Kel smiled and took a sip of his drink. The ice shifted, and he was forced to wipe a splash from his cheek with the back of his hand. "Saw you on CNN at the airport. What's that make? Two, three interviews? By the way, you really need some lessons on not scowlin' at the camera. It's not a good look."

"Screw you. Like you'd know."

"Ahh, see? If only you could get that sunny side of your disposition to come across on camera." Kel took another sip of his drink. "Actually, if you want to get out of television interviews, a buddy of mine says to just make sure to say the f-word every three words. He claims to have done a study of it and says they can't get any sound bites if they have to cut out every third word. Haven't tried it yet myself, but it sounds like it should work. And you'd be a natural, provided you could limit it to every third word." He took a drink. "So tell me, what's new with your Chaffee case? You figured out yet why the media is so interested?"

Levine shook his head and sighed. "Got me. Between CNN and the local media, I've given two-dozen interviews since I arrived here. Nothing new to tell them, but they want to keep rehashing it like it was news. They're still pushing that same Cuban bullshit angle. Maybe you can help put that to rest."

"As a federal employee, all I know is that Cuba doesn't officially exist. Somethin' to do with Desi divorcin' Lucy. Lord knows, I still have a hard time forgivin' that sonofabitch."

"Somehow, that was about the answer I was expecting from you." Levine took another sip of coffee and sat quietly for a moment and then cleared his throat as a prelude to shifting conversational gears. "I've been meaning to tell you. About that Elmore case . . ." He was referring to the case in Split Tree that the two of them had worked three years earlier.

Kel's mood darkened. "I'd rather talk about Desi and Lucy."

Now it was Levine's turn to shrug. "Hear me out. It wasn't an easy call. I know that."

"Sure was easy for you. I'm the one that ended up with a man's brains splattered all over me. All you had to do was dump the damn thing in my lap and run in the other goddamn direction. That must have seemed easy enough."

"Only because I knew you'd make the right decision." Levine momentarily broke eye contact. Normally, he wasn't the sort to break eye contact. "You made the right call. Somebody should tell you that, but I'm sure nobody did."

"That so? Then why do I feel so shitty about it?"

Levine recaptured McKelvey's eye. "Because life's the shit and sometimes that's the way it is." Levine paused. "But for what it's worth, you did good."

Kel nodded, unconvinced. He sighed and changed the subject. "Thanks. So, when do we get started? Tell me about this body you have."

"Skeleton."

"I taught you well, grasshopper. So tell me about this skeleton."

"You saw CNN. Bulldozer turned it up over at Fort Chaffee. You say you know it."

"I know Chaffee well. Elvis got his hair cut there when he joined the army."

"So you've already told me. So has everyone else."

"Bears repeatin'."

Levine smiled patiently, without a hint of humor to back it up. "Just how big is Fort Smith, anyway?"

"Hmm. Not sure anymore. Not as big as its population. Never has been."

Levine sighed. "You know, just for once, Doc, just once I wish you'd answer a goddamn straight question with a goddamn straight answer."

"I did."

"No you didn't. That wasn't an answer. Sometimes it's like you're a congenital half-wit."

Kel knotted his face. "Congenital means you were born that way. For the record, I work hard at being a half-wit. A congenital half-wit, now that would be my boss."

"Mister Neep?"

"Les? No, I meant the commander, Colonel Botch-it. Les isn't my boss . . . he's more like a . . . like a suicide counselor." Kel shook his head at the thought and sucked in another slug of caffeine. "Anyway. You made any progress in gettin' your jurisdictional angle figured out?"

"Well, now, I believe that's why I asked you here, professor. You're going to tell me whether he was buried before the base closed or not. Maybe I can still flick this off on someone else and walk away. Maybe still save my vacation."

"I guess we'll see, but why don't we focus on savin' your job first."

CHAPTER 18

Fort Smith, Arkansas

Wednesday, November 5

Levine had arranged with the Sebastian County coroner to have the remains laid out at the Hampton Brothers Funeral Home on Massard Road for Kel to examine; it was conveniently located to the McDonald's, and they left McKelvey's rental in the parking lot and drove together in Levine's government car. The cold front that had shagged through a few days earlier was now stalled out over Kentucky, and the weather that had fallen in behind it was more-or-less back to normal for an early-November day in western Arkansas. It was a pleasant afternoon; the skies were clear and the sun was warm and people were out clogging the road.

"I heard you were in Iraq a year or so ago. Not that I'm keeping track of you," Levine said, as much to take his mind off the traffic as to elicit information. "How was that?"

Kel shrugged. "Shithole. How's it supposed to be?"

"Hmmm," Levine acknowledged. "One of many in this world. Glad you're safe."

"You sound like my wife. Thanks. Say, Mike—" he was interrupted by the sound of Levine's cell phone ringing.

Levine answered it. "Levine. Yeah. Yeah." He looked at his watch. "On our way now, maybe five minutes out. Lot of morons on the road. Yeah. Thanks." He snapped the phone shut, dropped it into his lap, and sighed impatiently. "That was the guy at the funeral home checking to see if we were still coming."

"Hmm," Kel acknowledged. "Same smooth telephone etiquette I see."

"Don't talk to me about phones, Doc. You still get hives when you have to use one?"

"Sometimes, but I see you're also tethered to one now. How long's that been? Thought you didn't like talkin' to people."

Levine glanced over his shoulder and muttered *asshole* as he changed lanes. He turned his attention back to McKelvey. "Wrong. I don't mind the talking, it's the people themselves I don't like, remember? You're the one that doesn't like talking to them."

"Only on phones. Hate phones." Kel nodded at Levine's lap. "But answer my question. When'd you start carryin' that? You weren't three years ago when I last saw you."

Levine drove silently for a moment, avoiding eye contact with McKelvey. Finally, he said, "My oldest daughter just started at Fordham."

"Really? Fordham? That's great. That's a Jesuit school, isn't it?"

"What are you saying?"

"I'm not sayin' anythin'; I think that was a question."

"My parents were Jewish; I'm not. Not a good Jew, anyhow. Besides, it's an excellent school."

"Sure it is. You read too much into that. I was just makin' conversation. That's great, Mike. Congratulations. That's really great."

"Right. Great." He looked at McKelvey and for a moment the sinew and gristle softened. "Goddamn, Doc; here's the deal, she's coming home for her first break, and here I am living in this friggin' exile. You're absolutely right; I do firmly believe that the world would be better off without people. But my family, my wife and kids, are different. They're my world, and now a part of my life is passing, and I'll never get it back, and here I am. Here." He gestured out the car window at the stalled traffic. He sighed. "Don't tell me you can't understand that. I know you're crazy about your kids."

Kel nodded slowly. "Not so much crazy. Insane, maybe. At least that's what I told the judge when they arrested me for tryin' to drown them both in the bathtub."

"Thanks for taking it so seriously."

"Sorry, Mike. Sorry," Kel added quickly. "I know what you're sayin'. Ours are still young; younger, anyhow, but I hear you. I know exactly what you mean. In case you haven't noticed, I don't get to spend much time at home either."

Levine nodded and laughed but without any trace of humor. "My wife says that I don't handle change well."

"Oh, bullshit, Mike. No offense to your wife, but that's crap. You were wounded in Vietnam. You've taken down congressmen. Hell, you've endured three years of exile over in Memphis—which for you might as well be on the dark side of the moon. Worse. You may be a ring-tailed prick, but the inability to handle change is not a flaw that I'd say you have."

"I can handle *situations*, Doc. I can deal with any shit you throw at me. That's not what I'm saying, I'm saying that my children have been my life for eighteen years and now that's over. My daughter's in college, and it'll never be the same again. The minutes are ticking by and I'm . . . here."

"So give it up."

"Can't afford to. And I won't let those pricks force me out either."

No further words were spoken. None needed to be spoken. Almost fifteen minutes later they pulled into the driveway of the Hampton Brothers Funeral Home and killed the engine.

"I wish I had some advice for you," Kel said.

Levine stopped him with a look that clearly indicated that no further discussion of his family was welcome.

Kel shifted the topic. "Well, another day, another funeral home," he said, hoping to break the funk that they'd settled in to. He undid his seatbelt and looked out the windshield. "I'll tell you what, thanks to you, I've seen the inside of more goddamn southern funeral homes in the last thirty-six months than I care to count. We gotta stop meetin' in places like this." The reference was to the earlier case that the two men had worked and the fact that they'd been forced to deal with a small-town coroner who'd also administered his office from his funeral home business.

Levine had already unfolded his long, six-two frame and was standing out on the concrete, politely waiting for McKelvey to finish talking before closing his door. "You aren't going to get an argument out of me," he replied, as if there hadn't been any personal conversation in the car. Any momentary gap in his armor was closed up. He adjusted the fit of his sport coat as if he were adjusting his outer shell.

Kel stood and arched a kink from his back. There was a muffled pop, like a distant gun shot, as a vertebra snapped back into place. He started to reach into the car for his own blue sports coat that had been wadded into a ball in the back seat, when Levine's figure caught his attention. They were both wearing khaki slacks and white, button-down collared shirts, and although Levine had on a striped red tie and a couple inches in height, together they looked like urban missionaries in search of a wayward soul. Matching blue sport coats would be way over the top. Besides, with the sun out and shining it was almost pleasant if you avoided the wind. Instead, he left his coat in a wad and closed the car door and began walking slowly up the sidewalk, knees stiff and still uncooperative from the long plane flight.

Levine got to the entrance first and paused, looking back, his eyes going between McKelvey and the car. "You lock it?" he asked. Levine's city-bred paranoia led him to keep his car door locked at all times.

Kel was slowly coming to an agreement with his back and legs and was almost to the door when he replied. "Don't start, Levine. This ain't New York. You're back in the friendliest place on earth. Besides, nobody in his right mind is gonna steal a car out of a funeral home parkin' lot in the middle of the day. You really do need to develop some faith in folks."

Levine pulled the keys from his pocket and aimed the electronic door clicker at the car. The car honked and flashed its lights in response. "When you've dealt with enough shitbirds, Doc, you'll know it's not the ones in their right minds—as you put it—that you need to worry about."

"Maybe," Kel replied. It was a losing argument. He reached past Levine to turn the knob on the front door as he smiled and gestured for the FBI agent to enter; they stepped inside.

It was quiet and warm and the air smelled of lilacs or gardenias or some other industrial aromatherapy. There was soft music coming from nowhere; soft enough that it took Kel a moment to realize that it was Andy Williams singing Christmas carols. As he closed the door behind them, a small, but otherwise quite normal looking young man rounded the corner, hand already extended in greeting. He was wearing a dark-blue sweater covered with too many smiling snowmen on it, and he walked like a man whose life was tidy and whose underwear fit comfortably.

"Happy Holidays," he said. "C'mon on in. What can I do for y'all?" He began shaking Levine's hand with considerably more enthusiasm than you would expect for someone in the funeral business. "I'm Mr. Russell," he continued as he grabbed for McKelvey's hand and began working it over. "Jack Russell." He smiled. "Like the dog. It's really John, but I go by Jack. I'm an associate director here at Hampton Brothers."

"Mr. Russell. I'm Special Agent Levine. FBI," Levine broke in. "I spoke to Mr. Parker earlier about looking at some remains recovered from Fort Chaffee. He was going to make arrangements for us to—"

"Oh, yessir, he told me about that. Mr. Parker's off tendin' to some early Christmas shoppin'. He's been so busy givin' interviews about the Chaffee Man that his head's a spinnin', and that's sayin' somethin'. But I guess I ain't tellin' you anythin'. I ain't never seen anythin' like it. Lord, you'd think we never dealt with a body before. Of course, you boys at the FBI are doin' all the big-time network shows; we've just been gettin' the local news. Been kinda fun, but to tell you the truth, I think Mr. Parker kinda needed a break. He was out of town and came home to this . . . actually, you just missed him. He went on down to the Supercenter to take care of some things for the missus.   She's been wantin' a new blender.   Taken to drinkin' smoothies."

"That right," Levine stated.   The inflection was not that of a question, it was more that of impatience.   "Mr. Russell—"

"Jack."

"Mr. Russell, this is Dr. McKelvey.   He's the one who is going to examine the remains—if that's alright."

"Oh, yessir."   He looked at McKelvey.   "Welcome, doctor.   Umm, we're all set up, if you want to go ahead and get started," he paused awkwardly and looked back at Levine.

"Then let's do that," Levine responded.

Jack Russell nodded and turned and began walking away toward the rear of the building.   "All righty then, y'all can come on back," he replied over his shoulder.   He paused long enough to ensure that he had a train hitched up behind him and then continued.   "Normally we arrange for autopsies to be done over at the Catholic hospital, but seein' how this is just bones, we figured we could accommodate you here just as easy.   This is just a cursory exam as I understand it; not an autopsy.   We got everythin' laid out best we could.   We don't get too many cases like this in here—just bones and all—so they may not be in the proper order."   He pushed open a door and held it until his two visitors were inside and then he accelerated past them into the brightly lit tile-and-chrome room.   "The doctor can work in here.   We set these two embalmin' tables up for you, but if they won't work we can rig up somethin' else."

"This is fine," Kel said.   "Hope we're not imposin'."

"Not at all.   As you can see, it's kinda light.   Two old folks from one of the nursin' homes didn't make it through the night.   I was in here until three in the mornin', but other than that, it's been kinda slow."

"Three?   Sorry to hear that.   You must be tired.   This shouldn't take too long."   Kel rolled his shirt sleeves another half turn; clearing his elbows.

"Take your time. Take your time. I'm here all day; nothin' scheduled, so it should be all yours—of course, like I was sayin', it's not like we can really schedule our business, if you understand—death and taxes, death and taxes—but as far as we know, we ain't got nothin' goin' on this afternoon. It's all yours." He stood in the room with his hands on his hips and nodded at the white embalming table. "Let me know if this won't do you."

"It'll do us just fine," Kel responded as he walked up to the side of one of the porcelain-clad steel tables. He put an extra shot of enthusiasm in his voice to compensate for Levine's poor manners. The tables were covered with brown paper bags, each folded flat, and on top of each bag was a muddy, brown bone. At the end of the table was a human skull—missing some pieces. "We're just gonna take a quick look-see today. Like you said, cursory. Nothin' fancy. Ahh," Kel paused and craned his neck around the room. "Tell you what, Mr. Russell, I could use some rubber gloves if you got any. Not sure if we're gonna need to do DNA on this fella, but we better be safe."

The little funeral director bent over and removed a small box from under a cabinet. "Yes, sir. I understand precautions. Will latex work? And call me Jack, if you want to."

"Latex is great, Jack. I'm Kel, by the way." Kel smiled as he pulled two beige latex gloves from the top of the box. He dropped his voice into a mock conspiratorial tone as he snapped on a glove and canted his head in the direction of Levine who was walking slowly around the second table looking at the remains arrayed on its surface. "And Special Agent Grumpy there is best left uncalled, period."

Jack Russell looked at McKelvey and then at Levine, unsure what to make of the situation. In the end, his thick good nature overcame his thin doubts, and he smiled and winked at McKelvey. "Well, you gentlemen need anythin' else—anythin' at all—one of y'all just hunt me down. I'll need you to sign in before you leave."

"No problem," Kel responded. "We'll be out of your hair shortly."

"Take your time. I'm in no rush. I'll be up front. We're tryin' to get our calendars mailed out well before Thanksgiving so everyone will have one to start the New Year with. Theresa's out this week with a couple of sick kids and all, so I reckon I'm all there is. I tell you what, though, I've licked so many dang envelopes this mornin' that I'm surprised my tongue ain't glued tight to the roof of my mouth. I'm glad for any little diversion."

"I hear ya," Kel replied. He glanced up at Levine to better savor his expression. Levine had a very low tolerance for human beings, and Jack's particular variety brought out the foul humors in him quickly, but to Kel's surprise, Levine seemed to have not heard a word. "We'll do that, Jack. If we need anythin' we'll come find you. Might come find you even if we don't need anythin' just to give your tongue a break from all that lickin'."

"You do that, Kel." Jack Russell replied as he headed for his office.

"Moron," Levine mumbled as the door closed behind Russell. He had been listening. "Is every friggin' small-town coroner in this state like this?"

Kel smiled as he slowly picked up the skull and began turning it over in his hands. "Show some charity. First of all, he's not the coroner—the coroner's off to Wal-Mart buyin' a blender for his wife's fruit smoothies—and second, he's a nice guy who's been nice to us, which is more than he can say about you. Besides, I'll take a small-town coroner over some of the big-city medical examiners that I've dealt with. You want to talk about egos."

"Hmm," Levine grunted; not in agreement but in acknowledgment. "You're in a hurry to get to Atlanta, remember? And I'm in a hurry to get out of here, so let's get on with this."

"Not in that big a hurry, Mike. Like I told you . . ." his voice trailed off as his attention soaked into the skull in his hands.

"Got something?" Levine asked after a moment when he realized McKelvey had stopped talking. When he looked over, McKelvey was holding the skull at eye level, examining it closely.

"What?" Kel mumbled, only half listening.

"You have something or not?"

"You know, you could have told me he had dental restorations. Wouldn't have wasted all that time speculatin' on it bein' prehistoric," Kel said.

"Restorations?"

"Dental restorations."

"What? You mean, like fillings in the teeth? No one told me." Levine walked over beside McKelvey.

Kel continued rotating the skull. "You're tellin' me that you've been workin' this investigation for three days, and you haven't seen these remains yet."

"And the point of that would be? It's not like I'd know what I was looking at if I had. So, tell me about restorations. What do they tell us?"

"There's a bunch of them. Kinda hard to see with all the dirt, but they're definitely dental restorations. His mouth is trashed. So much for bein' American Indian."

"So it's recent?"

"Sure as shit isn't ancient. But don't get too hopeful just yet. Just because it isn't a thousand years old doesn't mean it's not fifty. Or twenty."

Levine sighed. "Anything else?"

"Yeah. Maybe. Look here."

Levine edged closer to the table and bent his knees, trying to match his point of view with the anthropologist's.

"At least they were right about blunt force trauma," Kel said, as much to himself as to Levine.

"You're sure? That's what the professor said. How can you be so sure? It was run over with a goddamn bulldozer."

"No. This is perimortem trauma—at or near the time of death. This is unrelated, unless he was alive when the dozer ran over him. No, bone fractures differently when it's green verses when it's dry.

Plus, look at this," Kel traced the margins of the broken bone on the side of the skull. "What color is the bone?"

"Is this a test?"

"Sure is. Don't touch your pencils until I tell you to. You want my help or not? Just answer."

"Brown."

"Dark brown?"

"Yeah. You say so."

"I do. And how about the broken edges of the bone. Like here and here."

"Same. Brown. Dark brown."

"Right. Now, look at that humerus there." Kel used a nod of his head to point to one of the arm bones laid out on a paper bag. It was shattered, the midshaft represented by small slivers of sharp bone. "See the breaks? What color are the broken edges?"

"White. Whiter. Sort of off-white."

"Right. Kinda buff. Sort of a dirty cream color. That's the natural color of bone. All of this dark brown color is the result of bein' in contact with the soil, but not those fresh edges. They're still white because they were just broken the other day when the Cat ran over it. But these," Kel nodded again, this time at the skull in his hands, "These here are old breaks. The edges are the same dark brown as the surface color. What's more, there were at least two blows would be my guess. If we glue all the fragments back together we can probably figure out how many times he got whacked. From what I can see, though, I'd say at least two."

Levine was peering closely at the skull that McKelvey was holding like an odd-shaped bowling ball—one hand beneath to support the weight, the other on top to manipulate it. "I'll take your word for it, but how can you tell? Educate me."

Kel carefully rotated the skull a quarter-turn so that the fractures were face-on to Levine. With his right index finger he traced a long, spidery fracture that originated in a gaping hole in the side of the skull and radiated over the top of the vault. "Like Deep Throat said, you follow the fractures. These cracks radiate out from the point of impact. All the bone that's missin', this big hole here—actually I'm guessin' that most of the fragments are in that pile there on the paper bag—this hole is where the blow struck. The first one. Caved all this in, but there was enough force that the pressure resulted in these long radiatin' fractures. See, they run out like a spider's web."

"Yeah?" Levine's inflection implied McKelvey should continue.

"Now look at this one," Kel's finger shifted to a smaller tangle of cracks near the back of the skull. "Some more radiatin' fractures, but not as big because the skull was already compromised; already shattered. It dissipated some of the force, but it still cracked. This is the second blow. See what happens to this crack? It runs up here, takes a small bend and then continues until it hits that first crack— from the first blow—and then the force dissipates and it stops."

"Sort of like when you have a cracked windshield and you put a small scratch ahead of it to arrest the crack?"

"Yup. I never could get it to work with my car windshield, but it sure as shit works with skulls."

"Okay. Interesting, but how old is it?"

"Gimme a minute, will you?"

Levine made a show of looking at his watch.

Kel sighed. "All right. The answer is, I can't tell you. I can say this is a very white lookin' skull. This guy was about as white bread as you can get. Average height and build, I'd guess. Can't tell you exactly until I take some measurements—which I'm not goin' to do today, you understand? I'm on leave, and this is all unofficial. If you want a written report, you'll have to make a formal request for help, and we need to get this sent to Hawaii."

"Talk to your buddy, Jack, about that."

"Jack's boss," Kel corrected. "I will. If he's not agreeable, I might be able to generate a memo of my preliminary observations or somethin' like that, based on what I see today, but not an official report."

"I understand. How about age?"

"That'll take some time as well," Kel replied as he softly returned the skull to the table, careful not to let it roll. He looked over the remains and finally picked up one of the hip bones. He turned it over and brushed some dirt away with his gloved thumb. "Maybe late twenties. Give or take, I guess. I could narrow it down if I could get it cleaned up and pay it some attention."

"Twenties?" Levine squinted in confusion. "You mean 1920s?"

Kel laughed. "Duh. No, late twenties as in twenty-five to thirty years old when he died. That kind of twenties."

"Very useful, Doc, but what I really need to know is how old? I mean, when'd he die? Remember? If it's recent then it's a local problem. If it's prewar maybe I can wash my hands of it.

"No way that we can really be sure." Kel bent at the waist and put his face at table level to look at the teeth without picking the skull up again. "If we take this on officially, we may need to take a small bone sample or a tooth for analysis. That be okay?"

"Put the goddamn thing through a wood chipper for all I care. If it'll generate some answers."

"Hmmm. One of our dentists at the lab might be able to do some work with the fillin' material on those teeth. Look at the style; the elemental composition, maybe. They might be able to narrow it down to first half, or last half, of the century. Twentieth century." He shrugged.

"That it? Let me repeat in case you weren't listening the first two-dozen times I said this, what I really need to know Doc, is when'd he die? I still haven't heard that."

"Wrong. You just don't like what you hear. Like I already told you, a case like this, best indicator of time-of-death isn't the bones but what's with them. Your cigarette pack suggests 1942 or earlier. I don't think Chaffee was built until 1940 or 1941, so that's a pretty tight window."

"Assuming that it was really found with the remains."

"Assumin'."

"You're the one that was telling me how big Chaffee was during the war. Hell, there could be a thousand old cigarette packs buried out there. Doesn't mean ours was actually associated with this skeleton. Don't you have that carbon shit dating thing?"

Kel laughed. "Yes, we could do that *radiocarbon shit*, but it probably won't tell us much more. The dental fillings will probably put it in the late twentieth century. The error range on radiocarbon will be large enough that it wouldn't add much," Kel said as he peeled the gloves off of his hands and looked about for a trash can to toss them into. "Artifacts are always your best bet for datin' a case like this, though. The human skeleton hasn't changed much in the last hundred-thousand years, I'm afraid." He paused to take a jump shot at a trash can in the corner. The rubber gloves unfolded in flight and fluttered to the tile floor well short.

"Air ball," Levine remarked as he walked over and picked the gloves up. He snapped them a couple of times before tossing them away.

"Hmm. You can see why I wasn't on a basketball scholarship."

Levine sighed. "So what you're saying is it's not looking good for me, is it, Doc? I'm screwed."

"Well . . . no, it isn't lookin' good; not if you're lookin' to drop this hot rock any time soon. You've got a young, white male. Twenty-five to thirty. Probably medium height. Medium build. Blunt-force trauma to the head, at least two blows; one to the left side, one to the back near the base of the neck. No accident."

"All that and it still comes down to a dirty cigarette pack."

"Yeah, sometimes that's how it goes."

"I'm screwed. Say it."

"Okay. You're likely screwed, if that makes you feel better."

Levine nodded and sighed in resignation. "Anything else before we go?"

Kel looked at the remains laid out on the table. "Maybe," he said as he nodded at a small collection of bones piled on one of the paper bags like a bunch of dirty pencil stubs. "There may be somethin' else. Guy's right hand, there's some green stainin' on it."

"Hand? That? What kind of green?" Levine's interest was renewed.

"Yeah. See that bright green. Third, fourth, and fifth hand phalanges, couple of metacarpals as well."

"Translated means."

"Right hand. Probably right ring finger."

"Translated."

"He had a ring on."

"Had?"

"Well, I don't see it there now." Kel took a deep breath and held it momentarily before exhaling loudly through his nose. "That's about all I can do here, really."

"But you could do more if you had this back in your lab?"

Kel kept his eyes on the remains. "Of course, but maybe not what you're hopin' for. We could get a little more definitive on the age. Get a solid biological profile. Maybe do somethin' with the dental fillin' material. Then there are oxygen isotopes, that *carbon-shit* datin' thing, mitochondrial DNA. Maybe some other stuff." He shrugged and looked at Levine. "Depends on how much you want done and how long you can wait for it, and who's footin' the bill."

"And what would all that tell us?" Levine asked. He quickly caught himself. "Never mind. It's not like there are many other options. You can educate me later. So how do we get this to Hawaii?"

"I'll talk to the coroner, Mr. Parker, as soon as he gets back with his wife's blender. Unless he's got more money than he needs, my guess is he'll take us up on an offer for free help. And assumin' he transfers custody, we can have the funeral home box the remains up and ship them. FBI footin' the bill?" Kel asked.

"Why not. Sure."

"In that case, shouldn't be too difficult. We can ask Jack, to make the arrangements. Soon as we get a green light from his boss, I'll email the lab and tell them to expect it and let them know what to get started on."

"When can you come back?"

"Come back? You mean, *here?* To Arkansas? Hell, bubba, I just got here an hour ago and I haven't left yet. Kinda early to worry about comin' back, don't you think?"

"When?"

Kel laughed. "I don't know. Month. Six, seven weeks I guess. My wife and I are both from here; our whole families are still here, so we usually come this way for Christmas."

Levine looked at the remains on the table. "What do you suggest in the meantime?"

Kel put his hands in his pants pockets and looked at Levine. "Well, if I were you, I'd go get myself a library card."

CHAPTER 19

U.S. Army Central Identification Laboratory, Hawaii

Thursday, November 6

"Central Identification Lab," Davis Smart answered the phone. "Smart here."

"Hey. Is your refrigerator runnin'?"

"Yeah, I need to catch it before it runs away. Kel, thank God. When are you coming back? This paperwork is killing me."

Kel laughed. "D.S., I've only been gone two days."

"Yeah, well, they've been a busy two days."

"Colonel Boschet?"

"Who else? With luck we'll have him potty trained by the time you get back. When is that again? This afternoon?"

"Another week. Gotta head over to Atlanta first. Remember?"

"Thanks for reminding me. No offense, but I hope you freeze up and blow the interview."

"Can always count on you for support. You know, if I really wanted to piss you off, I'd tell you that I'm actually gettin' to work a case."

"Not funny. You mean with bones and everything? That kind of case?"

"And everythin'," Kel answered. "Kinda ironic, isn't it? That I have to keep leavin' the lab to get to work a case."

"A real case, huh? I'm pretty good with bones, you know. In fact, I used to be an anthropologist—before I went to work in Dr. McKelvey's House of Administrative Paper Horrors. You need some help?"

"I've heard that rumor—about you being an anthropologist. I just assumed it's like alligators in the sewers. Listen, partner, I need a couple-three favors."

"Anything. Provided you turn down that ATF job in Atlanta and come back this afternoon. I'll settle for one of those."

"We'll see. In the meantime, the favors."

"You got it. Is this like one of those 900-number things? You going to pay me to tell you that I'm not wearing any pants?"

"Yikes. I'm not sure that'd be much of a favor. How about some anthropology consultation instead?"

"Have it your way. Did I tell you I'm a nineteen-year-old cheerleader?"

"Great. Exactly the person I need to talk to. First, that case I mentioned—can I call you Bambi, by the way?"

"It's your dollar. Bambi works for me."

"Okay, I'm havin' this case sent to the lab. It'll probably get there before I get back; when it arrives, log it in as a consult case for the FBI. I'll supply the details later, but get it accessioned and get some folks workin' it, *wiki wiki*. And if you're good, I'll let you look at it; maybe even touch it."

"Anything special?" D.S. asked.

"Pull out the stops. Anthro, obviously, and odont. Have the dentists take a close look at the fillin' material and see if they can tell anythin' about origin, time period, that sort of thing."

"Got it."

"I'm not finished," Kel interrupted. "Pull a tooth and run oxygen isotopes on the enamel. Sample it for mitochondrial DNA, of course."

"Going to be expensive. Who's paying?"

"FBI. I hope. Otherwise we take it out of hide."

"Priority?"

"Yeah. Maybe not the top of the list, but let's move it. Gettin' late in the year, the DNA folks may be able to squeeze it in durin' some slack time."

"You're the boss. Is this something big?"

Kel laughed. "I sincerely doubt it."

"Then why are we pulling out the stops? Why are we involved at all, for that matter? You're the boss, but it's not like we have a shortage of work here already, or an excess of workers."

Kel was silent for a moment. "Hell, I don't know. Somethin' isn't right. Maybe I guess because the guy who's in charge of this case could use a break. He's a bit of a jackass, but . . . Agent Levine, you remember me tellin' you about him?"

"The nutcase from New York? The one you worked that old civil rights case with? The case that sort of blew up in your face?"

"Thanks," Kel said. "Yes, the one that blew up in my face, as you so delicately put it. Literally."

"No offense. So, are we in the business of helping out down-on-their-luck federal agents now? I didn't realize you were back on good terms with the FBI."

Kel sighed. "I'm not, but it's more than that, D.S." He paused. "Whoever this skeleton is, he deserves a name."

"You're going soft on me. They all deserve names."

"They do. They do." Kel went silent for a moment. "Hey, one last thing. I need to talk to Hugh. Is he in?"

"I haven't seen him, but I'm sure he is," D.S. responded. "Does he ever go home? He almost lives in that little windowless cubicle of his with all his books stacked up around him like stalagmites in a cave. Why, what do you need?"

"The material evidence they found with this case. I assume it's been analyzed?"

"Yeah. Prelim analysis anyhow. The final report hasn't been written. Don't tell me you need it already?"

"No. What's the bottom line?"

"It's a Lucky Strike package; pre-1943. The lighter's a Ronson; a model called Fine Line; they started making them in the midthirties; stopped when the war started. It could be either American or British."

"The lighter looked like it had some engraving; were they able to raise anything? Was it initials?"

"Yeah," D.S. said as he reached over and took a stack of paper off the corner of his desk. He shuffled through them until he found the one he needed. "Yeah. Initials would be my guess; fancy script. It looks like . . ." He turned to the second page of the preliminary report in his hand and examined a photograph of the lighter. "Looks like J-S-H-J. Maybe J-S-B-J. It's kinda messed up. The front is an Art Deco design in enamel over chromium plating, but the enamel's all pitted and flaked off. It was probably in contact with some other type of metal that set up a chemical reaction."

"Midthirties. Great. That's what I needed. Four initials, huh? Get Hugh on it. See if anyone from World War Two has those."

"Four initials doesn't sound like your average American: any chance it could be a Brit?"

"Given the context, I'd bet not. Let's assume it's an American," Kel said.

"Hmm, even so, I'm not telling you anything you don't know, but a lot of people served in World War Two. That's a lot of names to search."

"That's what computers are for. Tell Hugh this isn't an assignment, it's an—"

"Opportunity. I know, I know. I'm sure he'll see it that way. Who knows, four initials are a bit unusual so maybe we'll get lucky. Shouldn't be more than a couple of hundred, I'd guess—if we exclude the Brits. Fortunately for you, Hugh doesn't have a life."

"Fortunately. And it may only be a few dozen. The lighter was found on an army post, so I think—"

"So eliminate navy and Marines," D.S. said.

"Roger that. And then cross-check it against folks that went through Fort Chaffee. Start with 1943 and work backward from there. He'll know how to do it better than me."

"You want only the people who died there?" D.S. asked.

"No. From what I can tell, this guy was found under an old barracks. It smells funny. Figuratively, that is. I'm bettin' there's no record of death. No, we need to look at everyone who came into camp and see how many we can verify went out."

"How many would you think that is?"

"Could be a good number," Kel answered. "Chaffee was actually one of the busiest camps durin' the war. Quite a few men went through there."

"Hmm. The things I can learn from you."

"You got that right," Kel answered. "D'you copy all that?"

"Yes. Unfortunately, at my age the problem will be remembering it five minutes from now."

"Put a sticky note on your forehead. You'll see it when you brush your teeth tonight," Kel said. "And thanks. I've always said you're the man—even if you are a nineteen-year-old cheerleader named Bambi."

CHAPTER 20

U.S. Army Central Identification Laboratory, Hawaii

Monday, November 17

Matthew Hardy paced impatiently outside the door to Davis Smart's office. The young forensic anthropologist had come in early to finish his report before heading to the airport. He was off to Cambodia for forty-five days, and Davis Smart had made it clear that he'd better not leave without running the oxygen isotope test on one of the teeth that McKelvey had submitted. He had the preliminary results.

"Come on in, Matt," Davis Smart said as he hung up his phone. "Sorry, I was trying to deal with a travel voucher. I didn't mean to keep you waiting. Don't you have a C-17 to catch?"

Matt Hardy entered the office and held out his preliminary report. "Yes, sir, Dr. Smart, but you said you wanted this report before I left."

Smart looked at the paper in the young anthropologist's hand. "How long have you been working here?"

"Almost three years."

"So cut the *doctor*, you know how Kel feels about that stuff. It's D.S. remember?"

"Yes, sir, D.S."

"That's a little better," Smart said as he took the report. "So, what've we got?"

"Good results. Clean. Nice values."

The deputy scientific director smiled and shook his head. He was old school, completely at home with bones and fragments, and wholly uncomfortable with printouts and numbers. "Where's the tooth?" he asked as he read.

"Sir?"

"Hmmm. Cut the sir crap as well. Kel wanted the tooth sent to AFDIL when you finished. When can it be ready to send off?"

"Soon."

Smart looked up. His expression asked the question.

The young anthropologist shrugged in response. "We got good isotope readings, so we don't need to keep it any longer. I'll ask Chelsea to put it into FedEx tomorrow or the next day. They should have it by the end of the week."

Smart smiled and resumed reading the printout. "Good job. Now, humor me, Matt." He tapped the paper in his hand. "The boss gonna be happy with this?"

Matt Hardy looked uncertain. "I don't know what Dr. McKelvey—I mean Kel is looking for. All I know is that the numbers are pretty definitive."

Smart looked closely at the figures on the page. He was still shaking his head. He cleared his throat, a nervous habit. He looked at his watch. "I'm not entirely sure either. He'll be in soon—assuming he got back last night like he was supposed to." He fanned the paper back and forth for emphasis, "But you think these numbers of yours . . . you think they'll answer his question?"

Matt Hardy smiled. "Yes, sir, Dr. Smart. Assuming that the boss asks the right question."

CHAPTER 21

U.S. Army Central Identification Laboratory, Hawaii

Monday, November 17

Robert McKelvey's office had the appearance of having been decorated by a family of happy magpies who had watched too many television home make-over shows—clutter and chaos interspersed with bright, shiny baubles. On the walls, the shelves, the filing cabinets, open patches of floor, were the souvenirs and detritus of too many days spent away from family and home. Tribal masks from New Guinea and bamboo arrows from the mountains of Laos. An elephant tooth from Cambodia. Bottles of North Korean moonshine infused with dead snakes. Twisted fragments of aircraft wreckage from crash site excavations. And over it all, over everything, like a thin layer of dust-bowl silt, had settled a veneer of paper; reports and printouts; photographs and sticky notes; faded crayon drawings from his sons' youth. A disinterested observer looking at the clutter would be tempted to assume that the owner of the office probably had ADHD. He probably did, or would have if his Methodist mother hadn't made it clear when he was growing up that she would brook no sloppiness of mind or character—chemical imbalance or not.

He'd returned home from Atlanta the previous evening and slept late the next morning; rolling into the office after nine. It took almost an hour to delete the several hundred emails that had accumulated in the week-and-a-half he'd been gone, and another hour to clear the line of people who'd camped outside his door as if they were waiting for Rolling Stones' tickets. He'd simplified his morning some by ignoring his telephone completely—its message light blinking in his peripheral vision like the storm of an oncoming migraine.

Davis Smart had given McKelvey some space and waited until a few minutes before noon before he walked into his office. "Jeet?" D.S. asked, trying to mimic McKelvey's accent.

Kel looked up from his computer keyboard. "Naw. I think I'll skip lunch. Too much piled up."

"You had a chance to look at your FBI case yet?" D.S. knew that McKelvey hadn't made it onto the lab floor yet, so the question was rhetorical.

"Been tryin' to get out there all mornin', but these damn emails keep poppin' up faster than I can delete them. It's like swattin' roaches with a high-heeled shoe," Kel replied. He pushed back from his keyboard as if he'd just finished a large meal and was distancing himself from the dessert plate, and leaned back in his chair and locked his fingers behind his head. "Tell me about it instead."

D.S. sat down. "Some interesting stuff. Interesting trauma, but then you've already analyzed it."

Kel laughed. "I wish. I can't even start to say I analyzed it. Hell, I can barely say I even looked at it. Basic once over . . . Interestin' stuff, huh? How interestin'?"

D.S. stood up. "Compared to your emails?"

Kel conceded the point and got up and followed D.S. They pressed their access cards against the small sensor mounted beside the door to the laboratory and waited for the beep and click that indicated that the door was unlocked and their presence into the analytical area was properly logged. There were thirty tables on the main lab floor, each holding the fragmented skeletal remains of a missing U.S. serviceman. On any given day the tables held a mix of cases: Vietnam, Korea, and World War Two. The splintered human wreckage of three generations of men who'd gone into Harm's Way and hadn't returned. The CILHI was identifying about two men a week—scant progress when compared to the almost 90,000 still unaccounted-for—but progress. Kel often told people who asked him about the emotional toll of forensic work that his work, his lab's work, was a reminder of what was good about life. So much of forensic anthropology focused on the seedy underbelly of humanity—murders and rapes and molestations—and while there was something fulfilling about bringing monsters to justice, you couldn't help but end the day working cases like that without feeling soiled and ashamed to be a member of the human race. But the CILHI's work was different. As tragic and as wasteful as war could be, the nobleness of men who stepped into the bloody maw knowing that they might not return, couldn't be denied. And as much of a soul-sucking toll as Colonel Botch-It and the whole mind-numbing bureaucracy of government levied on him, Kel could go home at night not feeling soiled.

D.S. led the way to one of the tables near the back of the lab; it was covered with the same brown-paper bags that Kel had seen at the funeral home in Fort Smith. Both men tugged a couple of latex gloves from a box at the foot end of the table and snapped them on. "I wasn't sure how you wanted to handle this, so I told them to keep everything in the bag that it came in. If it's okay, we'll get everything laid out and photographed and then transfer it all to plastic evidence bags."

"Of course," Kel answered. He was moving around the table nudging each bag with a gloved finger. "Matt do the elemental analysis?"

"He turned in his report this morning; on his way to catch a plane," D.S. answered. "It's on your desk. Somewhere."

"Hmm."

"Maybe you can make heads or tails of it. Matt says it's a western value, if that makes sense."

"Good work. That was fast. What does that mean? Western? Like California? Oregon? What'd he say?"

"Western. That's what he says. He also says the sample is ready to send off to AFDIL for DNA testing. Ken's got the dental; Chelsea's doing the anthro write-up. They should have their reports soon," D.S. said patiently.

"Hmmm." Kel poked and nudged the bags some more. The long bones of the leg, the femurs and tibias, fit awkwardly in the large brown-paper shopping bags that held them. Most of the bags were small or medium in size—large enough to hold the twenty-seven bones of a hand or the thin, brittle plate of a shoulder blade—but no bigger than necessary. The leg bones, however, were too long; the hip end of the femurs poked out of the ends. "Just make sure to keep the provenience."

D.S. sighed. "Now, I'd never have thought of that."

Kel looked up. "What? Oh, sorry. Of course; I didn't mean . . . yeah, of course. Sorry. So, you said there was somethin' interestin'? You mean besides the trauma to the skull?"

"I did," D.S. replied as he picked up the two bags containing the legs and set them down on an empty adjacent examination table. He placed the one labeled *L. Leg (Fem, Tib, Fib)* to the head end of the table, and moved the one labeled *Right Leg (Femur/Tibia/Fibula)* to the foot end. After snugging up his latex gloves, he carefully opened the bag. Inside were the well-preserved bones of a human right leg. He removed the tibia and held it up for McKelvey, rotating it in the bright light of the lab. "You saw this, of course."

"All the reactive bone? Yeah. Knee's boogered all to hell. The left's a little worse than the right, as I recall."

D.S. nodded his head in acknowledgment as he handed the tibia to McKelvey. "It is, but what do you think of this?"

Kel took the long, slender bone and turned it over, running his fingertips along the midshaft. He couldn't help but shake his head as he looked at it for what might as well have been the first time. He'd examined them previously, in Arkansas, and had seen the obvious pathology of the knee, but his analysis had been cursory and focused on the question of whether they were recently buried or not. He hadn't been asked to really analyze the remains—not really—and that, combined with the working conditions and the jet lag and the fact that it was en route to a job interview had gelled into a plausible excuse for otherwise incomplete work. At least some compartment of his brain had formulated that story, and he was tempted to stick to it, but now, as he took the bone into his hands and looked at it, he wondered how much age and too many days sorting administrative headaches into the appropriate IN and OUT boxes rather than working at the exam tables, had eroded his skills. It was there, right in front of him. Ten years earlier, he would have seen it. He turned the tibia over, finding an angle that best caught the light. It had been broken through the midshaft, several years before death, and had healed well, but there was still evidence of a large, slick, calloused slab of bone bridging the old fracture. He hadn't seen it before, maybe because of all the reasons he could list, but most likely because of the thick coat of rust on his skills. It was there. Healed. Not easily visible, but there. "Damn," he muttered.

"You saw that before, right?" D.S. asked.

Kel paused. He answered in an embarrassed tone. "The truth? Naw, I wish I could say I did. Must be gettin' old, D.S."

"That's okay. Tell someone who isn't more senile than you," D.S. said. "You really missed that though?"

"Yeah, I guess I did."

Davis Smart smiled and graciously said, "You know what you need? You need me to work these cases with you. We'd make a good team; given all the brain cells I've retired, I can miss all the shit you don't."

Kel laughed. "Great. Together, it'd be like we never looked at the case at all."

"There you go. Teamwork."

"Except you don't miss much, and since you did see this, and I didn't, what do you make of it?"

D.S. took the bone back. "Bad break. Must have hurt like hell. Well healed though. Maybe an internal fixation."

"That'd mean a plate or screws, wouldn't it?" Kel asked. "None here."

"Hmm," D.S. muttered to himself, and then he looked at McKelvey. "Or wire. X-ray might tell. Whatever it was, it was probably removed later. There can be a real problem getting the tib to heal properly; I think the army protocol was to remove the plate once it started healing."

"Now that you say that, I think you're right, but I think that protocol changed again after Vietnam when they developed better implants. This is probably a generation before that."

"Well, that'd be my best guess," D.S. replied.   "Probably an internal fixation."

Kel nodded. "No way that wouldn't be in his medical record."

D.S. smiled. "Like I told you; pretty interesting stuff."

CHAPTER 22

Prisoner of War Compound, Camp Chaffee

Sebastian County, Arkansas

Friday, 31 March 1944

The room had been rearranged. The three oak desks, which normally were spaced around the inside of Building T58 to maximize working space, now formed a tight horseshoe in the middle of the room. A single, stiff-backed chair sat centered between the arms of the U.

Captain Bill Porter adjusted the angle of the witness chair slightly and stepped back, hands on his hips, to survey the arrangement one last time. Satisfied, he nodded to Dorothy Kramer, the young stenographer that Colonel Wiggins had assigned to him to assist in the interviews. "Ready, Miss Kramer?" he asked. He waited for her to nod a nervous response before turning his attention to James Jordan. "Captain Jordan, you ready for this?"

James Jordan crossed his arms. "Your show now, counselor. I'm just along for the ride. Remember?"

"Then let's ride," Porter said as he took the chair at the base of the horseshoe and opened his briefcase. As he removed a pad of paper and a fountain pen—one that his mother had given him when he graduated law school—he flashed a smile at the young stenographer and imparted enough body language to indicate that she should take the desk to his left. He avoided looking at Jordan, determined to ignore his dismissive attitude, and instead, nervously centered his pad of paper on the desktop. He took several breaths and rubbed his hands on his thighs, before clearing his throat and beginning. "Sergeant," he said, catching the attention of Tech Sergeant Elliott standing by the door, "I believe we're ready."

Technical Sergeant Charles Elliott wore the satisfied look that comes with flat brain waves. He looked at Bill Porter momentarily before shifting his attention to Captain Jordan. He hesitated. His eyes tried their best to pose a question.

"You heard the captain," Jordan responded, "Move out."

Tech Sergeant Elliott nodded quickly, looked back at Porter, and then opened the door and spoke to someone outside. He held the door open and stood slightly to the side as a tall, thin, angular German officer entered. His coveralls were faded and in need of repair. Elliott used several abrupt jerks of his head to indicate that the German was to take the chair in the middle of the U, directly in front of Bill Porter.

When the officer was seated, Bill Porter cleared his throat and spoke to the young woman. "Miss Kramer, you understand what is required? We're going to be conducting a series of interviews over the next few days, and while we're not swearing anyone in—at least not at this stage of the investigation—I still need an accurate account of what was said and who said it. Understand?" He smiled and nodded his head once to seed an affirmative response.

It worked, and Dorothy Kramer smiled and nodded in return. She was a modest woman, in both size and disposition, with dark hair and darker eyes and full eyebrows that appreciated her thin nose. Pretty. More than pretty when you took the time to notice her.

"Good," he said. "Just take everything down verbatim. I need as complete and accurate a record as we can get. Any questions before we begin?"

The young woman's smile looked troubled. "Sir, the problem is . . . I don't speak German."

Bill Porter laughed and reached out to pat her arm. "That, Miss Kramer, is why Captain Jordan is here. Captain Jordan will be serving as the official translator. He'll translate the German into English, and you'll translate the English into all those shorthand squiggles that you girls are so good at." He winked at her in a manner intended to be reassuring, then he turned to James Jordan. "You ready?"

"I have been. If you two decide to get married, remember to invite me to the wedding, will you?"

Dorothy Kramer blushed.

Bill Porter bit back the urge to respond, and instead took a couple of steady breaths. He re-centered his pad of paper on the desktop, wiped his palms on his thighs again, and spoke for the record. "Today is the thirty-first of March 1944." He looked at his watch. "It is oh-nine-fifteen hours local time. This interview is taking place in Building T58, Camp Chaffee PW Compound, Camp Chaffee, Arkansas. Present are Captain Bill Porter . . . ah, William Porter, interrogating officer; Captain James Jordan, translator; and Miss Dorothy Kramer." He paused to give the stenographer an opportunity to catch up and then realized her note taking was almost instantaneous. He smiled at Dorothy Kramer again and nodded, as much to himself as to her. "The first interview is with *Wehrmacht Oberst* Albert . . . ahhh," he looked at Dorothy Kramer, "Sorry. Wehrmacht means army, the German Army, and Oberst means colonel. We'll try to keep the ranks and terms to a minimum." He waited for her to indicate her understanding before he continued. "The interview is with German Army Colonel Albert Zimmerman." He paused and looked at the German officer who had been sitting quietly in front of him. He maintained eye contact with the German but now his words were for Jordan. "Introduce us. Tell him who were are, and then get him to state his name and rank—for the record. Also, make sure he understands what's going on here. This is not a court of law, or a military tribunal, not yet anyhow, so we're not taking any sworn statements. Therefore, Article 62 of the Geneva Convention cannot be invoked at this time; specifically, he is not entitled to counsel. Nevertheless, this is a matter of grave and serious consequence, and it is important that the witness understands that statements made during this investigation may result in formal proceedings at a later time. If at any time he is confused or unclear of what is being asked of him, he should request clarification before responding. Et cetera. Et Cetera." Bill Porter looked at Jordan. "Do you need Miss Kramer to read any of that back?"

James Jordan smiled. "Got it. Anything else before I begin?"

"No. Just make sure he understands."

James Jordan turned to the witness. *"Herr Oberst. Wir sind—"*

Albert Zimmerman raised his right hand, palm out, as if arresting traffic. "Perhaps," he said in English, "given what you say is the seriousness of this matter; we should conduct this interview in English so that there are no misunderstandings."

Bill Porter squinted to better understand what was happening. He looked at Jordan, who shrugged, and then back at the tall German. "Perhaps so, Colonel. So you speak English. Very good. You're comfortable doing this in English?"

Albert Zimmerman closed his eyes and nodded slowly. "Yes, Captain. Very."

"Your English is very good, sir. Very little accent."

"Thank you, Captain," Zimmerman replied. He crossed his legs and pulled a packet of American cigarettes from the pocket of his POW overalls. "May I?" he asked, holding up a cigarette.

"Certainly. Please."

The German lit the cigarette and blew a plume of smoke toward the ceiling before offering an explanation. "My mother died of the influenza in 1919. I was a boy of four. My father could not . . . let us say, he could not care properly for me, and so I was sent to live with my aunt and uncle in your state of Pennsylvania. I worked on a dairy farm there until I returned to Germany after high school."

"And now you're back here," Bill Porter said. "Strange world."

"Indeed. This is true." Zimmerman took another puff of his cigarette. He sighed. "But, Herr Captain, your investigation; I believe you have questions for me."

Bill Porter nodded slowly. "I do, I do. Sir. Ahhh, first, your full name and rank—for the record."

"Of course. Oberst Albert Peter Zimmerman."

"Very well, Colonel Zimmerman. You are the ranking German PW in this compound, true?"

"Indeed."

"Oberst Zimmerman, you are aware of the murder of Private Hans Geller?"

"Yes, of course."

"Would you care to elaborate?"

Zimmerman smiled and took a puff on his cigarette. "Elaborate? Perhaps, Herr Captain, given—as you say—the seriousness of this matter, perhaps you should ask of me specific questions."

"All right. For the record, Herr Oberst, did you personally know Private Geller?"

Zimmerman wrinkled his brow. "Know? Yes, yes, naturally. As you say, I am the ranking Wehrmacht officer in this camp. I have knowledge of all of the German soldiers, including Soldat Geller, but I do not think this is how you mean."

"Let me rephrase, sir. Did you know Private Geller prior to your, or his, arrival at this camp?"

"No."

Bill Porter reached down and pulled a file from his briefcase. He opened it and riffled a few pages, skimming for some information. "Where were you captured, Herr Oberst?" he asked as he set the file down. Any nervousness that he'd felt at the beginning was gone. The game was in his blood.

"In Tunisia."

"Bone, Tunisia, to be exact. I believe that I'm pronouncing that correctly. And you were captured on the thirteenth of May 1943. Correct?"

Zimmerman nodded, slowly. "Ja."

And you arrived at the port of New York on eighteen July aboard the American troop transport the USS *General Forrest Milton*. Correct?"

Zimmerman nodded again. "Indeed. This is so."

Porter didn't blink. He drummed the fingers of his right hand softly on the desktop as he thought. "Oberst Zimmerman, I am confused," he said. "Private Geller was also captured in Bone, Tunisia. Also on the thirteenth of May. He, too, arrived in New York aboard the *Milton*, and yet you did not know him? How can this be?"

The German took a final puff from his cigarette and looked about awkwardly for a place to extinguish it. Finally he dropped it to the floor and rubbed it out with his toe. "Your Army, they took many Germans prisoner that day. Perhaps I saw Soldat Geller. Perhaps on the boat, or the train, but you asked if I knew him. No, Herr Captain, I did not."

Bill Porter seemed to accept the German's answer. "Fair enough, sir. We'll come back to that. Tell me, Colonel, do you have any knowledge of why someone would want to kill Private Geller? Did he have any enemies that you were aware of?"

"Besides the American Army?"

"Point taken, Colonel. Besides the American Army."

"No."

"No? You seem pretty sure for a man who says he didn't know him."

"You asked of my knowledge. Of this I am sure."

Porter smiled. "So I did. So I did." He shifted gears. "Sir, are you aware of the murder of a German soldier in Oklahoma? Camp Tonkawa?"

Zimmerman nodded. "I have heard of this, yes."

"Any reason to believe the two killings are connected?"

"I think not. No, Captain, of this I have no knowledge."

"That's not what I asked this time, Colonel. I asked whether you had any reason to suspect that they are connected."

"No."

"Are you a Nazi?"

Zimmerman's eyes fixed on Porter's. He measured his response. "I am a member of the party."

"The National Socialist Party?"

"Ja."

"So, you're a Nazi?"

"I belong to the party."

"You're a Nazi."

"As you wish."

"How do you wish?" Porter countered.

"I am a soldier."

"And an officer. Tell me, for the record, Colonel, are there forces at work in this camp . . . forces that are furthering Nazi aims?"

"I do not understand what you mean by forces."

"Forces, you know, forces. Is there an organized group within this camp that is furthering Nazi aims?"

"I do not understand these aims."

Bill Porter paused and reassembled his thoughts. "Sir, you are a smart man. You also are the ranking German officer in this camp. You are a member of the Nazi party. If there is an active Nazi vigilante group within this compound, you would know of its actions, would you not?"

Zimmerman shook his head, uncertain how to answer.

"As ranking officer, you must shoulder the responsibility for what happens in this compound, isn't that true?"

"I am a soldier."

"And a Nazi."

"A soldier."

"A soldier that must assume responsibility for his men."

"For most of us, Herr Captain, the war is over. Finished."

"But not all, Colonel? Is that what you're saying?"

"Your questions are clumsy, Herr Captain."

"And your answers are decidedly not, Colonel."

Zimmerman looked down at the floor. When he raised his eyes, the uncertainty was gone. "Are you a religious man, Herr Captain?"

Bill Porter was surprised. He hesitated, unsure of the turn the interview had taken. "Not as much as my mother would like, Colonel. Why?"

"Are you familiar with the Holy Ghost?"

"*Halt diene verdammte Klappe!*" James Jordan erupted. He struck the desktop with his first and partially rose from his chair. His face was flushed with anger. "*Halt den Mund verdammt!*"

Bill Porter was too taken aback to respond quickly. James Jordan was standing now; his voice was calmer but remained sharpened to an edge as he continued for several minutes to speak to Zimmerman in measured German. Zimmerman watched him closely, his eyes flicking back and forth, unsure of how to respond. After a moment, Jordan relaxed his posture but his eyes stayed honed on the German's.

"That was quite a long monologue. Care to enlighten me, Captain Jordan? Better yet, care to translate it?" Porter asked after a pause.

Jordan didn't break eye contact with Zimmerman. "I basically told this sonofabitch to cut the crap, is all. This is too damn serious to dick dance around like it's a damn game. I told him that if he had anything relevant to say, then he should say it; otherwise, he can keep his goddamn Nazi trap shut. You want my opinion; you've got too much patience with these bastards."

Bill Porter looked at Zimmerman. "Is that true, Colonel? Were you told to *cut the crap?*"

Zimmerman hesitated and then nodded. "Jawohl."

Bill Porter then refocused on Jordan's eyes. "That for the record, Captain Jordan."

"For the record, Captain Porter."

CHAPTER 23

Prisoner of War Compound, Camp Chaffee

Sebastian County, Arkansas

Friday, 31 March 1944

Bill Porter called for a break and waited for Dorothy Kramer to leave the room before speaking to Jordan. "You want to explain to me what the hell that was all about?" he demanded.

James Jordan stood up and stretched. He yawned in a manner intended to convey boredom and then shrugged in a manner intended to convey even more boredom. "Nothing all that complicated, counselor. I just don't have your patience with these Nazi sons-of-bitches and their goddamn superior attitudes. I've dealt with them for a long time. Assholes like Zimmerman will jerk you around all day if you don't grab him by the nuts right off the bat and make it clear that you won't stand for it. They forget who's in charge."

"And that's what you were doing? Grabbing him by the nuts?"

"You're damn right. Someone had to. He was making a fool of you. Of us. Look, Porter, with all due respect, I know that you've got a job to do, but so do I. I deal with these Nazi hard cases every damn day. They may be here in the middle of the good old U-S-of-A, but that doesn't mean the war's over for them. That was a line of bullshit he was feeding you about the war being finished for them; they're still fighting and they'll take every little opportunity—like your interview for instance—to try and win a victory. No offense, but if you let them, they'll take the interview away from you and next thing you know, you're answering their questions. You won't even know it's happening. It came damn close to happening just then."

"Nothing more than that?"

"Nothing more."

Bill Porter listened closely, his face expressionless. He waited until he was sure that Jordan was finished speaking before responding. "I appreciate your advice, Captain Jordan. Your experience working with these prisoners is valuable, but we have a long couple of days ahead of us. I want to try to interview all of the officers today so that I can focus more on the enlisted tomorrow and the next day. This is a legal matter, and as you've pointed out, you're neither a policeman nor a lawyer. I need you to translate what I ask you to and nothing else. Am I clear?"

James Jordan sniffed derisively and shrugged. "You're the boss, *Mein Herr*. Knock yourself out."

Bill Porter looked at James Jordan closely. He started to say more but held up; there would be time for that later. "Fine," he replied after a pause, "Now, if you'll tell Miss Kramer to come on back in, we can proceed with the next interview."

CHAPTER 24

U.S. Army Central Identification Laboratory, Hawaii

Monday, November 17

Kel walked down the hall to the other end of the building, through a half-dozen rat-maze turns and two secured doors, and into Hugh Rooney's small office. "Man, you might want to think about some air fresheners," he said.

The five-foot-six-inch Rooney was sitting in his windowless box in Hawaii, surrounded by stacks of books and printouts and wadded-up yellow balls of legal-pad paper that had missed the trash can and were mounding up like autumn leaves under a clear florescent sky. A graduate of the military history program at The Ohio State University, Rooney had been widely regarded as one of the up-and-comers in the field, and it had been something of a coup when Kel had convinced the previous CILHI commander to hire him five years earlier. But that was in the good days—the pre Colonel Botch-it days—when the historical section actually did historical research. Rooney now spent most of his time mailing out his résumé in hopes of being rescued from the monster's labyrinth. Every time they talked, Kel had to bite back the urge to apologize to Rooney for dead-ending a promising career. "I heard you were back," Rooney said as he looked up momentarily. "Atlanta? What were you doing there?" He refocused on the papers he'd been reading.

"Maybe some of those little pine-tree lookin' ones; like you hang from your car's rearview mirror. It's kinda rich in here," Kel dodged the question. He had no intention of any more people knowing about his job interview than were necessary.

Rooney understood that no answer was coming his way. "How's your German?" he asked. If McKelvey wasn't going to talk about is trip, Rooney wasn't going to discuss the air quality of his office.

"Umm, better than my Hungarian, but not as good as my English. Why?"

"You speak Hungarian?"

"Not a lick."

"Okay. Sooo, if I said *Heilige Geist* to you, what would you respond?" Rooney continued.

"I might try, *Gesundheit.*"

Rooney smiled patiently. If nothing else, the last three years or so had taught him restraint in the face of fools. "You want to humor me with a second guess?"

"Ahhh, sure. Heilige Geist. Well, then I guess I'd say you're either a Catholic or a German Lutheran. Not a whole lot of difference really unless you're nailin' your thesis on a door."

"Very good. You're on the right track. It means Holy Ghost."

"Very interestin'."

"Yeah, it is," Rooney said, "Now, hear me out. You're the one who wanted this information, remember?"

"I am?"

"Yeah, you am. Dr. Smart said you wanted me to run down anyone with the initials J-S-H-J or J-S-B-J that might have been at Fort Chaffee. Remember?"

"Yeah, I remember that. It's the Heilige Geist part that I seem to be drawin' a blank on."

"Well, that's because you didn't ask about it."

"Of course I didn't. How stupid of me."

"That remains to be seen."

"So, does this mean you found somebody with those initials? That was fast."

"Oh, hell no," Rooney responded. "That'll take a little longer."

"I see. Ahh, Hugh, no offense, but this conversation isn't makin' much sense."

"Oh yeah? Try dealin' with Colonel Zombie for an entire afternoon, and then talk to me about making sense."

Kel winced.

"Anyway," Rooney continued, "before I could track down your initials guy, I wanted to do a little research on Fort Chaffee—it was called Camp Chaffee during World War Two, you know?"

"Uh-huh. Grew up near there, actually. Close by anyhow."

"Yeah, well, okay, so you know it was a pretty busy place, and not just with GIs. It was also a big holding camp; a POW camp for German prisoners."

"I assume this is where the Heilige Geists come in, right?"

"Right. The Holy Ghosts—the Heilige Geists—they were a . . . ahh . . . they were kinda like a vigilante group—groups, actually—there were a number of them that operated in the U.S. prisoner-of-war camps during World War Two. They were more organized early on, you know, when the fanaticism meter was pegged out, but their influence and organization waned in direct relation to the number of German defeats, so that by the end of the war, their—"

"Vigilantes?"

"Yes. Like informal Gestapo types. They were true-believers that kept the other prisoners faithful to the Führrer. Even in the prison camp, no back was sliding allowed."

"How'd they manage that? I'm guessin' not with hall monitors and demerits?"

"Sort of, except these hall monitors carried blunt objects and had sour dispositions."

"You should have gone to high school in the South, son. They did where I went to school as well," Kel said.

"Well, that's sort of why we're having this discussion, isn't it? We're talking about German POWs in Arkansas, right?"

"If you say so. I really haven't followed much since I asked about gettin' some air fresheners. Go on. What's this got to do with the guy with four initials?"

"Absolutely nothing, but humor me, will you? God, Kel, it's not like I get to do any historical research anymore, and this is neat stuff—from an historical standpoint, anyhow."

"Yeah. You're right. It does sound interestin'. Go on." Kel tried to make his voice smile. He leaned against the door jamb, crossed his arms, and took shallow breaths through his mouth.

"Well, as I just told you, Camp Chaffee was one of the big POW camps for German soldiers. From early on in the war. The government wanted to keep the bad guys well in the hinterland so that if any escaped, they couldn't do much damage."

Kel found himself nodding. "Yeah. Did the same thing with the Cuban boat people in the eighties. Chaffee also housed some of the Vietnamese refugees in the seventies—though in their case it was just a matter of logistics and not so much the need to isolate them. Chaffee had a lot of unused barracks, at least until a big fire a couple of years ago."

"Yeah, well in 1942, where to put all those German prisoners was a matter of national security. The early POWs were hard-core types— as in *Afrika Korps*. Rommel's boys. Real ass-kicker types—at least until they got their own asses kicked. Anyhow, the concern was that if they got loose in the U.S., they could sabotage railways and docks and factories. The solution that was settled on was to put them out in the middle of nowhere like—and don't take offense at this, Kel—but places like Oklahoma and Arkansas where the worst that might happen is that an outhouse might get blown up or some cows knocked down."

"Tipped," Kel interrupted for the record. "Not sure what y'all do up in Vermont, but where I'm from, you tip cows over. You don't knock them down."

"I heard you people knock them up."

"No, you tip them."

"Is there a difference?"

"Sure is to the cow."

"Anyhow, there was a big POW camp at Camp Chaffee and another one in some place called Tonkawa, Oklahoma. You ever heard of it?"

"Nope, but it sounds like it should be in Oklahoma."

"I'm not surprised. It was over by someplace called Ponca City. Not that I've ever heard of that either."

"Hmm. I have. Not much over in those parts, even today."

"I'll take your word for it. But that's the point, isn't it? There isn't much there, or at least there wasn't in the 1940s. That's why it was a good place to put all the good little Nazis. There was nothing there to sabotage. But that's also why there was such an organized cell of Geists. You had this initial band of hard cores, true-believers, but then as the war went on, you got more and more conscripts who needed some regular reminders that they were supposed to be good National Socialists."

"And you're sayin' there were some of these Holy Ghosts at Chaffee?"

"Very much so from what I've been able to find out. And these guys meant business. In fact," Rooney paused and shuffled through some paper notes. "Here it is. Yes, in fact, over at the Tonkawa camp, one of the POWs—a corporal by the name of Kunze, Johannes Kunze—was found dead one morning outside the dining hall—beaten to death. Apparently he wasn't being a good enough Nazi."

"Depends who you talk to. My father always said that the only good Nazi was a dead one."

"Right. Well then, your father would have gotten along fine with this one. Anyhow, the War Department convicted five German POWs at Tonkawa—all members of the Heilige Geist—of first-degree murder. Oh, and tell me this isn't cool beans: Guess who the prosecutor was?"

Kel shrugged as he answered. "No idea."

"Try Jaworski."

"You mean the Watergate Jaworski? Leon? The one that got Nixon?"

"The same. He was an army JAG officer at the time. And they brought him in to get some convictions."

"So what happened? To the POWs. I know what happened to Jaworski. And Nixon—for that matter."

"Now that's an interesting story," Rooney said. "Ultimately all five became what your father would have considered to be good Nazis. They were all convicted and sentenced to death."

"Death?"

"Yeah, murder is murder, even in a POW camp, but it's not that simple. After they were convicted, somebody at the War Department realized that executing German POWs might not set all that well with Hitler and his—"

"I wouldn't think hurtin' Hitler's feelin's would be much of a concern. Why'd we care? Wasn't killin' Germans part of the game plan?" Kel interrupted.

"Think."

Kel closed his eyes and tried the fit of some puzzle pieces. He shrugged. "Hurts to think. Help me out."

"Well, the Germans were holdin' American POWs at the time. The concern was that there might be reprisals against our men over in the stalags, so the executions were stayed until near the end of the war when it was considered safe. Then they took the five, plus some others as well, up to Leavenworth and quietly hung them all in an elevator shaft. July tenth, 1944."

"An elevator shaft?"

"Don't ask me, I just read the books."

"And this was over in Oklahoma?"

"The executions were in Kansas, but the Kunze murder was in Oklahoma, that's right. But as I was saying, the Holy Ghosts weren't only in Oklahoma. This is where it concerns you: In early 1944, a German private by the name of Hans Geller was murdered at Camp Chaffee."

"Really? More Holy Ghosts?" Kel asked.

"Apparently. They convicted a guy and sentenced him to death, too."

"Another elevator shaft?"

"No. That's what's funny. They hang the ones from the Oklahoma case, but the guy convicted at Chaffee had his sentence commuted. I'm still trying to track it down, but I'm not having much success. There are lots of records on the Tonkawa case, but the one at Chaffee is . . . I don't know . . . it's like there's hardly any record of it happening."

Kel thought for a moment. He wanted to ask Rooney about progress on the initials, but bit back the urge. Hugh Rooney always produced when asked, and if this little historical back alley brought him this much cheerful diversion, it was worth a short wait. "The victim—what's his name again?" Kel encouraged.

"You mean the one at Chaffee? It's Geller. G-E-L-L-E-R. Private Hans Geller."

"Like the guy who bends spoons?"

"You're showing your age, but yeah. Geller. I'm trying to track down some personnel records on Private Geller, but there doesn't seem to be many," Rooney replied. "At least not that I found yet, but I did track down a copy of his death certificate."

"Really? It list the cause of death?"

"Wouldn't be much of a death certificate if it didn't, would it?"

"Smart-ass."

"Yeah, it's got the cause of death; maybe you can make sense of it," Rooney paused as he searched his notes and produced the copy. He tipped back in his chair. "Nice, flowery sort of long-hand; nice cursive handwriting but kinda hard to read. Let's see, says here that the cause of death was—and I'm quoting this—compression of brain, comma—"

"You mean coma?"

"No, comma. I'm reading the punctuation as well. So . . . ahh . . . comma, severe, comma, left temporal and parietal lobes, comma, blah, blah, blah . . ."

"Blah?"

"Well, I'm not reading all of it. The blah-blah part is editorial. Do you want to hear this or not?"

"Yes, comma, please continue, period."

"That's better. Okay, ahh, there's a period after that last blah, and then it says, severe extradural hemorrhage from the left middle men . . . men-in . . . men . . ."

"Meningeal."

"Thank you. Yeah. The left *meningeal* artery, then some more blah, blah, blahs, due to comminuted simple fracture of the skull involving the temporal. End quote. Make any sense to you?"

"Yeah," Kel answered, reaching for the paper. "It means someone beat his damn brains out."

CHAPTER 25

U.S. Army Central Identification Laboratory, Hawaii

Monday, November 17

Kel retraced his steps back to his office and sat in his chair, staring at his computer, watching email-after-email tally up on the screen— twenty-seven new ones in the time he'd spent talking to Hugh Rooney—thirty-five if you counted the various financial opportunities being offered by the Bank of Nigeria, generic Viagra sales, and religious chain letters. The DoD SPAM filters actually worked, but only at blocking emails from other government agencies, educational institutions, and anything else remotely essential to McKelvey's job. After a couple of minutes of steeling his nerve, he fished into his pocket and removed a small ball of paper that Levine had given him as they were leaving the coroner's office almost two weeks earlier. He uncrumpled it and flattened it and smoothed it out on his desk, then he took a deep breath, picked up the phone, and punched in the numbers written on the paper. The phone clicked and beeped and began ringing.

"Trader residence," the voice came out of the telephone's earpiece. It was a warm voice but it had a sticky crack to it, as if its owner had been asleep or too long quiet.

"Yeah, umm, I'm tryin' to reach Professor Trader, Pat Trader," Kel responded.

"That's me. What can I do for you?"

"Professor Trader, sorry to bother you. My name's Robert McKelvey, and I got your phone number from Special Agent Michael Levine, FBI. Agent Levine is workin' a case down in Fort Smith that you had some involvement in."

"I assume you mean that skeleton that we excavated last month."

"Yeah, that's it. I have a few questions about it, and I was hopin' you could answer them for me."

"I guess so. I'll try," Trader paused, "Ahh, no offense intended, Mr. McKelvey, but do you mind me asking who you are, and why this concerns you? I mean, like I say, no offense or anything, but from what I've been seeing on TV, I think that maybe the Sebastian County coroner or the FBI are the people you should be talking to. I'm officially out of the picture. It's a forensic case, as I understand it."

"Well, I think you're right about the case being a forensic one. You're right about that. And for the record, I have spoken to the coroner, and I'm actually workin' with the FBI on this—with Agent Levine; like I said. You see, I'm a forensic anthropologist."

"Really? Not from around here though. I know most of the anthropologists around here. Are you with the FBI?"

"Naw, not by a long shot," Kel laughed. "They'd make me wear a tie. Almost as bad though. I run the army's Central Identification Laboratory in Hawaii."

"Really? You the people who recover and identify dead soldiers?"

"Yeah, that's right."

"Cool. Are you in Hawaii now?"

"Sure am. I was in Arkansas a few weeks ago, but I'm back in Hawaii now"

"I'm jealous. Another cold front is supposed to roll through tomorrow. I think I've seen you guys on the Discovery Channel. Pretty fascinating stuff—at least compared to collecting arrowheads in the Ozarks."

"Can be. Sure can, but don't sell what you do short." Given a chance, Kel might have gladly swapped his administrative chores for the opportunity to collect arrowheads again. Those days seemed long past.

"You think that case I dug up is a war casualty?" The doubt registered in his voice. "I know it was on Fort Chaffee, but I don't see how."

"Seriously doubt it," Kel responded. "Kinda long story. Without gettin' into it, I worked with Agent Levine on another case a couple-three years ago; when he hooked this one on his line, he asked if I'd take a look at it for him. I did. Unofficially really. That's all. No need to read anythin' into it."

"So you say, but it must be important enough to get someone to leave Hawaii to come to Arkansas."

"Spoken like a man who doesn't do a lot of paperwork for a livin'," Kel laughed. "I'd go that far just to pick up a loaf of bread if it got me away from my desk. Give me a dead body any day."

"I hear you. I'm just an assistant professor, but I do my share of paperwork, Mr., ahh . . . I suppose it's Dr. McKelvey?"

"I suppose it's Kel. Least ways that's what my mother calls me."

"Well, I'm not your mother, but it's good enough for me. So what can I do for you, Kel? Call me Pat, by the way."

"Thanks. Well, Pat, tell me about the skeleton you excavated."

"What do you want to know? Something specific?"

"Yeah, actually. What can you tell me about the hand—the right hand—you notice the stainin' on it?"

"Of course. Copper salts. Pretty much isolated to the right third finger. Some sort of ring would be my guess."

"Yeah. I reckon you're right; that's what I figure as well. But y'all didn't find a ring or anythin' like a ring. I mean, overall preservation's pretty good, at least for the bones and a cigarette lighter that was purportedly found out there, so I'm assumin' that the ring should have been there as well. But I'm guessin' y'all didn't find one. That right? The copy of the report that I saw isn't all that detailed."

"Nope," Pat Trader answered. "I offered to write a regular archaeology report, but the coroner wanted only that one-page summary that I guess you saw. You're right, it doesn't say much, but no, to answer your question, we didn't find any evidence of a ring—except the green staining. As for the cigarette lighter, we didn't find that either. I heard that the construction crew turned that over. We did recover a cigarette wrapper or something."

"About the missin' ring, y'all checked the area thoroughly?"

"We did. We excavated a good meter or so beyond the soil stain. Well out of the burial pit. We'd have found it if it was there."

"Screened everythin'?"

"Quarter-inch hardware cloth. This may be backwater Arkansas, Dr. McKelvey, but we know how to do archaeology."

"Sorry," Kel offered up quickly. "Didn't mean that the way it came out. Thinkin' out loud mostly."

"That's okay. Yeah, for the record, we checked. No ring."

"Any chance the bulldozer got it? I noticed that one arm got pretty dinged up, and I figure that was from the dozer."

"Not a chance, least as far as I'm concerned. The right hand was a good ten, fifteen centimeters below the surface. The dozer caught just the left shoulder as best as I could tell. Shattered the humerus and pulled some of the bones out of the ground, but didn't disturb much else. All the finger bones were still there. That ring should have been there too."

"So the body was on its side? With the left shoulder up, nearest the surface?"

"Sort of. The body was flexed somewhat, but not like the flexed burials you see with Native American remains. The face was down, hips and legs prone, but the torso twisted with the right side down, left side up."

"How were the arms? Symmetrical?"

"Nope. The best I could reconstruct it, the right arm was to the back with the hand behind his ass, palm up I think. Left arm was flexed and over his head."

"But no ring," Kel said.

"Nope."

"And other than the damage from the dozer, you say it was undisturbed when you got there?" Kel mumbled his thought. No answer was expected.

"Well, now, I didn't say that," Pat Trader answered anyhow.

CHAPTER 26

Fort Smith, Arkansas
Monday, November 17

"Fifty bucks," Byno Pruitt said.   The dozer operator phrased his question as a statement.

"Try fifteen," Jeff Cooper replied.   "And that's because we're related. Sort of."

"Aw c'mon, Jeff. The thing must be worth a hundred at least."

"Like shit it is," the pawnshop owner said as he handed the ring back to Pruitt. "Fifteen."

"Thirty."

"Ten," Cooper responded.

"Whoa, whoa, whoa, we're headed in the wrong direction here," Byno Pruitt pushed the ring back across the scratched-glass counter top. "What happened? You were fixin' to gimme fifteen?"

"I don't dicker. Ten. Keep it up, and I'll offer five."

Byno Pruitt crumpled his face into a ball that looked like a knot of dirty twine. "But the damn thing's probably solid gold."

"The damn thing's mostly copper. Look at how it's corroded," Cooper's voice had taken on an air of dismissal he usually reserved for winos and his wife's worthless brothers.

"It'll clean up. A little Brasso, and it'll shine like Sunday mornin'."

"Yeah, it'll clean up all right—when you melt it down to make a key chain. That's the only real value. Look, Byno, it's just a hunk of cheap metal. You can't even see the design anymore. Nice craftsmanship, maybe; in its day. But to be honest, it's probably of more value as an antique or to a collector than it is for the metal, and even then . . ."

Byno Pruitt picked the ring up and began turning it over in his fingers, his visions of a big weekend at the Choctaw casino over the state line in Oklahoma beginning to swirl down the drain.   The corroded signet design on the face caught the fading light that sneaked past the bars of the pawnshop windows.   He was thinking, and with Byno Pruitt that required lots of time and very few distractions.

"Family?" Cooper asked.

"What?" Pruitt looked up, interrupted.   Now, he'd have to start thinking all over again.   From the beginning.

"Is it a family ring?   An heirloom?   Where'd it come from anyway?"

"Why you ask?" Byno Pruitt flared quickly.   "What difference's that make?   Can't a guy try and sell a ring without it bein' a friggin' offense?"

"Hey, cuz, go screw yourself."   Jeff Cooper raised his hands in mock surrender, but his eyes focused on the red face of his cousin's husband.   "I don't need this shit.   I was just makin' polite conversation here.   Last time I checked, you were in my store, not the other way around.   You want to sell that piece-of-crap ring, I'll give you five dollars.   And just for you, I'll shove the money up your ass—one shiny penny at a time.   You don't want, I'll show you the way to the door— for free."

Byno Pruitt stood and stared.   The gristle of his jaw pulsing as he clenched his teeth.   He had a mind that was well suited to moving piles of dirt, but anything else required a focused effort that he couldn't summon up without an appointment.   "Ten dollars," he said as he flicked the ring back across the glass counter.   "And no damn pennies."

CHAPTER 27

Prisoner of War Compound, Camp Chaffee

Sebastian County, Arkansas

Friday, March 31, 1944

Bill Porter emerged from building T58 into the glare of the setting sun. Captain Jordan, flanked by his two steady companions—Tech Sergeant Elliott and Sergeant David—had left thirty minutes earlier, soon after the day's interviews had concluded. Miss Kramer had stayed for a while to tidy up her notes. That had been the only pleasurable part of his day, watching her shift in her seat and cross her long legs and occasionally look in his direction with a blush and a smile. Otherwise, he felt wrung-out like an old gym towel. The day's work had been long and tiring and wholly unproductive, if not unsettling. Jordan had been on relatively good behavior for the rest of the day, having suppressed his smugness, but none of the sixteen German officers that they'd interviewed had any knowledge relating to Private Keller's death—or so they all steadfastly claimed. They were German officers and did not associate with the enlisted prisoners—or so they claimed.

Bill Porter was sure that the next morning would bring another round of denials. The interviews were taking longer than he'd planned, and there were another thirteen officers to question. He stood on the top step of the building and took a deep breath. He arched his back and lolled his head on his neck, trying to unknot the muscles in his back.

"You got the look of a man who could use a drink," said a voice. It was a sloppy sort of voice; the words took their time to get to a finish as they stretched out like warm hand-drawn taffy.

Porter looked up. Across the street, leaning against the front fender of a green '40 Chevy, was an angular young man wearing the uniform of a captain in the U.S. infantry. His hands were cupping a lighter as he put flame to an unfiltered cigarette, and the hank of thick black hair that tumbled down over his left eye obscured most of the rest of his face. For a moment, Porter wasn't sure the man was the source of the voice, but a quick glance up and down the empty street suggested no alternative. "If you're talking to me, I'd have to say you're pretty astute," he responded. "I could use a whole lotta drinks." He crossed the street.

The captain had finished lighting his cigarette and was holding a lungful of nicotine as he eyed the lawyer walking toward him. He smiled and blew a stream of smoke to the side and spit a fragment of stray tobacco before responding. "Then it's your lucky day there, Captain Porter. I just so happen to be a man that knows where to find a whole lotta drinks." He held out his hand. "I also happen to have use of the colonel's car."

Porter shook the captain's hand while he looked over the car. "Name's Bill. How's it going?"

"Mac. Fair to middlin'."

"Something to go with that, Mac?"

"Just Mac."

"Well then, good to meet you, Mac." He nodded at the car. "Is it safe to assume that Colonel Wiggins knows you have his car?"

Captain Mac smiled. "Safe to assume, Bill. The fact is, the colonel sent me to fetch you up. He figured that a day spent with Captain Jordan and a slew of Nazi hard asses would be more than a Christian man should have to endure. Told me to take you out and get you good and drunk."

"The colonel said that?"

"Yes sir, counselor, practically an order."

Bill Porter laughed and smiled. "In that case, Mac, I guess I don't have much of a choice in the matter. I don't want to be insubordinate."

Mac opened the driver's side door and motioned with his head for Porter to get in the passenger side. He fired the ignition.

Porter threw his briefcase into the back seat and settled quickly into the passenger side. "So where we headed? I hope you were serious about knowing where to find a lot of drinks, because I sure was serious about needing them."

Captain Mac smiled. "Ever been to Indian Country?"

CHAPTER 28

Moffitt, Oklahoma

Friday, March 31, 1944

Mac turned off the car and slowly unfolded his tall frame from behind the steering wheel. It was a study in origami in reverse. Bill Porter did likewise, though the number of folds was somewhat fewer. He looked at the ramshackle building in front of him and then back over the hood of the car to where Captain Mac stood, arms akimbo, smiling, his grin like a picket fence in spring.

"Welcome to Oklahoma," Mac pronounced.

"Quite impressive."

"Don't let appearances deceive you." Mac paused to light a cigarette and then nodded at the building. "Fort Smith's dry as a boar's teat. No hard liquor by the drink. Now the Blue Ginger here, while it may not live up to its exotic name, is a veritable drinkin' man's oasis. Provided that drinkin' man don't give a shit about taste. Or his liver."

Porter glanced at the building and then back at his companion. "Is something wrong with the officers' club?"

"Nothin'. Provided you don't want to talk in private and don't mind if you're around stuffed shirts more worried about promotion points than winnin' the war."

Porter smiled and nodded, as if that answer made sense. "Well, normally I'm quite discriminating about my choice in alcohol, and the health of my internal organs, but in the interests of being neighborly, and avoiding stuffed shirts, I'll make an exception. Lead on, Captain Mac."

The two men walked across the gravel-and-weed parking lot and through the front door of the building. The interior and the patrons gave the impression of a cattle auction taking a well-deserved break. Sawdust and plank floors. Mismatched chairs and tables. A metal bucket near the center of the room, presumably to catch drips when it rained, but currently filled with a slurry of spit and cigarette butts. A lens of blue-grey smoke undulated at shoulder level like a spring tide going out. The room was filled with large-browed men with few teeth and fewer regrets. No one looked up at the newcomers; it wasn't the type of clientele that inserted itself into other's concerns, and when they did, a pick handle or a knife was usually involved.

Mac mounted a bar stool with the ease and satisfaction of a cowboy astride his old horse. He made a small motion with his head and then quickly dropped his look to the rough counter top carved with a hundred odd initials and even more attempts at capturing the essence of the female form. "Best not make eye contact if you can avoid it." The words quietly slipped out of the side of his mouth, along with a stream of cigarette smoke.

"What?" Porter asked. Too loud. He looked around and caught sight of the bartender. An eclipse of tough corded meat and gristle, with long hair slicked back on his head and black eyes that were almost lost under the shadow of a glowering brow. He had all the appearance of a 300-pound hammer in search of a new nail. Porter quickly focused his look on the bar top. "*Shit*," he said.

Mac laughed. "Got that right."

The bartender worked his way down the counter and centered himself in front of the two men. He didn't speak. He simply loomed, like a building spring thunderhead.

"Boilermakers," Mac said. He eyes stayed focused on his hands, which were rolling a cigarette lighter back and forth on the bar like a flat-sided tire.

The bartender stood motionless for a moment and then slowly moved away—an exercise in plate tectonics. The two men emerged from his shadow as if a storm cloud had passed.

Porter snuck a quick look. "Holy shit," he repeated with emphasis.

"Half redbone, half mongrel dog. Some Choctaw, I think. Not really as bad as he looks. He'd like you to think he is, but as long as you don't annoy him, he won't mess with you. Problem is, you never know from one minute to the next what he finds annoyin'. Sometimes simply breathin' seems to meet the requirement."

"I take it you come here with a certain regularity."

Mac shrugged. He took a final drag on his smoke, stubbed the butt out on the underside of the plank bar, and dropped it to the floor. "Wouldn't say regular, but some. Got to remember counselor, I've been here now almost eight months."

Porter started to respond but sensed a movement in the air on his blind side. He paused and looked down while the bartender placed beers and shots in front of the men. He left a half-filled bottle of bourbon with no label. When he'd drifted away, Porter spoke. "Eight months? So, can I assume you're not from this area? With your accent, I just thought . . ." The sentence trailed off.

Mac lifted his shot glass and smiled. "To victory and bowlegged women."

Porter clinked his glass against Mac's and tossed the contents down his throat, avoiding his tongue as much as possible. He blinked hard. It was foul stuff.

Mac's eyes shifted to a target past Porter's right shoulder. "Tell me, Bill," he said, shifting conversational gears, "you married?"

It took Porter a second to realize that the topic had moved on. He blinked hard again. "No," he managed a croak. "But not for my mother's lack of trying. You?"

Mac nodded at what he was looking at, in a manner designed to prompt Porter to follow his gaze. The object was a small fireplug of a woman, attractive in a comfortable sort of way, who'd just stood up from a stool at the end of the bar and was walking toward them. "Cinch up your rucksack, partner. April Kennedy," he said as he smiled and momentarily caught Porter's eye. "Be careful if you want to stay single. She's trollin' for a ticket out of here, and her hook's pretty sharp."

Porter looked quickly down at the bar as April Kennedy edged in between them. This was becoming a place where he spent a good deal of time averting his eyes.

"Buy a pretty girl a drink, Mac?" the woman asked. She brushed against Mac's back and shoulder like a long-tailed cat. "Who's your friend?"

Mac smiled at her and slapped Porter on the shoulder. "Miss April Kennedy, this is Bill Porter. Bill, this is Miss April Kennedy."

"Pleased," Porter turned enough to make eye contact. He smiled and nodded.

"As am I," April Kennedy acknowledged. She spoke slowly to disguise any accent that might creep through. "Haven't seen you before. New in town, or do you just not get out much?"

"Little of both, I guess," Porter answered.

April Kennedy smiled. It was an attractive smile. Perhaps showing some hardship. "So now there are two handsome young military officers who can buy me a drink."

Porter was at a loss for words. Mac spoke up. "Don't know about handsome, Darlin', but I do know about that drink." He stood up as he motioned for the bartender to pour her a drink, then he lit a cigarette and handed it to her. "Sweetheart, would you do me the honor of lettin' me escort you back to your seat?" He held out his arm and winked at her. "If I don't act first, my buddy Bill here will edge me out for the honor."

She took his arm without protest, and he led her back to her stool. He stood beside her for a moment, speaking to her in a low voice. Smiling. Nodding. Touching her elbow. Before returning to his seat, he reached into his pocket and pulled out a ten-dollar bill that he secreted into her hand as he was shaking it goodbye.

Her face brightened, and her eyes moistened.

Bill Porter watched the whole affair. When Mac rejoined him, he said, "You two seem friendly. Not that it's any of my business."

Mac remounted his stool and refilled the two shot glasses. He looked at Porter and flashed an enormous grin. "There is no business." He looked past Porter and winked at April Kennedy.

She returned his wink with another smile.

Mac shifted his attention back to Porter but nodded in the direction of the woman, who by this time was half way through her drink. "Sad story. Got to feel sorry for her. I do, anyway. She's a Yankee. Her husband moved her here about eighteen months ago and then went off and got hisself killed on some God-forsaken island in the South Pacific that she can't even pronounce. Only then did she find out that he was previously married—previously, as in he never bothered to get divorced. Now she's stuck here. Got a young boy that won't ever know his daddy; won't even have a legitimate name. Her family up in Iowa has mostly disowned her. She doesn't get any of her husband's death benefits." He paused and threw back a shot that he followed with a swallow of beer. He blinked hard and shook his head. "I was wounded overseas." He tapped his chest and shrugged his left shoulder. "Big chunk of shrapnel. By all rights, I should be dead." His thought trailed off momentarily until he hooked it and reeled it back in. "Somethin' like that makes you think. Makes you feel for the ones left behind. Like her. She didn't ask for this. Nor'd her little boy."

"Not sure she's going about the solution the right way, though. I assume she's hooking?"

Mac frowned. "Strong word. Easy for someone like you to toss around. Survivin' is better. But, yeah. Maybe. Probably. I'm sure most guys around here would be happy to use her to that end." He took another shot and refilled his glass. "Most guys won't take the time to see her as a person. If you do, you'll see she could be your sister."

Porter looked back at his companion. He saw that Mac was looking down at the bar again, rolling his lighter back and forth. April Kennedy was no longer the topic of discussion. They sat silently for almost two minutes. Porter finally spoke. "You a baseball fan?"

Mac tossed another shot and chased it with a swallow of beer. He wiped his lips with a pinching motion of his thumb and index finger as he screwed up his brow. "Baseball? Naw. Can't really say that I am. Why?"

Porter shrugged and swallowed another shot of his own. "I thought I saw you playing baseball with some of the PWs. It looked like you, anyhow."

Mac laughed. "Then it probably was me, counselor. Probably was. I knock some balls around once and a while. Therapy for my shoulder, mostly. I'm here on a recuperative assignment, until they decide whether or not to send me back overseas." He took another sip of beer and then lit up another cigarette. He blew a column of smoke off to the side, away from Porter, and then turned back. "You?"

"Why am I here?"

Mac laughed again. "No, I work for the colonel, remember? I knew why you were here before you did. No, I meant baseball. You asked."

"Baseball? Oh, no . . . well, I follow the Browns some, I guess. It seems like you can't live in St. Louis without following either the Browns or the Cardinals. The Brownies almost had two winning seasons in a row. This might be the year. We'll see." He took his first sip of beer and flinched.

"Should have warned you. The beer's worse than the mash. The Browns, huh? No offense there Bill, but they stink."

Porter took another sip. "No argument. I guess I'm drawn to underdogs. Or whipping boys. Or are those the same things?" He held his glass up and looked at the world through the amber liquid. Things were floating in it that he didn't recognize nor did he want do.

"Could be. So, how'd it go today? Any progress?" Mac refilled the shot glasses and downed his. He took a long drag of his smoke.

"The Browns aren't the only whipping boys. It's easy to figure out this is a no-win assignment," Porter paused and looked at his companion, suddenly unsure. The drink was having the effect of mushing his brain, and he wondered how much of their conversation would find its way back to Colonel Wiggins.

Mac seemed to read the confusion and quickly offered, "Off the record, counselor."

Porter blinked and processed the information. He shook his head quickly in a vain attempt to clear his thoughts. He smiled. "In that case, I can humbly say, today might have been one of the biggest wastes of the taxpayers' money that has ever been witnessed in the Christian era. Interviewed . . ." He paused and frowned and set his drink down to count up on his fingers. "Questioned sixteen German officers today. Sixteen, and not a single one had anything useful to say."

"Hmmm," Mac acknowledged as he refilled Porter's drink. "None?"

"None. Not one. And I suspect that the dozen or so scheduled for tomorrow will be equally unenlightening, thank you." Porter emptied his shot glass again and chased it with the remainder of his beer.

Mac refilled the glass and motioned to the bartender to top off Porter's beer. When that was accomplished, and the shadow of the bartender had passed away, he spoke. "Don't know about the law, but I reckon a case like this is pretty near hopeless under most circumstances."

"Not if you're worth a shit as a prosecutor. They got five," Porter held up the splayed out fingers of his right hand, "five convictions over at Tonkawa. All death sentences. Five." He took a swallow of bourbon. "Not like there's any pressure on me to deliver. No sir."

The silence returned. Finally, Mac brushed the flop of hair back from his brow and fixed his eyes on Porter. He studied him for a moment. "I see you're workin' with Captain Jordan. How's that goin'?"

Porter looked up and blinked. His eyes weren't focusing as well he might want. He took a long slow breath and considered the question. He didn't know the relationship—if any—that existed between Jordan and the man seated next to him. He used his legal training to sidestep the answer. "His German's pretty good."

"That so?" Mac replied. "Since I don't parley the stuff, I'll have to take your word for it. Goin' okay between you two, is it?"

Bill Porter smiled. "You work with him much?"

"Me? Shit, son. I work for the colonel. That's the agreement I have with the army."

CHAPTER 29

U.S. Army Central Identification Laboratory, Hawaii

Monday, November 17

Davis Smart passed his access badge across the sensor beside the lab door. There was a metallic click and the door lock disengaged and his entrance into the lab was logged. He stepped onto the lab floor, where McKelvey was seated at one of the examination tables, a report open on his lap, staring at the human bones arranged in anatomical order in front of him. "I think you're the last one," he said. It was almost six, and his wife was waiting for him in the parking lot, and he didn't intend to initiate a conversation that would delay him—not that McKelvey appeared to be in the mood for a conversation.

Kel didn't look up. "Got it. Have a nice evenin'."

"Remember to set the alarm."

"Got it."

"You often forget," D.S. continued.

"Got it. Have a nice evenin'."

D.S. sighed. "The logbook is full of alarm violations where you didn't get it. We have a re-accreditation inspection coming up, and the last thing we need is more violation reports on the lab director. Just saying . . ."

"Hmmm," Kel mumbled. Distracted. "Glass half full. Shows the system works. Shows that we police ourselves. Besides, I said, *I got it.*" He reached over and picked up one of the bones from the table. "Hey, D.S., before you go. Got a minute?"

D.S. looked at his watch and calculated how long his wife had already been waiting. He walked over to McKelvey and the skeleton on the table. "Something I need to see?"

"Um hmm." He put the bone he'd been holding back onto the table. He'd read and reread the anthropology report. Its author, Dr.

Chelsea Brianne, was good. Very good for her age, but sometimes her lack of experience still showed. He turned as D.S. approached the table. "You looked at this report yet?"

"Not yet," D.S. answered. "She only finished yesterday, and I haven't had the time. It hasn't even been peer reviewed yet."

Kel pointed at the skeleton's right knee. "What do make of that?"

"Osteoarthritis. Same as it was the other day when we looked at it." D.S. bent over, arms behind his back. "Why? What'd Chelsea say?"

"Osteoarthritis. I know that, but what do you make of it?"

"She give a probable cause?"

"Nope. This guy's too young for that much damage; don't you think? It isn't age-related."

"Could be trauma induced." D.S. straightened up. "He's got that bad tibial break we talked about. Maybe it messed with his knee as well."

"Could be, except it's bilateral. He'd have to have had the same type of trauma to both knees."

D.S. bent over again. His face was inches from the bone. "It could be occupational. Prolonged trauma to the menisci. Is that what you're thinking?"

Kel nodded. "I am, but what would cause that?"

"Could be almost anything."

"C'mon, D.S. You're the bone guy."

"So are you."

"Hell, in a prior life, maybe. All I do anymore is sign the bone-guy's timesheet. C'mon."

D.S. sighed. "Well, it'd be something that requires prolonged time on your knees. Probably starting when you're young."

"Like a White House intern?"

D.S. smiled patiently. "Gee, I wonder why we all have to sit through mandatory sensitivity training every year." He straightened up and tilted his head back-and-forth while he thought about the bones in front of them.   "Hmmm, it could be what they used to call Housemaid's Knee."

Kel sat back and crossed his arms. He looked at the skeleton and then at D.S. "Why do I think this guy was no housemaid?"

CHAPTER 30

Fort Smith, Arkansas

Monday, November 17

Michael Levine's eyes were on the engineering map in front of him. It was spread out on the table, stacks of books pinning the curls at the corners. "Here in Arkansas?" he asked.

"Missouri and Oklahoma, too," Bill Grant replied. The assistant librarian was leaning forward, elbows on the table, and his eyes were pinched into slits to compensate for the glasses that were sitting on his bedside table rather than on his nose. "The thinkin' was that if any German POWs escaped, they'd be easy to hunt down."

"Hmmm," Levine said. "I thought Arkansas was supposed to be filled with friendly people."

"You bet it is, unless you're an escaped Nazi," Grant responded. "Then your opportunities for friendship would have been limited, at least back in 1943. Lots of good ol' boys out there with way too many guns and not enough targets to point them at." He chuckled. "Some things never change."

Levine leaned back in his chair and took in the open expanse of the Fort Smith Public Library's Genealogical Room. After McKelvey had left for Atlanta and Honolulu, Levine returned to Memphis for a few days; long enough to check his mail, pay his bills, and wash his socks. He was back now in Fort Smith and had taken McKelvey's advice to visit the library and read up on Fort Chaffee's history. As his eyes wandered the room, he couldn't help but replay the librarian's comment in his head. He'd been in the Memphis field office for what was starting to resemble a lifetime, and escape seemed like a pretty good idea. He was wondering if anyone would bother to hunt him down. Not the Bureau, that much was for sure. "It makes sense, I guess," he said, filing his personal thoughts away. "But how about the building I asked you about? You find it?"

Bill Grant scrunched his eyes again and surveyed the map. "Ahhh, yeah. Should be here somewhere." He drummed his fingers on the corner of the paper, near the U.S. Army Corps of Engineers stamp. "Camp Chaffee was a big place. *Is* a big place. It should be . . . here . . . . ahh . . . Oh, now see this buildin' right here?" The assistant librarian tapped an inked rectangle near the center of the map.

Levine leaned forward quickly and looked. "That it?"

"Nope. Even better. That's building 803. That, Mr. Levine, is where the King got his hair cut off. Elvis the Pelvis himself. Bet you never heard that story."

Levine's response was preceded by a deep breath. "Why, yes, actually I've heard that. Quite the historical marker." He smiled patiently. "Would that happen to be anywhere near the building I'm interested in?"

"No, no, no," the assistant librarian responded. "No, what you're lookin' for is way over here." His finger skated to another inked rectangle near the far edge of the map. He tapped the paper. "It was right here. It's long gone, but you can see that it was there in 1941."

"Forty-one?"

"Forty-one."

"And it was gone by when?"

"Well, for that you gotta go to another source." Bill Grant stood up and walked to a nearby map case. He read the labels on the drawers before opening the third one from the bottom. He returned a minute later with another large roll of paper. He fluffed it like a bed sheet and let it slowly settle down on top of the first one. After rearranging the books to hold the corners from curling, he pointed to an area near the center. "This one's oriented a bit different, and the scale's different, but this here's the same area. See, it's gone. Must have been a temporary structure."

"Temporary?"

"That's a relative term. You know, considerin' that many of those old temporary buildings are still out there, seventy years later. At least they were until the fire a year or so ago."

"What's the date on that one? That map."

Bill Grant lifted his forearm and looked at the map-maker's legend. "The Corps drew this map here in late 1950 in response to new construction for the Korea build up."

"So it wasn't there long. Forty-one to fifty."

"Or less. We know your buildin' was gone by fifty, but it could've been torn down even earlier than that."

Levine sat back in his chair again and ran his hand through his hair while he thought. After a moment he reengaged the librarian's eye. "Interesting. Your map say what the building was used for?"

A puzzled look curtained across Bill Grant's face. "Well, of course, Mr. Levine. That buildin' was to hold all of those Nazis."

CHAPTER 31

U.S. Army Central Identification Laboratory, Hawaii

Wednesday, November 19

Hugh Rooney walked into McKelvey's office and dropped a FedEx box into his lap. It had been opened. "You owe me. Big time," the historian said.

Kel looked up from the report he was reading. He sighed. "No doubt. What this time?"

"How long do you think it took me to walk here from my office? Go on. Guess."

"Your office? The one that's what, oh, maybe all of five hundred feet from here? I don't know Hugh, I—"

"Four-hundred-and-sixteen feet, exactly," Rooney cut him off. "But before you do the math, I'll give you a hint: It's a trick question, because I have to walk by Colonel Botch-it's lair."

Kel winced. He could see it coming.

"An hour and forty-six minutes, Kel. To walk four-hundred-and-sixteen feet. An hour and forty-six minutes that I'll never get back. All so that I could hear that we're driving a Cadillac."

"Not the Cadillac lecture?"

"Yes. The Cadillac lecture." Rooney's voice took on a staged air of importance. He jutted his belly and puffed his cheeks and began waddling in a tight circle like a penguin. "Pretty nice organization we have here, Mr. Rooney. In fact, a real Cadillac of an organization. But," he paused for emphasis, "as stewards of the taxpayers' money, maybe we shouldn't be driving a Cadillac. Maybe that's too showy. Too many luxury features. Cup holders, power locks, heated seats, automatic transmission. A real gas-guzzler. You know, Mr. Rooney, a Ford Escort is a perfectly good car that—"

"*Escort?* You're kiddin'? Last time I got the talk, it was at least a Buick Regal, now—"

Rooney held up an open hand to silence the interruption. "Yes, a Ford Escort, Mr. Rooney. You may not know this, my friend, but an Escort will get you where you want to go without all the bells and whistles. Dependable. Reliable. Cheap to maintain."

Kel started laughing. "Goddamn, Hugh. It'll be an AMC Pacer next. An Escort?"

"Yeah. Go ahead and laugh. It's easy for you. I'm the one that was stuck in there for two hours. Where were you?"

Kel laughed again and started extracting the contents of the FedEx box. A stack of file folders secured with a large rubber band. "I know better than go down to that end of the building. *There be monsters.*"

"There be morons."

"So, how'd you get out? Chew your leg off?"

Rooney sat down in the chair in front of McKelvey's desk. "I'll tell you how, when he finally took a breath, he noticed that." He nodded at the box in McKelvey's lap. "He asked me what it was, and I said that I was doing some research for you. Boom! That was it. Good God, the minute he heard your name, he began to spit and sputter. I thought blood was going to come out of his ears. The next thing I know, he said something awful about my mother and kicked me out of his office."

Kel was still laughing as he thumbed through the files. "See? It does pay to know me." He furrowed his brow and shifted gears. "What about these anyhow?"

Rooney leaned forward, careful to not touch McKelvey's desk for fear of initiating an avalanche of stacked-up papers. "These are the records for your Chaffee guys. They arrived this morning. The way you travel, I figured I better get them to you before you take off again."

"Thanks. That was fast. What do they say?" He held them up and gestured with them. "I assume you read them."

"Of course. You asked me to research them. If I knew more about what you were after, I could answer that question better. Best I can determine, those are the only seven men with the initials J-S-B-J or J-S-H-J, or anything reasonably close to that, who went through Fort Chaffee during World War Two. Some of those files are pretty sparse, but from what I can tell, none of these guys is your man. All are accounted for."

"Hmmm," Kel mumbled. He'd opened the first file to the middle and was skimming it. "Damn. Thanks. Good work."

"What can I say? I'm as dependable as a Ford Escort."

Kel looked up and smiled. "Son, if you had a couple of cup holders, you might even be a Buick Regal."

CHAPTER 32

Fayetteville, Arkansas
Thursday, November 20

Levine had been sitting in his car for thirty minutes, drinking a flat Diet Coke and fogging up his windshield with impatient sighs. His always thin patience was particularly brittle. He'd spent part of the morning doing a phone interview with an NPR reporter, who sounded all of fourteen. She was from somewhere that she swore was Pittsburg State University—what state that was in, he couldn't have told his mother on her deathbed, but he was reasonably sure it wasn't any Pittsburg that he was familiar with. The television interest had died down in recent days, only to be replaced by print and radio stories obtained through numerous mind-numbing telephone interviews. He took another swallow of flat Coke and looked at his watch again, willing McKelvey to get to his office. From working with him previously, he knew that the anthropologist was not a morning type. Nevertheless, starting at eleven a.m., seven a.m. in Hawaii, Levine had left two dozen or more messages on the anthropologist's work phone—each one spaced five minutes apart—until he exceeded the voicemail memory limit. Then he set upon McKelvey's cell phone with similar vigor. He knew that he shouldn't expect an answer from the latter, but it satisfied the need to do something. In the age of increasing connectivity, McKelvey had honed the waning art of being out of touch—at least electronically—and always managed to forget his cell phone no matter what the circumstances.

Levine looked at his watch: One thirty p.m.—eight thirty in the Hawaiian morning. He dialed McKelvey's office number again. It rang four times. This time it picked up.

"Central ID Lab," Kel answered.

"Shit, Doc. About damn time."

"Well, if it isn't Special Agent Dale Carnegie. And here I thought my mornin' might get off to a bad start."

"Morning? It's what? Eight thirty there. Sometimes I can't believe the government pays you for a full day's work."

"Me either. But then we can't all be prized human assets to our organizations the way you are. Tell me again what hot-bed of crime have they got you stationed at again? Fargo?"

"I wish. At least I've heard of Fargo. Now, I'm currently sitting in the friggin' parking lot of the university down here in Fayetteville."

"*Up.*"

"What?"

"Up. You were in Fort Smith. Fayetteville is *up* from there. What in the world you doin' there anyway?"

"If you say so. I'm *up* here to use the library. This will no doubt surprise you, but the vast library holdings in Fort Smith don't seem to include much on Fort Chaffee. They suggested I come up here. The university is supposed to have some special Fort Chaffee collection."

"Yeah? Findin' anythin'?"

"Fuck-if-I-know. I spent an hour trying to communicate with the back-up banjo player from Deliverance. The whole time he was drooling on his sweatshirt, which, my hand to God, had a red pig on it."

Kel laughed. "Razorback."

"Huh?"

"That was a razorback."

"Oh, shit. Well that changes everything, doesn't it. I guess I owe him an apology for thinking he was an idiot. I don't get it, Doc. You're from here originally and sometimes you seem to have at least half a brain."

"Well, gosh, I guess at least one of my parents needs to thank you."

"No, I'm serious. It's like I talk and talk but none of these half-wits can understand a thing. I mean, if I hadn't been living in Memphis for three years, I'd never have believed any of this. Gimme a break. And now I have to wait for the head librarian to come back from lunch so that I can ask about this friggin' special collection that is supposedly housed down here—*up here*—at the university. Goddamn."

Kel laughed again. "Poor, poor Job. How the Lord does try you."

"Screw you."

"Do us all a favor, Mike; when you talk to the librarian, check your attitude at the door. Okay?"

"Meaning what?"

"Meanin' your bedside manner leaves a great deal to be desired. You're not in New York anymore. Remember what I taught you in Split Tree—tried to teach you anyhow. Go slow. They're good folks there. Build a relationship. You can't steamroller people down there like you tend to do."

"I think I can handle talking to a librarian."

"I've seen you in action, remember? I can see this gettin' screwed all slam up. Don't say I didn't warn you."

Levine bit back his first response and took a deep breath. "Don't worry." He shifted gears. "Speaking of getting screwed, how'd your trip to Atlanta go? You do that interview?"

Six thousand miles away, Kel unconsciously shrugged a response. "Yeah. Who knows? Okay, I guess," he answered. He really didn't want to talk about the matter, but appreciated Levine closing his vents on his opinion of Arkansas IQs.

"Shit, Doc, take my advice. I'm telling you, stay away from the ATF. They're nothing but a bunch of FBI wannabes."

"Kinda like you."

"I mean it."

"Advice noted. So, what can I do you for anyhow? I assume you didn't call just to check on my career status."

"I'm checking on my case. What do you have for me?"

Kel laughed. "What do I have for you?"

"Yeah. You got anything yet?"

"Yet? Well, let's see. You know about the Lucky Strikes. The lighter dates to the midthirties, so that's consistent with what we know. It's a Ronson, and they stopped production once the war got underway. So that's consistent. What else? Ahhh, we also got some records for everyone who went through Chaffee during World War Two with the initials that we got off the aforementioned lighter. Seven guys. Though our historian says they're all dead ends. I haven't had a chance to really go through the files yet. Other than that, we're workin' your case as fast as we can, given that it's all bein' done under the table somewhat. Got the anthro report yesterday, but with all the other stuff we're doin', it'll take a while. We're throwin' the whole damn toolkit at it. How's that?"

"You haven't told me anything."

"Right. I forgot that we've been sittin' on our ass, and it was the FBI lab that figured out the Lucky Strike package and the date of the lighter."

"I meant, you haven't told me anything new. You said all along that that stupid lighter was probably from before the war. Okay, you were right. I want something new. Progress. Don't you guys do dental x-rays on the teeth?"

"On the skeleton? Yeah, but we need to have somethin' to compare them to."

"You said you had records on the guys with the initials."

"What we have are summaries of their military careers. Also basic data on age, height, and so on. No dental records yet. Those have to come from another location. But even then there are almost never any dental x-rays from that era. We'll compare the teeth to the paper records when we get them, but it may not be conclusive one way or the other. Besides, like I told you, all of them are accounted for."

"In other words, we got nothing."

"Didn't say that. The good news is that there's some very interestin' stuff goin' on with the skeleton. If you can get us some better leads, there's enough that we can possibly make an ID.

Remember, though, some of the analysis is destructive. We've had to cut one of the teeth for DNA. You said that was alright."

"Good. Do whatever you need to. Grind the whole frickin' skeleton up if you have to. Then my problem is over."

"Easy for you to say. As I said, we're flyin' this under everyone's radar. I haven't seen a letter from you makin' this official, which, ahh . . . that's a problem. I have to admit that I'm a little uneasy about cuttin' these samples and handlin' the evidence given the Gonsalves case and all."

Levine cussed under his breath. "Thought that issue was all behind us."

The Gonsalves case had been an FBI case that had gone sour, and the press had drawn the CILHI into it, and tarred both organizations with the same brush. There were people in both organizations that still held a grudge.

"Maybe. Still . . . I'd like to see somethin' in writin'. I'm out on a limb for you," Kel responded.

"What do you need?"

"Like I said, we're far enough down the road that we need somethin' more than a phone call to make this an official consult case. I FedExed some forms to your office this mornin'."

"Sounds like a plan, except that I won't be back to Memphis for a couple of days. You have a verbal go-ahead. That's as good as I can do for now. What else? How'd your talk with the college professor go? You called him, didn't you?"

"Yup."

"And?"

"Went okay."

"Okay?" Levine impatiently prompted.

"Yeah. We had a nice chat. He confirmed what I figured. The skeleton probably had a ring on it when it was first found."

Levine sighed. "That's something, anyhow. I guess I need to track down this phantom ring. What are you thinking? You mean, like a wedding ring or something?"

"Ahhh, or somethin'. Yeah, weddin' maybe, but I seriously doubt it. It was on his right ring finger, remember? I mean, he could be a European, I suppose. Don't some Europeans wear their weddin' rings on their right hands?"

"I ever give you the impression I'm European?"

"Well, you sure aren't from anywhere I grew up, but regardless of where you're from, I doubt it was a weddin' ring."

"Why?"

"The stain. Remember the stain? The green is from copper salts. Don't know about you, but if I'd given my wife a copper weddin' ring, well, I wouldn't have two kids right now." Kel paused and reflected. "Not that would necessarily be a bad thing, you understand?"

"Maybe a class ring or something. If we get lucky, maybe it'll have an inscription or something. Right? It could confirm the initials on the lighter."

Kel shrugged again, as if Levine could see him.

Levine continued. "Any chance it could have rusted away? Maybe it's just gone?"

"The ring? Nope. I mean, technically, copper doesn't rust. No iron in it. It oxidizes, but I doubt it would have oxidized completely away."

"Maybe those college kids overlooked it. They're kids, right?"

"They didn't overlook anythin'. And, no, they're younger than us, but they aren't kids."

"I'll bet the bulldozer drug it away. You think it would be of any use to go out there with a metal detector?" Levine's mind was starting to race through contingencies.

"You could try, but it ain't gonna do you much good."

"You sound pretty damn sure."

Kel sighed. "Well, where was the skeleton found? What were the conditions?"

Levine thought for a moment before he responded. "Out at an abandoned military base."

"*Abandoned* would seem to be the key word here. What's goin' on out there?"

"They're tearing down some buildings. What hadn't already burned down. Get to it."

"Bingo. Now just how many million goddamn nails do you suppose are out there? A metal detector would scream like a yellow cat dipped in kerosene, and it wouldn't be because of a cheap copper ring."

"So, we simply forget about it?"

"I didn't say that."

"But?"

"But," Kel quickly continued, "but this: The professor says he found the bones of the right hand well below the graded surface. Understand? That means the dozer never touched it. And those college kids, as you call them, did a good job of excavatin' that skeleton. They didn't miss anythin'—includin' the fact that someone else had been diggin' around the burial."

"What d'you mean? Digging? You saying—"

"I'm sayin' that someone intentionally took that ring before Professor Trader and his students got there, yes, sir. Now, you figure out who that might be, and I suspect you'll find your ring."

CHAPTER 33

Fayetteville, Arkansas

Thursday, November 20

Levine hated the thought of McKelvey saying, *I told you so*, and he was glad the anthropologist was six thousand miles away at the moment. Things were rapidly getting—as Kel might say—screwed all the slam up.

"Let me get this straight in my mind," Levine forced each word out as patiently as he could manage. "This is a library."

"That's correct," replied Jane Rich. She had a tight bun and a pinched, angular face that you could slice a loaf of bread with, but she maintained a smile even while she spoke. "We are the premier research library in the state of Arkansas, and one of the most-respected in the mid-South."

"I'm sure that's saying something." Levine drummed his fingers on the counter. "So, at the risk of repeating myself, this is a library, and you're a librarian."

"Actually, no. I'm currently the acting assistant manager of special collections."

"You're a librarian."

Jane Rich maintained a smile.

Levine continued. He nodded and enunciated slowly. "This is a library. You're a librarian. And I'm someone wanting to see your books. From this side of the counter, it looks like all of the stars are aligned here, so maybe you can explain what the problem is."

"Well, sir, as I've tried to explain, and as I understand Cody tried to explain—"

"Cody? That would be the kid with the pig on his shirt?"

"Razorback. Yes, sir."

"Right. I'm told there's a difference."

Jane Rich nodded politely. "Yes. As Cody tried to explain, unless you can be a bit more specific, I'm not sure how best to assist you."

"For the record here, Cody couldn't stop breathing through his mouth long enough to explain anything. Look, I drove down here from Fort Smith because—"

"*Up.* Fayetteville is north of Fort Smith. Generally, north is referred to as *up.*"

"*Up.* I drove *up* here because the people *down* there said you people *up* here had the books I needed."

"Well, no offense to the fine folks down there in Fort Smith, but we have a great many books here, and as I told you earlier, without some more details on what you're lookin' for, I can't really help you."

"And as I told you, I'm after records for Fort Chaffee. I assume you've heard of it."

Jane Rich smiled politely again. "Of course. It's where Elvis Presley was inducted into the army. In fact, if I'm not mistaken, it's where—"

"He got his hair cut off. Yes," Levine completed her sentence. He bit back more of a response. "Let me guess, if I were to ask you if you had any records on Elvis Presley's hair, you could probably help me out."

"Possibly. I could if we had any special collections relating to Mr. Presley. This is special collections, not the general reference section. Havin' said that . . ." She typed a few keystrokes and tapped her computer mouse several times. "Searching for the key word *Chaffee* does return one collection. Sixteen linear feet plus photographs. It doesn't appear that it's been checked-out in quite some time. Years actually."

"Sixteen feet," Levine repeated.

"Plus photographs."

Levine took a deep breath. "Well, that's a start. Where can I find these sixteen feet? Plus photographs."

Jane Rich squinted at the computer screen. Her nose twitched as if there were an unpleasant smell in the room. "I see it's the Wiggins Collection."

"Great. Where is it?"

"I'm afraid you can't see it."

Levine leaned forward and slapped his badge and ID on the counter. He hadn't mentioned that he was with the FBI, or that he was on official business, but he wasn't accomplishing much except to erode his patience. "Any particular reason why not?"

The acting assistant manager of special collections shifted her look from the computer to the badge to the man. She smiled in the way that's taught on the second day of assistant librarian school. "Because, Mr. Levine, you don't have permission."

CHAPTER 34

Alma, Arkansas

Friday, November 21

Michael Levine sat in the wooden chair, with his back to the sweating bank of windows spanning the front of the Cracker Barrel outside Alma, Arkansas, northeast of Fort Smith. He drew in a deep breath and held it, feeling the muscles of his chest tighten, and then slowly released it as he cranked his spoon around the inside rim of his ceramic coffee cup. He drank his coffee black, and the rhythmic motion of the spoon was more to keep his hands occupied than to actually stir the contents. It was a fine-motor skill substitute for the lack of a cigarette. He cleared his throat and maneuvered the sharp sliver of an almost dissolved cough drop into his cheek.

And he waited.

Patiently.

His trip to the university library the previous day had been a total waste of an afternoon. Maybe there was a collection—sixteen linear feet—plus photographs—that held some useful information; Levine doubted it, but he didn't know. Wouldn't know, unless he received permission. *What kind of goddamn permission do you need to see a public library collection*, he thought. *And from a frigging law firm, on top of that.*

Now, he was sitting in a room that smelled of wood smoke and bacon grease, staring at a man who probably counted tying his shoes as a major educational milestone.

Byno Pruitt took a bite of sausage patty. He chewed and stalled.

"Mr. Pruitt," Levine finally reengaged with forced patience. It wouldn't hold up for long; the strain of being so far from his family, so far from anything that mattered in his life, the tax of a career almost tapped out, was beginning to take its toll. Not to mention that he had an appointment in Memphis in a little over six hours and would have to hustle to make it on time. He contrived the semblance of a smile and carefully tried to cloak the exhaustion in his voice. "Look, I'll be blunt. Quite frankly, I don't give a rat's ass about the hows or whys. I really don't give a shit. Maybe I should, but I don't. We need to be clear on that fact. Understand?"

The dozer operator chewed and looked down at his plate where he was trolling the crescent moon of a half-eaten pork sausage patty through a thick puddle of maple syrup. He blinked quickly, several times, as if the movement would shake free a suitable fleck of mental lint. "I guess," was all that drifted loose.

"Good," Levine said. His eyes focused on the frayed top of Byno Pruitt's Oklahoma Sooners baseball cap as he tried to picture what lay inside of the man's skull. Like a frame in a cartoon, Levine pictured a long red brick with three holes in it hovering above the man's shoulders. "As long as we're clear on that, maybe we can make some progress here." He tapped the spoon on the tabletop and sipped his coffee before continuing. McKelvey had armed him with enough information about various unmarked-burial laws to run a bluff if needed, but after meeting Byno Pruitt, he realized that any effort would be wasted. When Levine had called to ask if they could talk, Byno Pruitt had answered the phone like a man with an appointment to have a rusty nail driven through his tongue. Now his body language suggested that if you blew on him lightly he'd confess to the Lindbergh kidnapping or the disappearance of Jimmy Hoffa, assuming he knew who either of them was. Levine blew lightly. "You want to tell me about it?"

"Shit," Pruitt replied with the first thing that bubbled to the top of his skull. Then he took another bite of pork and chewed.

"Well, that's a start," Levine smiled. His patience was still holding for the moment, but a familiar old red-and-purple migraine throb was beginning to corkscrew its way in behind his eyes. It hadn't been there for over a year, but over the last week it had begun hinting at its return. From past experience he knew that soon both Mr. Pruitt and he would wish that he didn't have ready access to a firearm. "Care to elaborate?"

Byno Pruitt wiped his mouth with the napkin and adjusted his ball cap, pulling it down tightly over his head with both hands with the same effort that he might use to wrestle a tomcat into a shoebox. "I can, but . . ." His eyes flickered, but the end of his sentence snuffed out.

Levine waited and then sighed as he pushed his coffee cup to the side of the table and leaned forward. His patience gone, he picked up a knife from off his napkin. His voice was low and honed to a sharp sliver, like broken glass. Time to click the ratchet. "Look, Mr. Pruitt, I told you I don't care about the hows and the whys, and that's quite true. It is. But what I do care about is finding that goddamn ring. I intend to do that, and if I have to take this butter knife and spread what little brains you have out on this table top to see what you're hiding, I will. I swear to God I will."

Pruitt's eyes flickered again. "S'not like it was worth much, you know." He defended after a moment.

Levine looked over the tip of the knife blade at the bulldozer operator. *This is what my career has come to,* he thought. *I lived through a year in Vietnam; I carried shit for over twenty goddamn years with the NYC Police Department and another twenty in the Bureau; I survived growing up in Brooklyn, for god's sake; for this? To threaten a half-wit construction worker with a butter knife?* He slowly set the knife down. "I'm sure it isn't, Mr. Pruitt. I'm sure not. But you understand, don't you, that the monetary value isn't what I'm interested in."

Pruitt nodded, though whether out of understanding or nervousness, Levine couldn't have guessed.

"So," Levine continued. He willed one last thin veneer of patience. "What can you tell me about the ring?"

Pruitt shrugged, paused, and shrugged again. Nervously. The conversational sluice gate finally opened. "Well, like I told you, it ain't worth much. Looks like gold to me, but my buddy who knows all about such shit says it ain't, and I'm tendin' to believe him even though I think it looks a lot like gold to me, but he knows about shit like that, ya know? And anyhow—"

"Slow down, slow down," Levine said. "Take a breath there, Mr. Pruitt."

Byno Pruitt did as he was told and took a breath. He blinked at the FBI agent waiting for further instructions

Levine watched him. *Now, Simon says pat your head and rub your belly at the same time*, he thought, surprised at the newfound compliancy. "Okay, let's back up a bit, shall we? First, you did find a ring while you were knocking down those structures out at Fort Chaffee, is that correct?"

Byno Pruitt nodded and looked at Levine. Once, his third wife had made him go to a modern art show in Tulsa. His eyes had assumed the same involuntary squint then.

Levine synchronized his nodding head with that of Pruitt's. To Levine, it looked as if Pruitt had to pee and was stuck in church, and then he realized that Pruitt was still holding his breath. "Okay, ahh, now this . . . you can breathe now, Mr. Pruitt, just relax."

Byno complied.

"Now, was this ring on, I mean, did you find this ring on the skeleton that was exposed? The one you uncovered with your bulldozer," Levine continued.

"Yes, sir," Pruitt nodded and blinked and then reassumed his squint. "It was there by the bones, and all."

"And all? On the skeleton? Or near it? Which is it?"

"Well," Byno Pruitt paused and considered his words. He readjusted his ball cap and swallowed. "It was kinda on them finger bones. Like a ring."

It is a ring, you imbecile. Levine nodded and smiled. "In direct association?" As soon as he said it he realized that the vocabulary was all wrong. "I mean, it was there on the finger. Directly on the finger? The finger bone was sticking through the ring? Is that's what you're telling me. For the record, as it were."

A nod.

"Okay, now, this ring, this looks-like-it's-gold-to-you-ring, after you took it . . . removed it from the skeleton, you did what with it? You took it home? Is that right?"

Another nod.

Levine reimagined his image and saw not one, but two red bricks sitting under Pruitt's ball cap. He nodded and continued, "And then what? You took it home, but you say that a buddy of yours looked at it and evaluated it. Is that right? Who is this buddy?"

"I'd rather not say. He's kinda kin and all. He's my wife's cousin, Jeff."

"Okay, okay." Levine took a long swallow of cold coffee and reaffixed his patient smile. "I understand. Look, Mr. Pruitt, as I said earlier, the ring is what I'm after. It's probably not going to mean much when I find it, but it might. Do you understand? It may be evidence. I can't say where this case is going to go, but I have to cover the bases. I'm not trying to screw somebody to a wall here, not you, not your family, but this is a potential homicide case; you understand that? Murder case. And I am from the Federal Bureau of Investigation. You do understand what I'm saying? The FBI. I need answers, and I think you may have them."

Byno Pruitt nodded and blinked.

Levine took a deep stabilizing breath and mentally checked his navigation. *Hardball? Softball?* "Let's try this again. Do you know where this ring is? Right this very minute?" He tapped his fingertip on the table.

Byno Pruitt nodded.

Levine nodded. Between the two of them, there was a lot of nodding going on. "That's excellent, Mr. Pruitt. At the Bureau, they call that making progress. Let's build on that, shall we?" He decided to pursue the softer route for a little while longer. "So, you know where this ring is?"

"Yes, sir."

"Yes, sir. That's good. Very good, now, and you . . . you didn't . . . you didn't sell the ring."

Byno Pruitt nodded slowly, nervously. "Tried to," he stammered. "Weren't worth nothin'."

Levine nodded again. "So you've said. And just where might this ring be at this moment? This very moment. Do you know?"

Byno Pruitt blinked and looked at the FBI agent. For the first time since Levine had pulled up a chair and sat down, Pruitt seemed finally to understand what they were talking about. He reached into his pocket and pulled out his balled-up fist. When he opened his hand, a ring rolled off his palm onto the table. "Right here, Mr. Levine."

CHAPTER 35

Memphis, Tennessee

Friday, November 21

After finishing up with Byno Pruitt, Levine stopped at a branch post office in Fort Smith and put the ring in an express box bound for Hawaii, then he'd driven ninety-miles-an-hour from western Arkansas to downtown Memphis—arriving with ten minutes to spare. Arkansas State Troopers had stopped him twice, a fact that hadn't improved his mood. Neither had the hour-and-a-half wait once he'd arrived, nor the fact that he had three voice messages on his phone from newspaper reporters wanting updates on the Chaffee Man case.

He was finally shown into the office by an attractive young woman who was way too aware of how attractive she was. She was the same one who'd announced him through the telephone almost two hours earlier and who had been avoiding eye contact with him ever since, whether out of embarrassment or general disdain, Levine couldn't quite tell. Levine stepped past her into an office that was large and open and finished with a dark striped wood paneling that looked African or Amazonian and definitely endangered. Shelves filled with law books and photos of prominent politicians and celebrities covered two walls, and there was the smell of pipe tobacco and leather and furniture polish mixed with smug.

"Please, take a seat," Martin S. Gilbreath said. He met Levine in midroom and walked with him to an enormous slab of desk that looked as if it were best used for sacrificing large animals with a stone knife. It was angled in front of the large window that overlooked downtown Memphis. Gilbreath looked intentionally at his watch and waited for Levine to sit down before taking his own seat behind the desk. Gilbreath was a small, concentrated sort of man, with thick white hair brushed back from his forehead as if he were facing into a stiff breeze. His pitted nose twitched like a rabbit's. Five years earlier, a *US News and World Report* article on the top-fifty lawyers in the country had noted that his warm avuncular appearance belied the beating heart of a pit bull. As if to prove the point, Gilbreath sued the magazine for defamation and won. "What can I do for you, Mr. Levine?" he asked.

"Thank you for agreeing to meet with me on such short notice," Levine responded. He returned the gesture and looked intentionally at his watch. He restrained himself from saying, *and go screw yourself for parking me in your waiting room for an hour and a half.* Instead, he said, "I'm sure you're a busy man."

Gilbreath smiled. "Too busy, my wife says." He didn't look at his watch again, but he adjusted the band to convey the same message.

"Well, this shouldn't take much time. It's just a formality, I'd guess. You see—"

"You're not from around here, are you?" Gilbreath interrupted. He stretched out his avuncular smile and blinked his pit-bull eyes.

Levine laughed involuntarily. "Well, I almost made it through the day without someone making that astute observation. No, I am most definitely not. But I'd guess you are."

"Do you mind if I ask, who do you work for, Mr. Levine?"

Levine sighed and smiled and took another patient breath. "I'm with the Federal Bureau of Investigation. Temporarily with the Memphis office here. Same as I was when I called you. Same as I was when your secretary announced me two hours ago. Probably the same as I'll be thirty minutes from now."

Gilbreath cocked his head to the side to better size up the man in front of him, but he didn't respond.

Levine continued. "I'm investigating a body—a skeleton—found on the old Fort Chaffee military reservation in Arkansas—"

Gilbreath held up a hand to interrupt. "Does Lawrence Frank know you're here?"

Levine was caught off guard by the lawyer's knowledge of the FBI's personnel structure. He was caught off guard by the palm in his face. He regained his presence. "Well, Larry wouldn't be much of a Special Agent in Charge if he didn't. Yes, in fact, he assigned me to this case."

"What I meant, Mr. Levine, is this: Does Special Agent Frank know that you're *here*? In my office?"

Levine took a figurative step back. He wanted to say Larry wouldn't know his head from a bowling ball except that a bowling ball wouldn't fit up his own ass nearly as easy. Instead, he answered, "Let's just say, Larry's a busy man—as you and I both are—and I try to not bother him with details of my investigation. Why? Would it make a difference?"

"I see," Gilbreath responded as he swung his chair to the side and began typing on his computer. He glanced at Levine and affected a light-hearted tone. "Please, go on. I may not be as young and agile as you, but I can still perform two things at once. Please, continue."

Levine watched the lawyer. Levine's eyes were not what they once were, and he couldn't make out clearly what was on Gilbreath's computer screen, but it appeared to be some sort of electronic address book. He waited until the older man had found what he was looking for and, with a mouse click, minimized the screen image. "As I was saying, I'm investigating the discovery of a skeleton on Fort Chaffee ground," Levine replied.

"Yes, indeed. I believe I've seen you on television. Several times. You seem to be quite a celebrity. You're most photogenic."

Screw you, Levine thought, but he said, "My fifteen minutes of fame." He leaned forward. "Look, you're busy, I'm busy, so I'll cut to the chase. I have reason to believe that certain records up at the University of Arkansas are—"

"*Over*. I believe the University of Arkansas is west of here. You mean *over*, not *up*."

Levine wanted to wring the old man's throat. "Over. Spoken like a man who parses words for a living, counselor. My apologies. Now that we've oriented the map, maybe we can actually make some progress. I've been informed that there's a special collection at the university that may aid in my investigation."

"Indeed," Gilbreath answered. He still had a smile on his face. "Is that a fact? Do you mind if I ask who told you this? And what precisely they told you?"

"Not at all, counselor. Two people. First, there was Cody, a kid with a pig on his t-shirt for one—you might have him in your computer address book there—and then there was the acting special manager for super-secret special collections for the other. She's the one who said I had to talk to you." Levine matched his smile to that on the lawyer's face. He held his hands palms up in a mock expression of confusion. "And, so, here I am. Having the pleasure of talking to you. All so I can check out some library books."

Gilbreath made a point of looking at his watch again and then fixing Levine with a look that, if Levine hadn't been twenty years younger and a foot taller and not Michael Levine, might have made the FBI agent flinch, or throw the first punch. "Does this special collection have a name, Mr. Levine?"

Oh, goddamn, Levine thought. *How many special collections over at the University of Arkansas do you have control of?* Instead he said, "I've got it right here, counselor." He reached into his shirt pocket and made a show of withdrawing a slip of paper. He knew the name, but he read it from the paper as if he'd just learned of it. "The General M. Fritz Wiggins, Jr., Wartime Papers. I assume that rings a bell."

"And why do you wish to access these papers?"

The reality is that Levine had no idea why he needed the papers other than he was otherwise dead-ended, but he wasn't about to admit that to Gilbreath. He replied, "Let's just say, they may point me to a killer."

"As I recall, those records date to the early 1940s. That was some time ago."

"As I recall," Levine said, "there's no statute of limitations on murder, but I'm sure you'll correct me if I'm wrong, you being the lawyer."

Gilbreath looked at his watch and rose from his seat. He smiled again. "Indeed. Well, I'll take your request under advisement."

That was the last thing Levine expected to receive as an answer. "Advisement? I was hoping to handle this informally. I'd hate to have to seek a court order."

The lawyer actually laughed. "Court order? I don't think there's much chance of that, do you, Mr. Levine? No, I'll take your request under advisement. You see, while the Wiggins papers are on loan to the university, they remain the property of the late general's heirs, and they have imposed certain guidelines and restrictions on their use. I suspect that all this red-tape seems rather silly to a . . ." he paused as if he were struggling to find the proper word, "to a man of action like you, Mr. Levine. Probably is, but it's red tape, nonetheless. There's a governing trust board for the Wiggins estate—and that includes his wartime papers. As attorney for the trust, I have certain duties, you understand, but I'll be happy to bring the matter up with the board at the next meeting and see what I can do. Now, you'll understand if I must bring this meeting to a close."

Levine also rose from his seat. "Certainly. Any idea when the next meeting is scheduled?"

Gilbreath knitted his brow as if the question was totally unforeseen. "Well now, I believe that would be in about seven months; next July, Mr. Levine. The board meets the first Monday of every July."

CHAPTER 36

Armed Forces DNA Identification Laboratory, Rockville, Maryland

Friday, November 21

Dr. Thomas Pierce stared out the window at the snow wisping through the air. The forecast was for an inch of accumulation and that meant highway snarl, and Pierce had already dismissed the lab staff and sent everyone home in hopes of letting them get ahead of the worst of the traffic. He was alone in the building and enjoying the quiet before hitting the hum and splash of the already slickening roads for his own long drive home to Manassas.

Then the phone rang.

"Armed Forces DNA Identification Laboratory, Dr. Pierce speaking," he answered. He half expected to hear his wife's voice. She knew that he was a soft touch and would have excused his staff early, and she'd be calling to urge him to come on home and beat the weather.

"Hey, bubba," Kel responded. "Your refrigerator runnin'?"

"Hey, yourself, Kel. Usin' the phone. Good for you. Must be a special occasion. I'm honored. So how's it goin', with you?"

"Fair to middlin'. You got a minute to discuss a case?" Thomas Pierce was one of the few people that Kel didn't mind talking to on the phone.

"Well, of course." Pierce's Old Dominion drawl was softer and had more rounded shoulders than McKelvey's lazy Arkansas accent. "Just sittin' here watchin' the snowflakes comin' down."

"Sounds pretty."

"Looks cold. The traffic's already startin' to back up." He shifted in his seat to better view the highway that ran in front of the laboratory. "It'll take me a couple of hours to get home, I'm guessin'."

"Then I won't keep you," Kel said. "This will just take a minute."

"Shoot," Pierce prompted.

"Okay. We're sendin' you a tooth. Too long a story to get into right now, but I need a rush job on it. If y'all are like us, most of your staff will be startin' to take leave for the holidays, and I know it's kind of hard to get much done until mid-January, but I was hopin' . . ."

"Yeah, that's true, but we've got a few new folks who don't have much leave time saved up. They'll be in. We might be able to jump on it as soon as it arrives. You already sent it? It's comin' now?"

"Yeah. Well, actually it went out a day or so ago. I'm surprised it's not there already; you should be gettin' it any time now. Here's the thing, like I said, I need a rush job. What's the fastest you can turn it around?"

"Hmm," Pierce verbally shrugged. "That depends."

"On?"

"On what it is you need. Considerin' I don't know anythin' about it, it's hard for me to say. What exactly do you need? A full report? Comparison to a reference sample? I'd say two, two-and-a-half months is reasonable. Assumin' it's a routine sample. Normal turn around. Can you tell me more?"

"No, no, no. That won't work. Look, all I need is a prelim. No comparison. I don't have a clue who it is yet. I don't need a report either—at least initially. Just a verbal. This is totally a fishin' expedition, Tom. I just need somethin' quick and dirty."

"Okay, I won't ask, but if you don't need a report, then, ahh, I don't know, cut that in half; maybe a month. Let's say a month and a half; to be safe"

"No can do. How about a couple of weeks?"

Pierce burst out laughing. "Sure, why not? In fact, we'll just make up the results, and I can send you a report this afternoon. We don't even need to wait on the sample to arrive. You just tell me what you want it to say. Better yet, write it yourself."

"C'mon, Tom, work with me here. I need preliminary results only. Like I said, I'm fishin' here, and I need to know if I'm usin' the right tackle."

Thomas Pierce took a deep breath and let it out slowly as he looked out the window at the growing line of red tail lights on the highway. "You just want it rough?"

"Don't we all."

Pierce paused. "I assume you want mitochondrial, not nuclear."

"Yeah. I'll take what I can get. Yeah. Ultimately, both. Maybe. This is a potential forensic case, so it may have to go into CODIS and NCIC. We'll need nuclear for them, if it comes to that." The Combined DNA Index System and the National Crime Information Center were FBI-run databases.

"Whoa, whoa. Time out here. CODIS? Whose case is this?" The AFDIL was established to identify American war dead and not to assist criminal investigations. Pierce didn't relish getting into a turf battle with the FBI or his own legal department.

"Mine. Call it mine."

"Call it bullshit. Excuse the language."

"Don't ask, don't tell, bubba. I'm the one submittin' it. My name's on it. I'll take the heat."

Pierce paused again. Longer this time. Finally, he sighed. "Maybe. The research section is experimentin' with a new procedure and is looking for some test samples. We haven't completed the validation tests on it yet, but if you're willin' to let us run your sample as a test case, and if you're willin' to take the results as they come out of the machine, without bein' replicated, verified, cross-checked, or anythin' else resemblin' normal procedure, then, . . . ahhh . . . maybe we can get you somethin' in," he paused while he weighed his response, "a month. Maybe."

"Week?"

"Maybe."

"Days?"

"Don't push your luck."

"Hey, a week is great. Would that be a calendar week or a work week?"

"Don't—"

"Roger."

"But hold on. There's a string attached. This can't go into CODIS. No FBI. You gotta promise me that you won't use these results for anythin' other than your own fishin' expedition. I'll disavow all knowledge of it. I'll disavow any knowledge of you."

"Cross my heart. Fishin'," Kel replied.

"I'm serious. These results will never hold up in court. These will not be official AFDIL results. Understand?"

"I owe you, bubba."

"I'll add it to your tab."

CHAPTER 37

Pyatt, Arkansas

Friday, November 21

Dennis Viktor spelled his name with a *k* because he felt it had an air of sophistication. Of power. Of will. Of great potential.

Not that it really mattered how he spelled his name. His name wasn't really Viktor—or at least it hadn't been until he joined the *Blood, the Thorn, and the Sword of God*—it was Vaughn. Most times anyway. Denny Vaughn, aka Doug Vaughn aka David Victor and Eddie Voight, and a slew of others, but usually Vaughn. His birth certificate actually read Dennis Lee Vaughn from Port Arthur, Texas; Mother: JeanElla Vaughn; Father: Unknown, but Viktor, no matter how it was spelled, seemed somehow more fitting, more charismatic, especially after he picked up the tattered remnants of the church and bent them to his will. Viktor sounded like Victory.

Dennis Viktor was the sort of man that women with shapeless figures and pointless minds found irresistible. He was taller than average and slimmer than average, with a live-wire hum to his limbs. He had thin, short hair the color of whole-wheat bread that graded into long pointed sideburns that mirrored the slope and angle of his narrow, pointed nose. His blue-grey eyes, which somehow seemed to pulsate when he talked, were the color of faded denim. He wore tight shirts and even tighter pants, held up with a large silver-buckled leather belt, the excess tongue of which lapped at his hips like that of a yellow dog on a hot day.

His critics liked to whisper that he'd killed a man. Viktor could only smile at the rumor. He knew it wasn't true. The truth was that he'd killed six men. One accidentally and five intentionally.

He'd joined the Blood, the Thorn, and the Sword of God fifteen years earlier after meeting Brother Reeder at a gun show in Fort Worth.

Within a year he was part of the inner council, and by the time Brother Reeder—who was by then calling himself *The Prophet*—moved the church to Pyatt in the steep-sloped mountains of north-central Arkansas, Dennis Viktor had ascended to the position of elder and chief of security.

It had been almost ten years since the federal government had tried to crush them. February 3, 1998. The FBI and ATF and every swinging dick in a county uniform and a shiny badge had descended on their compound, guns drawn and warrants waving. Fortunately for them all, *The Prophet* was a pragmatic man not enamored with the idea of physical martyrdom, and he saw no need to replay Waco. The takedown was handled without loss of life or tangible property. In fact, the only injury on either side of the arrest occurred when a state trooper put a nail through the sole of his foot when he stepped into some tall grass to relieve himself.

The Prophet spent the next seven years and two months in federal prison. Kidnapping, statutory rape, and interstate flight to avoid prosecution had all been on the table but were bargained away in return for a guilty plea on weapons possession and tax evasion. He'd been released eighteen months ago, and Dennis Viktor met him outside the Federal Correctional Center in Bastrop, Texas, and drove him the 680 miles home to the compound. *The Prophet* certainly looked healthy when he arrived home, and so it came as a complete surprise to all the faithful, all except Elder Viktor, when he died two weeks later as the result of undisclosed congestive heart failure—or so Viktor tearfully reported to the congregation. The dutiful servant to the end, Viktor had then secreted *The Prophet*'s body in an undisclosed location to await the spiritual cleansing and resurrection of the corporal body that *The Prophet* had foretold. That was eighteen months ago and the resurrection hadn't occurred yet, at least as of last night, at least as Dennis Viktor told the faithful every morning.

He was no longer Elder Viktor. He was the anointed and chosen one—though the awaited resurrection of *The Prophet* did present a logistical, or at least protocol problem with regard to a formal succession.   While he waited clarification from on high, he was the *Dear Leader*, a title that he'd read one day in a newspaper article about the leader of North Korea.   He'd tried it on almost as a joke, like slipping on a floppy hat and looking in the mirror for laughs, but was surprised with how comfortable it felt—and how well it fit.   A few of the old guard, men who'd been with *The Prophet* since the early Texas days over twenty years ago, balked and jockeyed in opposition, but most of them were gone now; a couple having left to join another movement in eastern Montana, another one arrested on a questionable drug charge that he claimed was a frame up, and four who just disappeared.

The *Dear Leader* was staring into his refrigerator and scratching when the phone rang.   He checked his watch: 3:42 p.m.   He thought for a moment about letting it go and took a quick glance down the darkened hallway, into the bedroom, where he could see a slender brown ankle and foot dangling off the edge of his bed.   The phone rang again.   The ankle twitched.

"The faith of Jesus be with you," he said into the phone.   He took one last look into the refrigerator and then closed the door.

"Cut the crap," came the response.

Viktor held the phone tighter against his ear and tried to place the voice.   It was southern, but not trailer or back road.   It had a polish to it.   It was smooth and thick and coated the listener like warm honey.   Viktor didn't respond.

"You there?" the voice prompted.

"I am," Viktor responded.

"Good, because I'm offering you a chance to settle an old debt."

Viktor recognized the voice now, and he wasn't happy.   Some dogs are best left asleep.   But he also recognized the prospect of an opportunity in the making.   "I believe all my debts have been settled.   Or perhaps I'm forgetting something."

"Perhaps you are.   Most assuredly you are.   You think that living in the hills makes you invisible?   It doesn't.   I've been keeping tabs on you, my friend. You're The Prophet now, I hear. I believe things have worked out rather well for you."

"And for you," Viktor challenged. "For both of us. But if you've been keeping tabs, then I guess your sources are poor. There is only one Prophet, and we await the day when he will arise, cleansed and freed of the chains forged of human sin, to take his rightful place at the side of Lord Jesus and lead his—."

The voice laughed. "As I said, Dennis, cut the crap. I'm not one of your toothless followers who looks the other way when you bed their fourteen-year-old daughter. I'll make you a deal; how about I won't treat you like a yokel, and you don't treat me like one of your fast marks? Deal?"

Viktor looked down the hall at the slender ankle, and then turned away and padded softly into his living room where he sat on the couch. "As long as it runs both ways," he replied. "It's been a while. I can't say I'm too surprised, though."

"I am," said the voice. "Frankly, I'd hoped to never have dealings with you again, but something has come up and now is a chance for you to settle your debt. Some of it, anyhow."

"I'm listening."

There was a pause, then the voice said, "There's an FBI agent that has become . . . let's just say, bothersome."

"Bothersome?" Viktor laughed. "They usually are, aren't they? And what? You want my help?"

"I do."

"He must be some kind of bothersome for you to call me. Beyond bothersome, I'd say. What's the matter that you can't handle this? I'm a simple preacher now; you're the big shot. Since when can't you control an FBI agent?"

"Let's just say . . ." the voice hesitated, "let's just say that it would be better if someone else dealt with this situation. I would prefer that my fingerprints not be found when the dust settles."

Viktor laughed again. "Is this being taped? This could be a set-up, couldn't it? What am I supposed to say, huh? Is this where I'm supposed to ask you if you want this guy dead? He that big a bother to you?"

There was silence on the other end of the line, and for a moment, Dennis Viktor thought that the phone might really be bugged. He listened for any suspicious pops and clicks.

Finally, the voice responded. "No, he's not that big a bother. More of a nuisance. The man needs to be encouraged to mind his own business."

"FBI agents are pretty good at following orders as I recall. You tried just telling him to back off?"

"Yes, but he's proving to be quite stubborn; he needs to be dissuaded from what he's doing."

"And just what is he doing?"

"I told you," the voice answered. "He's not minding his own business."

CHAPTER 38

Fort Smith, Arkansas

Friday, December 19

Michael Levine was midway into his third beer when Kel pulled up a stool at the Varsity Grill on Garrison Avenue, and sat down beside him, plopping an opened FedEx box onto the counter. There was a noisy football bowl game on the dozen or so televisions mounted around the room and clots of young and middle-aged men and women were talking loudly to compensate.

"Suppose you could have found a louder place to meet?" Levine grumbled between sips of beer.

"What? Can't hear you."

"I said, suppose . . ." Levine caught McKelvey's smile and realized it was a joke. "Screw you."

"Gotta buy me a drink first, sailor," Kel replied as he nodded to catch the bartender's attention. "Coke Cola, diet," he mouthed slowly so the bartender could read his lips.

They sat amid the noise without speaking until McKelvey's drink arrived, and then Levine stood up and looked around the room until he spotted a couple vacating a booth. He jutted his chin to indicate to McKelvey that they should move. A minute later they were seated near the wall, the high back of the seat booth blocking out some of the bar noise and allowing effective, if not comfortable, conversation.

"When'd you get in?" Levine asked. "You could have let me know."

"Yesterday afternoon. My apologies for not callin' you right away. I selfishly decided to see my family, take a shower, and get some sleep first," Kel answered as he took a sip of his Diet Coke.

Levine waved the comment off with his hand. "You done anything productive since you arrived? God knows I haven't accomplished shit since we last talked."

"I told you, I visited my family. Not sure where that ranks on your scale of productivity, but yeah, I like to think it was productive."

Levine took a drink. "For once, Doc, I actually envy you."

"Bullshit."

"No bullshit. I do. I was going to fly home to Maryland for a week or so. Instead I spent it in Memphis doing some work. Filing expense vouchers, mostly. Now I'm back here." He took another swallow and looked at the contents of the bottle momentarily. "My wife and kids are flying out here in a few days. Not here, but Memphis. I'll drive back over; get to spend a couple of weeks with them."

Kel raised his glass as if in a toast. "Good for you. I'm glad. I am. Say, we saw you on TV again last night. I don't watch much television, but dang if you haven't been on just about every time I pass one. Suppose I should get your autograph while I can. Does the FBI have rookie cards? I'd like to get yours before they get too scarce."

Levine sighed. "Gimme a break, will you? It's been unbelievable. Picked up again. Every couple of nights some Gomer wants an interview—and it's not just the local hick shows. I can't even start to figure out what all the interest is. I thought it'd died down. There's nothing new to tell them."

"Tell me about it. It happens to us every once and a while. Some story grabs their attention for some god-unknown reason, and the press is on you like a bad dose of chiggers." Kel took a sip of his drink and wiped his lips with a pinch of his thumb and index finger. "Of course, what gets me is that they always treat whatever case it is like it's an anomaly; like it's never happened before in the history of the world and won't ever happen again. We identify two men a week; forty-seven from World War Two this year alone, and yet, here they are pesterin' you about this one like it's King Tut's long-lost cousin."

"You got any advice?"

Kel shrugged. "Buckle in and ride it out. Pretty soon they'll announce the next celebrity DUI and all this will be old news."

"Yeah. Hasn't happened yet." Levine nodded. Then he abruptly changed directions. "You get that ring I sent?"

"Yup. Folks at the lab are tryin' to get it cleaned up as we speak."

"What's that?" Levine nodded at the FedEx package.

"Uh-uh. You first, cowboy. This is a two-way street. Fill me in on what you've been up to."

Levine took the last swallow of his beer and centered the bottle on the cardboard coaster before answering. "I don't guess I've told you, but I spent some time at your library here." Somebody scored a touchdown and the assembled patrons erupted in cheers. Levine waited until the noise subsided before continuing. "I talked to a librarian. He was sort of a local historian. He showed me some old Corps of Engineers installation maps for Camp Chaffee."

"Yeah. And?"

"There was a building near where our skeleton was found, but it was only there for a few years. Forty-one to fifty. Actually it was gone sometime before fifty."

"Cool," Kel replied. "That fits nicely with that 1942 Lucky Strike package, doesn't it?"

"Yeah, that does. But what doesn't sync up too well is what the building was used for."

Kel arched his eyebrows to indicate a question.

"That was an American lighter, right? And American cigarettes?" Levine asked rhetorically.

Kel arched his eyebrows again. "The smokes were Luckies. The lighter's a Ronson. Might be English made, but go on."

"Well, the skeleton was found under an old German POW mess hall or barracks."

"German? German? Well, shit, Mike, kinda changes everythin'," Kel erupted. His mind started running the calculations. He went silent for a minute and then started up again. "Suppose you could have told me? How long have you known this? It might have a bearin' on all the damn research our folks are doin' for you."

"Or not."

"Remains to be seen. I wish you'd have told me. How long have you known this?"

"I've been busy," Levine fired back. He started to say something but paused. He took a breath. "You're right. I should have."

"Damn right. I've got folks workin' overtime searchin' for a missin' American."

"Look," Levine flared again, "You want an apology, or you want to argue? Because I'll be happy to do the latter. Damn if you're not like my wife. I said I was sorry. Some things . . . have come up."

"Yeah, like?"

Levine caught the attention of the waiter and pantomimed the need for another beer. "The library here sent me over to, *up to*, the university. Remember, I called you from their parking lot?"

Kel nodded impatiently. He wanted to hear what was so important that Levine hadn't seen the need to communicate such an important piece of information.

"I was told they had some additional records. Some sort of special collection that related to Fort Chaffee, and so I drove up there. And . . ." Levine seemed at a loss for words. "I tell you, Doc, something's not right with this case."

"You're just now figurin' that out? Shit, I could have told you that the minute I heard they assigned you to it. That was clue one," Kel said as the waiter brought Levine's beer. Kel held up his empty Coke glass and a finger to indicate the need for a refill. "What's not right?"

"For one thing, the university has this special collection, but no one—including the FBI—is allowed to see it without the permission of this big-time law firm in Memphis."

Kel shrugged. "So? It's a special collection. My guess is that that may not be so uncommon. Libraries have rules just like the FBI. I assume you asked the law firm for permission."

"That's the thing," Levine responded. He leaned closer. "That's why I went back over to Memphis. I get an appointment and go to see this schmuck lawyer, okay? Older guy. Full partner. You know. One of the top-fifty lawyers in the country—according to some magazine article he has framed in his office. Also has pictures of presidents and shit. Big office, lots of glass and dark wood. Helluva better view than mine."

"And? Get to it."

"And he tells me that he'll take my request under advisement. Submit it to some governing board and maybe they'll get around to it seven friggin' months from now."

The waiter brought Kel's drink, and he took a swallow before replying. "Okay, I'll humor you; that's a bit unusual, but still I'd—"

"That's not all. This lawyer then asks who I work for. Not in a general way, but what field office. I say, *Memphis*, and he nods and says *Lawrence Frank*. He's the SAC. This guy knows the name of the friggin' SAC. And then he looks up an address on his computer. I'd swear it was Frank's."

"Well, you'd know better than me, but if he's a hot-shit Memphis lawyer, I'd think it'd be normal for him to know the local FBI SAC. Especially if he does criminal law. In fact, it'd probably be unusual if he didn't. Right?" Kel was still hot but was starting to cool off.

"Yeah, maybe, but when I got back to my office—less than two hours later—the same Larry Frank calls me into his office and says that I'm now off the case. He tells me that I should take a couple weeks of vacation and go home. I'll bet that SOB lawyer called Frank before I got back to my car."

"What?" Kel almost yelled this time. "What? Wait. Wait, you're tellin' me that I've had folks jumpin' through flamin' hoops for the last month to figure out your case and you're not even on it anymore? Vacation? Well, if that's not the cork in the damn bottle. This is an FBI case, but let me get this right, no one in the FBI is workin' it? Do I have that about right?"

"You're not listening to me."

"Oh the hell I'm not. I clearly heard you say you're off the case."

"No, I didn't say I'm off the case."

"Well, are you?"

"Technically."

"Well then, technically you can go pound sand."

"I said technically I may be off it. Something's fishy here. Frank's trying to screw me somehow."

"Really?" Kel took an angry drink. "Tell you what, Levine, I'd like to bend you over this table myself right now."

"No. Listen. Frank hates my guts. He put me on this snipe hunt in the first place to screw me over; same as he did sending me over to Split Tree a few years ago. He never gave two shits about solving that one, and he doesn't care about this one either. But now, I start asking questions, and all of a sudden this same guy wants me to take some vacation. I don't think so. Two hours after I meet with the lawyer who won't give me access to the library file? I don't think so."

"You're goddamn paranoid. I swear to God, if you start to tell me you were abducted by aliens, I'll—"

"I'm not paranoid. You don't know Frank. Something's not kosher."

Kel sat and stared and Levine for a moment. Finally Kel said, "So, technically, if you're off the case, what are you doin' here? More to the point, what am I doin' here?"

"Technically, I'm on vacation."

"And technically, what are you doin' on your vacation? Besides drinkin' beer."

"Well, for one, I'm planning on going back to pay that lawyer a visit. I want to see those records. I left a dozen messages, but he hasn't returned my call. It's time for another visit, appointment or no appointment."

"Hmm," Kel grunted. "And what's changed since he last told you to go fuck yourself?"

"Nothing. Except that now I'm pissed. I figure I'll go back and let him know that we can do this easy or we can do it hard, but I'm going to get those records."

McKelvey laughed. "I'm sure the threat of a vacationin' FBI agent gettin' pissed off will shake him up."

"Laugh all you want, but it should."

"Even if it does, you honestly think any public record housed up at the university will help out? Because I don't. You just told me that the skeleton was buried under the damn mess hall, remember? The POW mess hall. Or barracks. If what you're sayin' is true, then it wasn't an accident. People don't just fall through the floorboards like old coins. The skeleton bears that out, too."

"How so?"

"The head's all bashed in, remember? Plus, there's the posture. The professor who dug it up said that the body was in an asymmetrical posture. Arms askew. And it was shallow. That means whoever buried him was in a hurry and didn't give a damn about him, and that usually means foul play. No, if what you're sayin' is true, then it's obvious that someone didn't want this guy found, and if that's the case, it won't be in someone's goddamn public papers. I don't care how special they are."

Levine leaned forward. "Not necessarily. Think about it, Doc. Maybe there was an official investigation. A search. These papers belonged to some general. Maybe it was big news at the time that someone was missing."

"That's a big maybe."

"You got other suggestions? Because I'm tapped out of ideas. Besides, that lawyer got under my skin, and I feel like making his life unpleasant."

"Well, that's always a good reason. So, you plan on doin' what? Throwin' your weight around?" Kel laughed. "I can see that workin'. C'mon, Mike, if he's one of the top-fifty lawyers in the state—"

"Country."

"Oh, even better. If he's that good, he'll eat you alive and not even burp twice. Besides, you just told me he has your boss on speed dial; the same boss that just told you to take a vacation."

"I still don't hear you offering any alternatives."

Kel sat back and looked at Levine for a moment. He took a deep breath and let it out slowly while he thought. Despite it all, despite himself, he felt sorry for Levine. He leaned forward again. "Tell you what, maybe there's a way to get those files. If it was me, I'd start by filing a FOIA."

"Come again?"

"F-O-I-A. Freedom of Information Act. If those are public records—they probably aren't but since they're housed at a state university you can make an argument that they are—then you have the right to obtain them through a FOIA. We get FOIAs all the time; there's even a fixed timeframe that we have to respond within. It's set by law. Technically, FOIA is a federal law, but Arkansas has a state version of it."

"And he'd have to turn them over? Just like that?"

"Oh, hell no. Hell no," Kel laughed. "FOIA probably doesn't apply, plus, he's a lawyer. My guess is that even his janitor could think of a hundred reasons to stall your ass. You'll never live long enough to get them through a FOIA."

Levine looked confused for a second and then he started to look mad, figuring his chain was being jerked again.

Kel held up a hand to avert an outburst. "I said that I'd start by filing a FOIA; didn't say I'd expect it to work. Too many ways they can delay and screw with you. No, you file it, or at least be ready to, say you're goin' to, but what you really do is rely on your new found celebrity status for leverage."

"I'm not following," Levine said.

"Look, right now, you and your Chaffee skeleton are a hot news item. What do you think would happen if you held your next press conference and said, ladies and gentlemen, key documents that would lead to the resolution of this homicide—have you publicly called it a homicide yet?"

"No."

"Well, start. It's a homicide now, and you say that the key documents, which are being curated at taxpayers' expense, are being withheld from you—the FBI—by Mr. Joe Dokes esquire, or whatever his name is. Follow? Here's what will happen, I can guaran-damn-tee you that every muckrakin' sonofabitch out there will start beatin' on his door because every one of them will want to get their hands on these key documents before you do. Your lawyer friend will be inundated with angry letters and calls. Not to mention that you'll have a hundred reporters turnin' over every which kind of rock. If you're right—and I'm not sayin' you are—but if you're right that somethin' is fishy, then gettin' the press involved is the last thing he wants. He might just decide it's better to deal with you rather than them."

"You think that'll work?"

"Probably not. Maybe. No. Sure. Drop a reference or two to Gitmo while you're at it. Make it sound like he's defending some Muslim extremists. That may win him points up where you're from, but down here—hell, his windows will be shot out by the time he gets home for dinner."

"God," Levine said, shaking his head. "You ought to work for the FBI."

"I was thinkin' the same about you," Kel replied.

CHAPTER 39

Fort Smith, Arkansas

Friday, December 19

When Kel returned to the booth carrying another beer and a Diet Coke, Levine was looking through the contents of the FedEx package. He looked up at McKelvey. "What's this?"

"Not sure you have a need to know—considerin' that you're off the case." Kel sat down and pushed the beer toward Levine. "But technically I'll humor you a little more. Those are the records that I mentioned; for the guys whose initials match the lighter. To be honest, I've been under the gun at work, and I still haven't had time to study them, but I did glance over them on the plane. There are seven of them."

"So I can count. Any of these look promising?"

"Not really, but then it all depends on what you mean by promisin', I reckon. Six of them are guys with the initials J-S-B-J and one is a J-S-H-J. The initials match the ones on the lighter—which is pretty damn amazin' when you think about it. I mean, I have to admit that that's about six more people than I thought would have four initials, and about seven more than I figured we'd find records for."

"So you think one of these might be our man?"

Kel took a sip of his drink and shrugged. "Didn't say that, Mike. Actually, aside from the correlation of the initials—which is pretty goddamn amazin' when you think about it—"

"So you said."

"Well, none of them look to be good candidates. Especially in light of you sayin' that they were found on the POW part of the base. Four of them, includin' the one J-S-H-J, all survived the war and lived to be old men. The other three died elsewhere and are accounted for."

Levine's face registered a question. When no answer was forthcoming, he asked, "How do you know that? That four of them survived?"

"Spent the mornin' on the phone to the VA. God, if that wasn't like havin' my fingernails pulled out with a pair of hot-dog tongs."

"The Veterans Administration?"

"Yeah, we've got some contacts there. We use them sometimes to help run down relatives of the guys we're lookin' for so we can get blood samples for comparison to the DNA from the bones. The VA has records on benefits; who got them, where they lived, who gets the death benefits. Pretty useful stuff if you're tryin' to track down someone's heirs. I ran the names past them. Turns out that . . . here . . ." Kel took the papers from Levine and sorted through them. He handed them back one at a time. "This one died in 1967 in Iowa; this one a couple-three years ago in upstate New York; this guy about ten years ago in Raleigh, North Carolina, and . . . here, this one committed suicide in Omaha with a Remington twelve-gauge shotgun the day Spiro Agnew resigned. Not necessarily as a result, you understand."

Levine nodded at the three files still in McKelvey's hands. "And those?"

"These are called I-D-P-Fs. Individual Deceased Personnel Files. These are the three men who didn't make it home from the war. This guy died in forty-three in the Pacific when the troop transport he was on took two torpedoes in the side. He's lost in the deep blue. This one a year later, also in the Pacific. And this one," Kel plopped the file down in front of Levine, "must have died somewhere in Western Europe late in the war. Record's not very clear where or when. In fact, other than orders showin' he was bein' sent to Europe, there isn't much. I can't even prove he was there, but he must have been."

"So none of these guys is the one we're looking for."

"If you mean, are they the owner of your Chaffee skeleton, then it would appear not. Not if they all died elsewhere. There's some obscure law of physics that says that one skeleton can't occupy two graves at the same time. Besides, the biological profile from the skeleton is a poor match for any of them."

"So, it can't be them?"

"Let's just say there'd be a whole lot of discrepancies that we'd have to explain away to make it work."

The crowd in the bar erupted in a loud moan suggesting that someone who shouldn't have scored a touchdown had. There was a smattering of mild obscenities that quickly subsided into quiet laughter and clinking glasses.

Special Agent Levine watched the bar's patrons with a sour disdain that he reserved for most breathing humans. He took a sip of beer while he waited for the noise to dampen. As he did so, he shuffled the files, looking at each one but not really seeing them. His thoughts were working themselves into a question. "So now what? It's not these guys, and neither one of us figures that your FOIA idea is going to lead anywhere soon. To my thinking, this case is about dead-ended."

Kel answered, taking a sip of Coke first, "I think it was pretty well dead-ended from the get go. Isn't that why your boss assigned it to you?"

Levine looked out the window at the traffic that coursed Garrison Avenue.

Kel continued, "Maybe it's time to pull the plug—technically, that is. Sometimes that's the way it works out. Your boss seems to have given you a ticket out of here by telling you to take some vacation. Isn't that what you wanted?"

"Except there's a man dead—whoever the hell he was—and there's no statute of limitations on murder."

Kel rattled the ice in his glass and then turned sideways in the booth, stretching his legs out along the seat. "Murder's a big word. Hard to prove."

"You're the one who says the skull was bashed in," Levine replied. "And, even if one of these guys isn't our skeleton," Levine dropped the files onto the table to punctuate his statement, "that doesn't mean he couldn't be involved somehow. Does it? I mean, one of these seven could be the killer. Could have dropped his cigarette lighter when he was digging the grave to dispose of the body."

"Lots of coulds."

"Doesn't mean it isn't true."

"Except."

"Except what?"

Kel took a drink and squinted. "Well, as you just said, there's the small detail of the dead body. Even if one of these guys killed someone, before you can prove anythin' you'll likely still have to figure out who died. And that's what's presentin' the real problem, right?"

"That's why I want to see those records at the university."

"Which aren't goin' to tell you shit."

"So, what do you propose we do?"

"Me? You're the special agent, Mike. Do somethin' special."

"Cut the crap," Levine said as he resumed looking out the window. After a minute he looked back at McKelvey and smiled. "I'm on vacation, remember? How about a little help?"

Kel bobbed his head in exaggerated agreement. "Sure. Why not? It's not like I haven't been helpin' up to this point."

"Just a joke between friends. You're too damn sensitive."

Kel held up a hand to head off any additional explanation, or insult. "Okay. So let's just say that this problem can be figured out. Where do we start? We can assume that whoever it is, someone didn't want the body found. That's a given; so we start from there. From what you told me a few minutes ago, I'd say we got three choices." He spread out the fingers on his left hand and ticked the first one off with the other hand. "First, could be a civilian. Someone who worked on base. There might be a missin' persons report from sixty-five years ago. If you could ever find it. Maybe somethin' in the newspaper archives. My gut says it isn't a civilian, though. Not where it was found." He nodded at Levine to make sure he had his attention, and then he ticked off a second finger. "Or it could be a dead GI. Someone who isn't listed as dyin' there. Maybe someone who's listed as a deserter. We kinda learned that lesson with that case in Split Tree. Unlikely, but we don't want to make that mistake again."

Levine nodded.

"Or third," Kel tapped his ring finger, "it could be a dead German POW. After all, the remains were found under the old POW mess hall or barracks, or whatever."

"But how about the cigarette lighter and the smokes? They're American."

"How about them? The lighter is English and American cigarettes wouldn't be hard to come across. Besides, aren't you the one who just said that maybe someone else could have dropped them? Now, the ring, that might just pan out to be somethin'. I should have some information on that in a couple of days, but I wouldn't hold your breath."

Levine looked at McKelvey for a moment without responding. Finally, he spoke. "Sounds hopeless."

"Yeah, it does. To be honest, looks like you got a variety of dead ends to choose from."

The group at the bar erupted again and momentarily evoked Levine's displeasure. With a sigh he turned his attention back to McKelvey. He nodded in agreement as he absent-mindedly peeled the corner of the label off his beer bottle. "I want out of here, but not like this. Dead ends or not, I need to run these leads to ground. Need to check these seven guys out." He looked back at McKelvey. "Maybe I should also look into who was in charge of the prison camp. See if that shakes any leads free."

"Good luck. We're talkin' over sixty years ago as it is, and anyone who was in a position of authority would have been in their late twenties or early thirties at the youngest. Even if you find anyone, they'll probably be doin' good to remember their danged names, let alone anythin' about bodies under mess halls."

"I didn't say I was expecting to question anyone. I said that maybe I ought to look into who was in charge. Like I said, that's where the library records come in. Maybe there's some diary, memoir, something like that. Maybe some long-lost after-action reports. Maybe there were some in-house investigations that dropped through the cracks and have been forgotten. I sure-as-shit have written my fill of memos that get read once and then filed away and lost. Haven't you?"

"Wouldn't be worth my salt as a government employee if I hadn't."

"So, I'm assuming that the POW camp was headed up by a full bird colonel, maybe even a brigadier. Maybe even that general who's associated with those special library records. You can also figure that whoever it was had an aide, probably an executive officer as well. Somebody must have generated some paper."

"Maybe."

"It's time to find out what's so special about that special collection over in Fayetteville."

"*Up.*"

"Up, in Fayetteville. I'll give that prick lawyer one last shot; in the meantime, I'd like to take a look at whatever's available on these poor sons-of-bitches that you found." Levine glanced down at the files and then nodded a question at McKelvey. "Are these the complete records on them?"

"These three dead guys? Nope. These are the IDPFs; just the records relatin' to their death."

"I assume there are full military records somewhere? Can you get hold of them?"

"Yeah, I already got them. I was fixin' to start reviewin' them later tonight, but if you want to do it instead, knock yourself out. You won't find much useful in them."

Levine wrinkled his brow. "You already have them?" He gestured to the folders on the table as if to ask McKelvey why he hadn't brought the other files.

"They're electronic. We have access to all the World War Two records. They've been scanned. You have a computer?"

Levine shook his head. "Not here. Got one back in my office in Memphis."

"Well, that isn't much help to you here."

"I've been using the one in the business center at the hotel."

"The files are way too big. You'd be sittin' in there all night." Kel took a deep breath and held it momentarily while he thought. "You can use mine, I guess. I mean, it's a government computer, and you're a bona fide G-man. Sort of. I'll show you how to log on to our system and read the files. Just stay off the porn sites and don't tell anyone I let you use it."

"What about you? Don't you want to review the records?"

"My father-in-law has a computer. Not exactly state-of-the-art, but it'll do for accessin' some files. I'll bring my laptop by your hotel tomorrow mornin' first thing. You be there?"

"Unless I'm headed to Memphis to see that cocksucker lawyer. Thanks, I'd appreciate that."

"Don't thank me until you see the records. Plan on spendin' a day or two—especially if your computer connection is slow. They're pretty thick and very unorganized, and they won't tell you much."

Levine turned to the window again. "Fortunately for me, I don't seem to have anything else to do with my vacation time."

Both men sat quietly, listening to their thoughts and the noise of the room as the football game played on. Kel replayed his conversation with Hugh Rooney. He thought of the Holy Ghosts. Suddenly he sat up and began searching the files which were fanned out on the table top like giant playing cards. "I tell you what, partner, if I was you," he picked up one of the files, "I'd start with this one right here."

Levine turned to look at McKelvey and took the file from him. "James Jordan, Junior" he read. "Why him?"

Kel nodded his head at the six files still on the table. "Those guys, they were all combat arms—all but one anyhow. Three were infantry: two field artillery and one quartermaster. Plus they were all low rankin' Joes. Privates mostly, couple of corporals; I think maybe a tech sergeant. They were all at Chaffee for trainin' before gettin' shipped overseas."

The FBI agent began looking more closely at the file in his hands. "And this one?"

"Military Intelligence."

"MI?"

Kel nodded. "And a captain."

Levine looked up from the file. "Okay, but I'm missing your point."

"You were in Vietnam, right Mike?"

A nod.

"Infantry right? Twenty-fifth Infantry Division as I recall. Around Cu Chi."

"And your point?" Levine picked up his beer bottle as Kel leaned forward.

"My point, Mike, is this: You ever take any Viet Cong prisoners?"

Levine sighted down the length of his bottle at McKelvey. He took a long sip, but his eyes were locked and unblinking. "I killed a crap ton of them. Never saw the need to take any as prisoner," he responded.

Kel momentarily broke eye contact before regaining it. "Okay. Let's try this again. Your unit ever take any VC prisoners?"

"Some." Levine put his bottle down, but kept his eyes on McKelvey's.

"Okay, you ever interrogate any VC prisoners? Not you personally, we've already established the nature of your relationship with the VC, but your unit. Your buddies? They do the questionin'? Besides some quick in-the-field questions."

"No. We were an infantry squad. They didn't give me a rifle so I could make conversation. And your point?"

"My point is, if your squad, your platoon, didn't interrogate the prisoners it captured, who did? Who'd you turn them over to for questionin'?"

Michael Levine looked back at the file in his hands. "I see your point."

CHAPTER 40

Fort Smith, Arkansas

Friday, December 19

"Sorry to bother you at home on your day off, Hugh, and so late too," Kel started the conversation. He was sitting in the parking lot of the Varsity Grill talking on his cell phone after saying goodnight to Levine.

"Hey, don't worry about it. I only took leave to get away from the office, not to get away from the work, and it's not that late. It's only seven o'clock here," Hugh Rooney replied. "Besides, it must be important to get you to use a telephone."

Kel laughed. "Hey, I'm tryin'. Twelve-step program, plus, Mary Louise said if she caught me leavin' the house without my phone one more time, she'd take a big stick to me. I reckon if I gotta lug the damn thing around, I might as well use it for somethin' other than puttin' a bulge in my pocket."

"Welcome to the twenty-first century."

"Yeah, I've turned into a regular George Jetson."

"Tell it to someone who doesn't know you. Mary Louise might make you carry it when you leave the house, but it'll take more than that to get you to use it without a gun being pointed at your head. This must be important."

"Actually, not sure how important it is, but I've got another favor to ask of you."

"I'll add it to your bill."

"What's with everyone addin' crap to my bill? What bill?"

"The one that's labeled Poor Hugh answers all of Colonel Botch-It's asinine questions so that he doesn't come back to the Lab and bug the living shit out of Dr. McKelvey. That bill."

"Ahh. Have I ever told you what a bang-up job you're doin'?"

"No. I'll remind you to do that sometime. By the way, you get to look at those records I sent you yet?"

"Yeah, thanks. I was just discussin' them with an FBI agent."

"I hope they're useful. I should be getting the complete medical and dental records on the three dead guys in a couple of days. Now, you said favor. So, what's it this time? More initials?"

"Wish it were that easy. No, now I need a different kind of information. I'm not sure even you can track this one down though."

"Should I be insulted?"

"Not at all; not at all. I have tremendous confidence in your abilities; it's the subject matter that I'm doubtful about. I'm lookin' for two groups—one should be easy, one hard."

"Challenged accepted. What's the easy one?"

"Fort Chaffee again. This time I need a list of everyone who's listed as AWOL or as a deserter from there."

"Both?"

Kel paused. "Hmm. Guess not. On second thought, only deserters and only those who never resurfaced. AWOLs would have either been accounted for or would have been reclassified as deserters. Right? So, I guess I'm lookin' just for deserters."

"You got a time frame?"

"Forty-two plus or minus a couple."

"Got it. And the hard one?"

"A missin' German POW."

"Hmmm. POW? Doable, but my guess is that you've got them reversed."

"How so?"

"POW will be easy, or at least easier."

"That doesn't make any sense."

"Sure it does. Deserters will require going through unit morning reports—and there'll be a truckload of them. Then they'll have to be cross-referenced to see what finally happened to them and so on. Lots of files. Most of that stuff has been scanned, but the indexing sucks, absolutely sucks. We're talking weeks, and that's if I don't do anything else."

"But German POWs . . ."

"Well, I shouldn't say it'll be easy, but in fact, it'll probably be easier than tracking down a set of initials and a whole lot easier than tracking down a list of deserters from sixty-five years ago."

"I still don't see."

"The fire, remember? The 1973 fire that took out the top floor of the National Personnel Records Center in St. Louis; it destroyed most of the World War Two army files. There're still lots of records floating around, but they're harder to track down, and they're incomplete when you do find them. German POW records on the other hand, I'll bet they're all in one place—not sure where, but they're somewhere, I'd guess. I'll have to do some looking, but when I find them, you can bet they'll be in one place and unburned."

"So you're tellin' me you can track down an individual German POW?"

Kel could almost hear Rooney smile on the other end of the telephone. "If there's a paper record, I can find it. What's this German's name anyhow?"

Now it was Kel's turn to smile. "Now, that's the challengin' part, Hugh. That's the challenge. I want to make this fun. I don't know his name."

CHAPTER 41

Fort Smith, Arkansas

Friday, December 19

The house was still. With the thermostat turned down to sixty-five, there was no hum of the furnace. The children were asleep so there was no hum of adolescent mayhem. The street was quiet. In the absence of ambient noise, every creak and crack of the settling house seemed like gunshots. Kel sat in bed, his back propped against pillows, reading through the IDPF for Captain James Stuart Biddlecomb Jordan, Junior. He'd dimmed the bedside lamp and had to tilt the papers at an angle to read the faint Xeroxed copies. Even though it was late, he couldn't turn off his brain, and the conversation that he'd had earlier in the evening with Michael Levine kept running through his head.

"I'll be damned," he muttered out loud. In the still of the house, it sounded almost like a shout.

"Hmmm," his wife responded. "Probably so." She was a light sleeper under most circumstances, and the bed in her parents' guest room was oddly lumped and unforgiving of anything but uncompromising exhaustion.

Kel looked at the curve of her body under the blankets. "Sorry, honey," he said quietly. "Go on back to sleep."

"You go to sleep yourself. It's late, Kel," came another mumble.

"I know," he responded. "Soon." He reached out and patted her hip.

His wife sighed and rolled over; putting her head onto his shoulder. "What's the matter?"

"Nothin'. Go on back to sleep."

"Kel."

"Nothin' really. It's just this old file doesn't make any sense; one of these guys that Hugh tracked down for Agent Levine . . ."

"What about him?"

"Well, I don't know. He was supposed to have been killed in Europe late in the war."

"Umm, so what's the problem? Lots of men were killed in the war. That's what you men do in wars, isn't it? Kill each other."

"Somethin' isn't quite right. These records are usually pretty detailed, but this one has this Captain Jordan fella goin' to Europe . . ."

"Mmm."

"The problem is that there's no record of where he died, or how, or even when, for that matter. No record of what unit he was with. Nothin'. Orders sendin' him there, and then nothin' except some forms sayin' that a skeleton came back in early 1947 and got buried in California. Sacramento."

Mary Louise McKelvey adjusted her head into her husband's shoulder, working around the bone until there was an accommodation. "I don't know; you're the anthropologist in this bed, but if his skeleton came back way back then, then I'd say he must be dead."

Kel laughed and kissed the top of his wife's head. "Oh, I guess I overlooked that fact. Thank you for pointin' that out."

"I always said I was the one who should have gotten the PhD."

"Can't argue with that," he said as he reached up and turned off the light. He slid down under the covers and hooked his arm over his wife's hip. "Only thing is, Professor . . . the skeleton that came back in 1947 doesn't seem to have been his."

CHAPTER 42

Prisoner of War Compound, Camp Chaffee

Sebastian County, Arkansas

Wednesday, April 5, 1944

Bill Porter was exhausted. At the end of five days, counting Saturday, he'd interviewed every German prisoner in the compound who might have possible connections to Private Geller, and at the end of five days he knew nothing more than he did when he started. He looked at his watch. It was almost midnight, and he had a meeting with Colonel Wiggins in less than seven hours to update him on the status of his investigation. He'd worked all day, through lunch and dinner, and had even foregone the regular visit to *Indian Country* with Captain Mac—a nightly ritual that he'd come to look forward to—in order to review the interviews once more. Miss Kramer was proving a valuable asset, delivering typed transcripts every day before leaving for her home at seven p.m. He also didn't think it was entirely his imagination, or ego, that she was spending as much time sneaking glances at him as he was at her.

His vision was blurry and for the last half hour he'd read, and reread, the same page. It was page four of the third to the last of thirteen interviews he'd conducted the previous day. Most were vacuous and easily glossed over, the individual either not knowing Private Geller, or having very limited familiarity with him. This one was no different. The prisoner being questioned in this file—Albert Majewski—was an ethnic Pole who'd been in the camp for less than two months. He had little to offer, recognizing Geller only from having heard the name at morning muster, and from serving with him on a short two-day work detail repairing a rock wall near the base chapel.

Porter wasn't aware of falling asleep at his desk, though he assumed that he must have. Momentarily at least. Suddenly, he was aware of reading the same page again, and this time a name jumped out that hadn't during the interview or during the first three, four, five readings. Maybe it had simply been lost amid all the Horsts and Gunters and Johanns that had been questioned in the last week. Maybe his mind had so turned to jelly that connections wouldn't stay connected.

Toward the end of the otherwise uninformative interview, Majewski had mentioned that Hans Geller was often on work details with an older soldier: Obergefreiter Dieter Ketel. Porter had noted Ketel's name during the interview, but it was only in rereading the transcript that he realized that the interviews were now complete, and he didn't recall questioning Corporal Ketel. He reread the page again and then took up the bundle of file folders neatly stacked on the corner of his desk. Each one held one day's worth of transcripts. Paperclipped to the inside cover, however, was a typed list of the men to be questioned; each named crossed-out in pencil when the interview was concluded. He started with the first folder, scanning the list for Ketel's name. Not there. He scanned day two. Day three. Yesterday's. Finally, he turned to today's stack. Ketel's name was on none of the days' lists. He went through them again.

He drummed his fingers on the desk for a moment and then stood up and opened the top drawer of his filing cabinet. In the front was a thin folder holding eight pages of onionskin: The master list of men to be questioned. Porter walked back to his desk and drew his finger down the typed list of names. They were grouped by rank, alphabetically within each group. On page six, near the top of a group of twelve corporals, was what he was looking for: KETEL, Dieter.

He slumped in his chair and laid his head backward, resting it on the chair back. With his eyes closed, he tried to reason through the finding. He'd compiled the master list his first day on the case. After that he'd let Captain Jordan handle the logistics of scheduling the interviews and rewickering the prisoners' work assignments to get them in and out with a minimal amount of disruption. In fact, Jordan had taken the task upon himself without Porter having to ask.

How had Ketel fallen off the list? Were there others? He collected up his file folders and tallied up the interviews. He did it twice. Eighty-three both times. Then he counted the names on the master interview list. He did it twice. Eighty-four both times. Ketel was the only one who'd dropped off the list.

Porter looked at his watch: 12:07. He drummed his fingers some more as he thought, and then looked at his watch again. "Screw him," he mumbled as he picked up his phone and instructed the base operator to connect him through to Captain Jordan's quarters.

It took six rings.

"Yeah," James Jordan answered. His voice clearly indicated his opinion of a midnight call, though it also betrayed no thick-throated sounds of sleep. "Captain Jordan here. Who's this?"

"Sorry to bother you, Jim," Porter responded. He wasn't a bit sorry, but he said what needed to be said. He intentionally made his voice sound casual. "It's me. Bill. I've gotta question for you."

"Porter? Question? Must be a helluva question."

"Hmm. Probably not, but I've got to update the colonel in a few hours. I'm here at the office going over the interviews from the last few days, and I noticed something, probably nothing, fact I'm sure it's nothing, but, you know how it is. How the old man is."

"No, I don't. But, I'll tell you what, I'll be in a little after six. You can ask me your question then."

"Well, since I've got you on the phone, I don't see why I can't ask you now," Porter responded quickly to keep Jordan from hanging up. "It concerns a German prisoner that we didn't talk to."

"It's late, Porter. You need to give it a rest. We talked to everyone, so I suspect you've overlooked something. Why don't you head back to your quarters and turn in, and I'll help you find your error in the morning. See you then."

"Wait," Porter interjected. "I don't think I overlooked anything. I'm assuming maybe you did. The man's on the master list, but he doesn't show up on any of the daily schedules—the ones you arranged. I'm sure it's simply an oversight. A corporal. Name's Ketel, K-E-T-E-L. Dieter Ketel. I need you to have him in my office first thing tomorrow morning. Make that this morning. Before I meet with the colonel."

There was a long pause. Jordan sighed into the receiver. "That explains it, counselor. Should have told me who it was right off. Ketel's no longer here at Chaffee. He was transferred out."

"Transferred? Where? When?"

"Can't recall offhand. You're lucky I can barely remember the name at this hour."

"Who authorized the transfer?"

Jordan chuckled. "Who you think? Colonel Wiggins, of course."

CHAPTER 43

Fort Smith, Arkansas

Monday, December 22

Kel was driving home from the hotel when his phone rang. He'd dropped his computer off with Michael Levine, along with instructions on how to log onto the CILHI records system and search the World War Two files, but he hadn't told the FBI agent about the discrepancies in Jordan's mortuary record. It probably had nothing to do with Levine's Chaffee case, but if the body had been misidentified back in 1947, it was a matter that Kel—as scientific director of the CILHI—would have to deal with. Kel would tell Levine all about it later, but he wanted to review the file again before voicing any conclusions. No use spooking him down a rabbit hole. Besides, Levine was finishing a confrontational phone conversation with Martin Gilbreath's receptionist when Kel got to the hotel, and now Levine was headed over to Memphis to confront the lawyer in person. It hadn't been the best time to talk.

The streets were wet. It had rained overnight, but now the early-morning sun was out and the windshield was filmed over from the mist kicked up by the cars in front of him. Kel hit the windshield wipers and washer, successfully homogenizing the haze into a film resembling skim milk. His cell phone was on the passenger seat next to him when it rang. He flinched and looked at it. After the second ring, he pulled into a metered parking space on Garrison Avenue, put the vehicle into park, sighed, and picked up his phone. The number showing on the screen was Hugh Rooney's office at the CILHI.

"Hey," Kel answered. He took a quick look at his watch under his coat sleeve; calculating the time in Hawaii. "Don't you ever sleep?"

"Plenty of time for that later. Besides, it's not all that late here. Surprised to catch you, though. I assumed I'd have to leave a message. You don't normally like to get up before noon, do you?"

"Not normally. Had some errands to run for my in-laws. Plus I had to see this FBI guy I'm workin' with before he headed out of town. Actually, though, you must have been readin' my mind. I was plannin' to call you today."

Hugh Rooney groaned. "What now?"

"Easy stuff. Real easy."

"You said that the last time. I'd be careful about cashing in all your favors before you get back here."

"True. It just goes to show how much confidence I have in you. This time I need you to see about runnin' down the mortuary file on the remains that were identified as James Jordan. He was one of the ones you found with four initials. He was processed through Strasbourg."

"I remember."

"Great. Think you can?"

"You mean his file or the initial X-file?" Rooney asked. Long before there was even television, the government had begun amassing X-files, only these files represented unidentified remains of U.S. servicemen. Before Jordan was identified, the remains would have been given an X-file number by the lab in France. It would detail the anthropological analysis of the skeleton, not just the summary results that Kel had read the night before.

"The X-file. I want to see what they said about the skeleton back in 1944."

"Sure. I can probably access a scanned version on the computer. The quality won't be great, but it'll get you started. I'll order the hard copy from the archives, but that may take a couple of days. They're probably on a holiday schedule, so it'll take at least that long. In fact, it may be faster if I have them send it straight to you there in Arkansas. You at your mother's house?"

"Great. Do it. Yeah. We're movin' back and forth between my mother's and my in-law's house. Have it sent to my mother. D.S. has the address."

"Okay. I'll also see if I can get you an electronic version before I go home tonight . . . this morning . . . whenever."

"Owe you."

"Sure do."

Kel laughed. "Acknowledged. Now, unless I'm mistaken, you called me this time."

"You're right. As you'll recall, you challenged my ability to track down some historical records last night. I couldn't sleep with that hanging over my professional manhood so I came in right after we got off the phone," Rooney said.

"Manhood? That's a bit of an overstatement."

"I am my job. You want this information, or not?"

Kel reached up and turned the car's ignition off. "Jesus Christ, you got it already? Overnight?"

"Overnight is easier, usually," Rooney replied. "The internet doesn't sleep, but the five-hundred million numbskulls who clog it up do."

"Hell yes, I want it. Is this about the list of deserters?"

"Nope. I told you that'll take some time, even for me. Weeks, maybe. If ever. No, this is about the German POWs."

"Great. What've you got?"

"Good news or bad news."

"Ahh, now there's the second shoe droppin'. Let's start with the good."

"Well, the good news is that I was right that the POW records are fairly detailed and all in one place. The government kept very good records on the status of POWs in this country, which makes sense when you think about it. We were going to have to repatriate all the POWs after the war—no matter who won—and no one wanted any Geneva Convention violations. Also, the Germans were all sent home together, or at least in specific groups. Very organized. Returning U.S.

soldiers, on the other hand, they sometimes came back helter-skelter depending on their discharge points. A few here; few there. But the POWs were tracked very carefully. Lots of lists, lots of roll calls, lots of check marks."

"And you found these records?"

"Of course."

"So what'd you find? I assume that was the good news."

"Maybe. You wanted to know if any German POWs at Camp Chaffee are unaccounted for, right? From what I can tell, everyone went home to Germany after the war."

Kel sighed. "Shit," he said. "All of them?"

"Almost. As best I can determine anyhow. There are a few confirmed deaths, including that Hans Geller guy that I told you about. The one that got his brains knocked out by the Heilige Geists."

"Yeah. Do we know where he was buried?"

"I don't know where he's buried now, but at one time he was buried at Camp Chaffee in a designated POW cemetery. After the war his body was taken back to Germany. There's no record of where in Germany he's buried, or at least no U.S. record that I've found yet. In fact, almost all the POW bodies were exhumed and returned home. The ones executed up at Leavenworth are still buried there, but the rest went home, I think."

"Includin' the ones from Chaffee?"

"Yeah. That much is very well documented."

"And all the live ones went home as well?" Kel asked.

"Now, that's the bad news. Of course, the big answer is, *yes*, they all went home, but as detailed as the records are, there are five from Chaffee that I can't track. Yet."

Kel sat up straighter. "Five?"

"Yeah, but before you get too excited, I think it's simply a gap in the records. Five out of several hundred isn't exactly something to get too concerned about. It's probably just a lost file folder. The records indicate that all five of these missing guys were transferred out of

Chaffee during a five- or six-month period in late 1943 and early forty-four."

"You're sure they left Arkansas?"

"Yeah. That's pretty well documented, too. I found copies of the transfer orders; all signed by the camp commander."

"All to the same place?"

"You mean, sent to the same place? Yeah. Same, same. Transferred to a smaller camp up in Missouri. That's the extent of the good news. Now the bad—their records are complete blanks after that."

"Administrative black hole?"

"Maybe. I thought that at first, but . . ."

"But?"

"Now I'm not so sure. The thing is, it's odd. I searched all of the other POW camps in Missouri, Oklahoma, Nebraska; everything in a couple state radius of Chaffee; searched them all—until well after midnight. There's no record of any of the five of them ever arriving at the camp they were sent to, or any other camp for that matter. That could be a lost file folder, except that there's also no record of them going home after the war—alive or dead. That would mean two lost folders. And you know what's really odd?"

"What?"

"We have very good records on them otherwise. Their in-processing forms. Their original fingerprint cards. I mean, we even have some medical records for one of them when he was treated in a couple of U.S. hospitals for a gunshot wound to the leg. But when it comes to what happened to them after they leave Arkansas, not nothing. Zip." Rooney paused. "I wish I could be of more help."

"What? No. Jesus, you've been great. Just great." Kel thought for a moment. "Hey, Hugh, can you send me what you've got?"

"Their records? I've got the originals being overnighted here, which means with Christmas, it'll be next Monday before I get them, but, sure, I can send you some scans before I go home. Gimme a couple of hours, but, hey, like I was saying, don't get your hopes up; there isn't much concerning what may have happened to them."

"Except that they left Camp Chaffee."

"Well, yeah, I guess. If you can believe the records."

CHAPTER 44

Pyatt, Arkansas

Monday, December 22

Dennis Viktor reached for the small digital recorder that he'd purchased the day before at a pre-Christmas special at the Wal-Mart in Flippin. It was $29.95 and a miracle of modern technology; he'd bought it when the phone calls kept coming. He hit the Record button, verified that the green LED was blinking, and held the recorder up to the phone receiver. "You want to repeat that? One of us is dropping out," he said. "I'm only hearing every other word."

"I said," the voice repeated, enunciating slowly, "That our Mr. Levine is becoming a real nuisance, and I want him taken care of. Now."

"I'm trying. You need to learn some patience."

"Patience is for losers. You may settle for that; I do not. I want him off this case and out of my business. Immediately."

Viktor paused the recorder. "I'm trying to persuade him that life is too short to put up with unnecessary aggravations."

"Is that all that you're doing? Aggravating him?"

Viktor hit the Record button again. "What is it that he did that you want him eliminated so badly? If I can use the word eliminate?"

"That's my business," the voice replied. "All you need to do is get rid of him."

"If you say so. How do you want it done?" Viktor asked. "Kill him?"

"That would be one way to stop him. What you've done up to this point certainly hasn't worked."

Viktor smiled. He hit the Pause button. "That makes two of us. Thought you were going to get him pulled off the case. What happened?"

"He's proving stubborn," the voice replied. "He doesn't take orders well."

"That's my impression. You know what that means, don't you? Means that short of killing him, I may have to take some extreme measures."

"That's acceptable."

Viktor turned the recorder back on. "So, you want me to take," he paused for emphasis, "extreme measures to get rid of Mr. Levine?"

"I want you to do whatever it takes."

"Whatever?"

"You heard me."

Dennis Viktor smiled again.

CHAPTER 45

Memphis, Tennessee

Monday, December 22

Levine looked at his watch for the third time in five minutes. He cleared his throat and spoke. "I suggest you check again?"

The attractive young woman—the one who was too aware of how attractive she was—spoke without making eye contact with Levine. "As I tried to tell you on the phone earlier, Mr. Gilbreath has a very busy schedule this mornin'. I'm not sure that he'll be able to work you in." She paused and finally looked up from her desk. "But of course, you are certainly welcome to keep on waitin'." She blinked, smiled, and looked down again at the magazine she was leafing through.

Levine stood up and walked to the edge of the young woman's desk. She wasn't much older that his oldest daughter; midtwenties perhaps. He leaned forward, straining the shoulders of his jacket, his knuckles on the desktop, and spoke quietly—like a stern father. "Here's the situation. Mr. Gilbreath's a busy man; I'm a busy man. The real difference between the two of us is that I'm losing patience rapidly, and I carry a badge. Now, I've watched you take at least three cups of coffee into his office in the hour that you've had me parked out here. Sooner or later, your boss is going to have to go to the can, and when he does, I'll follow him in there and unzip his goddamn fly if that's what it takes." He could see her slender arms tense, but she kept her head down. He raised his voice, loud enough to ensure that it carried through the wall. "So, here's what I want you to go in there and convey to Mr. Gilbreath; tell him that I'm prepared to sit out here for another hour. After that," he said as he looked at his watch, "I'll call another CNN press conference. You go tell Mr. Gilbreath that no matter how busy he thinks he is, it'll be a good idea for him to take a break about then and turn the TV on. You got that?"

The young woman nodded but kept her head down and didn't make eye contact.

Levine was still standing at the desk, looking at the young woman, when her desk phone buzzed. She answered it. "Yes, sir," she said. "Yes, sir." She flashed a quick look at Levine and nodded her head in acknowledgment of something being asked her. "Yes, sir. I understand." She cradled the phone and stood up. She was tall and in her expensive do-me heels almost met Levine eye-to-eye. She blinked quickly. "Mr. Gilbreath has freed up five minutes to see you now," she said.

Levine didn't pause to respond. He walked quickly past her into Gilbreath's large office.

Gilbreath was seated behind his desk, working, or at least appearing to work, on some papers. He motioned for Levine to take a seat. "Mr. Levine," Gilbreath began. He moved a stack of papers to the side of his blotter and sat back in his chair, rocking it back as he sighed—whether from fatigue or impatience wasn't clear. "I dare say that I didn't expect to see you again. I was led to believe you were on vacation."

"That so?" Levine responded as he sat down. He reached forward and took a gold-plated cigarette lighter off the desk and leaned back, flicking a flame. "Mind if I ask who led you to believe that?"

Gilbreath smiled and watched Levine closely. He hadn't become one of the top trial lawyers in the country by not being able to read people. He shrugged. "I can't rightly recall. Perhaps I made that up." He nodded at the lighter. "Help yourself; if you wish to smoke. Feel free. This is not a federal office building; we still have the freedom to indulge offensive behavior."

Levine stopped flicking the lighter and returned it to the desk. "Gave it up. Still have the craving, but so far, the will power is holding up." He nodded slowly. "That's the funny thing about will power; sometimes I can control myself. Sometimes I can't."

Gilbreath rolled his eyes. "Indeed, I'm sure you must be a willful man. So, Mr. Levine, as I have already noted, I didn't expect to see you again. Not again so soon, certainly. Do you have new business? As I told you at our last meeting, I have your request under advisement and will take it to the trust board when it next meets."

"In six months or so?"

"In six months. Yes. So, you do remember."

"Unacceptable."

The lawyer laughed. "Is it now? I'm so sorry. I'm afraid, however, that that's the way it is. The trust board won't meet again until July. But I'll make you a promise, the next time I set up a trust, I'll be sure to consult your appointment calendar first."

Levine leaned forward and rested his elbows on his knees. "About that trust board. Funny thing. I spent some time calling around. From what I can piece together, the trust is made up of a guy name Wiggins who lives in Missouri, a woman who's up in New York, and you. Just you three. I'm thinking that you could have an ad hoc meeting right now." He pointed to the telephone. "I'll bet you have their numbers around here somewhere."

Gilbreath didn't blink. "I agreed to give you five minutes." He glanced at a small clock on his desk rather than his watch. "And I'm afraid your time's up. I'm sorry. Now, if you'll excuse me."

"I'm sorry, too," Levine said as he stood up. "You're going to force me to FOIA the records. Do you understand what that means?"

"Do you? Freedom of Information Act?" Gilbreath laughed loudly. "Really? I'm a lawyer, Mr. Levine, and a good one, but please, please entertain yourself. Entertain us both. You do realize, however, that even my receptionist can probably think up a thousand ways to block your FOIA if we wanted to do so?"

"So I've been told, though the person who told me that said it'd be your janitor you'd have think up the different reasons."

"A smart man, your friend. Whoever he is, you should listen to him."

"That's what he says. So, is that what you want to do, Mr. Gilbreath? You want to try to block my FOIA?"

The lawyer smiled, but didn't respond.

Levine nodded. "Perhaps I will listen to my friend. You know what else he suggested? He suggested that I call another press conference. God knows it wouldn't be hard; I have CNN on speed dial nowadays. And here's what I'd say, I'd say, vital records relating to this homicide over at Fort Chaffee are being withheld at the direction of you. Key information. There may even be a Gitmo connection that you're attempting to cover up."

"Homicide? So it's a homicide now? It wasn't long ago that you were tellin' the press that it was some prehistoric Indian find of some sort. Or am I wrong? Did you decide to classify it as a homicide, Mr. Levine? I didn't realize you're a medical examiner in addition to your other many talents."

The FBI agent put his hands in his pockets and tilted his head to the side. He'd dealt with a thousand pricks like Gilbreath in his life, and it usually hadn't ended well for any of them. "I'm not, counselor. In fact, I was trained in accounting. I'm a numbers guy. That's my talent. We had a saying when we were investigating a white-collar crime—*cui bono*. As you say, you're a lawyer, I assume you're familiar with it."

"Indeed. From Cicero, I believe. *Who benefits*? Tell me, do you think someone is profiting from something here, Mr. Levine?"

Levine turned and slowly walked to the door, his hands still in his pockets. He stopped and looked back at the lawyer. "I do, Mr. Gilbreath. Not sure yet who or how, but I do. I'll figure it out; you can count on it."

CHAPTER 46

Fort Smith, Arkansas

Monday, December 22

Even with the sound muted, it was obvious that the Channel Ten AccuDoppler weatherman was foretelling a New Year's warming trend. He was pointing at a bright yellow sun wearing sunglasses and a jagged grin bouncing across the green screen behind him. If the forecast held true, it would be in the midsixties by Thursday, Christmas Day, and even warmer by the weekend. In the silence, Kel sat slumped on the couch in his mother's den, his stocking feet propped on a stack of magazines piled on the coffee table, eyes closed, thinking about the X-file that he'd been reading. The one that Hugh Rooney had emailed him. The one for the remains finally identified as James Jordan.

Kel sighed. It was an unconscious act, and he'd been doing it regularly for the last half hour.

Kel's wife was also laying on the couch, head in his lap, half-moon glasses on the end of her nose, working through the newspaper. She was thinking that if her husband sighed one more time that she'd strangle him with her bare hands and gladly take her chances with a jury of her peers.

On cue, Kel sighed again.

"Robert Dean McKelvey, if you don't sound like the little engine that could. What in the world requires all that sighin'?" Anne McKelvey, his mother, asked. She was sitting in an upholstered chair next to an end table. There was a large ceramic ash tray on its scuffed top, despite the fact that no one had smoked in the house in years, and a cylindrical green plaster lamp that was showing four or five decades of nicks and chips. In its dim yellow light, Anne McKelvey was reading an Erle Stanley Gardner novel. She'd read it a dozen times before; in fact, she had a bookshelf filled with mystery novels, and she'd read each one of them numerous times, but at her age she now could enjoy them again and again as if each time were the first time.

"Thank you, Anne," Mary Louise McKelvey said as she turned onto her side and set the newspaper aside. "You may have just saved me from doin' twenty-to-life for manslaughter."

"What?" Kel said, opening his eyes. "Did I miss somethin' here?"

"What's botherin' you, Kel?" his mother asked.

Kel blinked and looked around. "Nothin'. Why? What'd I miss?"

"You've sighed more tonight than your boys at a long church service. What's botherin' you so?"

Kel crumpled his brow and considered. He shrugged. "Sorry. Just thinkin', I guess."

"An act that apparently requires considerably more effort for some of us," Mary Louise said. She looked up at her husband and smiled.

"Love you too," Kel smiled back. He looked back at his mother. "It's this case I'm workin' on."

"The one for the FBI? The one out there at Fort Chaffee? Or do you have another one?"

"Yes, ma'am. That's the one. One's enough."

Anne McKelvey closed her book and focused her look in such a way as if to say, *so tell me.*

"Well," Kel responded, "they found this skeleton out at Chaffee. There was an old Lucky Strike green wrapper with it."

"Green? Oh my. Luck Strike Green goes to war," Anne McKelvey said, recalling the old advertising slogan. "That was fairly early, as I recall."

"Yes, ma'am. Good memory. Sometime in 1942. There was also a 1930s era cigarette lighter with it that has some initials engraved on it." He nodded slowly as he sequenced the events in his mind. "Kinda corroded, but you can read them. The lab searched all the Chaffee records and came up with a short list of six or seven men with the same initials who served out there durin' the war."

"Six or seven? That sounds pretty promisin', given all the young men that passed through there," Anne McKelvey responded. "Mercy, there were so many of them. All so young. But that all sounds promisin'; so why all that sighin'?"

"One of them was an intelligence officer who worked for General Wiggins."

Anne McKelvey closed her eyes at the name. "Old Fist Wiggins," she said, more to herself than anyone else in the room. She opened her eyes and looked at her son. "Haven't heard that name in a long time. He was a very popular man around here for many years. Even after the war. But that doesn't explain all the sighin'."

"The sighin' is because this intelligence officer is the best match of the whole bunch, but he died in Europe and accordin' to the records, he's buried over near Sacramento."

His mother nodded and opened her Perry Mason novel. "Well, I'm not an anthropologist, but if he's buried in Sacramento, then my guess is he's not buried out at Fort Chaffee."

Mary Louise McKelvey laughed.

"Well there's another fact I seem to have overlooked," Kel said sarcastically. "What would I do without y'all's uncanny damn insight?"

"Mind the language, Kel," his mother admonished.

"Yes, ma'am."

Mary Louise giggled again and picked up the newspaper.

"Seriously, mom," Kel continued, "it's the fact that he's buried in Sacramento that's got me doin' *all that sighin'*, as you say."

Anne McKelvey put her book down again and folded her hands. "I'm still listenin'."

Kel sighed again, this time in order to rewind the story before hitting the play button. "Captain James S. B. Jordan, Junior. Twenty-six years old in 1945. Raised in the Sacramento area. Bachelor's degree in European history from Princeton at age nineteen. Master's from Yale. Spoke a half-dozen languages. I think we can assume that his folks were probably well-to-do. Anyhow, he joins the army on December eighth, 1941—day after Pearl Harbor. Immediately assigned to military intelligence. Probably a natural for it. You with me?"

His mother smiled patiently.

"Okay," Kel answered quickly. He hadn't meant for it to sound the way that she took it; he adjusted his tone. "He was assigned to a post over in Oklahoma and then Fort Chaffee," he continued. "And then the next thing you know, he's over in Europe. No real record of when, where, why, or how he died. All we know is that after the war, his body gets shipped back to his father in Sacramento."

"Certainly makes me want to sigh," Mary Louise said as she feigned reading the newspaper.

Kel ignored his wife and continued, "But the problem is that, unlike you two experts, the folks that examined the remains back in forty-seven were anthropologists. Pretty good ones, too. I don't have the complete file yet, it's comin' from Washington, but I have a scanned copy of their findings, and their analysis of the skeleton suggests that it was an eighteen-nineteen-year-old male who was about five three in stature. Short little guy. Just a kid, really."

"So many of them were," his mother said softly. She had been listening closely. "And your boy from Sacramento, you say he was twenty-somethin'?"

"Yes, ma'am. Twenty-six in 1945 when he was sent to Europe."

"Any chance the estimate of his age is wrong? Just how accurate can you be when all you've got are some old bones?"

"Sure, there's always room for error. It's possible, but not likely. Not with that age. There's a big difference between the skeleton of a teenager and someone twenty-six. They didn't miss the estimate by that much, even with the techniques available to them at the time."

"And the height?"

"His stature? That's the other thing. Captain Jordan is listed as five ten, five eleven. Big difference from the five three estimate they got from the skeleton."

Anne McKelvey sighed.

"See?" Kel responded. "See? Sort of brings out the sighs in a person, doesn't it? And there's another piece of the puzzle. Captain Jordan was an athlete. Rowin' team. He even played football at Princeton his senior year—halfback—at least until he blew out a knee.

The records don't specify which leg, but it says he had to have orthopedic surgery. In fact, it was bad enough that he had to get a doctor's letter certifying that he was fit to join the army."

"And does that body in Sacramento have a broken leg?" his mother asked.

"I didn't say his leg was broken. The record just says trauma to the knee, but to answer your question, no, the file on the skeleton in California doesn't make any mention of trauma to either leg."

"So where does that leave you?"

Kel smiled, without much amusement, and shook his head slowly. He stroked his wife's hair for a moment as he thought. "Leaves me thinkin'," he paused. "It leaves me thinkin' that the skeleton in Sacramento was misidentified; plain and simple. And if he was misidentified, then I gotta ask: Where's the real Jordan, and who's really buried in California?"

Anne McKelvey opened her book and resumed reading. "Too much of a mystery for me. You just go ahead and sigh. All you need to."

CHAPTER 47

Fort Smith, Arkansas

Monday, December 22

His hotel room was clean and moderately spacious and smelled of bottled oranges. In fact, it was only slightly smaller than the entire three-room brownstone box in Brooklyn that Levine had grown up in, the one that he'd shared with his mother and father and the ever-roaming ghost of his older brother, Lowell, who'd died in 1952 from complications of the polio epidemic that had scythed through the city that summer. It was only slightly smaller than the apartment he rented in Memphis, the one he shared with no one.

Michael Levine sank lower in the chair as he took in the room. He'd returned from Memphis a few hours earlier, tired and hungry and totally at a loss for what to do next. As soon as he could summon the energy, he'd head for the lobby bar—as was now his habit—but for now he sat and sank. At least he felt as if he were sinking lower in the chair, but perhaps it was an illusion; an impression; a manifestation of his state of mind. If he let himself, if he closed his eyes and let his mind untether, he was sure that he would feel the yawing movement as he swirled down the drain into the darkness. If he let himself. The television was on, its volume muted, and a black-and-white movie was showing; a British actor whose name Levine couldn't recall was walking down a rain-soaked city street in a bent-brim hat and tweed overcoat. It frustrated him that he couldn't recall the actor's name, not because he really cared who the actor was, or what the movie was. He didn't care much for movies. What bothered him was that this movie, and this actor, were his wife's favorites and he couldn't recall the name of either.

He closed his eyes and felt the swirl and began the roll call.

Increasingly in the last year, he'd become aware of a slipping memory. There had been a time when he could recall everything with crystal clarity. It had been a strength. A force. Now, he found himself struggling more and more frequently to retrieve even the names of friends and family. He always managed to recall them, eventually, but not always at will and often only after diverting his thoughts and accessing his memory sideways.

Like now.

He called the roll: Shipman, Dale; Skinner, Roger; Smith, Brion. Early on he'd only have to call a few names, never more than a half-dozen, just enough to get the brain side-tracked, and whatever, whoever he was trying to think of would literally pop into his head. Sometimes it'd take as many as a dozen, but lately, and with increasing frequency he found himself having to run the whole company. All the men that he'd served with in Vietnam. Those that came back. Those that didn't. Those that should have. Those that shouldn't have.

Tonight, the roll call was stuck. He felt the swirl as he kept repeating the same name: Levine, Michael; Levine, Michael; Levine, Michael.

When the phone rang, he almost didn't hear it, having lost himself in the hypnotic mantra of the roll call. It was on the third ring, and ready to switch over to the hotel's voice mail, when he picked it up. The voice on the other end was soft and indistinct, almost ghostly in its lack of physical substance. "Give it up," the voice said, and then there was silence. And then a click.

Levine almost thought that it had been a ghost; one of the long lost answering the muster. Almost, that is, until he went out to his car the next morning and found all four tires had been slashed.

CHAPTER 48

Fort Smith, Arkansas

Tuesday, December 23

His wife kissed him gently on the forehead; a warm soft touch that made him want to sink further into his pillow and never emerge. He could feel her warm breath on his ear as she whispered, "Why don't you shut up now?"

Kel watched the words swim around through the early morning molasses inside his head. He wasn't aware that he'd been saying anything. "Ummf?" he responded.

"What?" his wife asked.

"Why do I need to shut up?" he mumbled.

Mary Louise McKelvey was already starting to make the bed, tugging up the comforter on her side and smoothing out the wrinkles with her hand. She could finish as soon as Kel got up. "I said, why don't you get up now? Day's gettin' away, and you promised to take the boys shootin' today. You don't get on with it, you'll run out of time." Kel had let his twin boys open one of the presents early—twelve-gauge shotguns—and they'd both been anxious to try them out, especially with the weather warming. It was an hour's drive over to the state shooting range in Franklin County, and the days were short.

"Lord. What time is it?" he asked.

"Almost eleven. You need to get on up."

"Ummf." It was a statement this time; not a question.

"What time did you come to bed, anyhow? You on the computer the whole time?"

Kel exhaled deeply. "Dunno. Late." Actually he did know. It was almost four thirty in the morning when he'd signed off his father-in-law's computer. "I was searchin' some army records. Tryin' to track down somethin' more on that James Jordan guy."

"The one buried in California?"

"Or not."

"Find anythin'?"

"Naw. Not really."

"Sorry," Mary Louise said, and she meant it. She was standing, hands on her hips, watching her husband. She puffed and blew back a thick strand of hair that had worked its way out from behind her ear and had cascaded over her face. "Come on now, get up. The boys are anxious, and besides, that FBI buddy of yours has called here a good dozen times already. Started at six this mornin'. Woke up mother."

"Levine?"

"How many other FBI agent buddies do you have here in Fort Smith? Yes, Levine. He always so gruff?"

"Only to humans," Kel responded as he swung his legs out of bed. "From what I can tell, he's pretty damn charmin' otherwise." He squinted hard and rubbed his eyes with the balls of his hands. "What does he want?"

"You, I gather, but don't ask me why. Now get up so I can make this bed. You go call him back."

Kel groaned. "God I hate telephones."

"Hold on. Hold on," his wife said excitedly. "Where's my calendar?"

Kel groaned again. "I don't know. Why?"

"Because I want to mark this day down. My husband went all of two minutes before tellin' me that he hates telephones."

Kel stood up and stretched. He looked at his wife. "Did I ever tell you 'bout that case I worked for the New York State Police? The one where the man killed his wife of over twenty-five years because she drove him crazy one mornin'? Tragic."

"I'm sure it was," Mary Louise responded as she returned to making the bed. "Did I ever tell you about the husband who joined the monastery? The husband that figured that since he was facin' a life of painful celibacy, he might as well join a support group."

"Don't believe you did, sweetheart." Kel got one leg into a pair of blue jeans before hanging up the other and losing his balance. He started hopping in a circle trying to unsnag his foot. "God I hate telephones," he muttered.

"Oh, now I definitely need to mark this day down. My husband made it all of sixty seconds before tellin' me a second time how much he hates telephones. Honestly, Kel, you really need to grow up and get over this silly aversion to—" she stood up and turned around in time to see him hopping in a circle. "Or not. You goin' on the warpath, Sittin' Bull, or is that just a rain dance?"

Kel finally maneuvered his second leg into his jeans and came to a stop. "You been here awhile? Because I was wonderin' if you might have seen what happened to my lovin' wife that kissed me so gently this mornin'. She seems to have completely disappeared," he said as he picked up his cell phone from the bedside table and began clicking through the stored numbers until he found Levine's; he pushed the recall button. As he listened to the phone ring, he looked at his wife and smiled.

"Would that be the same one that told you to shut up?" Mary Louise replied.

"That'd be the one. She said it lovingly, though," he responded just as Levine answered. He winked at his wife, and she smiled. After almost thirty years, her smile still made his whole body buzz.

"Goddamn, Doc. All you seem to do is sleep," Michael Levine answered the call.

"Good mornin' to you too, Mike. Always good to get a dose of your sunshine in the mornin'. I'm told you called," Kel replied. "And please don't call me Doc unless you're chewin' on a carrot."

"Yeah, yeah. Great morning, provided some punk kids don't slash all four of your car tires."

"Oh, man. Seriously? Sorry. All four?" Kel paused. "My sons have alibis. I think."

"Yeah. Four tires. I spent all morning getting them replaced. Forget it. Shit happens. You got anything?"

"On?"

"On our goddamn case. What else? You come up with anything more?"

"Ahh. Correct me if I'm wrong here, Mike, but it's not our case; it's your case. I'm willin' to help out here, but you're on the payroll, and I'm on vacation. Though . . . actually, I guess you are too."

"Bullshit, Doc. You may be on vacation, but you love working these cases. I know you better than you know yourself. You can't stop thinking about that skeleton. Can you?"

"Maybe; maybe not. I do know that I could do more, but you've got my computer, remember? I'd like to get it back, but, hey, speakin' of updates, tell me, how'd it go with your lawyer friend yesterday? Did your naturally sunny disposition win him over as easily as it does me?"

"What a prick."

Kel hesitated, then laughed. "Him or me?"

"Both. I'll tell you about it later."

"Can't wait."

"I read through the army files last night. You're right, there's nothing definitive, but your boy, that Captain Jordan, if he weren't already buried, I'd agree that he's the best bet. His record's pretty damn sparse, though. About the only thing that seems for sure is that he's buried in California."

Kel laughed. "Yeah. Maybe. I wouldn't be so sure about even that."

There was a silence on the phone that registered confusion. "Thought you didn't have anything new?" Levine questioned.

Kel shrugged. "Didn't say that. You're right, I've been doin' some thinkin' about this case. Lookin' over those files. With a slow computer."

"And?"

"And whoever they buried over in California . . . well, I don't know who that boy was, but I can tell you that it probably wasn't James Jordan."

"Say again."

"I can, but you heard me the first time. Don't need to chew my tobacco twice."

"You sure?" Levine's rising interest came through the phone line.

"Sure is a relative word. Without diggin' up that grave in Sacramento, no, I can't be sure. So, I'd have to say *no*, but havin' said that, *yeah*, I'm sure—so, I'd say *yes*." He looked up and caught his wife's eye. She was watching and listening to the one half of the conversation. She smiled and shook her head in amused confusion.

"If that's the case, then maybe we're on to something, aren't we Doc . . . Kel? Are you saying our skeleton from Fort Chaffee could be this James Jordan after all?"

"Maybe. Still unlikely, but he has to be somewhere, and if he's not in California, then that option is back on the table. I mean, the age of your Chaffee skeleton is about right. Stature's about right. Jordan had a bad knee and the skeleton from Chaffee has got a busted tibia and bad knees. Don't know if it's the same injury, but maybe."

"But it could be?"

"Like I said, unlikely, but maybe. I can't excluded him. Oh yeah, the isotopic value is western, so that's in the plus column as well."

"Isotopic value?"

"I'll explain later."

"So let's say it's him, how do we prove it?" Levine asked.

"It'll be easier to disprove it."

"I'd rather prove it."

"Well, that's a problem. Having better dental records would help. We're trying to get hold of Jordan's, but in the meantime, the DNA lab in Maryland is tryin' to get DNA out of one of the teeth. Of course that'll mean we've got to track down a suitable relative of Jordan's to get a reference sample for comparison. That'll take some time; may even be a bigger problem than findin' better dental records. I'm not sure he has any livin' kin left, and even if he does, they may not be the right ones to get DNA from.'"

"But it's possible?"

"That it's Jordan? Sure. I guess it's possible."

CHAPTER 49

Fort Smith, Arkansas

Tuesday, December 23

Levine was at the hotel bar. It was too early to go to bed, and he found himself, as he was increasingly finding himself, working his way through a scotch on the rocks and high-grading the cashews and stale cheese sticks from a bowl of mixed bar snacks. He hadn't eaten all day and he chewed slowly, allowing the alcohol to take full effect and numb the reality of his life. He was on his third drink when a man sat down beside him.

"This taken?" the man asked. His body language indicated his reference to the bar stool next to the FBI agent.

Levine gave a slight shake of his head, acknowledging the man as little as possible. He took a cashew and nudged the bowl with his fingertips in the direction of the stranger—not so much to be engaging as to be polite—and perhaps to preempt any additional interaction.

The man squirreled a handful of snack mix into his cheek and mumbled amid a shower of pretzel crumbs, "Man-oh-man, what a day. What a day." He swallowed loudly and pushed the bowl back toward Levine. "Vic Davidson, glad to meet you." He dusted the crumbs onto his pants leg before sticking his hand out and forcing Levine to shake it.

Levine reluctantly shook hands in reply and checked the level of his drink, evaluating the cost-benefit of leaving before it was finished. He made the decision to finish it and took a long swallow. He shook the ice in preparation for finishing it off.

"Man oh man, the life of a road warrior, right? And at Christmas time, too," the man said. He spoke too loudly for the confined space as he leaned forward and groped another handful of snack mix and

stuffed it into his mouth. He sniffed and intruded into Levine's space.
"You look familiar. You do. Do I know you?"

Levine took another swallow. Tossing the liquid back in his
throat. "No."

"Well, you sure do. You sure? You do look familiar." He made a
show of squinting his eyes as if he were staring across the hood of a
waxed car in the afternoon glare. "I'm good at faces. Have to be in
my line. I sell food flavorings. All kinds, but mostly the smoke
flavorin' that they use on chickens. Those grill stripes that you see on
frozen chicken breasts, that isn't real grillin' you know—that's smoke-
flavored paint most times. Most people don't know that. Big, big
seller with all the chicken processing around here—" He paused
abruptly and squinted some more, then he slapped the bar with his
palm. "Dang if you ain't that guy I've been seein' on all the news
shows. Dang. Dang. Dang. You're that FBI fella that dug up that
body out at the army base. That's you, isn't it? Sure enough."

Levine raised his right hand in an attempt to get the bartender's
attention. He wanted his tab. He stood and partially turned his body
to screen the stranger.

"I'll be ding-donged. How about that?" The man's enthusiasm
continued to grow along with the certainty of his identification. "Let
me buy you a drink." He turned his attention to the bartender and
upped the volume. "Hey, Pedro. You." He waited for the bartender
to turn his head. "Yeah, you. Another drink for my buddy here.
Whatever he's havin'. And make it the good stuff."

Levine held up a palm. "No, thank you. I'm going."

"No can do. Hey, Pedro. Dos drinkas, por-favor." He nodded
and winked as the bartender acknowledged him and then turned his
attention back to Levine. He lowered his voice. "Must be near his
siesta time. Mexicans every-dang-where. Am I right? Only good thing
is that they all answer to Pedro."

"Look," Levine said, "I appreciate the offer, but I'm leaving." He
bit back the urge to say more. Levine didn't like Mexicans. He didn't
dislike them either. But he did dislike this stranger.

"What? Shit. Leaving? Dang, I've gone and offended you, haven't I?" the man said. He shot a quick look at the bartender and then back at Levine. "Was that it? Hey, I'm sorry. No harm intended. Just that I have to deal with these folks a lot. Didn't mean anything by it. Sometimes I shoot my mouth off when I'm tired." He paused while the bartender put two drinks down in front of them. "You finish that drink and let ol' Vic pay for it. Tell you what, let me apologize to him as well." He nodded in the direction of the bartender. "Square it right up. No hard feelings. I'll even leave a big tip. How's that?" The man stood up and clapped Levine on the back as he walked to the other end of the bar. He talked briefly to the bartender, his hand and facial features in great motion, and returned to his seat. "Done. Square. We're best amigos now." He took another handful of snack mix. "So, you're the FBI man I've been seein' on television. My wife isn't goin' to believe this." He brushed his hair off his forehead and straightened up on his stool. "Hey," he shot an elbow into Levine's arm. "Crime scene photo."

Levine flinched and spilled his drink. He looked at the stranger.

The man smiled and nodded. "Smile."

Levine followed the man's eyes and saw the bartender holding a point-and-shoot camera. He was framing Levine and the strange man and the camera's flash was blinking in anticipation.

"Hold on—" Levine started.

"My wife isn't goin' to believe this." The man said through his smile, not breaking eye contact with the camera.

"Look—" Levine tried to respond, but the camera flashed and Levine was momentarily blinded.

The bartender set the camera in front of the man along with the drink bill and then stepped back.

"This has been great," the man said as he clicked the ballpoint and filled out the bill. He glanced up at the bartender. "Can I put this on my room?" Getting the confirmation that he needed, he nodded his head as he signed the bill and turned it face down. He looked back at Levine. "Listen, buddy, this has been super talkin' with you, but I gotta go meet some clients. Big-time chicken sellers. Not as important as FBI business, but it pays the bills. Anyhow," he said as he stood up and took Levine's hand, shaking it with fraternal enthusiasm. "It's been a real honor."

Levine avoided saying what flashed into his mind. Instead he managed a smile and a tip of his glass. "Thanks for the drink."

"My pleasure, my pleasure," the man said. He nodded at the bartender, and then winked and clapped Levine sharply on the shoulder. "Maybe we'll be meeting again. You take care now," he said as he turned and quickly walked away.

Levine didn't follow the man with his eyes, instead he sighed, finished his drink, and pushed the glass toward the back edge of the bar.

The bartender was collecting the glasses and the bill as Levine stood up. He looked at the bill and then at Levine. "Sir," he said.

Levine arched his eyebrows to indicate his attention. His look said *what?*

The bartender pushed the bill toward Levine. "Sir, your friend."

"He wasn't my friend. What about him?"

"The bill, sir."

Levine took the slip of paper and read it. It said: *Tires can be replaced. Next time it'll be your face.*

CHAPTER 50

Prisoner of War Compound, Camp Chaffee

Sebastian County, Arkansas

Thursday, April 6, 1944

"Bill, come on in here, son," Fist Wiggins said as he rose from his desk. He motioned with his good left hand for the young captain to take a seat, and then he looked up at the sergeant standing at the door. "Thank you, Sergeant. Hold everything for the next thirty minutes." He raised his eyebrows and nodded at Porter to confirm that thirty minutes would be sufficient time for their meeting.

Porter nodded in response as he sat down, positioning his briefcase between his feet.

The sergeant closed the door.

"Now," Wiggins said as he took his own seat behind his desk. "You've been busy, I hear. I hope productive as well. How's Miss Kramer working out, by the way? She's very . . ." he let the suggestion take form in the air as he smiled. "Efficient. Wouldn't you say?"

"Yes, sir," Porter responded. "Not bad to look at either."

"Really? Hadn't noticed." Wiggins winked. "Now, what do you have for me?"

Porter shifted weight from one hip to another and sobered his tone. He shook his head slowly to telegraph his apology. "Not much, sir, I'm afraid. I've finished the first round of interviews; almost ninety prisoners. Predictably, no one saw anything, and they seem to know even less."

"Not surprising," Wiggins responded. "They can be a tough bunch, even when they don't have rifles. I hope that doesn't deter you. We do know one thing for certain, someone murdered Private Geller, and we can reasonably assume one other thing, somebody knows who it was. The man didn't beat his own brains out."

Porter nodded. "Yes, sir. Agreed. The base doc who did the autopsy has been on leave for the last week, but he's back now, and I'm supposed to meet with him this afternoon to go over his findings."

Wiggins laughed. "To find out that Geller is dead?"

Porter shifted in his chair again. "No, sir. Ahh, a formal review of—"

Wiggins held up his good hand to silence the lawyer. "Your show. Run it like you need to." He shifted directions. "So, how is it going with Captain Jordan?"

Bill Porter hesitated, unsure how to answer. "His German is very good."

"Is it?" Wiggins responded. He looked at Porter for a moment and then picked up a fountain pen and twirled it in his fingers, a routine exercise designed to improve the dexterity in his remaining hand. A large smile broke across his face. "Don't underestimate me, Bill. I've spent enough time cross examining reluctant witnesses to recognize a non-answer when I hear one. I didn't ask about his German, did I?"

"No, sir."

"So how about an answer to my question? Or do I have to ask the judge for permission to treat you as hostile?"

Porter took a deep breath and released it slowly. "Permission to speak frankly?"

Wiggins nodded. And smiled again.

"Can't say we have the best working relationship. Not sure what the root problem is—aside from the fact that he thinks he's smarter than I am," Porter said.

"He thinks that about everyone, Bill. Don't take it personally," Wiggins laughed.

"I don't. Besides, I'm sure he is. That's not it." Porter looked down into his lap and nodded slowly as he formulated his response. He looked up, directly into the colonel's eyes. "Several times during the interviews," he sighed and reset this thoughts, "Well, sir, he's behaved inappropriately; in my opinion. Provided incorrect, at least incomplete, translations.   Stifled some responses; directed others. Bullied the witness.   Even outright threatened a few of them."

"And how do you know this?"

"Sir, I, ahh, when I said Captain Jordan's German was good . . . the reason I can say that is because I speak German myself."

"I didn't know that. That wasn't in your file."

"No, sir.   No reason it should be.   After my father died, I was raised partly by my grandparents.   My grandmother never learned English very well; German's what they speak at home.   A form of it anyway."

"I knew there was a reason I requested you for this assignment. Can I assume Captain Jordan also doesn't know you speak the language?   Can I assume you didn't bother to tell him either?"   Wiggins winked.   "Sometimes being smarter than everyone else can backfire on you."

"Sir, my German is very colloquial.   I didn't say anything because I assumed Captain Jordan's familiarity with the language is better than mine. I know it is.   But that's not it, sir.   It's . . ." he hesitated.

"Go on," Wiggins prompted. "You can't clam up now."

"Can I ask you a question, sir?"   Porter didn't wait for a response. "I've interviewed every prisoner in Geller's company but one: A corporal; Dieter Ketel.   That name mean anything to you?   Do you recognize it by any chance?"

Wiggins stopped twirling his pen.   He cocked his head.   "Should it?"

Porter swallowed hard and looked down at his lap again.   "The problem is that this Ketel was a friend of Geller's—at least from what I can piece together.   The two of them were on a number of work details together, and they were seen talking frequently."

"Just the sort of person you should interview."

"I agree.   And there's something else."   Porter bent forward and removed a sheet of paper from his briefcase.   He placed the paper on the desk in front of the colonel.   "Ketel wasn't here at Chaffee very long.   He was recently transferred in here for medical treatment that he couldn't get at his previous camp.   Complications from a burst appendix."

Wiggins laid his pen down and picked up the paper. "That's not uncommon. We have one of the best medical facilities in the area; men frequently get transferred here."

"Understand that, sir. It's where he came from that's interesting." Porter nodded at the paper. "He was transferred here from the camp at Tonkawa. That's where—"

"I see the point, Captain. That's where those five Germans were convicted of murdering a fellow prisoner." Wiggins handed the paper back to Porter. "You saying that you think this, this Ketel fellow is somehow involved in Private Geller's death."

"I don't know that I'd go that far just yet, but—"

"But he's worth questioning. Agreed. So, is there a problem?"

Porter reached into his briefcase and produced a second piece of paper. He handed it to Wiggins. "Yes, sir, there is. It seems he was transferred six days ago to the camp up at Leonard Wood in Missouri."

"Six days ago?"

"Yes, sir. The day after I began my investigation. That's a copy of the transfer order. It's signed by you, sir. Recall it?"

Wiggins looked up and smiled once again, but there was no humor behind it this time. "Careful, Captain. Your tone is a little too prosecutorial for your own good."

Porter nodded. "Unintentional, sir. Believe me. I was simply hoping that you might be able to shed some light on the situation. I mean . . ."

Wiggins stood up and tossed the paper in Porter's direction. It wafted in the air, drifting down in a lazy zig-zag motion before Porter snagged it. Wiggins remained standing. "This may surprise you, Captain, or perhaps it won't, but I sign a thousand pieces of paper a day, probably more; a great many of which I don't even read. Maybe I should. That's the case here, obviously. What you need to know, however, is that I simply approve orders of this type. Our friend Captain Jordan would have initiated a transfer involving a prisoner."

He turned and walked to his window and looked out into the yard for a moment before responding. "Perhaps you're right to have your suspicions about him. Almost certainly you are." He turned and looked over his shoulder at Porter.

"I try to not be too cynical, sir," Porter replied.

"Sometimes cynicism is healthy. This bears watching, but let's keep your suspicions about Jordan between the two of us for now. Understood?"

"Copy."

Wiggins returned his gaze out the window. After a moment, he asked, "What are you going to do about Corporal Ketel? Do you intend to track him down or let it go?"

"That's the real problem, sir," Porter replied. "I've been on the phone with Camp Wood since four this morning." He laughed nervously. "I think I woke up just about everyone on base before I was finished."

"A problem, Captain?"

"Well, sir, nobody at Camp Wood has ever heard of Ketel."

CHAPTER 51

Moffitt, Oklahoma

Thursday, April 6, 1944

"How'd your meetin' go with the boss?" Mac asked as he took a cigarette from behind his ear and lit it. He'd given the rest of the pack, along with some money, to April Kennedy a little earlier. The money he didn't miss; the pack of smokes he would before the evening was over.

Porter shrugged a response and downed a shot. He'd been looking forward to this nightly trip to the bar all day, though he'd made Mac promise to make an earlier evening of it. He hadn't slept last night, aside from dozing at his desk for a few minutes. He poured another shot from the bottle and moved the glass in little concentric circles on the bar, working up the nerve to drink it.

"That productive, huh?" Mac said. It wasn't really a question.

"Yeah. That productive. Wouldn't be so bad if I didn't feel like I was letting the old man down personally."

Mac downed his own shot. "Understand. He's got that effect on folks. How about the doc. Learn anythin' new about the autopsy?"

"Oh yeah. Veeery productive. I learned that Private Geller was killed."

Mac refilled his glass and lifted it in a toast. "Here's to progress, counselor."

Both men emptied their shots. Mac took another drag on his cigarette.

After a moment, Porter spoke up. "Can I ask you a question, Mac? You been here, what, almost a year?"

"At Chaffee? Eight months. Give or take."

Porter nodded at the answer. The shots, combined with no sleep or food, were beginning to have an effect. "Eight months. So, tell me, in your experience, how often are prisoners transferred to other camps? Is there much movement like that?"

"Of the PWs? Naw. Chaffee's one of the bigger compounds in the area. We get new prisoners in regular." Mac smiled. "But out . . . no, no reason to send anyone out. It's pretty rare, I'd reckon."

"How about for intelligence reasons?" Porter blinked back the alcohol cobwebs rapidly forming in his head.

Mac chuckled. "Naw. Most of our prisoners were captured early in the war. Not much useful military information to be mined from this bunch. Hell, we'll be liberatin' cat houses in France before the summer is over. Knowing the Afrika Corps' 1942 order of battle isn't really high on Ike's Christmas list anymore."

Porter seemed to consider the response. He blinked hard. "So what's Jordan's role here? I mean, really? What kind of intelligence is he gathering?"

Captain Mac stared at the bar for a moment and then stood up. He finished his drink and clapped Porter on the shoulder. "Gettin' late, counselor, and I believe I promised to get you home early."

CHAPTER 52

Fort Smith, Arkansas

Wednesday, December 24

It was a comfortable house, in a stable, uniform, A-Bomb-era sort of way. Big, blocky furniture that bespoke a sense of stability and easy permanence and immutable values. On the periphery, on the shelves and table tops and window sills, were the ubiquitous dust collectors that always seem to inhabit an old woman's home; ceramic figurines of chickens and cats and dozens of framed photographs spanning a hundred years of bloodlines and affines. It was a time capsule unchanged in Kel's five decades of life, and the twine holding it all together was his mother, Anne Elizabeth McKelvey.

"We're so happy you could join us, Mr. Levine," Anne McKelvey said, her voice, always soft and careful, precise and yet flexible, but having gone somewhat whispery over the years. She was sitting on the couch in her den, her old orange cat curled up and warming her knees. The house was decorated for the season with strands of garland and faded grade school ornaments of glitter and cotton and vaguely cruciform constructions of pipe cleaners and Popsicle sticks and painted macaroni noodles. They'd been hung from the same paperclip hooks, from the same doorknobs and cabinet handles, since the start of Eisenhower's second term; added to with each child and grandchild, but never, ever reduced. Working its way out of the kitchen was the smell of spice and ham and a Campbell Soup green-bean casserole that was as much a staple at Christmas as the tree and ornaments.

"Thank you, Mrs. McKelvey. It's nice to get out of the hotel."

She laughed and looked at the clock on the fireplace mantle. "You might want to hold that thought. When Kel's brothers and their families get here in a little bit, it can become a madhouse. A pleasant madhouse, but a madhouse all the same. Countin' his boys, there'll be almost a dozen little ones runnin' around. Some not so little anymore, but they'll still be runnin' around."

"Sounds wonderful."

"Don't know about that, but when Kel told us you were spendin' this night in a hotel room orderin' room service, I just thought that wouldn't be quite right."

"Thank you, Mrs. McKelvey. My plans fell through at the last minute. I'd intended to drive back to Memphis. My wife and two daughters were going to fly in from Maryland for a few days, but there were some weather problems—their flight was cancelled."

"That's what Kel said. I'm so sorry to hear that. I'm sure you miss them."

Levine nodded slowly. "I do, Mrs. McKelvey. More than I care to admit sometimes."

Anne McKelvey reached forward, careful not to disturb her cat, and patted his knee. "I bet you do. And my name is Anne, unless that makes you uncomfortable."

"Anne works fine for me—provided you'll agree to call me Mike."

"I think that'll work. So, Mike, what do you think of Fort Smith?"

Michael Levine paused for a moment. He had never been good at diplomacy. "You have a nice library."

Anne McKelvey laughed. "Is that the best you can say?"

He thought for a moment. "It's a whole lot better than Memphis," he answered.

Anne McKelvey laughed again, louder. The cat on her lap raised its head in annoyance. "Amen, but that's probably not sayin' much, Mike. I have to admit, I never thought much of Memphis myself."

"You're not from around here?"

Anne McKelvey laughed again. "Mercy, if I've heard that once, I've heard it ten thousand times. Lived here sixty-some years now, but I'm still an outsider to most of the folks around here."

"That's right; you're from Alabama or someplace like that. I remember Kel telling me that now."

"Biloxi. That's down in Mississippi. South and east of here. But you're not far off with Alabama. I spent some time there; I was a nurse in an army hospital in Mobile early in the war. That's where I first met Kel's daddy, actually. He healed up there for a while after gettin' hisself injured overseas. But when did my son find time to talk about my past?"

"A few years ago. We worked together on a case over in a little town in eastern Arkansas. A place called Split Tree."

"Oh, Lord. Now if that isn't fallin' off the face of the earth. I guess you know that's where Kel's daddy was from originally. You have my pity, Mr. Levine, if you've had to endure a day in Split Tree." Her laughter finally proved too much for the cat, who stood up, stretched, glared, jumped down from her lap, and disappeared under the couch. "Now that you say that, I remember when Kel was workin' over there a few years back, but I didn't make the connection with you. My, oh my, Split Tree. If that place isn't a waste of good dirt."

"Thank you," Mike Levine smiled. "My feelings exactly, but all your son could do was tell me that we were in God's country."

Anne McKelvey smiled her understanding. "Let me tell you somethin', Mr. Levine—"

"Mike."

"Mike. There's somethin' you need to understand. I'll try to put this into perspective. When he was a boy, Kel had a bird dog; big ol' English setter named Jack. Good dog, I guess, as far as dogs go, but dumber than a coffee can full of wet pea gravel."

"I have an Irish setter at home."

"Well then, I guess you know. Anyway, Kel's daddy used to always say that by comparison, Kel made that dog look like a New York banker." She noticed Levine starting to smile. "Now, I'm dead serious. Sometimes I wonder how my son can even walk upright. Bless his heart. And now he's been away in the middle of that Pacific Ocean so long that apparently even Split Tree is lookin' good to him."

Levine put his hands out to indicate that he had no intention of arguing. "I won't comment on that."

"You don't have to. He's my son, and I love him dearly, but . . . but anyway, tell me more about Memphis. You've been there a few years, Kel tells me."

Levine felt emboldened. "What is there to say? How can you like a city that deep fries pickles and lets ducks into its hotel lobbies?"

"Well, there're worse things, believe me, but you sound like me in my younger days. I love this town, but like I told you, I never thought much of Memphis . . . and not because of the ducks."

"What are y'all talkin' about?" Kel asked as he walked up on their conversation. He was carrying a glass of eggnog in each hand and offered one to Levine.

Anne McKelvey responded. "I was just tellin' Mike here about Jack."

"Jack the dog? Man-oh-man, he was a good dog. Smart as a whip."

Anne McKelvey smiled and sighed. After a pause, she said, "Mike tells me that the two of you worked together over in Split Tree."

"That's right. You remember. Year or so ago. Mike's first opportunity to see a little stretch of God's country."

"With that," Anne McKelvey laughed, "I'll be leavin' you boys to talk. Anymore of that eggnog in the kitchen, Kel?"

"Yes, ma'am. I'll get it for you. You sit."

"No. No. You stay here and entertain Mr. Levine. I need to check on the casserole and help that poor Mary Louise slavin' away in the kitchen. Plus, I need to work these old knees before they get any stiffer." She turned to Levine. "I'm afraid the bad-knee gene runs in my family. My father was all but a cripple by my age."

"Oh, hell, mom. Granddad was a coal miner. That's what did his knees in; not genes."

Anne McKelvey looked at her son and then back at Levine. "Mike, growin' up and livin' in the South, we hear lots of ugly things about New Yorkers. Tell me, do you ever swear around your mother?"

"No, ma'am," Levine replied reverently. "We simply wouldn't think of doing that."

Anne McKelvey smiled at Kel and walked into the kitchen.

"Like hell you don't," Kel mumbled.

Levine sat back and crossed his legs. "Nice lady. Smart. Very perceptive."

"Hmm," Kel responded watching his mother through squinted eyes. He took a sip of eggnog, painting his mustache white. He wiped it with a pinch of his thumb and index finger.

Levine sat forward. "Let's talk a little business. I'm going to take another shot at the library over in Fayetteville—"

"*Up.* Remember, Fayetteville is up from here."

Levine sighed with forced patience. "By the way, you didn't call me at two in the morning, did you?"

"Me? This mornin'? No. Why?"

Levine waved off the question. "Been getting crank calls the last few nights. Late night hang ups."

"They ask if you have Prince Albert in a can?"

"No."

"Then it wasn't me. But I'm flattered you assumed it was."

"That's not what I meant. Forget it. Probably kids. So," he said, trying to shift gears, "you mentioned isotopes on the phone. Explain it to me."

Kel sat down and took another sip of eggnog. He didn't really want to talk business, but he also saw that he wasn't going to get Levine away from it without giving it some attention. He wiped his mouth again and began. "Okay, we know that this Jordan guy is not really buried in California. Someone is, but not him. So he's back in consideration. Now, the skeleton from Chaffee shows some consistencies with his physical characteristics. It's not a dead-on match for him, but there're consistencies—nothin' definitive—but consistencies. And one of the consistencies is the isotopic analysis." He nodded his head at Levine to pose the question of whether or not Levine was following.

"Go on," Levine prompted.

"Well, oxygen atoms come in different forms, different atomic weights. These are called isotopes, and the ratio of these isotopic forms relative to normal oxygen atoms varies around the world. It's related to ocean temperature or somethin'. Now these isotopes get incorporated into molecules like water. With me?"

Levine nodded.

"Okay. And of course we drink water, and so these molecules become part of our bodies—including the bones and teeth." Kel paused and took another sip of eggnog. "Here's the best part, your tooth crowns finish formin' by age twelve, thirteen, fourteen; somethin' like that. That's it. They don't change after that, and that means that whatever oxygen isotope ratio you were exposed to in your first fourteen years or so gets captured in your teeth and is there forever; just waitin' for us to come find it." He sat back and looked triumphant.

"That's it?"

"Yeah, that's it."

Levine's expression registered a blank.

"Okay. It's like this. We can measure both the amount of normal oxygen and the isotopic form in a tooth usin' a mass spectrometer and from that you can calculate an isotopic ratio. That's what they did at the lab; they measured the oxygen values in one of the teeth, and once you know the isotopic ratio, you can compare it to known values from around the world, and that tells you where the person was during the first decade of life."

Levine was starting to understand. He leaned farther forward. "And you did that?"

"The lab did, yeah. It's not precise, but it'll put you in the general ballpark. I haven't had a chance to look at the report, but D.S. said— ahh, he's the deputy lab director—and he says it's a western value."

"Western? You mean California?"

"Last time I checked, California's in the west. Yeah." Kel was distracted by the sound of the front door bursting open and the sound of a child yelling *"Grandma!"* One of Kel's brothers had arrived with his young son. Kel stood up to go greet him.

"So our skeleton is this James Jordan guy?" Levine asked as he also stood up.

Kel smiled and shrugged. "I didn't say that, but like I did say, if Jordan's not buried in California, then he's still in consideration. There are lots of problems to work out, but it sure is startin' to look more promisin', isn't it?"

CHAPTER 53

Fort Smith, Arkansas

Thursday, December 25

Kel was sitting on the couch in his in-laws' den, his eyes were closed and his mind was thick and awash with tryptophan from the late afternoon turkey dinner. There was a fire in the fireplace, and the room was warm and his thoughts had drifted free of work and job offers and the long year's corked-up frustration of Colonel Botch-it. The chair was leather and overstuffed and comforting and in the onset of a stuporous doze, all the little odd-shaped puzzle pieces of life had seemingly been fitted agreeably together. At least for the moment.

And then the phone rang.

Kel flinched and pressed his eyelids together tighter as if bracing for a blow.

Fight or flight?

The phone rang again as Kel weighed the options. Only his twin boys and he were at home; his wife was visiting some college friends who were in town for the day and his in-laws were out for a late afternoon drive. He started to run the odds. It wasn't his house, and the chances were strong that whoever was calling was not trying to reach him anyhow, in which case it really wouldn't hurt anything for him to not answer . . . and if they were calling for him, then it was perfectly within his right to not answer . . . it was, after all, Christmas day . . .

He shut his eyes tighter as he parsed out the long interval until the third ring. *One Mississippi, two Mississippi, three Mississippi.* It didn't come. Instead, from the other end of the house he heard a loud yell. *"Daaad! For youuu!"* One of his sons had answered Pandora's telephone and spilled the contents onto the floor.

Kel mumbled a curse as he rolled out of his chair and stumbled toward the phone in the hallway. One of his feet had fallen asleep and was tingly and unresponsive to his will. He picked up the receiver and mumbled another curse before answering. "Hello," he dipped a toe into the conversational waters. He could hear the sound of crashing furniture bleeding over the extension that his son had left dangling in some distant room.

"Good morning, Kel," Les Neep, the CILHI's deputy commander said. *"Mele Kalikimaka.* I hope I'm not interrupting anything."

"Merry Christmas. What is it, Les?" Kel asked. A giggle and a choking sound filled the earpiece as his boys continued in their attempts at fratricide.

"Ahh, is everything okay? Maybe this is a bad time?"

"No, no. Don't worry."

"Are you sure? It sounds like you're in a barroom fight."

"Yeah, I'm sure. No, nothing so organized," Kel responded. "It's my sons. You ever see one of those National Geographic films where they show bear cubs wrestlin'?"

"Of course."

"Well, picture that in a bedroom with lots of antique furniture." Kel covered the receiver with his palm and yelled, *"Boys! Knock it off! And hang up the dang phone!"* There was the loud thump of a body hitting the floor in response. Kel sighed and returned to Les. "Sorry. Now, what is it?"

"Why does it have to be something? It's the holiday season. Maybe I wanted to pass along some Christmas cheer."

"Maybe you can just tell me what you want."

There was another loud thump followed by muffled laughter as the extension clattered into place.

"You're getting cynical, Kel," Les Neep said.

"I was born cynical, I'm gettin' impatient, that's what I'm gettin'. The last time you called me on Christmas was when a tsunami took out a big piece of Thailand. Since I'm keepin' up with the news this time, I know it's not a natural disaster. So it must be man-made. What's he up to now? Staple his tongue to his desk again?"

"Who?"

"C'mon, Les," Kel bit back a yawn. "Botch-It."

"Ahh, well, here's the deal. A V-I-P is coming here on Sunday."

"That right? Good for H-I-M. Wish him happy holidays for me. Or is it an H-E-R?"

"Ahh, Kel . . . ahhh . . . it's the Vice President."

"So? For Christ's sake, it's Christmas—ahh, no pun intended there. The Vice President has been to the lab before. He's been there enough, he can probably give the tour himself by now; besides, you should know the drill: Have the first sergeant get the cigarette butts picked up in the parking lot, and you'll be good to go."

"You don't understand, Kel. With Afghanistan and all, money is tight and the budget's under pretty tight scrutiny right now. I need some help. We don't want Colonel Boschet to—"

"Come to work?"

"That too. But I was thinking that we don't want him representing the Lab to the Veep."

"No, of course not. It's not like he's the friggin' commander—oh, wait a minute—he is." Kel sighed. "Why you callin' me anyway? Where's D.S.?"

"Not answering his phone."

"I trained him well. You know, Les, I'll bet you five bucks that the trip gets cancelled at the last minute."

"I don—"

"Make it ten."

"Okay. I'll take the bet, but do you want to take that chance? With the budget?"

"Crap."

"Kel?"

"Get me a ticket."

"Travel section's already working it. You've a flight out of Tulsa tomorrow."

CHAPTER 54

Prisoner of War Compound, Camp Chaffee

Sebastian County, Arkansas

Friday, April 7, 1944

Bill Porter cancelled the day's interviews. He'd intended to re-question several prisoners, whose answers now seemed incomplete, but it was Good Friday and he decided it could wait until next week. Besides, he was feeling the effects of yesterday's lack of sleep, and was partially hungover from the night before, so he decided to forego talking to any more Germans and instead focus his efforts on tracking down the whereabouts of the one German that he hadn't talked to: Dieter Ketel.

His morning was spent on the phone wearing out two base operators. He'd initially recorded the name, rank, and duty position of everyone he talked to, but after filling up three legal pages he stopped. By noon, when he finally pulled the plug, he could have sworn that he'd talked to everyone at Camp Leonard Wood below the rank of full colonel. For good measure, he'd even questioned a rather bewildered brigadier general who expressed his surprise, and concern, that there were German prisoners in the United States, let alone on the same base as he was stationed. Everyone he talked to had the same answer: No one had heard of Dieter Ketel. No one had seen Dieter Ketel. No one had processed any paperwork for Dieter Ketel.

After lunch, Porter took a lazy circuitous route from the mess hall back to the office. It took him past his room at the Bachelor Officers Quarters, where he needed to retrieve several file folders that he'd left on the nightstand next to his bed.

His head was throbbing when he got to his room, and he took the opportunity to sit down on his bunk and open up a BC headache powder, mixing it with some water from a pitcher by the bed. As he drained the glass and replaced it on the nightstand, his hand brushed against something tucked under the corner of the pillow. It was a plain white envelope. Sealed. No writing on it. He held it up to the light coming in the small window by the door but couldn't determine the contents. Without any more consideration, he tapped the envelope on his thigh, tore off a thin strip from the edge, blew in the end to inflate it, and then extracted a thin sheet of onionskin carbon paper. It took him a minute to realize what he was holding.

CHAPTER 55

U.S. Army Central Identification Laboratory, Hawaii

Saturday, December 27

The skeleton was laid out in front of him on one of the analysis tables, and Kel was staring as blankly at it as it was staring back blankly at him. He'd arrived the night before, after an eighteen-hour flight that routed him from Tulsa to Detroit to Atlanta to Honolulu—the sheer artistry of the government travel office being on full display. He'd spent the last ten-hour leg of the flight staring into the watery blue eyes of a three-year-old girl who hung over the seat back in front of him like a Kilroy-was-here drawing. By the time he'd collected his bag, it hadn't been worth going home, and so he'd come straight into the lab, showering in the locker room and sleeping on the couch in his office. The bright Hawaiian sun and a couple of noisy myna birds outside the window had awakened him way too early.

It was quiet, no one was in, which was why he jumped when he heard the lab door beep and unlock. He looked up to see Davis Smart, in an Eric Clapton t-shirt, cut-off cargo pants, and leather sandals, walk onto the lab floor.

"Hey," Kel greeted him. "Been a change to the dress code while I was away?"

"It's Saturday, Kel," D.S. answered. "The real question is, why are you here? The VP's visit was cancelled."

"So I heard when I landed last night. Les Neep owes me five bucks; maybe it's ten. At least the cigarette butts got picked up; parkin' lot looks clean enough to eat off of." He looked at his watch. Ten a.m. "Speakin' of butts, I suspect I'll get the feelin' back in mine just in time to get on a plane home in three hours. I was just fixin' to head off to the airport to try and salvage what's left of my vacation. Merry Christmas, by the way."

"Thanks. You, too. I figured you'd be here; that's why I came by. Thought you might want this." D.S. was holding a couple of file folders. He handed one to McKelvey. "Hugh received it a day or two ago. It's the complete dental file for that Jordan guy. The records center was able to find some additional information."

"That's great," Kel replied excitedly as he took the folder and started to open it.

Davis Smart cleared his throat nervously and put his hand on the folder.

Kel looked up at him. "What?"

Smart cleared his throat again. "Kel . . . ahh . . . we, ahh . . . that can wait. We need to talk."

"Talk as in talk?"

"Talk as in, we need to talk."

"This doesn't sound at all good." Kel placed the file folder down on the table and sat back in his chair. He sighed and stripped off his latex gloves with a snap. "Give it to me. Please don't tell me you're quittin'."

"I believe you're the one interviewing for jobs." D.S. hesitated and then pulled up a stool and sat down. "No, ahh, we have a situation that's come up."

"Situation? Crap. I've never known of anythin' good comin' from a situation. You sure it isn't a circumstance? Maybe an issue? Those I can deal with."

"No, I think this is clearly in the situation category," D.S. nodded.

After a pause, Kel asked, "So, what is it?"

Davis Smart looked at McKelvey for a moment. "More like who. Chelsea came to me a few days ago." He cleared his throat again. And again. "Ahh, she, ahh, she was peer reviewing a search-and-recovery report from a mission in Cambodia. Nothing unusual about the case. Typical aircraft crash . . ."

Kel was rubbing his eyes. "The *situation*, D.S. What happened?"

"It's Dr. Nolen's case."

"Ah, Shit," Kel threw his arms in the air. "Like I couldn't have guessed. Minute you said situation. Goddamn it. A situation, huh? And don't, for the record, don't ever use *doctor* and *Nolen* in the same sentence unless you're going to say that some doctor has pronounced that goddamn bastard dead."

D.S. held up his hands as if to ward off a blow.

Robert Nolen was, at best, a mediocre anthropologist who had been hanging drywall thirteen months earlier when his brother-in-law met Colonel Boschet at a Jiffy Lube in downtown Honolulu. Boschet, in what was either an example of incredibly poor judgment—even for him—or an example of effectively screwing with McKelvey, had taken advantage of McKelvey being in Iraq for ninety days and hired Nolen. It never seemed to have dawned on Boschet that really qualified forensic anthropologists tend to be working in other labs or universities and not rehabbing tourist condos on Waikiki. When McKelvey finally returned from his overseas assignment, it was too late.

Kel realized he was shooting the messenger and took another deep breath. "Sorry. Sorry. Chelsea, huh? Sorry for her, too. So, what'd she find?" he asked. He took a deep breath and let it out slowly to drain away the frustration from his voice.

"We're still looking into it. I was hoping to get some more details before I handed it to you, and I figured it could wait until after the holiday, but since you're here . . ." D.S. shrugged, "Bottom line, looks like Nolen falsified his field notes from his last mission. Worse, he lied about it when I questioned him. Sort of."

"Sort of? Sort of what?"

"Sort of lied. Initially he admitted it, then he left my office and called a lawyer, and now he denies it. Claims we're setting him up."

"Settin' him up? Why? How?"

Davis Smart smiled and shrugged. "He says you never liked him."

"Well, at least he got that right. I don't like lazy, lying, incompetent sons-of-bitches, and he seems to have all the blocks checked on that list. What's that got to do with anythin'? We're not talkin' about whether I plan to ask him to prom. Did he falsify his notes or not? That's all that matters."

"Yeah," D.S. nodded. "He did. That's pretty clear. We're checking now to see how long it's been going on."

"Then fire his ass. This is not brain surgery, D.S. We're a forensic lab in the credibility business. Zero tolerance. This drags all of us down. Is he on island? Hell, I'll do it before I leave town."

"I'm not sure where he is. I suggested he take some extended Christmas leave. I don't expect to see him again until January."

"Hope you pulled his badge. No access to any evidence. Hell, no access to the buildin' for that matter. He doesn't come back. Not now; not in January. Understand? Fire his ass." Kel didn't like the face D.S. was making. "What? What?"

Davis Smart cleared his throat. He took a breath. "You're going to love this. Ahh, he and his lawyer are claiming this is discrimination. There's even talk of his suing you."

Kel laughed. "Me? You, maybe. I just heard about this."

"Nope. He says this is all being directed by you. I'm just your stooge."

"You are my stooge, but that doesn't mean you're a good stooge; I can't ever get you to do anythin'. I wish I had half the authority around here that people assume I do. You know what? Maybe it is discrimination, bubba. We discriminate against lyin', incompetent people who should never have been hired in the first place. How about that? But last I checked, lyin' and bein' incompetent are not protected classes. How's he figure it?"

D.S. held his hands up again, in preparation for the response. "Well, like I told you, you'll love this: He says that he's a white male and that you're trumping up this minor mistake," he made quotation marks with his fingers, "of his so that you can pursue your plan to achieve a more diversified," more quotation marks, "workforce."

Kel just closed his eyes and shook his head.

CHAPTER 56

U.S. Army Central Identification Laboratory, Hawaii

Saturday, December 27

"Don't let it ruin your vacation," D.S. said. "Go on home. I'll deal with Dr.—ahhh, I'll deal with Nolen. A complete investigation will take a couple of weeks anyway." After a moment, he laughed. "But, hey, I do have some good news for you."

"Great. I could use some." Kel's eyes were still closed, and he was still shaking his head.

"Seriously, you'll like this. It's about that ring you had sent here," D.S. said as he nodded at the skeleton. "The one that goes with those remains. We tracked it down."

"We?" Kel was slow to respond. He'd momentarily forgotten about the case in front of him.

"Yeah, it ended up being a real group effort. First, it's a brass alloy."

"Brass? I thought copper was odd, but who the hell wears brass rings?"

"Hold on, you'll like this. It's brass, and, as you'll recall, very corroded. We tried everything to clean it up, but it's too far gone. Then, I think to x-ray it," D.S. paused and opened the other folder still in his hand. "You hear me?"

"Yeah," Kel responded. His head was still working the symmetry of how Botch-It's diversity plan was coming back to haunt him. "Yeah, I just don't understand you."

"That may be because you're in the presence of genius. When we x-rayed it, the corrosion product is less dense, so, we played around with the voltage and finally got it set to where it'd image. It may glow for the next ten years, but it worked. There was a design underneath, and it shows up real clear in the radiograph. You can see where the original metal is thicker and thinner. I sent you a JPEG by email, but you were already on a flight headed here." He dropped a photograph in McKelvey's lap. "It's a shield with a stag's head, a flame, and a pick-axe."

"A what?" Kel asked. His thoughts started to focus as he rotated the photo first ninety degrees, then one-hundred and eighty, then back to ninety. The image was hard to make out.

"You heard me." D.S. moved behind McKelvey and pointed over his shoulder. "That's a pick-axe. There's the stag and over here's the flame. But here's what's so neat: Did you know Chelsea was an art major as an undergrad? She specialized in jewelry making."

Kel sighed. "You're right. Neat. But, get to it, D.S."

"Well, she saw this when she came in to report the—that situation we just talked about—and she recognized it immediately. I mean, not the exact design, but she recognized it as a guild ring. She's got all these books on rings, and she says these things are real collector's items. In fact, she got on the computer for five minutes and found one almost identical to it for sale. Almost the same design but in silver." D.S. dropped a second sheet of paper in McKelvey's lap. It was a print-out of an eBay page; pixelated and slightly out of focus. "It turns out it's from a trade school. One for mining engineers. That's what the pick-axe is for, and the flame is a burning lump of coal—don't have a clue what the stag's head is all about. And you know what else?"

"No, but you're goin' to tell me quickly, or I'll find a pick-axe somewhere and kill you with it. I'm in a killin' frame of mind right now."

D.S. laughed. "Remember, yours is brass."

"Thanks. So are yours."

"I mean the ring. And that's important, because the school that made these only made brass ones for a short period of time; 1940 to 1948. Gold and silver were in short supply."

"School? Where?"

"A trade school. Hamburg, Germany. Now, ain't that neat?"

CHAPTER 57

U.S. Army Central Identification Laboratory, Hawaii

Saturday, December 27

"Germany?" Kel said. "You sure?"

"Absolutely. I have no idea what it means, but I told you you'd like it," D.S. replied.

Kel was quiet for a moment as he sifted through the layers of information in his head. Trained as an archaeologist originally, he tended to file things by strata, which meant that to recall something he merely had to estimate when it entered into the neuron parfait of his brain and then isolate the appropriate layer. "Goddamn, D.S., we've run down the wrong rabbit hole. This explains it." He picked up the file folder holding Jordan's dental records and opened it; fanned through several pages. "Shit. Shit. Look at this. Jordan was a rich kid. Look at this; great dental care. Makes sense. Not a fillin' or cavity in his mouth. No extractions." He pointed to the skull on the table; the one recovered from Chaffee. The mouth was full of silver amalgam fillings and several teeth were missing. "Even allowin' for dental work that might not be documented, there's no way he could have trashed his mouth like this. Not in the short time he was in the army."

Davis Smart nodded. "And this makes you happy?"

"It's not about bein' happy. It's about Germany."

"Yeah, but I don't see how a German ring has much to do with this guy." He gestured at the remains on the table. "What's the connection to Germany?"

"Remember the knees?" Kel started to pick up one of the leg bones with his bare hand, but stopped himself. Instead he pointed to it.

"Sure. Don't tell me you just figured out who this is?"

"Not if Matt's right. That's a problem we have to resolve, but . . ." Kel looked at D.S. "Where's his report? On the isotopic ratios."

"Matt's? Last I saw it was when I put it on your desk."

Kel jumped up and ran to his office. D.S. followed.

"Where?" Kel asked, looking at the drift of additional material that had accumulated on his desk, chair, and floor while he was gone.

"You got to be kidding me," D.S. laughed, looking around McKelvey's office. "Give me a month and a pitchfork and I might be able to find it." He touched a stack of light-blue folders that promptly cascaded off the edge of the desk and onto the floor. D.S. lifted his feet as if a wave had just broken on the shore and he didn't want to get his pant cuffs wet. "What's it going to tell us, anyhow?"

"The oxygen isotope analysis that Matt did; what were the values, exactly?"

D.S. shrugged. "Like I could remember? I know he said they were western." He moved a stack of yellow folders from the left side of the desk to the right.

The folders started to slide but Kel pinned them with his right elbow as he moved a stack of brown folders to the left side of the desk. They balanced precariously. "That's what you told me. You said it was a western value," Kel said.

"That's what Matt told me."

"Right. And I assumed it was a West Coast value, like California or Oregon or somethin'. That's why I went down the blind alley with that Jordan guy. He was from Sacramento, and without the dental record to rule him out . . ." Kel stood up and looked at the papers on the desk. "This is hopeless, D.S. Shit. Where is Matt anyhow? He in town?"

"Cambodia."

"Crap. That's right. He have a satellite phone with him? You could call him."

"I could, but it'd help if I knew what I was asking him."

"I'll tell you. What the hell time is it in Cambodia?"

CHAPTER 58

U.S. Army Central Identification Laboratory, Hawaii

Saturday, December 27

Davis Smart hung up the phone and looked at McKelvey. "Sorry," he said apologetically. "When Matt said western, I assumed western U.S. All he meant was western, as in non-Asian."

"That'll teach us to jump to conclusions," Kel said.

"My bad. We've never used isotopic analysis on anything except to rule out Vietnamese, so you can't blame him—"

"I'm not blamin' anyone but myself. I'm the one that jumped to the wrong conclusion. If I'd have checked, I'd have known the isotopes look more European than American."

"So, you still haven't explained what all this means."

"Not sure how much you've read on this case, but Hugh came up with a short list of U.S. soldiers that went through Chaffee."

"Yeah, from the initials on the lighter; right?"

"Right. The problem is . . ." he pointed in the direction of the lab floor, "this skeleton isn't a perfect match to any of them, but the closest one was from a guy who was born and raised in California—a western state—which explains why I latched onto the isotopic values."

Smart listened patiently.

"But," Kel said as he stood up and walked to his office door so that he could look out onto the lab floor, "there was somethin' fishy with his ID. In fact, I'm all but positive there was a mis-ID and that means whoever's buried in California is not James Jordan. Because of that, I've been tryin' to make the Chaffee case be Jordan; tryin' to hammer that square peg into a round hole. I figured it had to be him." Kel began to nod slowly. "But with the dental record you just gave me, we can now clearly eliminate him from consideration. Once and for all. Whoever died at Chaffee, it wasn't James Jordan."

Davis Smart nodded, but his expression conveyed confusion. "I was with you there for a minute, but now I'm confused again. If those remains out there aren't this Jordan guy, then who is it, and what does Germany have to do with anything?"

"Well, that's where the isotopes come in," Kel continued. "We know now it's not Jordan, and we've eliminated all the other Americans, but Hugh also found some other names. By accident almost. German POWs. German. A non-Asian *western* value as well, don't you see?" He rubbed his eyes while he tried to recall the information Hugh had compiled. "There were four or five German POWs that he couldn't track down, but one was way too old to be this guy. I remember that. He was fifty somethin'. Two others were way too short. Like five two and five four. Somethin' like that. But there was one . . . name begins with a *K*. Keitel. Kiser. Ketel. Yeah, Ketel, I think. Dieter Ketel. Ketel . . ."

"That explains your ring from Germany."

"More than that. If I'm rememberin' correctly, accordin' to his file, Ketel was a coal miner before the war. My granddad was a coal miner, so it caught my attention. Now you tell me that the ring's from a minin' guild. And think about the knees. You said they were Housemaid's Knee, remember? What else is it called? Think."

Davis Smart squinted and then nodded and smiled. "Some of the older literature calls it Miner's Knee."

"Yeah, and where do they call it that?"

Smart nodded. "Mostly Europe."

"Add in the tibia. Unless I'm mixin' them up in my head—which I'll admit is entirely possible—I think Ketel's record said he was treated in a U.S. hospital for a gunshot wound to the leg. One of the POWs was, and I think it was him. That'd explain that bad fracture. I'll bet he had some surgery to repair it."

Davis Smart nodded. Slowly at first, but more decisively as he thought the matter through. "Sounds good, but even if you're right, which is a long shot, how you going to prove it?"

Kel looked at his watch and calculated the time difference; almost three thirty in Virginia. He swiveled around in his chair to look at the wall behind his desk. It was wallpapered with Xerox copies of his left hand. Kel had the habit of writing notes on his palm and then, to avoid losing the information, he'd photocopy his hand when he got back to the lab and fasten it to his wall. He flipped through several taped one over the other. They passed for his address book. "What if we could get a DNA sample for this Dieter Ketel?" he asked as he found the one he was after.

"I'd say, good luck finding a family to get a reference sample from." D.S. said. "It's hard enough finding DNA donors for U.S. losses. It'll be almost impossible to find one from Germany."

Kel picked up his desk phone and began punching numbers. "Suspect you're right. My guess is that genealogical records in Germany can be problematic—especially from wartime. No, what I'm thinkin' is that—" Kel abruptly shifted conversational gears as the phone connected. "Hey bubba, sorry to bother you at home on a weekend. If you don't mind, I'll put you on speaker." He didn't wait for a response but hit the button for the speaker phone.

"Not a problem," Thomas Pierce's voice filled the room. "Why's my caller ID say Hawaii? Aren't you home in Arkansas?"

"I was, but I was runnin' low on frequent flyer miles and decided to have lunch with D.S. In fact, I'm sittin' here in Hawaii with him now, and we're talkin' about that case from Chaffee that we sent you."

"Hey, D.S. Merry Christmas."

"Hey, Tom. Same to you," D.S. responded.

"What can I do for the two of you? Is this about the tooth you sent us?" The AFDIL Director asked.

"That's it."

"We obtained a good preliminary sequence from it—unofficially, you recall. That was the agreement for the rush job."

"I remember."

"Now, if you can find a reference to compare it to, we'll be ready."

"That's why I'm callin'. Maybe we can." Kel looked up at D.S. and his confused expression and smiled. "What about a fingerprint card?"

"What about it?" Pierce answered. "You have one?"

"Yeah. If it's the person I think it might be, we do. Sure do."

"Then I'd say you're in luck if you have some fingers to go along with it. But I'd bet money you don't."

"Well now, you got that right, but I'm figurin' we might just have the next best thing. How about some skin cells?"

"Go on."

"If I'm right, this guy was a German POW—"

"POW?"

"Yeah. Hang with me. I think it was a German that was held in Arkansas durin' the war, and if I'm right, we've got the original ten-print cards that were made when he was in-processed as a prisoner. Been in a file folder for sixty-plus years."

"I'm not trackin', Kel," Pierce patiently responded.

"Okay. You know how all y'all are always gettin' after us for handlin' the bones without gloves?"

"Yes. Especially D.S."

"What can I say," D.S. leaned forward and spoke in the direction of the phone. "I'm generous with my DNA."

Kel smiled. "He's generous all right, but that's the point. You're always tellin' us that all it takes is a single stray skin cell from one of the analysts and the DNA is all contaminated. Well, obviously our guy sure wasn't wearin' any gloves when he was fingerprinted. So, what about his skin cells? Where are they?"

There was a long silence as Pierce thought through the angles. "Stuck to the paper. Is that what you're thinkin'? Maybe. But if they've been in a folder for all these years, there's no tellin' how many folks have handled those cards over the years, includin' you. I'm not sure how we'd ever sort out the reference cells from the contaminants."

Kel looked up at D.S and smiled again. "You've got my sequence on file. Hugh's too, and anyone else here that might have handled the card recently. As for the others, I'm thinkin' the ink. I mean, think about it, the ink is oily and sticky and would act like a glue. Right? Wouldn't it?"

"Maybe. Go on."

"So, the ink would effectively pick up any loose skin cells on the guy's fingertips and glue them to the paper. I mean, sure, lots of people must have handled the card since then, but not with inked fingers. Right? I admit that I don't understand your business, but I'm thinkin' you can pretty aggressively decontaminate the surface without washin' away the cells trapped in the ink. Scrape some of the ink off, and you'll get the cells along with it . . ."

There was another long silence on the speaker. "Possibly. We don't have any validated protocols for that sort of reference. It'll take months to get one in place."

"What if we didn't wait on a validation study?"

Pierce sighed. "C'mon, Kel. This is becomin' a bad habit with you. Don't put me in that position. We're an accredited lab just like the CIL. What's the rush anyway? If it's a POW, then this guy's been dead, what, sixty years or more?"

"If it's him, it's been almost sixty-five years, but if it's not, then hell, I don't know who he is or how long he's been dead. That's the problem. We don't know, and if it isn't this POW, then the sooner I know that, the sooner D.S. here can go back to the drawin' board and figure out who it is."

"Thanks," D.S. laughed.

"Seriously, Tom, what if you ran this as another experimental case? Give it to your research folks."

"I could, but the problem is, how would you know if the results are valid or whether you've sequenced an unknown contaminant?"

Now it was Kel's turn to be silent. "Well," he finally answered, "you said you have results from the tooth?"

"Unofficially."

"But?"

"But, yes. Preliminary results."

"So that's how. If you get DNA from the fingerprint card and it matches the DNA from the tooth, then it's got to be a legit sequence."

"Unofficially."

"Unofficially, of course, but, I mean, if the unofficial tooth sample matches the unofficial DNA sequence from the fingerprint card, then what are the odds of a random match? Unofficially speakin', that is."

"Remote. Very."

"Right. And if it doesn't match, well, then we sit back and wait on your validation studies before we figure out step two. What d'you say?" Kel looked at his watch. "D.S. can get the fingerprint card sent out today; he doesn't have much of a life anyway."

"The results would have to be reported out as experimental. Like the tooth. You understand that? We won't issue them as a formal findin'."

"Absolutely. Not a problem. We've got some circumstantial evidence, but what I need is a feel-good piece of the puzzle. I just need somethin' that gives me the confidence to move forward. Your stuff would be corroboratin', but otherwise unofficial. All the appropriate caveats. I'll even type out the identification papers with my fingers crossed if that'll make you feel better."

Thomas Pierce sighed again. "You know, it just might work."

CHAPTER 59

Prisoner of War Compound, Camp Chaffee

Sebastian County, Arkansas

Friday, April 7, 1944

"No interviews today. It would have been nice if you'd told me. I have other things I could be doing," James Jordan said from behind his newspaper. He'd arrived first and was sitting in one of the swivel-base desk chairs and had his legs up, feet on the corner of Porter's desk. Tech Sergeant Elliott and Sergeant David sat on opposite window sills, arms crossed. Their hooded eyes tracked Porter's movements as if he were prey emerging from the tall grass into the open flat.

"You understand correctly. I'm sorry you didn't get the message. None tomorrow either. I've got some other matters to attend to today," Porter replied as he pulled out his chair and took a seat. He thought once about swatting Jordan's feet off his desk but decided to let it go. It also hadn't gone unnoticed that neither non-commissioned officer had acknowledged his arrival when he entered the room. That too, he let go.

"No harm done. Good to hear you've other things to attend to. I thought for a minute you might be under the weather. You and Stretch have a long night at your watering hole over in Moffitt?"

"By Stretch I assume you mean Mac. I didn't know you were monitoring my activities, Captain Jordan."

"Captain Jordan? So formal this morning. Something I need to know? What happened to Jim?"

Porter stood up and leaned over his desk, pushing Jordan's feet off the edge. "Let me rephrase the question, *Jim*. I didn't know you were monitoring where I went? Or with whom."

Elliott and David shifted their weight but otherwise didn't move.

Jordan smiled. If having his feet pushed off the desk bothered him, he didn't let it show. He grinned and shrugged all in one easy motion. "Guilty your honor. Occupational hazard, I guess. When you're military intelligence, that's what you do to relax. Don't take offense."

"In that case, none taken."

"So," Jordan said as he slowly folded his newspaper and tossed it on Porter's desk. "These other things you're going to tend to, you think they'll be productive? Care to fill me in?"

Bill Porter picked up the newspaper and dropped it in the metal trashcan beside his desk. "Is this more intelligence gathering? For relaxation?"

"Have it your way, Captain Porter. I thought we were working this investigation together. I guess I know the rules of the game now," Jordan replied as he turned his chair so that it was facing away from the lawyer. He rolled it the five feet necessary to center it under his own desk.

Porter stared at the back of Jordan's head for a moment, and then he asked, "Did you interview Private Geller?"

"You talking to me?" Jordan responded after a calculated pause. He didn't turn around.

"I'm sure not talking to the Katzenjammer Kids here," Porter replied. He could feel the air thicken as Elliott and David tensed their muscles.

"Sorry. What was your question?" Jordan asked.

"I asked if you'd questioned Geller. In the course of gathering intelligence."

"Maybe. Probably," Jordan replied. He swiveled his chair to the side so that he could look in Porter's general direction. "I try to question everyone, though privates rarely yield much useful information. Now, if we're back to sharing information, mind me asking why?"

"Nothing special about him? Nothing that would make him stand out?"

Jordan pursed his lips as if he were giving the matter some extended thought. He shook his head. "Since I don't recall talking to him, I can't really answer that. And since I can't recall talking to him, I'd just be guessing. I'll say this though, if I did, then he must not have made much of an impression. Now," he said as he turned his chair the rest of the way so that he was directly facing Porter, "I've answered several of your questions; you've yet to answer mine: Why do you ask?"

"You know of any reason that would necessitate his transfer out of this camp?"

"None that I can think of, counselor. None that I can think of."

CHAPTER 60

Prisoner of War Compound, Camp Chaffee

Sebastian County, Arkansas

Friday, April 7, 1944

"Two office calls in two days," Fist Wiggins said as he reached forward and dropped a stack of forms into his *OUT* box. He took an equally large stack from the *IN* box and set it on the blotter in front of him. Then he leaned back in his chair. "I hope you have something more productive than yesterday."

Bill Porter was standing in front of the colonel's desk, having not been asked to take a seat. "That remains to be seen, sir. I need to ask you another question."

Wiggins nodded as he took up his fountain pen and began twirling it in his fingers. He nodded for Porter to continue.

"I need to know if you're aware of any reason why Hans Geller would be transferred out of this camp and sent to Camp Wood." Porter asked.

"I believe I answered that yesterday, Captain."

"No, sir. I asked you yesterday about Corporal Ketel. Now I'm asking you about Geller."

"Geller? Oh yes, our dead man."

"Yes, sir."

"No, Captain. I do not."

Porter reached into his left breast pocket and removed the paper he'd found under his pillow earlier in the day. "With all due respect, Colonel—"

"Your level of respect is noted, believe me, Captain Porter. Duly noted."

Porter momentarily dropped his gaze to the floor to register the reprimand. "No offense intended, sir." He unfolded the paper and dropped it onto the stack of folders in front of the colonel. "It's just that the rule of parsimony suggests that this isn't a coincidence."

"What is this?" Wiggins asked as he leaned forward and began scanning the paper that Porter had put before him. "Where did you get this?"

"It's a copy of a transit order. Hans Geller was to be transferred to Camp Leonard Wood. You signed it, sir. Same as with Ketel."

Wiggins looked up at the man standing in front of him. "I'm not sure I appreciate what you're implying. As I told you, I sign a great many things. In retrospect, it's clear that this is another one of the items I should have read. In retrospect, Captain. Where did you get this?"

"Understood, sir, but note the date. That order is dated the same day Geller's body was found. You might not remember signing one for Ketel, but don't you think you'd recall signing a transfer order for the murder victim? Whether you read it closely or not?"

Wiggins rose slowly to his feet. He spoke slowly, forming each word with great care. "What exactly are you insinuating?"

Porter swallowed hard, his mouth suddenly dry. "I can't prove anything, yet. But . . . what I'm saying, sir, is that I think our suspicions are well founded. Captain Jordan may have falsified these papers."

CHAPTER 61

Moffitt, Oklahoma

Friday, April 7, 1944

"What'd the old man say to that?" Captain Mac asked as he drove across the bridge in downtown Fort Smith, aimed at the rapidly setting sun, entering Moffitt, Oklahoma. They hadn't spoken in the last five minutes; not since Porter had finished explaining what he'd told Colonel Wiggins about Geller's transfer orders.

Porter remained quiet; his eyes were closed.

Mac cleared his throat and repeated his question. "He comment?"

"Not really?" Porter finally responded. "Asked me where I got it. How sure I was. What could I prove? He said that accusing Jordan of falsifying transfer orders was a serious charge. That we should keep an eye on it, but keep it under wraps for now. Jordan is well connected . . ." He went silent again, but soon muttered, more to himself than to his companion. "I'm thinking I shouldn't have said anything. Not yet. It was stupid. I need more evidence."

"Yeah? What kind of proof do you need?"

Porter sat up, using his hands to push himself erect in the seat. He adjusted the vent window to direct a stream of air onto his face. He also changed the subject. "What do you know about the Holy Ghost?"

Mac laughed. "Trick question, right?"

Porter smiled, but in the growing darkness its effect was lost. "I wish. No, I mean the Heilige Geist. What do you know about that murder case over in Tonkawa?"

"Not much. I hear folks drawing comparisons between us and them, but can't say I know much beyond scuttlebutt. You sayin' there's a connection?"

"I'm not, but one of the German officers I interviewed did—or started to anyway before Jordan threatened him."

"Threatened?"

"Yeah. Not physically, I suppose. Didn't have to. Jordan basically told him he'd spread the word among the other POWs that he was a homosexual. He made it pretty clear that that news wouldn't set well in the barracks. I have no idea if it was true or not, but the German certainly took notice and clammed up."

Mac nodded. "That's how Jordan operates. Keeps a file on everyone. Watch yourself around him."

Porter laughed. "You say that as you drive us to an off-limits bar in Oklahoma."

Mac leaned forward and spoke into the dashboard as if there were a hidden microphone. He enunciated slowly. "For the seventh night in a row, I might add."

Both men laughed and then fell silent. After a minute, Porter asked, "How well do you know him? Jordan."

Mac snorted. "I don't, and that's fine with me. I know his kind though; sure enough. He briefs the old man weekly. Top secret shit that I'm neither privy to, nor interested in. I usually go knock some baseballs around while they meet."

They drove on in silence for a few minutes more, until Mac pulled the big olive-green car into the gravel lot of Blue Ginger.

"Mac," Porter said as soon as the engine died. "I need to ask you something."

"Shoot," said the tall captain as he lit a cigarette and blew the first lungful of smoke out of the window and into the still evening.

"As the colonel's aide, do you have visibility on everything that he signs? Official things. Transfer orders and so on."

Captain Mac picked a loose piece of tobacco off the tip of his tongue and took another long drag on his cigarette. He turned sideways in his seat so that he could better look at the man beside him. "Do I look more like a secretary or a clerk?"

"I didn't mean—"

"Relax." Mac smiled. "Just givin' you a rash of shit. To answer your question, I'm his executive aide, not his secretary. Tremendous amount of paper goes across the old man's desk every day; unbelievable really. Not really my job."

"I guess I don't know exactly what your job is."

Mac took another hit of his cigarette, turning his head to blow the smoke out the window, before he responded. "Main job is to get myself healed up and back into the fight before it's over, but other than that, I guess I'm sort of a handy man. My job is to fix problems."

Porter nodded slowly as he considered the answer. "Did you slip that copy of Geller's transfer order under my pillow?"

Mac opened the car door and unfolded his long frame. He stubbed his cigarette out in the gravel with the toe of his shoe and arched his back. There were at least a dozen other cars in the lot, and from one of them came the sound of music from a radio. A slow, undulating song with clarinets and saxophones.

After a minute, Porter opened his door and got out. The two men looked at each other across the top of the car.

"Did it ever occur to you, Bill, that whoever slid that paper under your bed, they had their reasons for doin' it the way they did?" Mac stated. It wasn't really a question.

The lawyer closed his car door and leaned against the top. He tried to discern the look on Mac's face, to search for any tic or stray betrayal of muscle that would supply what the words had not, but the deepening shadows yielded no answers. Finally, he answered, "Yeah, in fact it did. What also occurs to me is that you didn't answer my question."

Mac snapped the lever and brought a spark to his lighter and cupped his hands around the flame as he lit another cigarette. He blew a long plume of smoke that mixed with his foggy breath and drifted lazily away into the night to join the music. "How about this for an answer, counselor, maybe you should focus on figurin' out who the bad guys are, not rootin' out the good guys."

"It's not always so easy to tell them apart."

"True. I know that. But here's somethin' else that I know: I know for a fact that there's some distilled spirits with our livers' names written on them waitin' for us yonder. We've talked enough business for one night."

CHAPTER 62

Fort Smith, Arkansas
Monday, December 29

"When'd you get back?" Levine asked. He took a swallow of his beer.

"Yesterday. Saturday. Who knows," Kel answered. He sat down at the bar in the hotel lobby and ordered a Diet Coke, then he swiveled his stool so that his back was against the bar.

"You could have called."

"Are you my wife or my parole officer? Not sure I'm required to call anyone else."

Levine held up a hand to head off any further banter. "Sorry. Sorry. Seems like everyone else is calling me up. Not that they ever say much."

Kel swung his stool around and took a sip of his drink, centering his glass on the oval coaster before changing gears. "Still gettin' those crank calls, huh?"

Levine nodded. He looked tired.

"You been here the whole time?" Kel asked. "Fort Smith, that is. Not this bar. Or maybe this bar."

"Hmm."

"Nice answer. Pithy, but nuanced."

Levine shrugged, took another swallow of his beer, and cleared his throat. "I saw the family for a couple of days. Too short, but—"

"Super, Mike. That's great. I'd like to meet them. They still here, or they go home already?"

"Here? No, ahh, no. They didn't . . . no, I went there. To Maryland."

Kel made a face and nodded slowly, as if he understood. "Sorry. Weren't they comin' here? Or at least to Memphis? Or did I make that up?"

"No," Levine replied. He intended not to elaborate, but changed his mind. "No, you had it right. We ahh . . . we . . . altered the plan."

Kel nodded again.

"There's some weird shit going on," Levine continued. His voice was like a tired growl. "The phone calls, tires slashed, someone busted my car window while it was at the airport parking lot." He drank some more beer. "I felt it was safer them not being around. Not that they were in danger, it's just . . ." His sentence trailed off.

"I hadn't heard about the window."

"Yeah."

"I understand."

Levine turned his head and stared McKelvey in the eye. "No, you don't."

Kel broke eye contact and shrugged. He was content to let Levine be the alpha male in the bar. "You say so." Kel took a sip of his drink and let a moment pass in silence before continuing. "Ahhh, well. Anyway, I've got some good news for you. If you're interested in bein' cheered up. I may finally have a handle on your Chaffee guy."

"That right?" Levine changed his tone of voice. It would pass for an apology, in the event one was needed.

"That's right. We're positive now that it's not that Jordan guy. The one from California that looked so good. We finally got some usable dental records. He was a total dead end." Kel took another sip of Diet Coke.

"I thought you were sure it was him. What changed? What's the good news? It sounds more like we're losing ground here."

"The dental records finally cinched it. That's the way it works. Back and forth. Sure; not sure. Pays to stay flexible. Like they say, *semper Gumby*."

"Is that what they say? Here's to progress," Levine offered a cynical toast.

Kel patiently continued, "We're still not sure how the body in California came to be mis-ID'd back in the forties . . ." He shrugged. "Who knows? There're some letters in Jordan's file. His father was fairly well connected and wrote anyone in the government who could read. My guess is that someone gave the father what he wanted: A body to bury."

Levine took another sip of his drink. "That happen a lot?"

"No. I hope not anyhow. Not really sure it happened here, but it makes sense. Army made a good effort, but there were still a lot of folks missin' back in the forties, and no shortage of unidentified bodies either. No matter how hard they tried, there was always goin' to be a whole lotta folks who never got their sons back. At some point, maybe someone figured, what the hell; this old man cares enough to pursue it; he deserves it as much as the next guy."

Levine signaled the bartender for another drink. When his glass was refilled, he said, "But you're sure it's not this Jordan character? He was the one good lead that we had."

"Yeah. Of course, provin' who someone isn't is always easier than provin' who it is. But in this case, we may have pulled a rabbit out of a hat."

"Wait, so you do know who this Chaffee guy is? Is that what you're saying?"

"Possibly."

"You've said that before."

"No, never did. I had a hunch. That was wrong. This is a feeling. Better than a hunch."

"Good enough that I can go home?"

Kel shrugged. "Wouldn't start packin' yet. In fact, while I think I know who it is, provin' it will require somethin' just this side of a miracle. But the good news, at least for you, is that if we're right, I think this is way out of the FBI's jurisdiction."

CHAPTER 63

Choctaw Nation, Oklahoma

Monday, December 29

Levine cussed the whole way there.

When the call came in, he'd started not to answer it. He was exhausted; not physically, for the fact of the matter was that he hadn't done anything strenuous all week; but emotionally and mentally. After the fourth ring, knowing that the hotel's voice mail was about to connect, he'd picked up. No one from the office would be calling, especially at eleven o'clock at night, especially never, for that matter; his wife would have called his cell phone; and he'd just left McKelvey, who was unlikely to use the phone unless someone had a cocked gun to his head. It was probably another hang-up call.

"Mr. Levine?" the voice had said. *Mister Lee-VINE.* It wasn't an old voice. Wasn't young. Wasn't really in-between. It was female and soft, but even so, there was a sticky husk to it that spoke of hard candy and cigarettes and mixed drinks the color of tropical sunsets. "FBI agent Levine?"

"Yeah," he'd replied.

"Mr. Levine," the voice had repeated. "I think I might have some information for you."

"What kind of information? Who are you?"

"You want to know about them bones?"

"Who is this?"

"You ever been to the casino in Pocola?"

"Look, I don't know who—"

"You want to know who cut your tires all up? I know that too."

"Who is—"

"I'll be here for another hour. Nickel slots. The last one on your right when you're comin' in the front door. I know what you look like. One hour." And then the voice had hung up.

Levine had asked at the front desk about a casino and a place called Pocola, only to learn that he was very near it. Less than eight miles away. Fifteen minutes if he didn't take a wrong turn.

Unfortunately, he did, and it took him almost forty-five minutes.

The inside of the casino was like a throbbing headache on a hot day; flashing lights and colors and bells and dings. It was as if Levine had stepped into the midst of a full-blown migraine. He wished he hadn't spent the last three hours in the bar at the hotel, it wasn't helping now.

She was easy to spot. Last nickel slot machine on the right, just like the voice on the phone had said. She was perched on her stool like a blue jay on a fence post, checking her watch and swiveling her head back and forth looking for Levine, as if she were afraid that he wasn't going to show. She was taking a sip from a plastic cup when she saw him, and the recognition that flickered in her eyes removed any doubt that Levine had that she was the voice on the phone.

It took Levine a full three minutes to walk the twenty-five feet from the door to the last nickel slot on the right. He could have walked straight to her, but he detoured past the video poker and the dollar slots, looking at the crowd, scanning for something or someone, though he didn't know what or who. He simply felt that he should. He finally bellied up in front of a brightly lit machine, second from the right, and watched it ping and flash as if it were being played by a ghost. He made no effort to play it or to look at the woman next to him. For her part, the woman watched him the whole time, trying to figure out what he was up to. She was thirty, maybe a little younger, though she looked a little older. There was mileage starting to show on the tread, but all in all she was a handsome woman: Cowboy boots, ponytail, tight jeans, even tighter rust-colored sweater that conformed to friendly breasts like a film of rainwater.

"You're Mr. Levine," the woman said. She turned to look at him. "I recognize you."

"Do you? And how would that be?" He watched the wheels on her slot machine click over and lock onto a grape, a shamrock, and a donkey's head. Levine finally looked at the woman. "Have we met?"

"From the TV," she answered as she swiveled her chair back to face the machine and punched the PLAY button again with a manicured index finger. There were 175 credits showing and she was playing five credits at a time. The machine pinged and blinked and the wheels locked down on two bananas and a well bucket. Somehow that won her four credits. She giggled, more out of nervousness than enjoyment, and took a small sip of her drink. "Want some?" she asked, looking up at Levine and motioning with her cup. She paused and brushed a stray wisp of mahogany hair away from her face, taking the opportunity to look over her shoulder. "They don't serve, you know, alcohol here. No firewater for the redskins. But if you know the guards, there are exceptions to the rules." She giggled again, again out of nervousness, and looked at her watch.

"I'm here because you called."

She took a small sip of her drink—just enough to wet her lips— and punched in another five credits. She giggled again and looked at her watch as the wheels spun and clicked. "I like these here nickel machines. I can play and play all night for just a few dollars. Beats the movies. Sometimes I even come out ahead."

"I'm sure you do," Levine replied. His patience was thin. He turned to face her, towering over her. "You called. You have something for me or not?"

The woman looked at her watch and swiveled in her chair so that her breasts were almost brushing his belt buckle. She swallowed hard and let out a staccato breath, then she took a small sip from her cup. "I said, *no*," she said in a loud voice. She looked around.

"What?" Levine asked. "No? What are you talking about?"

"*I said, no!*" she repeated. Louder. "No! Get away you creep!"

She stood up, the top of her head came to Levine's chin. She was so close to him that he reflexively grabbed her shoulders and pushed her back, holding her at arms' length. "What are you up to?"

"Leave me alone! Get away!" she almost screamed. She pulled one arm loose long enough to splash her drink in his face. It was vodka, or gin, and the liquid soaked into Levine's sport coat and the smell filled the air.

"What the—" Levine stammered. He recoiled from the drink and took a half step back. Then he grabbed at her arm. "What the hell are you—"

The woman screamed and pulled away from him. She screamed again.

Levine took a step forward and reached out for the woman, but suddenly he was flat on the floor, face pressed into the carpet. There was an enormous weight on his shoulders and back and his limbs were twisted and pinned.

"Take it easy, Mister," said a deep voice. "No need to get yourself hurt—which is what you're about to do." The voice was centered about an inch from Levine's left ear. It smelled like hot dogs and Ranch-flavored Doritos. "Shit," the voice suddenly grew excited. "Shit! The son of a bitch has got hisself a gun! A gun! A gun!"

There was a flurry of noise and motion and Levine took a bigger bite of carpet and his arms were twisted into uncompromising angles. Several sets of hands were grabbing him.

"Get the fuck off me," Levine mumbled into the carpet.

"Get the gun! Get the gun!" the voice said to someone. "Watch him!"

Levine winced. He could feel his gun being removed from its holster at his hip. "Get the fuck off me," he repeated.

"I'll get off you when you got yourself under control. Now, calm it down, cowboy. Ain't no reason to escalate this none." The warning was punctuated with a twist of Levine's arm that made his right shoulder pop as if it were about to dislocate.

"Okay, okay. Take it easy," Levine tried to say, but there was too much commotion for anyone to hear him. He sucked in a breath of carpet fibers and waited a moment. When he felt the weight on his back shift slightly, he worked his head to the side and said, as plainly as he could, "I'm a goddamn federal agent. Police. FBI. FBI."

The pressure was backed off his arms slightly. "Got proof?"

"My tin. It's in my left inside breast pocket. Inside my jacket."

The pressure ratcheted up on his left arm, straining his shoulder joint again but allowing access to his jacket pocket. Out of the corner of his eye, Levine saw a fist, the size of a trashcan lid, groping in his pocket and extracting his credentials.

There was some mumbling, most of which Levine couldn't hear due to an elbow in his ear, followed by the same large hands hauling him to his feet. He was facing the slot machine that the woman had been playing a few minutes earlier, but his arms were still bent behind him painfully.

"Looks like the real thing," another voice said.

"Yeah?" the voice smelling of hot dogs acknowledged. "Sure? Really FBI?"

"Looks like it."

The big hands let go of Levine's arms, and the FBI agent slowly turned around. His joints hurt to move, and it took him a moment to work them back into mobility. "Where's the women?" he asked the large security guard in front of him.

"This is the Choctaw Nation, Mr. FBI man. I'll ask the questions here."

CHAPTER 64

Camp Chaffee, Sebastian County, Arkansas

Saturday, April 8, 1944

It was past midnight when Bill Porter returned to his room at the BOQ. He'd stopped at the office for a few minutes, intent on tying up a few loose ends from the day, but as was becoming the norm, he'd drunk too much and eaten too little, and was feeling the effects of both. Instead, he headed for his quarters and the bunk that had seemed so unbelievably uncomfortable a week earlier but was now as enticing as a grandmother's lap. He tossed his jacket onto the small wooden chair by the window, loosened his tie another tug, and sat down heavily on the end of the bed—all in one continuous fluid motion. He started not to turn on the light, but he knew that his head was too fogged to untie his shoes in the dark, and so he reached out to flick the small chain attached to the lamp on the nightstand. As he did so, he fell forward, his head landing square in the center of his pillow. It was a well-executed, if unintended, change of plan. He closed his eyes and let out a breath that seemed to have been pent up all day awaiting this moment. He would have been asleep almost instantly had he not slipped his hand under the pillow and raked it across the sharp corner of another paper envelope.

Even with his compromised brain, Porter immediately realized the importance of the paper he was holding. As before, the envelope was plain, with no marking or writing to betray its source, and sealed. Inside was a single sheet of thin carbon paper. It was a copy of a transfer order, dated six months earlier, but not for a German POW. This one assigned Captain James Jordan to Camp Chaffee, Arkansas. It was signed by a colonel in the Military Intelligence branch in Washington. The colonel's name meant nothing to Porter, there was no reason it should, but something else did—*Line 5 Current Duty Station.*

The paper almost hummed in Porter's hands. Six months ago Captain James Jordan had been at Camp Tonkawa, Oklahoma.

Bill Porter had been unable to sleep after that. For a while, what seemed like hours, he'd lain in bed staring at the darkened ceiling in the vain hope his head would clear and allow him to think his way through this latest information. When that failed, he'd changed into a fresh uniform and wandered over to his office in search of a pot of coffee. He was still there, sitting at his desk, drawing circles and boxes and arrows on page after page of legal paper, trying to link up the disparate pieces of his puzzle, when Dorothy Kramer arrived for work.

Porter rose when Miss Kramer entered. He'd forgotten to tell her that there were no interviews scheduled for today. He smoothed his hair and greeted her warmly; he also looked at his watch: 5:38 a.m. Over the course of the last week, he'd noticed that the attractive stenographer was arriving earlier and staying longer each day. He'd also noticed, or at least told himself, that she spent as much time stealing looks at him as he did trying to avoid spending all his time looking at her.

"You're in extra early today, Captain Porter. Especially for a Saturday," she said. She'd taken the lid off of the coffee percolator in preparation for brewing the morning's first pot when she realized there was no need; the coffee was already made, though the pot now was half empty. She knit her brow, which had the pleasant effect of making her eyes sparkle more than normal. She turned and surveyed his uniform, which was in fairly good shape, and then the stubble on his chin, which was not. "Or should I say, extra late?"

Porter ran his hand over his face and smiled. "Both, I guess." He paused as the thought about how best to formulate his next sentence. "Miss Kramer . . . ahhh . . . seeing how you're not in the army, and I probably shouldn't be, don't you think that Captain Porter is a bit too formal? It would please me to no end if you'd call me Bill instead."

Dorothy Kramer cocked her head to the side and hesitated—so long that Porter began to stammer an apology. She held up a hand to silence him. "I'll do that on one condition, Captain Porter. Only if you agree to call me Dorothy."

"My pleasure. Dorothy it is."

"Then Bill, it shall be," she replied with a laugh. They both smiled at each other, awkwardly. Finally, she nodded at the scribbles on Porter's legal pad. "Anything I can help you with before the first interview?"

Porter was preoccupied looking at Dorothy Kramer and had momentarily forgotten what he'd been working on; with a jolt, he caught himself and looked at the papers strewn across his desk. "Ahh, no. No, not really. I was just trying to make sense of some of the information we've compiled over the last few days." He began to pull the papers together. "I can't say I'm having much luck, I'm afraid. Ahh, actually, I've decided to postpone today's interviews; not sure how productive they'd be anyhow, and I'm thinking I can better use my time trying to make sense of what we already have. I'm sorry; I should have notified you."

Dorothy Kramer looked crestfallen. "Oh," she managed to say.

"My apologies. I hope you didn't cancel any important plans to come in. I don't need an angry boyfriend coming after me."

She laughed. "Not much need to worry about that. No boyfriend. I don't have much of a social life, so it's not a problem at all."

Porter caught the tone and change in her demeanor and understood it immediately. He felt the same way and quickly responded, "Well then, in that case, Miss Kramer—"

"Dorothy. We agreed."

"Dorothy. Of course. In that case, Dorothy, while I'm not going to require your stenographer skills today, I certainly could use a pleasant face and a clearer head to keep me company. You're more than welcome to stay." He stepped to the side of his desk and held one of the wooden chairs by the back rest, his motion suggesting she should take a seat. "Lord knows I could use some help piecing this puzzle together."

Dorothy Kramer acknowledged the gesture and sat down, smoothing her skirt as she did so and folding her hands in her lap. It was a new dress, purchased from the Boston Store on Garrison Avenue; it had taken almost two-week's salary. She smiled and waited.

Porter cleared his throat. Twice. Three times. "Ahhh, Miss—" he caught himself, "Dorothy, may I ask you a question?" He didn't wait for a response. "You're employed by whom? Who do you work for?"

"I thought I worked for you," she replied.

Porter laughed self-consciously. "I think you do. No, I mean, before I got here. You work for Colonel Wiggins, don't you?"

"I suppose. I started out in the S-1. I was hired to do general clerical duties. Some dictation. Some filing. Scads of typing. But then, I don't know, a month ago, Lucy—that's Colonel Wiggins's secretary—found out she's pregnant. The colonel asked me to replace her. That's what I was doing when you reported for duty. And now I work for you."

"My gain," Porter quickly responded.

Dorothy Kramer laughed and touched Porter's forearm. They both felt a slight buzz, and she withdrew her hand quickly to her lap. They sat quietly for a moment.

Porter cleared his throat again and resumed. "What do you know about Captain Jordan?"

"Aside from the fact that he gives me the creeps?" she laughed again.

"That makes two of us," Porter responded with his own laugh. "Yes, aside from that."

She shrugged. "Not much, I guess. In the half year he's been here, I don't think he's spoken all of ten words to me—at least until I started working for you."

"But you know he's been here six months."

Dorothy Kramer searched Porter's eyes, trying to figure out where the question was headed. "I don't know. That's a figure of speech, I guess. Six months. Half a year. I don't really know."

"And you were originally hired to work in the administrative section. The S-1. You're familiar with personnel records? Transfer orders and so on?"

"That's what S-1 is. Personnel." Her tone had taken on a slight edge in response to the way in which she was being questioned.

Porter caught the tone and backed up. He went silent for a moment as he tried to decide where he was headed with his line of questioning. "Sorry," he said as he reached out and returned her earlier gesture, lightly touching her hand. He let the touch linger for a moment and then withdrew. "I don't mean to sound so much like a lawyer. Actually, I was wondering if I could ask a huge favor of you."

"Of course," she replied, intentionally removing the edge in her voice this time.

"Good. I . . . ahh . . . I assume you still have connections over in S-1. You still know some of the girls working there? I need some information, and I, well, let's just say it would be better if this information was obtained quietly. Without many people finding out. At least for now."

Dorothy Kramer nodded. She no longer seemed to be the focus of his questions, and that relieved her. "Anything, Bill. Just ask."

CHAPTER 65

Fort Smith, Arkansas

Tuesday, December 30

"Buy you a drink?" Levine asked. He set his tumbler down on the bar and motioned for the hotel bartender. "We can celebrate the end of this stinking year."

"Hmmm," Kel answered. "Thanks, but I'll pass. Promised my wife I wouldn't be gone long. I'm already late for dinner. Just stopped by to get my computer; if you're finished with it."

Levine picked up his glass and rattled the ice. He nodded. "Yeah. I'm done."

"*Finished*. Potatoes are done, people get finished," Kel corrected. "If you don't believe me, just ask my mother."

Levine looked at McKelvey. "Sometimes, Doc, you're a friggin' piece of work."

"Thanks."

"The rest of the time you're a friggin' prick."

"Ahh, God loves puppies and happy drunks."

Levine sighed and nodded. "Sorry. Not drunk, just . . . just ready to call it quits. Bad night last night." He made a writing motion with his left hand to signal the bartender to bring the bill.

"Last night? Weren't we right here last night?" Kel looked around. "Hell, same damn bar stools, even."

"Yeah. It really went to shit after you left." He waved McKelvey off. "I don't want to talk about it. Fuck it all. I'm not sure what the point is anymore." He picked up his glass and rattled the ice and put it down again. "Sorry. I don't suppose you have any developments to report that will get me out of here today? You identified our skeleton yet?"

Kel shook his head. "Nothin' new since last night."

"Didn't think so," Levine responded. The bartender laid a curled slip of paper on the bar and Levine calculated a tip, signed his name, and added his room number. He pushed his stool back and got up. "Let's go get your computer. I'm *done* with it."

The two men walked down the hallway without speaking. Levine's room was on the first floor, and they reached it quickly. Kel watched Levine carefully. He was telling the truth, he wasn't drunk, despite his best efforts.

As they neared the room, Levine fished a wad of crumpled bills from his front pocket and pawed through it. He didn't find what he was after and checked his other pocket and then the pockets of his blue sports coat. From the right side pocket he extracted the room key card and swiped it through the lock on his door. He had to pass it through the slot three times before it beeped and the LED flashed green. As he cracked the door, he froze in his steps. Sounds of someone were coming from his room. Muffled. Levine's right hand went quickly to the gun holstered on his hip and with his left arm he swept McKelvey to the side, away from the doorframe. With McKelvey out of the way, he placed his back to the hinged side of the door and slowly swung it open, gun ready.

McKelvey allowed himself to be brushed aside, but not without rolling his eyes. Levine might not be drunk, but he was definitely working on it.

The room was empty. It wasn't a large room and a quick look in the bathroom confirmed that no one was present. The voices were coming from the television; it was turned on and an adult movie was showing. The bed linens were wadded on the floor, the quilted surface of the mattress was exposed, and in the middle of the bed was an uncorked bottle of scotch on its side, most of the liquid having soaked into the fabric, wicking the fumes everywhere. Levine's suitcase was open on the floor underneath the window and the contents—mostly socks and underwear and a dozen seemingly identical white shirts— were scattered loosely around the room. The whole place had the look and smell of a freshman dormitory room on a Sunday morning. Levine stood in the middle and turned in a slow circle, taking it all in. McKelvey joined him.

"What the hell?" Levine said. There was a genuine tone of confusion in his voice.

"Too bad the FBI frowns on togas," Kel commented.

"What?" Levine asked. He looked at McKelvey and saw a grin calculated to piss him off. "Screw you, Doc. Someone's been here."

"Oh, those imaginary friends. I sure hope Pooh hasn't gone and stuck his head in the honey pot again."

"Go fuck yourself. This look imaginary to you?" He holstered his weapon and walked to the window. He kicked at his suitcase with his toe and then knelt down and started raking his things into it as his eyes continued to scan the floor, looking for anything else out of place. He was quiet for a moment, then he spoke. "First my tires. Then my car window. The calls. That bitch last night. It's gone too far. You know what, Doc? Someone is fucking with the wrong man."

"Hmmm. Or maybe two men."

"What?" Levine asked. He turned and looked up to see McKelvey, arms folded, standing in front of the television, head tilted to the side, at a ninety-degree angle. He was watching the adult movie on the screen. "Goddamn, Doc, turn that shit off."

"Nooo. On second thought, I think the other one might be a border collie."

Levine angrily snatched the remote control from the end table next to his bed and turned the television off. He threw the remote on the bed and grabbed some underwear from under the base of a chair and stuffed it into his suitcase. He pushed past McKelvey, who was still rooted in front of the darkened TV, and went into the bathroom where he grabbed a white shirt from behind the door and his toilet kit from the counter. "Checking out, Doc," he yelled out to McKelvey.

"Don't blame you. The sort of filth they make you watch on the TV here. Ought to be a law. And hey, don't call me Doc."

Levine bounded out of the bathroom and stuffed the remaining items into his suitcase. "Like I need this shit," he mumbled as he snapped it shut, picked it up, and started for the door, stopping only long enough to grab his cell phone from the dresser. "Your computer's on the desk. Don't forget the power cord," he said over his shoulder as he opened the door and headed for the lobby.

Levine was already at the registration counter by the time Kel unplugged his computer, wrapped up the cord, retrieved an overlooked pair of Levine's socks from behind the door, and made his way to the front desk.

"That's right," Levine was saying to the freckle-faced girl behind the counter. She wore an oversized sports coat, the sleeves obscuring all but the tips of her manicured fingernails, and she had an assortment of rings and plugs through her ears and nose that gave the impression that she'd just finished making out with her father's tackle box. She looked all of thirteen and seemed very confused by the loud man in front of her. "Just settle the damn bill." Levine tapped his index finger on the counter to emphasize each word.

"Our check out time—" she stammered.

"Yeah. I understand that I'm paying for the whole day. Keep it on my credit card, and take that damn movie off the bill. I didn't order it."

The girl peered closely at her computer monitor and then at the tall man speaking so harshly to her. She blushed, or perhaps her freckles just spontaneously congealed. "You'll have to speak to Mr. Jensen. He's the night manager." She smiled in a confused manner and quickly disappeared through a doorway behind the counter without further comment. She was gone less than a minute when she reemerged, trailing behind a pleasant looking man wearing the same color sport coat. He was short, with well-trimmed blond hair, and a smart mustache that twitched when he spoke.

"Yes, sir, Mr. Levine. I'm Mr. Jensen; what can I do for you?" he asked, but his eyes were on the computer screen and his fingers were clicking keys, seemingly at random. "I see you're not scheduled to check out until the eighth of next month." He turned and nodded at the young girl, indicating that that he had the situation under control and that she was free to return to the back room.

"No, I'm scheduled to check out as soon as you print my damn bill."

"Yes, sir. So I understand. I hope everything was satisfactory with your stay."

"Abso-fuckin-lutely. Aside from someone being in my room, just fine. Now, how about my bill?"

The man looked up. "Someone was in your room? Let me assure you—"

"The bill. And take that movie off."

"Someone was in your room?"

"Yes. Now, the bill; minus the movie. This isn't all that complicated."

The man looked at Levine and squinted his eyes in assessment. "Movie? Yes, sir. Which movie would that be?"

"The one I didn't order. That movie. The one that's probably still playing on my friggin' TV."

The man looked down at his computer screen, and then back at Levine. He smiled and nodded. "Yes, sir. I'll take that movie charge off of your billing. You probably ordered it by accident. It can happen."

"It can't happen. I didn't order it. I assume that the person who was in my room ordered it."

The man smiled again. "Of course. May I assume these other movie charges are correct?"

Levine leaned over the counter, trying to see the computer screen. "What movies? I haven't ordered any movies the whole time I've been here. What movies? When?"

"I'm not sure what movies, sir. The titles do not appear on your bill."

"Bullshit. You can see what movies. What are they?"

The man looked up and smiled at Levine, then he looked over at McKelvey, who had been standing to the side, computer tucked under his arm, watching and wondering how long it would take before Levine pulled his gun.

"The sort of movies that we don't list the titles of, sir," the man said, looking back at Levine.

"Bullshit," Levine repeated.

"He may have thought he was watching ESPN," Kel spoke up. "The one I saw sure looked like some sort of gymnastics competition."

The man grinned.

Levine spun around and glared at McKelvey.

Kel held up a placating palm to indicate he'd keep quiet.

"No problem, sir," the manager said. "How about the nightly lounge tabs? Would you like me to delete these charges from your bill also? Perhaps someone else ordered these drinks." The man's voice had more sarcasm than was healthy under the circumstances.

"Those are mine," Levine angrily replied. "I'll pay those, but I didn't order any goddamn movies."

The man nodded. "Yes, sir. I'm deleting the charge for tonight's movies. Also for the three movies yesterday, the three the night before, the two the day before that, the two . . ." His voice trailed off as he looked up and smiled. He punched a button on his keyboard, and the printer hummed. Shortly he handed Levine a copy of his bill. "I've removed all sixteen of the movie charges that were not ordered by you. Is there anything else that I can do for you, sir?"

Levine was about ready to scale the counter and beat the night manager to death, but Kel, having developed a sense of what Levine's limits were, intervened. He stepped forward, picked up Levine's suitcase, repositioned his computer firmly under his arm, grabbed Levine by the elbow, end gently tugged him in the direction of the main door. "Let's go, bubba. This has got disciplinary action written all over it. You've got enough grief without having to sit through a government anger-management class for the next six months." He looked back at the night manager and mouthed the word, *Thanks*.

Levine reluctantly let himself be led away. He continued to glare over his shoulder at the night manager, who had been rejoined by the young woman in the oversized jacket. A couple of times the manager whispered something to his employee that made her giggle and him smirk. Once Levine pulled his arm free and started back to the counter with the intention of killing both of them, but Kel regained control, and a moment later they were both in the parking lot, standing by Kel's car.

"Goddamn candy assed schmuck." Levine fumed, literally, as his breath fogged and drifted away. "Ought to sue this damn place. On second thought, ought to kick that goddamn little prick's goddamn ass, and then sue the place. Someone in my goddamn room, and that prick is smirking at me. Screw him. Try to charge me for a bunch of goddamn movies I didn't order. Screw him."

Kel was nodding. He knew better than to block a vent when the pressure was building. "Forget him, Mike. Don't sweat it. You think someone was in your room—"

"I know someone was in my room. You saw it."

Kel held up his hands. "Okay, okay. Someone was in there. Watchin' pay-for-view movies and tearin' up your bed. Worry about that instead. Any idea who it was?"

Levine leaned forward and placed his forehead on to the top of McKelvey's car. The cold metal felt good. He was silent for a long time.

Kel opened the rear passenger door and put his computer on the back seat. He closed the door and tucked his hands into his coat pockets. He'd promised his wife he'd be home in time to take her and the boys out to dinner. He was a couple hours late as it was and standing in the cold watching Levine melt down wasn't really the best use of his time. He took in a deep lungful of air, trying to detect the smell of alcohol. *Maybe he is drunk*, he thought. *Drunk's better than crazy.*

"No idea," Levine finally mumbled an answer. He stood up and looked at McKelvey with a lost look. The blank stare of a gambler who just lost his house, his car, and his children's education. He shook his head slowly back and forth. "No idea."

Kel nodded. He unconsciously synchronized his nods to Levine's shakes. "So, where now? Headin' home? Why don't you head back over to Memphis? No one would blame you none. You okay to drive?"

Suddenly the look in Levine's eyes hardened. He stopped shaking his head. "This isn't over, Doc. Not by a long shot. Someone's screwing with me, and I was slow to realize that. Not now. Not anymore. They started this, but I'm going to end it."

Seventy-five feet away, a car started up. Its headlights briefly illuminated Levine and McKelvey before it turned and drove away.

CHAPTER 66

Prisoner of War Compound, Camp Chaffee

Sebastian County, Arkansas

Saturday, April 8, 1944

Dorothy Kramer and Bill Porter sat across from each other at Porter's desk in Building T58. It was eleven o'clock. Porter was quietly chewing large half-moons out of a pickle-loaf-on-white-bread sandwich and staring at the paper in front of him; his eyes plowing furrows back and forth across the page. She'd taken less than three hours to track down the information he'd requested and had then spent the rest of her morning at home fixing sack lunches for the two of them: Bologna and mustard sandwich for her, pickle-loaf and ketchup for him, two moderately cool RC Colas, and two slices—one thick, one thin—of pecan pie. While he wolfed, she nibbled. Her eyes tracked him.

"How far back did you look?" Porter asked for the second time as he looked over the papers that she'd brought him. He sluiced a bite of sandwich down with a long draw of his RC Cola. It fizzed up into the neck of the bottle when he set it down.

"Two years. Twenty-seven months, actually," Dorothy Kramer repeated her earlier response. "The way we file things, to go back any further will take some time, and I won't be able to do it by myself. I'll have to ask for some help, and you said you wanted it done quietly."

He was nodding. "This is fine. This is . . . So, this is all? Just these five? You're sure?"

"That's all that we have records for. You want me to go back further?"

"Hmmm?" Porter mumbled. "What? Oh. No. No. This is fine. So these five prisoners were all transferred to Camp Leonard Wood, but none prior to . . . prior to . . ." he counted on his fingers. "Prior to six months ago? This all occurred within the last six months?"

Dorothy Kramer nodded.

He picked up the phone and dialed the base operator, who connected him through to the operator at Camp Leonard Wood. It took a couple of additional transfers, but he eventually got the person he needed. He hung up almost an hour later and looked at Dorothy Kramer. She'd sat quietly watching him the whole time. "I guess you heard most of that," he said. "The provost marshal at Camp Wood up in Missouri can't find a record for any of them. Not just Ketel, but none of the other four either. They left here, out of our system, but never got into their system." He paused and took a swallow of warm cola from his bottle. "How could five men just disappear?"

"It could be an administrative error," Dorothy Kramer offered up. She took a sip of her drink, and dabbed at her mouth with a small light-blue napkin. It came away with a faint trace of lipstick. "As much as I take pride in my work, I can't honestly say that mistakes don't happen. We run scads of personnel actions through the office every day. Some of the girls are more diligent than others. I guess, when you consider the hundreds of prisoners being held here, five isn't very many to lose track of. Is it?"

Porter laughed and took another large bite of sandwich. He mumbled through a full mouth, sufficiently lost in his thoughts that the rudeness didn't register. "Not prisoners. I can't think of a faster way to get court martialed than lose some Germans. You lose pocket change, you lose your keys, maybe, but you don't lose prisoners. Not one and sure not five." He shook his head, leaned back in his chair, and stared at the ceiling. "And you sure as shit—" He caught himself. "Ahh . . . sorry. You sure don't lose them all in one place."

Dorothy Kramer smiled and set her sandwich down on the sheet of waxed paper on the desk. She dabbed her mouth with the napkin again. "So, who lost them? Us? Or Camp Leonard Wood?"

"That's the question, isn't it?" Porter nodded.

"But Bill, doesn't that suggest that it's an administrative problem?" Dorothy Kramer asked. "It's just has to be."

Porter shook his head and shoved the remainder of his sandwich into his mouth. He squirreled it into a cheek so that he could talk better. "Nope. Maybe if they were all transferred at the same time, but these five were all shipped out over a five-, six-month period. And it's the men that are missing, not their paperwork." He slowly chewed and looked up into Miss Kramer's eyes. He swallowed. "You realize that these transfers were all initiated shortly after our friend Captain Jordan arrived here from Tonkawa."

Dorothy Kramer smiled. If the connection to Jordan surprised her, she showed no sign of it. She touched the remainder of her sandwich and adjusted its position on the desk.

"Five prisoners transferred out in the last six months," he repeated as he wiped his mouth with the back of his hand. "None in the previous two years, but five in the last several months. And none of them can be located now." Porter clasped his hands behind his head, butterflying his elbows to either side, and tipped backward in his chair, raising the front legs off the floor. He started to change the subject, intending to tell Miss Kramer what a wonderful lunch she'd prepared, when the door opened.

James Jordan stepped into the room. He wore an enormous grin, as if he were privy to something he shouldn't have been. Behind him, two steps back, were Tech Sergeant Elliott and Sergeant David. The former wore the blank expression of someone not expected to think and more than eager to comply with that expectation; the latter had his usual dour look of someone whose dog had just died for the second time in a week.

"Well, isn't this a surprise; finding the two of you here," Jordan announced. "I thought we were foregoing interviews today, but seeing Miss Kramer's beautiful face here, I guess I must be mistaken. Why else would the stenographer be here on a Saturday afternoon—if not to take some dictation." He walked over to the desk and stood, surveying the remnants of lunch.

Elliott and David took up flanking positions on either side of the door.

Porter brought his chair down and leaned forward, gathering his papers and moving them to the side of the desk, beyond Jordan's easy view. "No," he replied, "you were correct. No interviews today. We won't be needing your interpreter skills. Don't need the sergeants either."

"We?" Jordan observed. He was standing over them. Smiling. "But you still need a stenographer, I see."

"Doroth—Miss Kramer knew I intended to work today. Through lunch. She was kind enough to bring me a sandwich. Sorry. They were so good that I ate the extra one, otherwise I'd offer to share."

Jordan held up both hands in a gesture of mock surrender. "No need to explain."

An awkward silence ensued. Finally Dorothy Kramer stood up and pressed the wrinkles out of her skirt with her hands. "Well," she said cheerfully, "I really need to be getting on. I should take advantage of a down day here to catch up on some work for the colonel." She nodded at Jordan and then looked at Porter, who was rising from his chair. "Thank you, Captain Porter, for keeping me company at lunch. I assume you'll let me know if there's anything you need from me."

Porter started to respond, but Jordan beat him to it. "Oh, I'm sure Bill will be giving you a call to discuss his needs, but, please, don't feel as if you need to rush off on my account."

"Miss Kramer was just going," Porter quickly interjected. He turned to face Jordan.

"In that case, why don't you let Sergeant David drive you over to the colonel's office?" Jordan let his eyes slowly work their way down Dorothy Kramer's body, stopping at her feet. "Those are quite pretty, but they don't look like walking shoes. Besides, I'm sure the sergeant would love your company for a few minutes."

"That's not necessary," Dorothy Kramer replied. "Really."

"Nonsense," Jordan answered. He gestured to David, who straightened up and opened the door. "He has a car outside. It's clouding up; might rain, and you wouldn't want to ruin that pretty new dress. It is new, isn't it?"

Porter started to say something, but Dorothy Kramer stopped him with a small shake of her head. "Perhaps, you're right," she responded to Jordan. With a smile she started to gather up the remnants of their lunch.

"I'll get that," Porter said.

"That's right. We'll take care of cleaning up here. Only fair," Jordan said as he took Dorothy Kramer's elbow and walked her to the door. "You made the lunch, let Bill there clean up the mess. He likes to clean up messes." He looked at Sergeant David, "*Now, you take good care of this lady.*" He let go of her elbow and nodded his head at her. "I hope you get caught up on all that work for the colonel so that you can get back to helping Bill here."

She glanced quickly at Porter, catching his eye as if to say that everything was all right, and then she stepped outside.

Jordan watched her climb into the car with Sergeant David. He waited for the engine to turn over before shutting the door and walking slowly back to Porter's desk.

Porter cleared the lunch debris, depositing it in the trashcan beside his desk, and turned the list of missing prisoners over so that it was not visible.

"Pretty woman," Jordan said. His voice had the tone of a locker room companion.

"I suppose," Porter replied as he sat down.

Jordan laughed. "Suppose my ass. Suppose? You're like that song. How's it go? *Barney Google, with the goo-goo googly eyes.* Something like that. You may have some competition though." He looked at Tech Sergeant Elliott, who was still standing by the door. "What do you think, Tech Sergeant, you notice how Miss Kramer was looking at Sergeant David? There's definitely something there. I think he's got a real shot. What do you think? It's not a long drive, but you never know; they may not make it to the colonel's office. He may be rounding first base right about now."

Porter looked up. Too quickly. Jordan was baiting him, and it had worked. Porter dropped his look to his desk blotter and a stack of transcripts from several days earlier. "What can I do for you, Captain Jordan?"

"Why don't you tell me, Captain Porter?" His voice dropped a few degrees in temperature, despite emanating from behind a warm smile. "The rumor has it that you're poking around in some new directions. Non-productive directions from the sound of it."

"Rumor? And where'd you hear these rumors?"

"Oh, come on, Bill. What kind of intelligence officer would I be if I didn't have my sources? Confidential sources. Besides, the *who* doesn't matter; only the *what*. I consume rumors the way you consume Miss Kramer's sandwiches."

Porter began leafing through the transcripts in front of him. After a few pages, he stopped and pretended to read. "That's all they are. Just rumors," he said. "The fact of the matter is that this case is going nowhere fast. I wish I had some new leads." A shadow crossed the papers in front of him.

Jordan was leaning on the desk. "Let me give you some advice, counselor. While you were off getting your law degree at East Jesus State, or wherever it is you went, the rest of the world has been fighting a war. One that's far from over."

"Is that right?" Porter said as he looked up.

"That's correct. And you don't seem to appreciate who the enemy is."

Porter leaned back in his chair. "It's not the Germans? I think that's what's in all the papers I'm looking at. Maybe you're right; maybe I should get out more."

"Germans aren't the enemy."

"So you said. Anyone told Ike?"

"Joke all you want; they're beaten. The Germans aren't the ones you need to worry about."

"There are worse?"

Jordan stood up, and before Porter could react, he reached over and took the missing prisoner list that Dorothy Kramer had obtained.

He smiled as he read the names, and then he looked Porter squarely in the eye. "Oh, yes," he said. "Much worse."

CHAPTER 67

Fort Smith, Arkansas
Tuesday, December 30

After McKelvey left, Levine walked across the street to a public parking facility. The garage had been almost full earlier in the day, and he'd been forced to park in a far corner, about as far away from the exit as possible. It was almost empty now, and his car sat, alone, steeped in the shadows.

He walked first to the rear of the car. It took a moment to locate his keys and pop the trunk, but soon he had his suitcase stowed away. He walked around the car and checked the condition of the tires, and then he stood for a moment and breathed the cold air in deeply. It felt good and cleansing and opened his head like a whiff of ammonia. He closed his eyes and relaxed his shoulders and thought, wondering where to go. The first order of business was to find another hotel for the night. There was a Marriott nearby, but if someone was targeting him, moving next door wouldn't deter them long. He needed some distance; needed to regroup and think. He remembered seeing several motels east of town, on I-540. He passed by them driving to and from Memphis.

He was still thinking about where to go as he unlocked his car and got in. The interior lit up, casting a reflection on the windows, and it was only after he buckled his seatbelt and cranked the ignition that the dome light dimmed and he could see it through the windshield—a piece of paper, the size of a playing card folded in half, tucked neatly under the passenger-side wiper. At first he assumed it was an ad for delivery pizza or a therapeutic massage or religious salvation, or all three. He was tired and started not to get out and retrieve it, but he knew that the moist night air would require the wipers before long.

He turned the car off, unbuckled, and got out. He reached over the hood and grabbed the paper. It was damp from the night air, but even so it clearly was not cheap advertisement paper. That made Levine take a second look. He got back into his car and carefully examined the paper. It was a photograph. Of him. It took him a minute to place the surroundings. It had been taken in the hotel bar. He had a scowl on his face. The picture was enlarged and cropped, so that only Levine's unhappy face was in the frame; what was missing was the annoying guy who'd asked the bartender to take the photo.

Levine stared at the photo, trying to remember what details he could from the odd encounter with the chicken salesman—or whatever he was. The threat written on the bar bill. The car dome light timed out, and Levine opened and shut the door to turn it back on. He looked at the photo for a moment longer before turning it over.

On the back, in blue ballpoint block letters, it read: NOW THAT I HAVE YOUR ATTENTION MAYBE IT'S TIME FOR US TO MEET.

Levine immediately reached up and flicked the switch that killed the dome light. His hand went to his gun as he tried to look around, but by now the windows had started to fog and he couldn't see out. He wiped a circular smear on the driver's window with his coat sleeve, and that gave him some visibility. The parking garage was almost empty, and the few cars still there appeared dark and quiet.

Levine cranked the ignition and turned on the defogger, blasting cold air into the car. He looked around once again and then put the car into gear and headed for the garage exit, watching his rearview mirror the whole way.

That's when his phone rang.

Levine pulled his phone from his pocket and looked at the caller ID screen, expecting to see McKelvey's number. Instead he saw a number he didn't recognize. An Arkansas area code. He hit the TALK button. "Yeah?" he said tentatively. Very few people had his cell number—and the one showing didn't match any that he recognized—and the crank calls had all been to his hotel phone.

"Got my message?" a voice asked. A man's voice.

"Who is this?"

"I'll take that as a *yes*," the voice responded.

"How'd you get this number?"

"Please, Agent Levine, don't waste our time. Getting a phone number is the least of my accomplishments."

"That so?"

"That's so. Now that we've agreed on that, I think it's time we meet. Formally, this time."

Levine checked his rear view mirror as he pulled to the curb. He didn't see any other moving cars, and it didn't appear as if he were being followed. "I can think of nothing I'd like more. But you haven't answered my question. Who is this?"

"I'll repeat, Agent Levine, don't waste my time. I'm the person who's been a thorn in your side, that's who I am, but since flat tires and late-night phone calls don't seem to be much of a deterrent with you, I guess it's time to sit down together and come to some sort of business agreement."

Levine used his handkerchief to wipe the fog off his window and the passenger's window. He scanned the street, sidewalk, and adjoining parking lots for signs of his caller. "Sure. How about my hotel? Lobby bar? I'll buy you a drink. Come to think of it, I guess I already did."

"How about not," the voice replied. It had an impatient tone. "You know where the National Cemetery is? It's close to your hotel."

"I've seen it."

"Good. Follow these directions: Drive like you're headed to the cemetery, then left on Wheeler Avenue, couple blocks, right on F Street, left on Sixth. Got that? There'll be a metal-and-concrete building next to some oil tanks. Front door will be open. All the way in the back." The voice paused. "And Agent Levine, without meaning to sound melodramatic, come alone."

Levine laughed. "Right. I'm supposed to come without some backup? To meet some nut-ball who slashes my tires and threatens me? That's not going to happen."

The voice sighed impatiently. "First, if I wanted to do more than annoy you, if I wanted to kill you, you'd be dead by now. Understand? You've been like a duck on a pond all week. Second, don't bullshit me, Agent Levine; you don't have anyone who could back you up, and you're unlikely to arrange for some in the next few minutes. So, do us both a favor. Follow the directions. Come alone. I'm a business man. This is business. We need to talk. Nothing more. Just talk." The phone went dead.

Levine was caught off guard by the sudden disconnect and struggled to recall the directions. Fortunately, they were relatively simple to follow. He exited the parking garage onto Seventh Street, which terminated at Wheeler Avenue, by the flagstone perimeter wall of the National Cemetery. He remembered the voice saying something about F Street, but he didn't recall the need to turn onto Sixth Street, and that necessitated several loops on back streets until he found it—a metal and concrete building. Next door to it were two large gasoline storage tanks. He pulled into the small concrete parking pad in the front of the building, under a busted street lamp, killed his engine, and dialed McKelvey.

CHAPTER 68

Fort Smith, Arkansas

Tuesday, December 30

Mary Louise McKelvey was sitting on the couch in her parents' den when Kel tried to sneak past. She glanced up, looking over the top of her reading glasses, her fingers continuing to work at her needlepoint. "I hope your story involves a beautiful woman with a foreign accent. I'd hate to think you stood me up for dinner for some grouchy, middle-aged man from New Jersey."

Kel stopped. He put his hands in his pockets. "Hey, Hon. Sorry. It got kinda complicated and took longer than I expected," he said. "You got the grouchy, middle-aged man part correct, but it's New York."

"Well, at least I was right about the foreign accent."

"Yeah. You were. Are. So, where are the boys?"

"Prison probably. Maybe a juvenile work camp."

Kel didn't pursue the topic. "What about dinner?"

"You need to go get it in about fifteen minutes."

"We're not goin' out?"

Mary Louise set her needlepoint to the side and clasped her hands. "That was the plan about three hours ago. Now the plan is for you to go pick up some pizzas that will be ready by the time you get there."

"Do I have time to get a couple of aspirin?"

"No, but you do have time to answer your phone."

Kel made a show of patting down his pockets.

"Don't even try, mister. It's in the bedroom. You seem to have forgotten it again."

Kel smiled. "Must have fallen out of my pocket when I was makin' the bed this mornin'."

"Like you've ever made a bed in your life," Mary Louise replied. "It's been ringin' all evenin'. Seems that I'm not the only person that can't get hold of you."

Kel hung his head in an attempt to look like a beaten dog, in hopes of generating some sympathy. He'd found that it sometimes worked and was preferable to apologizing—especially for apologizing for something he wasn't really sorry for, such as leaving his cell phone at home. He walked back to the bedroom, cussing under his breath the whole way, found his phone, and began paging through his missed calls. There were a dozen. Six from work—those he'd ignore, they'd call back again if it was really important—and he could ignore them a second time if they did; four from his wife; one from Thomas Pierce, the Director of the DNA lab; and the last one from Levine. Kel looked at his watch. Levine's call was stamped less than ten minutes ago. It probably wasn't important, there hadn't been enough time elapsed since Kel left the hotel for anything of importance to have occurred, unless maybe Levine had gone back and strangled the hotel manager and needed bail money. Pierce's call was stamped a little more than an hour earlier; after work hours. That suggested importance. First things first. He scrolled through the contact numbers, selected the one he was after, and hit the TALK button. It took two rings to connect.

"Hello," Thomas Pierce answered.

"Hey, bubba. It's Kel."

"Kel, how you doin'? Happy New Year, a few days late,"

"Same to you. Sorry I missed your call."

"Like I believe that," Pierce laughed.

"No, really. You're one of the few. So, tell me, what can I do you for? Or did you just call to say happy New Year and complain about Virginia's weather?"

"Just wishin' you a happy holiday, and, oh . . . since I got you, I'll ask if I can be a coauthor?"

"Of course. What are we writin'?"

"The article on gettin' usable DNA sequence data from a sixty-five-year-old fingerprint card."

Kel almost shouted. "No shit?"

"That's right, and fairly clean sequence, too. You were correct, we were able to aggressively decontaminate the surface without affectin' the skin cells embedded in the ink."

"Already? That was fast."

"We have a couple of new analysts without much leave time yet, and there isn't much for them to work on with everyone else takin' time off."

"And they match? It matches the DNA from the tooth?"

"Unofficially, as we agreed, yes, it's a match. I assumed you'd want to know the results ASAP."

"Shit, son, this will be a happy new year."

CHAPTER 69

Moffitt, Oklahoma
Saturday, April 8, 1944

Bill Porter had stewed after Jordan left. After repeating *sonofabitch*, *sonofabitch*, *sonofabitch* over and over in his head for the better part of an hour, he finally got up and wandered over to Colonel Wiggins's office in search of Mac. Instead, he found Dorothy Kramer still at work.

She smiled broadly when he entered.

"Miss Kramer," Porter said. He too smiled at seeing her face.

She returned a frown. "I thought we'd agreed on Dorothy."

"Dorothy." He returned an even wider smile. "Pleasant surprise. Glad to see you survived your ride with Sergeant David. I'm so very sorry. Sorry to put you in that position."

She laughed. "Thank you. I feel like I need to go home and shower all the drool off."

"I'm glad you can laugh about it. I certainly didn't like the way Jordan talked to you, and I sure didn't like the way they all looked at you."

She blushed. "Thank you, but it wasn't your fault. Now, what can I do for you?"

"Keep smiling for one thing. It brightens my whole day. It's about the only thing that does these days."

"That all?"

"That's enough, but you can also tell me where Mac is."

"Captain Mac? I believe the colonel sent him on a mission over to Camp Robinson in Little Rock. I don't expect him to return until later this evening. Anything I can help you with?"

Porter looked disappointed. "No. Just needed to ask him a couple of questions. It can wait. I guess it'll have to."

"Sorry," Dorothy Kramer replied. She evaluated the look on his face. "So, what are you going to do next? On your case."

"I wish I knew. I need to think. Try to keep putting the pieces together." He pointed at the colonel's door to inquire if he was in.

She shook her head. "Boss is at a meeting with the post commander. Something big is happening, but I don't know what."

Bill Porter sat down next to her desk, happy for the privacy. He nodded as he resumed his train of thought. "Dorothy, help me make sense of this. We know Jordan was at Tonkawa when the prisoner was killed there. Though he denies it, or, at least claims not to remember being there—which is even more suspicious. We know this German, Ketel, was also at Tonkawa at the time of the murder and was transferred here recently, and we know that he knew Geller. Now Geller's dead and Ketel's missing, and we have transfer orders for both of them, plus four other men, that sent them all to Missouri—except that none of them seems to have made it there. All initiated in the last six months. The same time Jordan gets here. Am I crazy to smell something fishy?"

If any of this information surprised Dorothy Kramer, her face didn't telegraph the fact. She sat quietly, watching Porter slide the puzzle pieces around in his head. After a moment, she repeated, "You're not crazy. I don't think so."

"Thanks. I'm worried that I might be letting my dislike for Jordan cloud my judgment."

"Your judgment is just fine. So what now, Bill?"

Porter rubbed his face with both hands. "Dunno. The fact that I haven't slept in two days doesn't make this any clearer."

"Maybe you should go take a nap."

Porter looked up. "Maybe I should," he said.

He wasn't in any hurry. He made small talk with Dorothy Kramer for another half hour, until she received a telephone call from Colonel Wiggins that required her to hand carry a file to him at the post headquarters. Porter walked her part of the way there before breaking away. He enjoyed her company, but he also sensed that it may not be in her best interest to be seen with him outside of her official duties as his stenographer. After watching her smile and wave and hurry off on her errand, he ambled his way back to the Bachelor Officer's Quarters, trying to sift the newest information through his head, but succeeding only of thinking about Dorothy Kramer. When he finally reached his room, he opened the door and stepped on a piece of paper in the middle of the floor. Unlike the earlier messages that had been left for him, it wasn't under the pillow, wasn't in a plain envelope, and wasn't a carbon copy of an administrative document. It was a single sheet of paper, folded in half with a single crease. Typed was the message:

> 2000 hrs
> Blue Ginger
> Come alone.
> I have something you want.
> Stay in car.

Porter wanted to talk to Mac, but that wasn't going to be possible until later that night. He looked at his watch. It was 4:12 p.m.; he had a little less than four hours to take a shower, catch a nap, if he was going to, and secure a car from the motor pool. In fact, it took almost the whole time to fill out the paperwork to obtain a car and both the shower and the nap were sacrificed.

It was closer to eight thirty by the time Porter pulled into the gravel lot outside the Blue Ginger. He'd gotten lost twice on the way. Despite going to the Oklahoma bar every night for the last week and a half, it wasn't until he started to drive himself there that he realized he'd never paid any attention to how they got there. The fact that Mac often took a different route each night didn't help.

He parked on the edge of the lot under a water oak, its leaves beginning to bud in the waxing days of spring. He killed the engine and rolled the window down and sat, waiting, listening to the night noises emerging from the trees and smelling the cool evening air. The lot was partially full, but no more or less than on the previous nights.

Occasionally a car came or went, but overall it was quiet. He stayed in the car, as he'd been instructed.

Another five minutes passed before anyone approached the car. Porter watched the small figure work its way toward him from the front of the bar. It was a woman's form, and she seemed unsure of what she was doing, pausing and looking in several cars. In the dark, he couldn't discern any features, at least not until the passenger door opened and April Kennedy quickly got in.

"God, I thought you were never going to get here," she said. It was said with a laugh. She rubbed her hands together to warm them.

"Yeah. Sorry. That'll teach me to maybe draw a map next time," Porter said, doing his best to cover his surprise. He'd spent the last four hours compiling a list in his head of who might have left the note; April Kennedy hadn't made the top fifty. Not even the top one hundred.

They sat silently. Each with their hands in their laps.

April Kennedy broke the silence. "Where's Mac? I thought he'd be with you?"

"Mac? Ahh, he's over in Little Rock. He'll be back later. Tonight. Tomorrow, maybe."

April Kennedy seemed to consider that for a minute, then she asked, "So, do you have something for me?"

Porter thought about the money and cigarettes that he'd seen Mac slipping to her every night. He hesitated and then reached into his pocket and withdrew a five dollar bill. It was all he had. He handed it to her. "Here. Sorry, I've got some money, but I don't smoke."

The woman took the money and made a confused, embarrassed face. "That's not . . . thank you . . . that's not what I meant. I mean, I meant," she shrugged to indicate her confusion.

Porter arched his eyebrows to indicate his own.

"I mean," she continued, "about the note."

"Right. Your note said you had something I'd want."

"My note?"

Porter's eyebrows went from an arc to a confused frown.

"My note?" she repeated. "Your note. You left a note for me, remember?" She reached into the pocket of her dress and produced a sheet of paper. She handed it to him.

Porter opened the paper and angled it out the window to catch the little moonlight that was available. It was typed, similar to the one he'd received. It read:

Can you meet me tonight at 8:00 at the Blue Ginger?
I'll be waiting in my car. I have something for you.
It's very important.
Bill Porter (Mac's friend)

He readjusted the angle of the paper, to catch more of the moon—as if that would somehow make it more understandable. He reread it.

Suddenly it was illuminated by a bright circle of yellow light from a flashlight. "Need some help, Captain?" said a familiar voice.

CHAPTER 70

Fort Smith, Arkansas
Tuesday, December 30

Levine turned his phone off after leaving a message on McKelvey's voicemail and tossed it onto the dashboard. He sat in his car a minute or two longer, looking for movement; listening for sounds. The longer he sat, the more his windows fogged up and the less he could see. Finally, convinced that he'd seen everything that he could see from the interior of his car, he reached up and verified that the dome light was switched off, and then opened the door. He drew his pistol as he did so and worked the slide as quietly as he could to chamber a round. He then closed the car door, silently, and stood still, listening. There was no movement; no traffic visible.

His eyes had begun to adjust to the darkness, and slowly he began to make out details of the building. It was actually several buildings, one sprouting from another. The main structure, which appeared to be some sort of office, was metal-sided with a glass door centered under the peak of the roof. He could make out a large rectangular area of darker-colored siding adjacent to the door, as if a sign had been removed. To the left was a flat-roofed concrete-block structure. It had wide doors and what looked like a loading dock. Adjoining that was another metal structure. It too was flat roofed, but no doors and windows opened to the street. Amorphous piles of what might be construction debris littered the lot.

The caller had said the front door was open. Levine assumed that didn't mean the sliding doors above the loading dock, so he focused his attention of the glass door leading into the office building. He turned his head slightly to the side, looking at the door with his peripheral vision, and detected light. It was dim, but detectable; not originating in the office, but filtering out from further back in the building, just like the caller had said: *Front door open—all the way in the back.*

Levine kept replaying the phone conversation—what he could recall of it—over and over in his head. He wasn't comfortable being here. Not alone. It defied both training and commonsense. He'd been so dismissive of the locals, and of the make-work nature of the assignment he was on, that he'd been slow to realize that maybe he was dealing with someone who really meant him harm. But then, as the voice had said, whoever was targeting him could have hurt him at any time over the last week. He didn't need to lure Levine to an empty building to do him harm. It all seemed so silly to him, but still this had a different feel.

Levine slowly climbed the three concrete steps leading to the office door—each crunch and squeak that his shoes made echoing like gunshots in the still cold. He stayed to the right of the door, pressing his back to the metal siding. There was definitely a light on, somewhere in the rear, but there were no sounds or signs of movement. With his left hand he reached out and tested the door. It gave; it was unlocked. Just as the voice had said it would be.

He took two deep steadying breaths and opened the door only wide enough to slip into the office. Once in, he flattened against the wall. The floor was linoleum tiles; the walls an inexpensive wood-grained paneling. There was a wooden desk and a couple of wooden chairs in a corner. Some empty cardboard boxes were stacked like children's blocks, one upon another against one wall; a broom and a dried-stiff mop leaned quietly against another. On the wall next to the door was a calendar labeled Port City Oil; opened to the month of July 1988. The first sixteen days had been crossed out with a heavy black marker. Nothing visible in the faint light gave the impression that the office had been used or occupied recently. It was so silent all he could hear was the ringing in his ears.

Directly opposite the front door were two interior doorways, equally spaced in the wall. The one on the right was closed; the one on the left open. It was from here that the faint light emanated.

Levine tightened the grip on his 9 millimeter and worked his way slowly around the perimeter of the room; quietly until he was at the edge of the open doorway. He crouched down and quickly stole a look around the doorframe. He didn't see anyone. He rose up and took a slightly longer look. There didn't appear to be anyone in the room—just a lamp on the floor, a couple of wooden chairs similar to the ones in the office, and a pile of brown tarps near the corner.

With one quick movement he stepped to the other side of the door. He waited and listened and then looked past the doorframe again, this time checking the other side of the room. There were some paint cans and a couple more broken down cardboard boxes; otherwise nothing. He replayed the phone conversation through his head again. Did he have the wrong building? He'd only heard the directions once, and he hadn't been ready for them. He thought about what had happened at the casino. Was he getting his chain jerked again?

He slowly eased around the doorframe and found the light switch. He flipped it; nothing happened. "Shit," he mumbled. That's when he heard it; a soft click like a door opening. He immediately thought of the other door in the office, the one that was closed. The one that he hadn't checked. The one behind him. He turned in time to see a form and the glint of a shiny gun barrel a split second before it impacted the crown of his head and dropped him to his knees.

CHAPTER 71

Fort Smith, Arkansas

Tuesday, December 30

Kel walked back into the den. "So, where are these pizzas I'm supposed to pick up?" he asked.

His wife smiled. "You look happy. Good news?"

"Great news. Just talked to Tom Pierce. I know who the Chaffee guy is."

Mary Louise set her needlepoint aside again. "So? Tell me. Are you sure this time? Or are you and Tom throwin' darts at names on the wall?"

"We prefer a Magic-8 Ball. Yes, we're sure. This time. I'll explain it over pizza. Where am I goin'?"

"Hog Barn. Out past the mall."

Kel patted his pocket to confirm that he had his car keys. "Okay. Back in a few minutes," he said as he turned and headed for the garage.

"Kel," Mary Louise called. "Forgettin' somethin'?"

Kel poked his head back into the room. He feigned a puzzled expression. "Oh, right," he said. He walked back to the couch, bent over, and kissed his wife on the top of the head. "See ya."

"Nice try. I was referrin' to your phone. Take it."

"You know, I'm only goin' be gone a few—"

"Kel."

"It's just a short—"

"Robert."

"Ma'am?"

Mary Louise pointed at his face and made a small twirling motion with her index finger. "Why don't you do that beat-dog thing with your head and then slump off to the back and get your phone."

Kel did as he was instructed. He returned a minute later, holding his phone up as if it were the trophy head of a fallen enemy. "Happy? I have my ankle bracelet," he said as he bent down and kissed his wife again. As he did so, he slid the phone under a pillow on the couch. He stood back up and smiled. "Fortunately for you, I'm so love struck that I obey like a mindless zombie." He held his arms out stiffly and took a couple of heavy-footed steps like Frankenstein's monster. "Back in a few."

"Kel"

"Ma'am?"

"Big mistake. Take your phone, and turn it on."

Kel looked at his wife through squinted eyes. His voice took on a mock menace. "There are things that can be done so that a body is never identified, you know," he said.

"Really?" Mary Louise replied with a smile, holding his phone up for him to take. "What besides havin' you work on the case?"

Kel took the phone. "No more kisses for you," he said. "I'm cuttin' you off."

It took less than ten minutes to reach the pizza place, and a couple more to run the credit card and sign the receipt. As he was getting back into his car, placing the boxes on the passenger seat, Kel noticed the words written along the edge of the box: *Try Our New Authentic New York Style Pizza*. That struck him as funny given that he was in authentic Arkansas, and that, in turn, led to a thought train that ended with Authentic New York Style Michael Levine. He'd forgotten to return his call.

He took his phone out of his pocket and dialed his voicemail. He listened to the synthesized woman's voice tell him that he had ten saved messages and one new message. He punched the number seven to access the one new one.

Doc. Me, Levine. Ahh, listen, right after you left I got a phone call. I think it's the same nut job that's been such a pain in my ass. Prick says he wants me to meet him. I'm at—ahhh—shit; I'm somewhere dark is where the hell I'm at.

Sixth Street. Not far from the hotel. Don't see a number. Kind of a run-down building, like a construction warehouse or something. Couple of gas tanks next door. Ahhh, there's a big square building close by that's got a big-ass OK, written all over it, whatever the hell that means. Ahh, listen, Doc, I can handle this. Alone. [laugh] Like there's an option, right? But just in case, ahhh, you know, just in case, I wanted someone to know. Talk to you later.

Kel replayed the message twice. He looked at the pizza boxes. He looked at his watch. "Ahh, crap," he said as he started the car and put it into gear.

CHAPTER 72

Prisoner of War Compound, Camp Chaffee

Sebastian County, Arkansas

Saturday, April 8, 1944

"It's a bit ironic, don't you agree?" James Jordan leaned back in the chair and let his head roll on his neck in a lazy circle, like an exhausted prize fighter in his corner between rounds. He almost seemed on the verge of dozing off.

Fitz Wiggins was pacing back and forth in front of his office window, twirling a pen between the fingers of his remaining hand. It was almost eight p.m., and the camp was quiet; more than normal for a Saturday evening; it was the night before Easter Sunday. "Not sure ironic is how I'd describe the situation," he replied.

"Oh, ironic is exactly the word. You did hand select him, after all."

"Precisely. I hand selected the biggest under achiever in the entire U.S. Army Judge Advocate Corps. I hand selected the one lawyer I could count on to screw up the whole investigation, and now look at where we are."

"That, Colonel, is exactly what the Greeks called irony. Your own hand-picked boy is going to unspool the whole thing. The Goddess Nemesis always punishes hubris."

Wiggins stopped pacing and turned to face the younger man. "You sound awfully smug for someone about to go to jail."

Jordan laughed. "You got that wrong, old man. The last time I checked, your name was on all those transfer orders; every last one of them. Look at my shoulder and then look at those shiny birds on yours; you're in charge of the camp. I'm a mere captain, a subordinate. I just follow orders."

Wiggins stepped behind his desk and squared his body to Jordan's. "Don't even try, Captain. This is your program."

Jordan rolled his head some more. His eyes were closed, and he didn't bother to look at Wiggins. "That's where you're wrong. This is not my program. I'm simply a small cog in the big machine. This goes way up; as far up as you can get. Roosevelt may not know it, but you can be sure some of his people know what we're up against. Winning the war will turn out to be the easy part; it's what comes after that will be hard."

"Easy? Why is it always the ones in the pressed shirts that call it easy?"

Jordan sighed dismissively, but didn't respond.

Wiggins resumed pacing. "The president has called for Germany's unconditional surrender. The Nazis will be cleared out of the postwar government," he said. "How about that? That's sort of a hitch in your plan, isn't it?"

"That's that Jew bastard Morgenthau's doing," Jordan spit. He was referring to Roosevelt's Treasury Secretary. He looked at Wiggins. "That Shylock's been pretty up front with his plan to cripple Germany for generations. We can't let that happen."

"Is that such a bad thing? I can't say I have much love lost for the bastards myself." Wiggins reflexively grabbed the stump of his right arm.

"It depends on whether or not you want to hand postwar Europe over to the communists. You don't have to love them, but you can be damn sure we're going to need the Germans before this is all over. Good, strong Germans. Good, strong, anti-communist Germans. Fortunately for all of us, there are still people in this government that understand that. I don't think much of them myself, but I'd rather have them between the Soviets and us. We sure can't depend on the lousy French, or feckless Brits."

"And that's where your Ghosts come in?"

"That's right. At the rate we're going, we'll level that friggin' country by the time this war's over. Hell, we'll have leveled the whole continent. Someone has to rebuild it. Someone has to run it; the telephones, the factories, trains, the power stations. It needs to be up and running as soon as the ink's dry on the surrender papers. Reds love a vacuum. We can't let that happen, and that's going to require organization. And that'll be in pretty short supply over there. It'll also require a certain ruthlessness."

"Your Ghosts?"

"They're not mine. They organized themselves. They maintain order. But yeah, they're part of the solution; at least in the short term. If we can use them, turn them to our end, then the end justifies the means. I know that. Others do too. You think I thought all this up? Sooner or later, Roosevelt will see it as well. If not him, then whoever replaces him."

"Unless Porter stops you."

"Porter can't stop shit—unless you lost your balls in the war as well. He can set things back a little, but he can't stop anything. Convicting those bastards over in Tonkawa didn't stop anything, did it? Won't here either."

"Perhaps not, but it forced you out of the woodwork."

"Temporary setback. Chaffee's a bigger camp; it's easier to fix things here. It won't stop anything."

"No, but carelessness can. Geller's death was as stupid as it was unnecessary. It served no end."

"No argument. It was an accident. They were only supposed to send a wake-up call. Someone got carried away."

"Carried away? That what you call beating a man's brains out?"

"I call it an accident," Jordan repeated.

"And what about the other men? Were they accidents as well?"

"They were necessary."

"And the most recent one? Ketel?"

"Ketel knew me from Tonkawa. He was in the wrong place at the wrong time. That's all. We couldn't risk him connecting the dots for your boy Porter."

"We?"

"Yes, Colonel. Damn right, *we*. You're in this up to that fancy medal you sometimes wear around your neck. Don't pretend otherwise."

"No, Captain Jordan. Don't tar me with your filthy brush. I've acquiesced to too many of your activities. I've even helped clean up your messes from time to time, but there have been too many accidents recently. It needs to stop."

"Activities? Such a proper word under the circumstances. Have it your way if that's what you need to sleep well at night. I did what was necessary. As for Geller, his death was an accident, but even then it could have been minimized. Another thirty minutes and the body would have been disposed of. No trace. Like the others."

"Ah, yes. Of course. Transferred to another camp in Missouri. As if no one would notice when the war is over."

"No one will give a shit about five dead Krauts when the war is over. There'll be a million of them when we get finished over there. What will matter is that we're positioned to fill the postwar vacuum before the Reds do. That's what will be noticed. I'll be the one wearing the medals then."

"But Geller's body wasn't disposed of, was it? That's the problem. No, it was found by one of my officers. And now Porter has copies of the bogus transfer orders, and he can place you at Tonkawa at the time of the other accident. And now there's this Ketel; I don't even want to ask what happened to his body, but you can bet Porter will. He's dumb but not stupid. You seem very calm given the shit storm that's about to come down on your head."

"And you seem very jittery for a supposed war hero," James Jordan replied. "Besides, the problem's being handled." He looked at his watch. "Right about now."

CHAPTER 73

Fort Smith, Arkansas

Tuesday, December 30

A light exploded behind Levine's eyes. A bright strobe that originated on the inside and snaked its jagged way to the edges of his skull. The blow to the top of his head hadn't knocked him out, but the pain and surprise momentarily incapacitated him. His scalp was split and blood flowed down his forehead. Even worse, he'd dropped his gun. Before he could regain his focus, someone grabbed him from behind, lifting him to his feet by his hair. A cold gun barrel was screwed roughly into his right ear.

"Don't even think about it," a man's voice said. Not unpleasant, but serious. "You struggle, you'll lose." A hand went into Levine's jacket and removed his badge.

A bell was clanging loudly inside Levine's skull. He complied.

"Why don't you take a seat," the voice continued. The man pushed him forward toward one of the two chairs. "Here, right here. You aren't looking so good, my man. Better take a load off. But first . . ." Levine felt the gun screw tighter into his ear as a hand undid his belt. "Let's drop them drawers," the voice said. Its tone was almost joking. The hand fumbled momentarily but succeeded in loosening Levine's pants and dropping them around his ankles. "Wouldn't be much of a party if we didn't make ourselves comfortable," the man said as he grabbed the chair and pulled it around behind Levine, lifting it slightly, just high enough to thread one of its legs through Levine's right pant leg. Then he pushed Levine down into the chair. "Arms on the chair arms, if you don't mind." The request was punctuated by the gun barrel pressing harder into Levine's ear.

Levine did as he was told. His vision was beginning to clear, and the pain in his head was evolving from a sharp crack to a dull, pounding thump. "Who are you?" Levine asked. "What's going on?"

"We'll get to that. All in due time," the voice replied. "But, first things first."

The gun momentarily left Levine's ear and shortly the man—Levine still hadn't seen his face—began taping Levine's right forearm to the chair with a roll of red Duct tape. After a dozen wraps, the man began taping his left arm. The man completed his task by taping Levine's elbows to the chair arms as well, completely immobilizing his arms. Only then did Levine realize that any opportunity he might have had to resist or break free was now passed.

The FBI agent now fully restrained, the man walked to the doorway and retrieved Levine's gun from the floor, and then he slowly walked around in front of Levine, pulling the second chair into his line of sight and taking a seat.

Levine tried to focus. The pain in his head was making it difficult. The room was lit by a crook-neck desk lamp on the floor, its metal shade bent over and almost touching the linoleum so that the light flowed along the floor like a low fog and cast everything above it in shadow. In the dim light it took him a moment to recognize his captor—he was tall and thin, with pointed features and pointed sideburns, a broad grin, and a light khaki-colored canvas jacket over a western-cut shirt—it was the man from the hotel bar.

Levine allowed his eyes to flick away from the man's face briefly, to survey the room and his situation, but the pain from moving his head, or even his eyes, almost made him pass out. The wooden chair was heavy and substantial, and with his wrists and elbows taped, and his pants wadded up around his ankles and threaded under one of the chair legs, Levine couldn't have stood or moved without falling on his face.

The man continued to smile. He was seated in a similar wood chair, not quite directly in front of Levine, and far enough apart that even if Levine had been able to lunge forward he wouldn't have reached him. On the floor to his right was a pile that Levine had initially thought was a wad of paint tarps but now he realized was a body wrapped in a tangle of rust-colored cloth. It was a woman's body, judging by the shape of the bare leg that was partially uncovered, the rest was hidden under the swales and folds of cloth, but he couldn't tell whether she was alive or dead. After a second painful flick of his eyes, even in the poor light, Levine recognized the pattern of the cloth. It was his hotel bedspread.

The smiling man saw Levine's eyes glance to the body and back. He winked at Levine. "Nice, huh?" he said as he winked again. His hands were in his lap, and he had a loose hold on his gun. He wore thin latex gloves.

"What's going on here? You know who I am?" Levine demanded, but it was feeble and without teeth. His head was still pounding and his focus was slow in returning.

The man laughed. "Well, *duuh*," he responded. "If that isn't about the dumbest question under the circumstances. Does the FBI train its agents by having them watch crappy cop shows on TV? Give me some credit, Agent Levine. You think you'd be here if I didn't know who you were? God almighty." He leaned forward, elbows on his knees, gun dangling loosely between his legs. "The real question is, do you know who she is?" He nodded his head at the shape on the floor.

Levine's eyes went to the unconscious body and then back to the man.

The smiling man cocked his head to the side, as if he were draining water from his ear. He winked again and slowly, without breaking eye contact with Levine, reached down and lifted the edge of the bedspread. He did it slowly, as if unveiling a prized possession, exposing the woman's other leg, inch by inch. He watched Levine's face the whole time, until the woman's body was uncovered. Then he stole a look. "Like I said, nice, huh? Not a bad ass for a mother of two. And that rack of hers could take a ribbon in a state fair." He looked up at the ceiling in mock reverence. "Thy breasts are like two young roes that are twins, which feed among the lilies." He shook his head slowly, back and forth, in quiet appreciation. "Song of Solomon. Pretty racy stuff, I guess; for the time. What the hell is a roe, anyway? I keep meaning to look that up." He looked back at Levine and flashed an enormous grin. "It'll be easy for folks to understand what you saw in her. Lonely, middle-age man far from home. Suffering from a midlife crises, probably." He glanced at the body, shook his head again in admiration, and let the bedspread drop. He looked back at Levine's puzzled expression. "Still don't recognize her?"

Levine looked at the woman and the tangle of cloth. Then he looked at the smiling man.

The man knit his brow, as if he were trying to solve a difficult puzzle. "In fairness, of course, I don't guess you ever got to see her from that angle." He stood up and walked over to the woman's head. He laid his gun down and grabbed her by the hair and shoulder and lifted her up, turning her head slightly so that Levine could see her face. When he saw no recognition in Levine's eyes, he knotted his brow again. "Lord, Jesus, where are my manners. Of course. You never formally met, did you? Special Agent Mike Levine," he paused a moment. "I can call you Mike, can't I? Good. My name's Dennis, by the way; Dennis Viktor. I had a drink with you a few nights ago, as you'll recall. Well, Mike, let me introduce Miss Jane Noel of Pryor, Oklahoma. Jane, this is my friend Mike; he's from . . . well, as they like to say in these parts, he's not from around here." He held her head up a little higher and brushed a curtain of mahogany-colored hair away from her face. There was a flicker behind her eyelids, and for the first time it was clear to Levine that she was alive. "You remember Mike, don't you, Jane?" The man looked at Levine and finished his sentence. "He's that lecherous old man who was hitting on you at the casino the other night. I believe you threw your drink in his face." He laid her head down and patted her, as if he were putting a sleepy child to bed, then he reached into his coat pocket and extracted Levine's gun and badge, which he placed on the floor, to the right of the woman's head. He adjusted their position once, twice, picked up his own gun, and with a small sigh, he stood up, walked back to his chair, and sat down heavily, as if he were tired, though his mannerisms suggested otherwise.

Levine blinked his eyes; slowly at first, but ever quicker. "What's going on? Who are you? What's—"

Viktor held up a hand, palm out, to silence him. He took a deep breath as a prelude to his explanation. "Let me try to clear things up for you Mike, seeing how we don't have all night. It's like this, you're going to be dead as a doornail in about . . ." He paused to look at his watch. "Lord God, it's later than I thought. Time flies. Ahh, you need to be dead in about an hour. Give or take."

Levine started to twist and strain at the tape holding his wrists.

Viktor watched him and shook his head disapprovingly. "There really isn't anything you can do about it. God's will, and I'm . . . I'm sort of his designated agent here. Closest thing you'll meet, anyways." He paused and looked at Levine for a moment and then reached down beside his chair where there were three brown-paper bags. He picked up one and continued talking as he extracted a bottle. "Yeah. You're going to be dead, but what you can control is how easy the passage to the Great Beyond will be; or wherever it is that your people go when they pass over." He peeled the seal off the bottle cap and unscrewed the lid. After inspecting the label, he took a swallow and made a face. He looked at the label again. "I'm not much into scotch, but I know you are, and I'm nothing if not a good host." He turned the bottle around so that the Dewar's logo was visible. "I even splurged for the expensive stuff. Now, I need you to drink a good portion of this, and I'm afraid we don't have all the time in the world. So," he said as he gestured the bottle in Levine's direction, "Cheers." He stood up and stepped toward Levine, moving the bottle to the agent's lips. Levine clamped his mouth tightly shut and turned his head aside. The smiling man chased his lips around in a circle a couple of times and then stood up, free hand on his hip. He sighed and shook his head and chuckled. "This really doesn't have to be so unpleasant," he said, and then he gripped Levine's face, pinching his nose shut and forcing the neck of the bottle between his lips. He waited for Levine to gasp for breath before tipping the bottle up and pouring the liquid in his mouth. "That's better," he commented as he held the bottle up and assessed how much the level had dropped. "Much better."

Levine coughed and spit as much of the liquor out as he could, but he couldn't help swallowing some.

Viktor smiled and repeated the process three more times, each time evaluating the level of the contents. Each time Levine was forced to swallow more. "We're making some progress here," he observed. "You're spitting out more than you're taking in, but that's okay." He nodded to the paper bags under his chair. "I hate to waste good liquor, but we've got two more bottles if need be." He set the bottle on the floor and sat back down, as if taking a well-deserved break.

"Whatever you're trying to do, you can't make me drink enough," Levine said. Despite the bravado, he sensed that maybe his brain was starting to thicken. He'd managed to spit most of the alcohol out, but nevertheless, he'd been forced to take several gulps—each the size of a shot jigger.

The man laughed. "All I need is to get your blood alcohol level elevated a tad; just enough to demonstrate you've been drinking. You've been doing a lot of that recently, I understand. Earlier this evening, even. No, I don't need you drunk," he said as he reached into his coat pocket and pulled out a brown prescription pill bottle. He rattled the contents almost as if he were shaking a pair of dice. "That's what these are for. You'll be taking a few of . . ." he paused and squinted in the dim light at the label on the bottle. "Oops. These were for her." He looked at Levine and grinned. "Yeah. These are what I—make that, *you*—gave her about an hour or so ago. *Roofies. Rohypnol.* It's your date-rape drug of choice for women who reject your advances. Couple of these, and she was out like a light. Yeah . . ." He stood up and leaned forward, slipping the bottle into Levine's coat pocket. "I guess you wanted to make sure she didn't throw another drink in your face. You had to teach that bitch a lesson, right?"

Levine struggled with his bound wrists. "No one's going to believe I gave that woman anything. I'm a federal agent. I—"

Viktor pulled a handful of pill bottles from his other coat pocket. "Now these," he continued, as if Levine hadn't said a word, "these are your basic mother's-little-helpers." He shook the bottles and then held one up, label facing Levine. "*Seconal.* Fast acting." He held up a second bottle. "*Phenobarbital.* Goof balls, I believe you hop-heads call them. Takes a little longer to start working, but it'll keep you out for twelve hours or so. More than enough." He held up a third bottle. "I believe—whoa . . ." he said as he looked closer at the label. He winked, and slipped the bottle back into his shirt pocket. "On second thought, maybe I'll keep these little bastards for a rainy day."

Levine struggled some more.

Viktor took a deep breath and sighed as he squinted at the FBI agent squirming in front of him. He opened one of the bottles and poured a handful of red capsules into his palm. He recapped the bottle and opened a second, pouring a half dozen yellow pills into his hand. He recapped the bottle and stood up. He looked down at Levine and cocked his head. "Here's the plan, you're going to swallow these bad boys. Just like the alcohol. One way or another." He held his hand out, offering the pills. When Levine turned his head aside, the man stepped behind him and grabbed his hair, jerking Levine's head backward. Levine's split scalp, which had started to close up, reopened and the blood began flowing fresh. "I'd really prefer no more bruises than necessary, but as I said, one way or the other. You know the drill." With that, he locked a forearm under Levine's chin, keeping his head tilted backward; with his other hand, he worked the pills deeper into his palm freeing up his thumb and index finger. He pinched Levine's nose and held it as Levine tried to jerk his head free. Finally, Levine gasped and the man shoved a mass of capsules and pills into his mouth. Reds and yellows spilled onto the floor, but a number made it into Levine's mouth. The man then constricted his forearm, forcing Levine's mouth closed.

"You're worse than giving my dog a heartworm pill. Do I have to wrap them in a piece of bacon?" He tightened his grip some more and pinched harder. "Sooner or later you'll swallow. Give it up."

Finally, Levine audibly swallowed and gasped for air.

Dennis Viktor held Levine's head in a lock a few seconds longer, until he gasped for air a second time, and Viktor was sure he'd swallowed the bolus of pills. "There," he said as he returned to his seat. He looked at the sleeve of his jacket and brushed at a dark smear. "Damn. Went and got blood on this. Damn. I like this jacket, too. Now I'll have to put it in a dumpster somewhere." He puffed his cheeks and sighed loudly. "Oh, well; shit happens," he said as he looked at his watch and wagged his head back and forth like a clock pendulum as he calculated. "I'd say we have about fifteen, twenty minutes before the Seconal really kicks in. Maybe a little sooner." He rubbed his palms on his thighs. "So if you've got any questions, better ask fast."

"You cocksucker."

"That a question or a comment? Clock's ticking."

Levine worked some particles of a partially dissolved pill around his mouth and spit them out.

Viktor shook his head and laughed. "Gonna deny me the satisfaction of explaining all this? Come on, ask me why."

"No one is going to believe this."

The man seemed to consider that, but then shrugged it off. "I think you're wrong. I'm banking that they will. You've made sure of that, haven't you? You see, you're a screw-up. People expect the worse from you, and all this does is prove it." He sat back in his chair and crossed his legs casually and brushed again at the blood smear on his jacket sleeve. "Here you are, a man your age . . . you a vet? Vietnam?" He looked closely at Levine's face. "You are, aren't you?" He clapped his hands in delight. "That's super. The FBI shrinks will love that. What is it? PTSD? Post-Traumatic Stress Disorder? Another psycho vet flips out." He nodded his head in mock understanding. "Tragic. We really should have seen this coming. The signs were there all along. The drinking. The drugs. If only we'd seen them . . ."

Levine shook his head trying to clear the rapidly accumulating cobwebs. "No one will believe you." It sounded as hollow as the first time he said it.

"Mike, Mike, Mike. You're not listening. When you going to understand that you're an embarrassment to the FBI? They'll believe it, because they'll want your sordid little escapade swept under the rug as soon as possible. You're a stain on the good men and women of the Bureau. No one's going to ask too many questions." The man leaned forward and slapped Levine on the knee. "Hey, how'd you like the little scenario in your hotel room? I thought the porn movies were a nice touch. I'm a bit of an artist, but I can't take all the credit. One of the maids is a member of my congregation—I'm a man of God, in case you didn't know—and that was actually her idea. She'd turn on your TV and order a movie while she was cleaning your room. Then she'd turn the TV off and you'd never know, but it'd show up on your account. She tells me you had a real thing for teenage cheerleaders and Asian stewardesses. It started out mild and got progressively kinky, and by the time your rubber band snapped, you were indulging in two, three of the foulest skin movies a night. Just the way you guys escalate your perversion until it culminates in something like this," he paused and gestured to the woman on the floor. "Until the devil seizes you with both hands, and pornography alone won't quell the need. As I said, the signs were there all along, if only we'd looked." He winked.

"You're crazy."

"Wow, that's profound." He looked at his watch and then stood and thumbed one of Levine's eyelids up to evaluate the size of the pupil. "Starting to get sleepy? I'll bet. Had a couple of shooters at the hotel, didn't you?" He sat back down and crossed his legs and brushed at his sleeve again. "Where was I? Oh, yeah. Here's the plan for the rest of the evening. In a few minutes, I'll finish undressing you, and then I'll lay you out next to your . . . your . . . what do we call her? Your girlfriend, let's call her that, and then I'll use one of your cigarettes—that reminds me," he said as he removed an open package of Marlboros from his pocket and tossed them on the floor near the woman's body. "Post-coital smoke that got away from you in your stupor." He gestured at the ceiling with his hands and looked around the room. "The whole place went up like an oily rag. All the old paint cans and shit." He looked back at Levine and smiled. "But don't worry, they'll still be able to identify you quickly. Take some consolation in that. Your car's outside; your melted ID and badge will be found near your charred remains; your gun is here." His expression changed to one of mock concern. "Now, your girlfriend, she might be a bit harder. I'll give the local authorities until . . . what is today? . . . Tuesday? With the holiday and all, I'll give them until next Tuesday to figure out who she is. That's a full week. If they haven't got it by then, they'll get an anonymous call telling them that a friend of mine—Jane Noel—was at the Choctaw Casino last Monday night, and I haven't heard from her since. I'm worried about her; just worried sick. They'll get to checking, and they'll discover her car is still in the parking lot at the casino—same place it's been since she was last seen—on the security tape of course—throwing a drink in your face and telling you to leave her alone. The casino security guards will surely remember you. Even the local police can add up two-plus-two. You followed her outside and abducted her. Horn dog like you, spurned in public; you drugged her up and brought her to an abandoned warehouse near your hotel. Privacy. No one to hear or interrupt you. It's got some holes, I'll admit, but like I said earlier, the FBI will be happy to tie this up as quickly and quietly as possible. A bad apple that finally rotted to its core."

Levine's head was swimming. He shook his head, trying to clear it, but his eyelids drooped. He blinked rapidly and hard. "Why?" he managed to ask. "Why?"

CHAPTER 74

Fort Smith, Arkansas

Tuesday, December 30

Kel knew he'd be in trouble if he didn't get home soon. He'd already stood his wife up for dinner, and now he was headed home with rapidly cooling pizza, but Levine's phone message kept gnawing at him. He was sure that whoever Levine was going to meet was harmless, and even if they weren't, Levine was more capable of handling the situation than Kel certainly would be. Still, there had been something in the FBI agent's voice; not fear, more of an uncertainty. Kel couldn't help but recall when they'd first worked together at Split Tree a few years earlier. Then he'd been the one that got into a bad situation, and Levine had been there. Levine had come; had found him.

Kel wasn't sure where Levine was, but he had a general idea. In his message, he'd said Sixth Street. That's a lot of street to cover, but he'd also said it was close to his hotel and that he could see a square building with OK written on it. The tall, white OK Feed Mill tower was a prominent landmark on the western edge of town, and that narrowed down the geography. He'd also said that the building looked like a construction warehouse, and there were gas tanks nearby. While Kel didn't know where the building was, he also knew that it shouldn't be hard to find.

It wasn't. Traffic was almost non-existent at that hour, and it took less than fifteen minutes. There were no cars moving on that stretch of Sixth Street, and he spotted Levine's dark blue Monte Carlo on his first pass. It was parked in a small lot beside a metal-and-concrete building—what could be a warehouse—and the OK Feed Mill tower loomed over it in the dim and gathering fog. The lot next door had what appeared to be a gas storage tank sitting in the tall dry grass.

There were no people in sight, no cars, no sounds, no activity, no light apparent in the building.

Kel parked his car next to Levine's, killed the engine, and got out. He looked into Levine's car. The hood was still warm. It was empty. He tried the driver's door. It was locked—naturally. The night was getting colder; it was wet and a mist was building. Kel buttoned his coat and shoved his hands in his pockets while he turned in slow circles, trying to decide what to do next. A few cars driving past would make him feel better, but there were none. Though it wasn't obvious at first, as his eyes adjusted to the dark, he made out a dim glow showing through the window of the front door of the building, as if a light was on somewhere in the back. He vacillated for a moment.

"Shit," he mumbled. He knew what he was going to do, even though he didn't want to do it and knew that he shouldn't. After adjusting his collar against the light breeze, he slowly climbed the three steps to the front door, careful to not make any noise. The glow was brighter, and looking through the window confirmed that the light was coming from a rear room. He started to knock, but then hesitated. The door was ajar and there was no movement. He put his ear to the opening and listened. Nothing definite.

"Shit," he mumbled again, and against his better judgment, quietly pushed the door open, listening all the while for the sound of any activity. His eyes stayed focused on the back room. There may have been shifts and undulations in the light, as if someone were moving about, or maybe not. It was hard to tell. He thought he heard a chair scraping against the floor, or maybe not. Someone may have been softly humming. Or maybe not. He stepped into the room, paused, and prepared to call out a greeting.

Then his phone rang.

CHAPTER 75

Fort Smith, Arkansas
Tuesday, December 30

"Why?" Viktor smiled, folded his arms, and nodded slowly at Levine. "Finally. I thought you'd never ask. Why? Well, don't take offense Agent Levine, but people don't seem to like you. In fact, you've really pissed a couple of people off. Important people, or at least people who think they're important."

Levine continued to blink. "I don't . . . understand. Who?" His words slurred.

"Well, a lawyer in Memphis for one. Your boss for another."

Levine shook his head hard. It failed to clear. "You're going . . . kill me because . . . pissed off . . . lawyer?"

Dennis Viktor laughed. "Oh, hell, no, Agent Levine. Hell, no. I'm going to kill you because it suits me." He paused, seeming to weigh whether or not he had the time to explain. He decided that he had nothing else to do for the next fifteen minutes. And he decided that someone really needed to appreciate his artistry. "It's like this, you're a nuisance to Mr. Gilbreath, the lawyer. He doesn't want you asking questions about that body found over at Chaffee. From what I understand, his grandfather was in charge of the POW camp during the war; the same grandfather that started that law firm. My guess is that he has a couple of ghosts that he'd just as soon stay asleep. Nothing more than that for him. He has some big business deal in the works and doesn't want the press running negative stories—even if it's a sixty-five-year-old story. He tried to get your boss to pull you off the case, but you're too stubborn. Or stupid. Which is it? Both?"

"Mouth dry," Levine mumbled.

"Yeah, that'll happen. You really shouldn't take so many pharmaceuticals. So, which is it? Stubborn or stupid?"

"They want me killed?"

"No. No. Of course not. You're not listening." He spoke slower, as if giving road directions to a foreigner. "Like I told you, they want you to go away; that's all. Go home. That's what I was asked to do; make you go home. Aggravate you enough that you'd give it up like you were told to. Slashed tires. Busted window. Telephone calls in the middle of the night. Nuisance shit. But you were either too stupid or too stubborn to take the hint, and then," he paused and grinned. "And then genius struck me like a bolt of God's righteous lightening."

"What?" Levine mumbled. He blinked hard, and tried to shake his head but it wouldn't respond. "Don't . . . understand."

"You're going fast, so listen carefully," Viktor continued. "Here's where the genius comes in; if I do say so myself. I'll give you the abridged version. Ten years ago, the FBI convicted the leader of a religious following—the newspapers like to call it a cult, of course— anyhow, they convict him of subversion, tax evasion, weapons possession, a whole smorgasbord of charges. The usual. All true, every last one of them, and that's just the ones they knew about. The problem is that instead of doing it the right way, the Feds took the easy way; all the evidence that was actually used in the trial was doctored. The testimony to the grand jury, including that of yours truly, was also cooked. It was coerced by an overzealous young FBI agent anxious to impress Washington. Follow? Well, the defense lawyer found out about it, after the fact maybe, but he found out, but instead of aiding his client, he opted to file it away for a rainy day. Are you following me?" He leaned forward and looked closely at Levine's eyes, assessing the effect of the alcohol and drugs. "Man, you're about gone; hang with me just a minute longer. So, the religious leader goes to prison, and the FBI agent—if you haven't fit the pieces together yet—he got a big promotion for breaking such a major case. Special Agent in Charge at the Memphis office. That'd be your boss." He smiled and took a breath to reload. "Starting to come together? The defense lawyer, now, he didn't become one of the top attorneys in the country by accident. He appreciated the value of having an important FBI official in his pocket. Sort of an insurance policy. So he kept mum as well. I really hope you can see the connections. Okay, so that leaves me, doesn't it? Well, I'm a little more complicated. I took up the shepherd's crook, and I've led my little congregation in our leader's absence. But, that's my problem. If the story ever got out that I'd lied to a grand jury and sent the dear old Prophet away, not only could I face some serious jail time for perjury, but I'd be cast from the fold, and, I don't mind telling you, it's a lucrative little fold to be the leader of. Now, my insurance policy is that if I go down, I could take your boss and the big-shot lawyer with me. You see, that's why it's complicated. What shook out in the end is a gentlemen's agreement to scratch each other's backs from time to time and not upset the balance. I do little favors for the lawyer now and then, he keeps the FBI off my back, and so on."

Levine blinked and stared at the smiling man.

The man continued. "You're not in any shape to fully appreciate this. Too bad. But when Gilbreath called and told me he wanted you scared off, I saw an opportunity to draw a couple more cards and maybe improve my hand. That's the bolt of lightning that struck me. His weakness, you see, is that he's too smart for his own good, and he assumes everyone else is stupid. I taped the last couple of phone calls he made. Steered the conversation where I needed it. Anyone listening to them would conclude that Mr. Big-shot Lawyer didn't just want you scared off, he wanted you dead. Understand yet? By killing you, and framing you for the sick, sadistic death of Ms. Noel here," he nodded at the body on the floor, "Mr. Gilbreath will be an accessory to a capital crime. Even if he can beat it, and believe me, if anyone can, he can, but his career would be in ruins. As for your boss, Special Agent Frank, now he can't afford for this to unravel either, so he'll assist in the cover up as well." He shrugged and smiled. "And I'll be untouchable after this. Now, and in the future."

"Why not . . . kill . . . me?"

"What's that? You're slurring your words Agent Levine. Why not kill you? Well, now, I'm going to. I think what you mean is *why not kill you outright*. Is that the question? Okay, listen up. If I just outright killed you, they'd be an investigation. Right? Much as no one appears to like you, you're still a Fed, and you don't kill Feds and get away with it no matter how much leverage you have. Making it look like a suicide is an option, and I gave it some serious thought, but you've got a wedding ring. That means there's the chance that your loving wife, who I assume does like you, probably wouldn't buy it. She could make enough noise that everything might still unravel. But this," he said as he gestured to the room and the woman sprawled at their feet. "This is ugly. And I mean ugly. This is sordid. This is embarrassing for everyone who knows you. Everyone, including the wife and family and whatever few friends you may have, they'll want this investigation over with as quick as they can. Sweep this trash under the rug and never talk about it again. That's the beauty, don't you see? The system will cover my tracks for me, and all it costs me is a few bottles of over-priced Scotch and some pills."

Levine's head dropped onto his chest.

Viktor stopped smiling. He sighed and looked at his watch again, then he stood up and checked Levine's eyes. Satisfied that the pills had taken effect, he pulled a pocketknife from his pocket and slit the Duct tape holding Levine's arms. He hummed while he peeled the tape off and balled it up, putting it in his pocket. Then he removed Levine's tie and pushed his jacket off of his shoulders and extracted his arms. Finally, he ripped off the top two buttons on the FBI agent's shirt and unbuttoned the rest. Throughout the process, Levine's head lolled on his chest.

Viktor then pulled aside the bedspread, exposing the woman on the floor. He admired the view momentarily, and then he grabbed Levine under the arms and lifted and pulled him out of the chair and onto the woman, partly on, partly off her. He pushed the two chairs to the side and then straightened up and surveyed his work. Levine's pants were still on, but were wadded around his ankles as if he were a man whose passion had allowed no delay; his shirt undone, partially rent through passion or struggle. The bodies tangled. He wasn't sure how much evidence would survive the fire he intended to set, but it paid to be detail oriented.

He made a few final adjustments, moving the angle of an arm or weaving together two legs, and then he retrieved some rusty cans from the adjoining warehouse. Paint solvents of some sort. He positioned them casually against the wall, not too close to be suspicious, but close enough to ensure a quick and consuming fire.

Satisfied, he smiled and reached into his pocket for a cigarette lighter. He flicked it open and struck a flame.

Then he heard a phone ring.

CHAPTER 76

Moffitt, Oklahoma

Saturday, April 8, 1944

"I said, need some help there Captain?" It was Tech Sergeant Elliott. He'd approached the car unnoticed and taken up a position alongside the driver's side mirror, shining his flashlight first on the paper in Porter's hand and then in Porter's face. His companion, Sergeant David, was on the other side tapping on the passenger window and making a circular movement with his hand, instructing April Kennedy to roll the glass down.

"Is that you Sergeant Elliott? How about you get that damn light out of my face," said Porter angrily as he threw his left arm up in front of his eyes.

Elliott moved the focus of the flashlight down to Porter's throat, out of his eyes but high enough to still make his point. "You were right, Sergeant David," Elliott said with a tone of mock incredulity. He returned his attention to Porter. "My partner here said that he thought that it looked like you driving this official car, but I says, no, no, that can't be right. Captain Porter's an officer. He wouldn't be over here in Oklahoma frequenting an off-limits bar. But, damn if he wasn't right. Here you are. And tapping the hired help, too."

His partner was playing his flashlight in a lazy path back and forth over April Kennedy's lap and chest. She reflexively slid along the seat, edging closer to Porter.

"Yeah, it's me. Now you know. So kill the lights," Porter ordered.

Elliott turned off his flashlight. As Porter's night vision slowly returned, he could see that Elliott and David were wearing MP bands on their arms. While they were military police, he hadn't seen them in armbands before.

"We seem to have a problem here, sir," Elliott said after a slight pause.

"No problem," Porter replied. "Go about your way, and I'll forget any of this happened."

Elliott laughed. David laughed a moment later. And then Elliott slammed the butt of his flashlight into the center of Porter's face. There was a muffled crack as Porter's nasal bones gave way and blood spurted from his nose.

"You goddamn moron," Porter cried out as he grabbed his nose. "What the fu—"

Both doors suddenly were jerked open, and as Porter was pulled from his seat, he was aware of a struggle on the seat next to him. April Kennedy was also being pulled from the car. She was protesting, but the ringing in Porter's ears precluded him from understanding what she was saying.

Porter couldn't see, his face was swelling rapidly and in grabbing his nose he'd smeared thick blood into his eyes. All he could do was struggle vainly as Elliott wrestled him a few feet away from the car. Toward the front of the car he heard April Kennedy start to scream, but then he heard a dull slap, a crumpling sound, and she went silent.

"The problem I was referring to, Captain, is that we have us a U.S. Army officer drunk off his gourd and screwing a cheap hooker," Sergeant Elliott whispered in his ear. "A hooker that he then savagely beat to death." He spun Porter around and put him in an half Nelson. He continued holding him as Sergeant David walked over and began pouring something on Porter's chest. It was whiskey.

"What the hell," Porter mumbled through his swollen nose. He'd blinked some of the blood from his eyes, and he could make out the blurred form of Sergeant David as he tossed the near-empty bottle into the rear seat of the car and walked back to the front of the car and stood, looking down at April Kennedy's body. He saw him pull his baton from his belt.

As Porter watched, Sergeant David prodded April Kennedy with the toe of his boot, and when she didn't move, he raised his baton to strike her. Time slowed. Then a third form appeared to materialize from the darkness. A man, holding something. Swinging something. Maybe. Porter couldn't be sure what was happening. He heard another thud and sharp cry, and he thought he saw David's body drop to the ground. Porter felt Elliott's grasp loosen, and he spun sideways to break free. He was at an arm's distance from the MP when he caught the movement of Elliott's arm in his peripheral vision and felt the dull crack of the flashlight striking the side of his head.

CHAPTER 77

Fort Smith, Arkansas
Tuesday, December 30

In the tense silence inside the building, the phone ringing sounded like a fire klaxon screwed to the inside wall of his skull. Kel grabbed for it, but he'd buttoned his coat to the neck, and his surprised fingers couldn't find their way through the fabric in time. It rang again, sounding even louder the second time.

Kel heard a startled sound from the back room and saw a shift in the light. He didn't wait to find out who it was. He retreated out the door and stumbled down the steps, unbuttoning his coat and grabbing frantically at the cell phone in his shirt pocket. He'd silenced the ringing by the time he reached his car and paused, hand on the driver's door handle, back on familiar turf, surveying the situation when he saw a figure appear at the front door of the building. It looked smaller than Levine's form, at least thinner, but in the dim and mist, Kel couldn't be sure it wasn't him. Certainly, the figure appeared unconcerned, even casual as it slowly walked down the steps toward him.

Kel tossed out a greeting. "Hey." If it was Levine, there'd be a growl in response.

The figure didn't reply; it just kept walking slowly toward the car.

Kel tightened his grip on the door handle. "How ya doin'?" he said.

The figure, a smiling man now that he was close enough for Kel to discern his features, walked to the passenger side of the car and stopped. His arms were to his sides.

"Can I help you?" the man asked.

"Ahh, no. Just leavin'," Kel replied. His eyes shifted to the building for any sign of Levine, and then quickly to the blue Monte Carlo. He was certain that it was Levine's car. The doors were locked, just like Levine would do, but he wished now he'd looked at the plates—Levine's would have Tennessee tags. The smart thing to do was to drive a block away and call Levine on the phone and ask him if everything was okay.

"Mind if I ask what you're doing here? At this hour? This is private property."

"Here? Ahh . . ." Kel stammered as he opened the car door. The dome light went on, illuminating the pizza boxes on the passenger's seat. He shrugged. "You know, I'm ahh . . . deliverin' pizza." He laughed and nodded at the boxes. "And they're gettin' colder by the minute."

The man bent and looked into the passenger side of the car. "No one ordered pizza here."

"Yeah, well, sorry. Lookin' for 1105 Sixth Street. It's too dark to see the address," he pointed to the building. "I take it this isn't the eleven-hundred block?"

"No," the man replied, "this is eight-hundred."

Kel laughed again. "Figures. There goes my tip. Thanks."

The man put a forearm on top of McKelvey's car. "You don't look like a pizza boy."

"Hey, this economy, you do what you have to do. Gotta keep the kids in ipods and Nikes," Kel replied as he started to get into the car. "Thanks for the directions."

"In fact," the man replied, his smile having left his face, "you look a great deal like someone a friend of mine hangs around with. In fact, I'm sure of it." A gun appeared on the roof of the car. The man sighed. "I'm afraid things just became very complicated for both of us."

CHAPTER 78

McKelvey's arms were taped to the chair with Duct tape. His elbows were similarly bound, as were his ankles. The man hadn't said much; hadn't needed to. After pressing the short barrel of his revolver hard into McKelvey's ear, he'd conveyed, through body language and a few impatient shoves, his instructions. Kel had complied, in part because there wasn't a really a good response to a cold gun barrel in his right ear, and also because, until he was seated and taped to the chair and able to survey his surroundings, he didn't realize how high the stakes had been raised. Anthropologists are more accustomed to tick bites and paper cuts than gun barrels in their ears. The light in the room was dim, but bright enough that he could make out the tangled elements of a bizarre situation. Levine, partially disrobed, was sprawled out on a pad of blankets, and was partially intertwined with the limbs of a naked woman. Neither of the two bodies was moving, and at first Kel didn't know if either was alive. Only after a minute did he hear a low groan escape Levine's throat.

After he finished taping McKelvey to the chair, Dennis Viktor pulled the other chair in front of him and sat down. He was shaking his head, but wore a lazy grin that gave McKelvey reason to hope, despite the scene displayed at his feet. "I'm telling you what, this complicates things considerably, and I'd be less than honest with you, Mr.—" he stopped short, "I'm afraid I don't know your name."

Kel didn't respond.

Viktor waited a moment and then shrugged. "No matter. Have it your way. I'll just call you, *Mike's Friend*. That alright? Well, as I was saying, Mr. Mike's Friend, I'm not real happy with this development. You see, I had this all planned out down to the minute; I'm sort of anal that way. And now this. Okay, let's review the biddin'. Here's what we have: Agent Levine here, sad, lonely, bitter Agent Levine, finally went off the deep end and abducted and then raped this poor woman. Even more tragic is that the two of them—make that, the three of you now—had to die when he accidentally set fire to this place in his drug and alcohol diminished state." He caught the look in McKelvey's eyes and almost chuckled. "Yeah, sorry to be the bearer of sad tidings, but you're about to burn up with these two other lost souls. That's the problem. You see—"

With a groan, a semi-conscious Levine rolled off of the woman and onto his back. He lay still.

Viktor paused and looked at Levine over his shoulder. He shook his head and looked back at McKelvey. "You can see the problem, I'm sure. Agent Levine flipping out is one thing, but I'm not sure how to weave you into this little tableau that won't cause too many questions, and I'm afraid I don't have much time to figure it out." He looked at his watch, tilting it to better catch some of the dim light. "In fact, I have a nice little alibi waiting for me—a nineteen-year-old alibi with green eyes and an amazing ability to speak in tongues, actually—but I need to be out of here in less than thirty minutes to make that timeline work. So that's the problem." He turned in his seat and looked at Levine again and at the woman on the floor, tilting his head as if he were a tailor evaluating the proper width for a lapel.

Kel tugged impotently at his bound wrists. He contemplated yelling for help.

The movement caught Viktor's attention. He smiled again. "Don't waste your energy. Yeah, sorry. You gotta die. That's easy, but here's what I have to decide, and I'll take suggestions if you have any: What's your involvement? I mean, were you part of this? I got to make it sort of believable. Were you and your buddy Levine tag teaming her? Or, did you stumble on to Mr. Hyde, and he flipped out and killed you? It's sort of like that game *Clue*, isn't it? Did Agent Levine kill you in the parlor; outright—with his gun over there—or did you die of smoke inhalation when the place went up. Did he tie you up

and make you watch first? Or did he let you get a piece of the action?
See what I mean? Fitting you into this scenario at the last minute is a
bitch." He looked down at the floor and was quiet for a minute while
he thought.

"No one is goin' to believe this," Kel finally said. "Look, you—"

Viktor held up a hand to silence McKelvey. "You sound as stupid
as your friend, and I didn't think that was possible. Now, be quiet, and
let me think. See, I think the pizzas are the real problem. My guess is
that someone's waiting for you, right? You may have a bit of a gut on
you, but I doubt you were going to eat two whole pizzas all by yourself.
It doesn't make much sense that you would have stopped off here to
shag a piece of ass with your friend while someone's waiting on dinner.
Leastways I'll give you the benefit of the doubt that you wouldn't do
that. No, I'm afraid that option won't hold up under scrutiny." He
nodded as a solution began gelling in his head.

Levine moaned again and partially rolled to his side.

Viktor looked at him and then at McKelvey. "No. No. Now,
here's what I think happened. Not perfect, but I think this will work.
Somehow, you suspected that Levine was a live wire about to short
out. You've been watching him, and somehow you figured out what
was going on. Maybe he said something to you or something—I mean,
you did find him here, didn't you? So, somehow you tracked him
down and walked in on his little depraved spectacle. But by now he's
too far gone to reason with." His voice took on a sing-song cadence.
"He's drunk. Popping pills like there's no tomorrow. He's got a gun.
You're a wimp. No offense. He ties you up," he paused and then
smiled. "Even better, he dopes you up so he can finish with her before
he has to deal with you." Viktor nodded slowly. "Not perfect, but it
just might work. Just might." He stood up and picked Levine's coat
off of the floor. He rummaged through the pocket and removed the
brown bottle he'd put there earlier. He read the label before he opened
it and shook out a couple of pills. Then he recapped the bottle and
replaced it in Levine's coat. "He forced you to take some Rohypnol—
just like he gave her," he said as he held the pills to McKelvey's mouth.

Kel clamped his lips shut and turned his head aside.

Viktor sighed. "Like I told your friend here, I'd take these if I were you. I really would. You see, in about fifteen minutes, this place will be the Devil's own oven. You can either be wide awake for the event, or out like a light. Now, if I were you . . ."

Kel looked at the man and saw his intent. He tugged at the tape holding his wrists and struggled vainly for a few seconds, but in the end, he reluctantly opened his mouth and let Viktor drop two pills on the back of his tongue. He swallowed hard.

"Much better," Viktor said. "I really hate for you to suffer. I do. I got no beef with you. I mean, I don't even know you, but—we're too far down this path to back the bus up, aren't we?" He stood up and arched his back. It popped, and he smiled. "Just to show that there's no hard feelings, I'll give those a couple of minutes to start working and then—" He stopped in midsentence. He saw McKelvey's eyes go wide in the dim light and he heard a moan behind him. Viktor slowly turned around.

Levine had managed to rise up on one elbow. In his right hand he held his 9 millimeter, which had been lying next to the woman's head along with his badge. The gun was swaying in a large figure-eight, sometimes pointing at McKelvey, sometimes at Viktor, sometimes at the wall, sometimes at the ceiling. Levine's head was lolling on his breast and his eyes were hooded and glazed.

Viktor took a step toward Levine.

As Kel watched, Levine opened his eyes.

The big gun swung in its lazy arc until it was pointed directly at McKelvey's chest. There was a flash and a roar as it went off.

CHAPTER 79

Camp Chaffee, Sebastian County, Arkansas

Wednesday, April 12, 1944

Bill Porter opened his eyes to a blurry world of light. He blinked and tried them one at a time—right, left, right. His right eye seemed to be functioning somewhat; nothing was clear, but at least there were shapes and lights and smudges of color. Through his left eye, all remained dark. He continued—right, left, right. Then he heard a voice.

"Well, look who's decided to rejoin the livin'." It was a soft, woman's voice, with a syrupy laziness to it. Southern, but deeper south than Arkansas, at least the part of Arkansas that Porter had become accustomed to hearing. "Bless your heart, if you didn't have us startin' to wonder if you were ever comin' back. You went and missed Easter completely," the woman said as she removed a thermometer from under his arm, read it, shook it down, and made a note in her chart. "Anythin' I can get for you, Hon?"

Porter's vision had improved somewhat, at least out of his right eye. He could see her now. Dressed in white. She was very pretty, with kind eyes and a warm smile. "Yes," he croaked. It was a dull croak with no resonance. He tried to swallow and repeated. "Yes. Some water."

She patted his hand. "Of course. I'm sure you're pretty dry. The doctor took the cotton out of your nose this mornin'; poor thing, you've been breathin' through your mouth for the last three days." She picked up a pitcher next to his bed and swirled the contents. "Let me go get you some fresh." She patted his hand again and turned to go. *"Not too much. He shouldn't talk too much for now."* The latter instruction was clearly directed to someone outside of Porter's field of vision.

"That's alright. He's not much of a conversationalist under the best of conditions." A male voice responded with a laugh.

Porter recognized the voice. "Hey, Mac," he said.

"Hey, bubba. Like the nurse said, you gave some folks a scare."

Porter blinked more, trying to clear his vision. His left eye didn't improve, and it wasn't until he reached up and touched the large ball of gauze encircling his head and nose and covering his left eye that he realized why. He probed through the padding until a sharp pain made him wince and pull his hand away.

"Broken nose. Broken cheek bone. Concussion. They say you'll recover," Mac said. He moved from the foot of the bed to the side so that Porter could see him without having to turn his head.

"Feel like shit," Porter said.

"Then you'd better not look in a mirror for a while because you look even worse."

Porter blinked and stared with his one working eye. He was trying to clear the cobwebs from his brain. "The woman," he croaked. He cleared his throat. "She okay?"

"April Kennedy. Yeah. She's got a couple of good sized bruises, but nothin' like you." Mac looked at his watch. "In fact, if the bus is on time, she and her little boy should be pullin' into Kansas City about now. From there she'll make connections to Iowa City or somewhere. She has a sister up in those parts that she's hopin' will take her in."

"How'd she manage that?"

Mac shrugged. "Dunno. Guess someone has been sneakin' her some spare change now and then. She finally saved up enough to get a bus ticket."

"But where's she going? We'll need her back for the court martial."

Mac went silent. He sniffed and looked out the window for a moment before he answered. "And what court martial would that be, Bill?"

Porter tried to sit up but winced as a crack of lightning shot through his head. He settled back into his pillow and waited for the throb to subside before he spoke. "What do you mean? Elliott. David."

Mac sniffed again and grabbed a chair. He pulled it closer alongside Porter's bed and sat down. "There isn't goin' to be a trial. Not now. Not ever."

"Those bastards attacked me, and they planned to kill her and make it look like I did it. She can testify to it." Porter paused as a thought flickered in front of him. "Who found us? I remember seeing a . . . a . . . form . . . a man. I think."

"That'd be me. You can buy me a drink later to thank me. Not sure where though; you went and got the Blue Ginger closed down permanent."

Porter tried to nod but it hurt too much. "So . . ." He formed a thought. "You can testify. You know. We won't need her," he said.

Mac took a deep breath and let it out slowly. "Look, counselor, get it through that cracked head of yours, there isn't goin' to be a trial. You don't want a trial. It's not about what I know, it's about what I saw, and what I could testify to. I know that Elliott and David are shitbags. I know that. But what I saw was this: I saw an MP standin' over an unconscious woman, another MP strugglin' to restrain a drunk Captain Porter. That's what I could testify to under oath."

"I wasn't drunk."

"Okay. But there're plenty of people, me included, that could testify you've been drinkin' at the Blue Ginger regular, and you sure as shit smelled like a distillery when we got you here."

"But that's not what happened, and you know it."

"True, but here's what Elliott and David will argue: They're sworn MPs. They'll say that they were doin' a sweep of an off-limits bar when they found one each, Captain Bill Porter, drunk and workin' over a prostitute. They confronted you, and you flipped out when they tried to arrest you, and maybe, just maybe they'll admit to goin' a little overboard in subduin' you, but who could blame them. It was you that resisted arrest."

"No one will believe that."

"You sleep through evidence class in law school there, Mr. Lawyer? Of course no one will believe that, but then they don't have to. All there has to be—correct me if I'm wrong—is a sliver of doubt."

"But the woman could testify. That's why we need her back."

Mac sighed again and leaned in closer. "Listen to me very carefully, Bill, there isn't goin' to be a trial. Win, lose, or draw, all that would be accomplished is that your military career—shit, your legal career—will be in shreds, and April, well, the defense will spell *whore* six ways from Sunday before it's over. She doesn't need that."

"So they get off? Scot free?"

Mac shrugged. "There are other forms of justice."

"Yeah? Like what?"

Mac paused before answering. "Well, David is about three doors down that way," he said as he pointed to the wall behind Porter's head. "Docs say that once the cast is off, he may have a ten, fifteen percent chance of bending his leg normally. I wouldn't bet on it though. It's a wonder what a number thirty-four Louisville Slugger can do to a man's kneecap. In any case, he'll be medically discharged as soon as he limps out of here." He paused again and leaned forward, elbows on his knees. "And your good buddy Elliott—now he's about two doors that away," Mac said as he jerked a thumb over his shoulder. "Ugly as you with all the bandages, but he'll be okay, and as soon as they unwire his jaw in a couple of weeks, he'll be fit for his new assignment. I hear he's been transferred to the infantry and is headed for some god-forsaken Jap-held island with too many damn vowels in it. The general signed the paperwork this mornin'."

"General?"

Mac laughed and slapped Porter on the side of his leg with the back of his hand. "Lot's happened while you were sleepin' there Captain Van Winkle. Yeah, Wiggins came out on the general's list. That's why I was over in Little Rock the other day, to hand carry some paperwork back here. He won't get the pay for a while, but he got to pin on last Monday."

Porter's mood darkened even more. "He knew."

Mac took another deep breath and let it out slowly before he responded. "Did he?"

"You know he did. Wiggins knew. Jordan. Geller's death. He knew. Knew it all." Porter's voice had started to clear with use.

Mac stood up and walked over to the door, shutting it quietly. He returned to his seat. "Maybe so. Unfortunately, you might be right, as much as I wish you weren't. All I know is that I'm here because of the old man." He tapped his chest. "If he hadn't put himself in the way, the grenade that took his hand off would have done more than send a piece of metal through my chest. I owe that man my life."

"So you look the other way. You expect me to?"

"No," Mac shook his head slowly. "No. Can't do that. But I can weigh the options and do some simple math. You can try to prove what you suspect, or . . . or you can leave it be and let things sort themselves out. Two weeks from now, the general's bein' transferred out of here. They want him to sell War Bonds for six months and then," he held his hands up, as if he was surrendering. "Then he can retire and reopen his law practice. Live out his life happy. His son and son-in-law, if they survive the war, can join him. That's his plan. His dream. He's earned it."

"Just like that?"

"Just like that."

The door opened and the nurse reappeared, carrying the water pitcher. She saw the two men engaged in a tight discussion and hesitated. "You still want some water, Hon?"

"That'd be nice," Porter answered.

She poured him a glass of water and stepped between Mac and Porter, holding the glass to his lips for him to take a sip. She was aware of Mac's eyes on her as she bent over the bed. As she replaced the glass on the nightstand, she smiled at Mac. "Not much longer," she told him, touching him lightly on the shoulder as she did so.

Mac smiled back. "No, ma'am. About done." He reached up and briefly touched her fingers, which lingered on his shoulder.

"Potatoes get *done*. People are *finished*," she said.

Mac's smile grew larger. "About finished then."

She left and quietly shut the door behind her.

Mac watched her go and then continued looking at the closed door. "I may just marry that woman," he said. He looked at Porter. "She's the one that nursed me back to health when I first returned from overseas. She followed me all the way out to here when I transferred."

Porter acknowledged with a short nod but didn't respond.

The two men sat silently for a moment. Mac shifted his gaze to the floor between his feet. After a moment, he stood. "Well, Bill," he said, "I guess that's that. I'll check back in later. Meantime, I have a nurse to talk to. And don't take this the wrong way, but she's a whole lot prettier to look at than you."

"Mac."

Mac arched his eyebrows in response.

"Forgetting someone."

Mac cocked his head and squinted at Porter. "Mean you?"

"Me? Hell no. What do you mean, me?"

"Well. You're kind of a loose end, aren't you?"

"You sound like Jordan. Or Elliott."

Mac laughed. "Shit. Like I deserve that. No, my friend, it's just a statement of fact. You're a loose end. They've already cut the orders for a new JAG to replace you. He'll be here next week to take over the case; though my guess is that Geller's murder is so hosed slam up by now that they'll never get a conviction, and even if they do, they'll end up havin' to commute the sentence anyway. No, you don't have to be a lawyer to know that one's a lost cause. But you don't need to worry. I was goin' to wait a day or so to tell you this, but you seem to have perked up. Here's what's goin' to happen to you." He leaned forward, hands on the end of the bed. "They'll cut you free from here in a couple three days, then you're authorized thirty days leave up in Missouri. To heal up. Get some home cookin'. When you're done— *finished*—you're to report to your new duty station." He paused for effect. "London."

"London?"

Mac shook his head good naturedly. "Just temporarily. Seems they're assemblin' the best lawyers in the whole country to go to London, so they'll be ready to swoop down on Germany as soon as we get to Berlin. You're on that list. Hell, you may even get to cross-examine old Adolph before we hang his ass."

"London?" Porter repeated.

"Yup. Seems you have friends in high places."

"I don't have any friends. Certainly none in high places," Porter replied. The croak in his voice had started to return.

"I meant me, bubba. I typed up the orders two days ago, and the old man signed them this mornin'. And of course, you'll need an assistant. Also typed up those orders. Miss Kramer will be goin' with you. I think she's shoppin' for a new dress right now." Mac winked and turned to leave. "Don't forget to invite me to the weddin'."

"Mac."

Mac turned around.

"I, ahh . . . I guess I should say thanks."

"Get some rest. You're probably exhausted from . . . hell, you're probably exhausted from sleepin' for three straight days. Besides, I have a nurse to talk to. In case you hadn't noticed, she's kinda sweet on me." He turned and opened the door.

"Mac."

"Yeah?"

"Jordan."

Mac hung his head and laughed. "Shit. I almost made it out the door."

"What about him?"

"What about him?" Mac responded.

"He can't be allowed to just walk away from this."

Mac closed the door. "Who says he will? Who knows what'll happen to him? You're not the only one with connections in the personnel shop, and I have the ear of a new general. I wouldn't be surprised if there isn't a set of newly signed orders for him.   Maybe Germany."

"Doesn't seem like justice."

Mac took a deep breath and held it.   He let it go.   His voice was suddenly very sober.   "Like I said earlier, counselor.   Justice comes in different forms."

CHAPTER 80

Fort Smith, Arkansas

Friday, January 2

McKelvey's face was the first thing that Levine saw when he opened his eyes; at least the first thing he remembered seeing since the man calling himself Dennis Viktor had pushed some pills down his throat. His eyelids didn't stay open very long. Even with the blinds drawn, the sunlight streaming into the hospital room jabbed past his eyes like a dull butter knife, forcing them closed again. He groaned.

"Mornin' sunshine," Kel said.

Levine groaned again and forced his eyes open, first the right one then the left. "What the fu—" he began.

"Careful," Kel interjected quickly. "This is a Catholic hospital. You'll have to watch your manners, and your language, for the next few days."

"Hospital? How'd I get here? What are you doing here? How long—" It all sounded like one endless modulated groan.

"Happy New Year, by the way. Yeah, long story. You've been here almost two days, and for the record, before this gets too cuddly, I have not been sittin' by your bedside the whole time, readin' to you and beggin' you to come back to us. In fact, today is my first visit. I called earlier and your wife said you should be comin' around soon, so I decided to stop by for a little while and see. She just went down to the cafeteria to get some coffee. Nice woman, by the way. And, oh, the authorities, quote unquote, are pretty anxious to talk to you; I'm sure they'll be here as soon as they find out you're awake, so enjoy the peace while you can."

Levine started to shake his head to indicate his confusion, but the bone cracking pain that accompanied the movement stopped him short. "I don't understand," he managed to say.

"That's two of us, bubba. I was hopin' you could make sense out of what happened the other night, because shit was already slam crazy by the time I showed up."

Levine started to shake his head again but stopped. "You were there?"

"Afraid so. What's the last thing you remember?" Kel asked.

Levine sighed. "Not sure. I remember calling you, and then going into a warehouse or something." He paused. "I remember someone hitting me with a something hard." His hand went involuntarily to the crown of his head. He winced.

"Half-dozen stitches. They say you have a concussion."

"I believe it," Levine groaned. "I can't remember much else."

Kel pulled his chair closer to the bedside so that Levine could see him better. "Don't recall a woman?"

"Vaguely. Yeah. How is she?"

"Fine. They released her yesterday. She's admitted to helpin' set you up. Claims she was told it was a practical joke at first. That was before things went sour for her. How about a nutcase named Dennis Viktor? Remember him?"

Levine closed his eyes again and thought. "Yeah," he said. Another minute passed in silence. "Yeah. He was setting me up to look like I killed her. I think. Gave me pills."

"No kiddin'," Kel laughed. "Me too. But you got a whole bottleful. They pumped your stomach, but it was too late to do much good. That combined with the knock on your head is what kept you out for the last two days, but that much we know already. What you'll have to fill in is the why component."

Levine lay still again, and for a moment Kel thought he'd drifted off.

"Something crazy," Levine finally said. "Something to do with that case out at Chaffee and that prick lawyer in Memphis . . ."

"Hmmm," Kel responded. "I figured out who he was, by the way—the Chaffee guy. For certain this time. He was a German POW. I've spent the last day or so typing up the paperwork to get him identified and returned home. I can't see a connection with your lawyer, however."

Levine tried to shrug but winced instead. "German? Don't know. I think . . . what was his name?"

"Who? The German or the nutball? The German was named Ketel; the nutball was a guy named Viktor. Dennis Viktor."

"Yeah. I think he said the lawyer didn't want to be embarrassed by the Chaffee skeleton. I don't understand. I guess this Viktor guy will have to fill in the details."

Kel was silent for a moment, and then he cleared his throat. "That's goin' be hard to do, bubba. He's, ahh . . . you shot him. Dead. You really don't remember?"

"No." Levine thought about it. "Good," he said.

"Thought for sure you were goin' to shoot me by mistake. You had your eyes closed when you pulled the trigger. Fortunately, for me anyhow, your form's pretty poor, and you jerked at the last minute."

"Where'd I hit him?"

"Above the knee. He likely would have survived, but with the two of us doped up, he bled out before anyone could get there. There's some irony for you."

"Wish I remembered it."

Kel hadn't been sure how Levine would react to the news he'd killed someone. Now he knew. "Yeah. What's that old Groucho Marx joke about shootin' an elephant in your pajamas? They say you're the first FBI agent to shoot a kidnapper with his pants around his knees. Yours, not his."

"Pants?"

"Man, you have a lot to remember. Anyway, the press is eatin' this up with a spoon. Local and national both. Not only have you solved the Chaffee case—hope you don't mind, but a little bird leaked the news that we'd figured out who he was; figured you could use some good publicity."

"Thanks."

"Don't mention it. Like I was sayin', not only that, but you spoiled a kidnappin' and shot a would-be rapist. You're a regular Dick Tracy—aside from being stoned and having no clothes on for most of the activities. Sort of like college. There's even talk of you gettin' promoted to Special Agent in Charge of the Memphis office. Just what you want, right?"

"The SAC? What about Larry Frank?"

"If you mean Lawrence Frank, accordin' to the newspaper this mornin', this was his last case. He's retirin' after a long and distinguished career with the Bureau. Goin' to spend more time with his family—whatever that means in the FBI. With the DoD that usually indicates someone screwed up, but not enough to sustain an indictment."

Levine smiled. More of Viktor's explanation was coming back to him. The full story would fill in over the next few days, he was sure of it. "Who found me?"

"Found you? You mean found *us*. Actually, I found you, even though you were naked and in a stupor when I did. The real question is who found me?" Kel flashed an enormous smile. "As if I'll ever live this down; my wife found us. Ain't that some shit? She made me carry this," he said as he reached into his shirt pocket and pulled out his phone. "When I got to the warehouse the other night, she called me to tell me to stop and get some milk or somethin'. That's how your buddy Viktor caught me. The damn ringer. I tried to turn it off but ended up hittin' the wrong button and answered it by accident. My wife listened to the whole conversation, includin' me askin' him what the address of the buildin' was. She started once to hang up, but when the conversation started to sound kinda strange, she stayed on. Finally it got so strange that she called the police."

Levine laughed and then winced again. "Tell her thanks for me."

Kel laughed as well. "Tell her yourself. They say she'll probably have to come back in a couple-three weeks to testify. Just a formality, but they're scheduling an inquest to determine whether you were actin' in the line of duty when you shot that bastard. Just a formality. In the meantime, if there was ever any hope of me gettin' out of the house without my cell phone, that's gone forever."

Levine closed his eyes and smiled.

Kel stood up. "I'll let you rest a piece before the cops get here and start with the real questions." He patted Levine's shin. "Tell your wife to give me a call if she needs anythin'; anythin' at all." He smiled. "I guess I'll have my phone."

Levine opened his eyes. "I guess I need to say thanks, Doc," he said.

"I guess you do," Kel replied. He turned and started for the door. "And please don't call me Doc."

CHAPTER 81

Sebastian County, Arkansas
Wednesday, April 12, 1944

The jeep bucked over the rutted road. Captain Mac had chosen the jeep over the colonel's staff car precisely because he knew how bad the roads were—he'd been down them before. Earlier in the day. To prepare. For his part, Jordan simply looked straight ahead into the darkness, occasionally noting the wet splat of a fat spring bug intersecting the flat windshield.

Captain Jordan was a smart man who prided himself on getting a mental hold on a situation before anyone else could, or stealing the initiative back from them if they had a head start. He was trying to do that now.

His first inclination had been to tell this goober of a general's aide to go screw himself. As the situation had begun to unspool over the last couple of weeks, he'd done a fair job of damage control, but there were still loose ends to tie up and telegrams to send and phone calls to make. He still had markers to call in, and right now, he didn't have the time or patience to deal with either Wiggins or his Huck Finn aide. But, he also didn't have the situation well enough in hand to completely blow off the newly minted general. As little regard as Jordan had for Wiggins, pissing off a popular war hero with a shiny new star on his shoulder wouldn't make things go any smoother, and so, when Huck Finn showed up at his office and said that the general, wanted to see him, Jordan had reluctantly gone along thinking that he could spare ten minutes. That was twenty minutes ago and instead of a short ride to the general's office, they were bouncing down a rutted track of farm field out in the middle of a pitch-black nowhere. *If I never see another fucking tree*, Jordan thought, *I'll be a happy man.*

Captain Mac steered the jeep toward a dark mass ahead of them. A copse of trees. He cut the wheels sharply, jolting the vehicle out of the ruts and cutting across the tall Johnson grass that ringed the field. The headlights caught two parallel shadows in the grass, tamped down tire tracks from his visit earlier in the day. Mac downshifted from second to first as the jeep negotiated the uneven terrain. Fifty yards into the darkness he brought the jeep to a stop, near a stand of black oaks and shagbark hickory. He killed the motor, pausing a moment to let his eyes adjust to the darkness and to drink in the night sounds that slowly began to reemerge over the relative quiet.

Mac reached down beside his seat and fished out a flashlight and flicked it on. He thumped it against his palm twice to ensure that the on-switch was well seated as he got out and walked to the front of the jeep. He played the light against the trees—back and forth—until the beam settled on a narrow space between two hickory trees, the branches furry with new growth. He held the light on the space for a moment and then turned, focusing the beam on Jordan's chest, low enough to make his intent known but not high enough to completely wash out the other man's night vision. "We're here," Mac said. He flicked the light back and forth between the opening in the trees and Jordan's chest. "Let's go."

Jordan laughed. "Here? What kind of shit is this?"

Mac sighed. "Let's go," he repeated.

Jordan laughed again. "I don't think so. What's the matter? Am I such a damn pariah now that your general doesn't want to be seen with me? Screw that. He didn't seem to mind meeting with me in public when I was giving him the results he wanted. Screw this."

Mac walked to the driver's side and focused the light back on Jordan's chest, higher this time, but still not directly in the man's eyes. He took a deep breath and let it out slowly. "Look. You're shootin' the messenger here. Let's get somethin' out in the open. I don't particularly care for you, and I'm sure the feelin' is more than mutual, so we can stop all the bullshit. Here's what I know, the sooner you get your ass out of that jeep and into that thicket, the sooner I can get home and do somethin' more enjoyable. You hear me?"

Jordan sat and stared at the tall captain for a moment. "Shit," he said after a moment. He swung his legs out of the jeep and slowly stood up, arching his back and making it clear that he was complying, but on his own terms. Finally, he motioned in the direction of the break in the trees. "You seem to have the light. Why don't you lead away?"

Mac walked through the break in the trees, stooping to clear a tangle of dead briars that had bridged the trees at head height. He played the light along a path in front of him. Jordan followed.

The path was relatively straight, with only a turn or two necessitated by a clump of tanglefoot or early spring poison ivy that discretion dictated avoiding. After fifty yards it terminated in a small clearing only a couple of arm spans in width. Mac came to a stop and turned off his flashlight.

"What the . . ." Jordan stated to complain.

"Shhhh," Mac cut him off. "Listen. Hear it?"

Jordan heard nothing; at least nothing that he was remotely interested in hearing. There were croaks and buzzes and clicks of a thousand unseen things—none of which Jordan cared about. He looked around, but he'd been focusing his eyes on the flashlight's round beam as they walked and his night vision was temporarily lost.

"That's the Vache Grasse Creek. It's got quite a story to tell. You can hear it talkin' if you'll let yourself. Don't you know there's some fine catfish in there."

"Yeah. Maybe that's where your general is; down by the river fishing. What is this shit? What's going on?" Jordan's eyesight was adjusting and he was looking around at the shapes and forms in the dark as he sized up the situation.

Suddenly, Mac's flashlight was back on, its beam focused squarely in Jordan's face.

"What the— Cut the crap," Jordan said as he threw his arms up to block the light. "Maybe you've got time for these games, but I don't. Where's Wiggins?"

"The general isn't here," Mac responded. "But I guess you've figured that out by now."

"Yeah. I figured out a whole bunch of shit. I've figured out that I've had about enough of this. You can either drive me back to post, or I can take the goddamn jeep and drive myself back." He turned and started toward the path. Behind him he heard the metallic click of a gun being cocked. He turned, the light was still in his eyes but he managed to block enough of it with his forearms that he could see the .45 semi-automatic in Mac's right hand. Where it had come from, he didn't know. "Oh, like I really have time for this shit. Give me a break; you aren't about to shoot me, and we both know it."

"Do we?"

"Yes we do. What's the script read? Huh? Wiggins write this out for you, or are you making this up as you go? Huh? What's the script? You supposed to drive me out to Hell's half acre and try to scare me? Is that it? Give me a fucking break. What's the matter? Wiggins afraid that my little program will spoil his reputation as a war hero? Shit. About all that old man is good for anymore is as a paper weight. No one gives two craps about his career, so you can put that damn gun away."

Mac didn't move.

"Look, Stretch, I wouldn't expect your little pea-picking brain to be able to wrap around this, but what I did, my program, was sanctioned way up, and I mean *way the fuck up*. Far above the likes of you and your new tin-star general. Yeah, that stupid asshole Porter upset things a little, and Lord knows Elliot and David have made a real dog's breakfast of things, but there's no reason to panic. I've been here before. It can be managed, and your general doesn't even have to muss his hair. You and I can sort this out. The two of us. You're a fixer, just like me. So let's get this little melodrama over with, and get back to post before the frigging bugs eat us alive."

Mac didn't respond immediately. He simply tracked the flashlight beam to his right, revealing a deep hole, a shovel stuck in an adjacent mound of fresh earth.

"Oh, for God's sake," Jordan replied. "You're staging all the props, aren't you?" He laughed.

"No props. I aim to kill you."

"Shit. You don't have the balls. You're going to kill me? For what?"

"Because you need killin'. Because what you did was wrong and you need to be punished, and it isn't goin' to happen any other way. Because innocent men are dead on account of you and the system will cover it up. Because men like you are a cancer."

"Innocent men? Innocent? You hear yourself? They're friggin' Germans, you stupid asshole."

"No one hates Germans more than me, but they were in our care."

"And you're going to kill me for that?" For the first time, Jordan sounded uncertain. "Or is it Wiggins? You that loyal to Wiggins? You'd kill for that sonofabitch?"

Mac returned the flashlight beam to Jordan's eyes. "Not about loyalty. It's about duty. It's about payin' back debts. It's also about emptyin' the garbage."

"I'll be missed."

"Maybe. But bein' missed and bein' found is another matter. I learned that from you and that little shell game you've been playin' with the dead PWs. Your file shows you were transferred to Germany this mornin'. I typed the orders myself. Anybody misses you, they can start lookin' over there. Of course, that'll be a dead-end."

Jordan fished a package of cigarettes out of his shirt pocket and shook one free, taking it between his lips. His hands trembled. He started patting his pockets. "Must be some debt you owe. You're not a killer; at least not like this." He patted his pockets some more. "Shit. You got a light? I can't seem to find my lighter."

Mac didn't answer.

"C'mon. You don't want to do this. Your general has nothing to worry about from me. Let's go on back to the post. We forget all this. Let's go over to that place in Oklahoma you like; I'll even buy you a drink. Shit."

Mac raised the gun.

To anyone out gigging frogs on the river, all they heard was a loud pop, followed, ten seconds later, by two more pops in close succession. And then the sounds of the summer night started up again, embracing the darkness.

CHAPTER 82

OFFICE OF THE PRESIDENT OF THE UNITED STATES

December 12, 1946
General George C. Marshall
Chairman, Joint Chiefs of Staff

General Marshall:

You are hereby directed to locate, recover, and establish the identity of the remains of Captain James S. B. JORDAN, Jr., O321168, U.S. Army.

Information supplied by The Adjutant General indicates that Captain JORDAN was assigned to the European theater on, or about, August 1944. No other information is forthcoming at this time.

The President of the United States has expressed his personal interest in the swift and successful resolution of this matter.

You are authorized all resources necessary to accomplish this task and are directed to commence forthwith.

By direction of the President:

//SIGNED//

Matthew Sisson
Deputy Assistant Chief of Staff

tdh/MS

CHAPTER 83

Central Identification Unit, Strasbourg, France

Monday, January 6, 1947

Captain Wayne Harlan's bottle-glass-green eyes were bleary from too much red wine and unfiltered cigarette smoke the night before. He'd received word yesterday that his father-in-law's hard work, and not-insubstantial influence back home, was paying off in spades and that his name would soon appear on the promotion list for major—no small feat in the dwindling postwar army. More important, a promotion would come with a reassignment back stateside, most likely as the commander of one of the supply depots in his father-in-law's home congressional district in Kentucky. It had been more than reason enough for late-night celebrating with a few select friends, but now, as he settled into his desk, he had to blink repeatedly to focus on the paperwork that had accumulated on his desk since last Friday. It was all the usual stuff—requisitions for supplies, civilian time cards, weekly status reports—and he was just about to push it all into a corner of his desk and head off in search of a headache powder, when his eye caught the sender's code on an overnight radio message that was peeking out from under the stack. He didn't recognize the specific office symbol, but he knew the Pentagon's prefix when he saw it.

The envelope had already been opened, as it should have been. With the exception of letters from his wife, and mash notes from a certain, particularly well-curved, young woman who lived on the outskirts of Strasbourg; his secretary, Corporal Bobby Nelson, was under orders to screen—which involved opening—all mail.

He unfolded the thin, almost tissue-like paper of the message and blinked hard again to clear his vision.

It didn't work, and he laid the paper down while he tried to rub the grape skins from his eyes.

Early on, more so during the command of his predecessor, the brass in Washington had taken a very active interest in how the Central Identification Unit was faring. There had been constant cablegrams and radio messages requesting updates and projections, and the CIU staff used to spend almost as much time graphing their progress as they actually spent making any progress. Recently, however, the attention had waned markedly, and while the Pentagon and the White House were still interested—or at least willing to feign interest—in how the efforts to recover and identify its lost soldiers were going, there was not the smothering, looking-over-the-shoulder sense of daily involvement that there once had been. That was why a radio message from someone at the Pentagon was reason to pucker. It wasn't a gratuitous atta-boy.

Captain Harlan blinked hard again and shook his head before picking up the paper. His eyes skimmed over the words for a second time as he tried to quickly gauge the magnitude of the Oh-Shit factor. He didn't like what he was seeing and started over at the beginning, moving slower this time, his lips moving as he read, hoping that he'd misunderstood.

"Corporal Nelson," he yelled over the top of the thin paper as he began rereading the message for a third time. "Corporal Nelson, I need to see you, son."

"Sir?" Corporal Nelson responded. His quick appearance in the captain's doorway suggested that the summons was not entirely unexpected. He'd clearly read the message and had been waiting for the call.

"Corporal, what d'you make of this?"

"Sir?"

"This here radio message, son. Cut the crap, I know you read it. The one from the Chairman of the Joint Chiefs of Staff."

Corporal Nelson walked over to the captain's desk. "What I make of it, sir, is that the War Department thinks very highly of you. I would think you'd be pleased," he replied.

"Pleased? Is that what you think? No, Corporal, I'm not pleased. I don't like this one bit," Captain Harlan said, as he looked up at the corporal. "This is bad news. This must be pretty hot shit for the Chairman of the Joint Chiefs to direct an urgent radio cablegram to me. Who do you suppose this, this . . ." he looked back down at the paper in his hand and searched out the name, "this, James S. B. Jordan, Junior, is?"

Corporal Nelson shook his head. "I wouldn't pretend to know, sir."

"Aw crap, Nelson; I'm supposed to pin on major here shortly and head for home. I don't need this sort of trouble."

"Sir? Trouble?"

"You read me clear enough, Bobby." Harlan shook the slip of paper in his corporal's direction. "This has got cluster written all over it. C-L-U-S-T-E-R. Cluster—as in Cluster Fuck. And in pretty fancy handwriting, too."

Corporal Nelson took the radio message from his commander and read it; his face blank as if he was seeing it for the first time. He paused before answering. "It seems pretty straightforward to me, Captain. I'm not sure I fully understand what you mean."

"What I mean, Corporal Nelson," Harlan responded impatiently, as if he was talking to one of the many dull-witted French officials that he had to deal with on a daily basis, "is that as much as this may surprise you, General George frickin' Marshall does not make it a habit to cable me personally about some damn dead Joe whose body seems to be presently missing. And he sure as hell doesn't do it for a captain; damn, son, there must be twenty-thousand dead captains in this theater alone."

Nelson nodded in slow agreement as he handed the cablegram back to his boss. "Yes, sir. I'd guess you're right about that number. Maybe more. If I might hazard a guess though, sir, I'd wager that this Captain Jordan here was as well connected as you are. Somebody's turned up the flame on this one."

"Exactly," Harlan said. "That's the problem."

The young corporal sloshed his head slowly back and forth as if it was half full of water and wasn't well balanced on his neck. "Or the opportunity. It's all a matter of perspective."

Harlan went snake-eyed as he plumbed his aide's face. "I say problem, you say opportunity."

Bobby Nelson crossed his pale, pipe-cleaner-thin arms and leaned his hip against Harlan's desk. As he did so, his shirt sleeve rode up on his forearm exposing the bare legs of a hula-dancer tattoo. "Like they say, sir; Too-MAY-toe, Toe-MAH-toe; problem, opportunity," he smiled. "Two sides of a coin, sir. It's all in the point of view."

"Point of view?"

"Exactly. Me, sir, now I'm an optimist, myself."

"So educate me, Corporal. Explain how this here Toe-MAH-toe is good news." He fanned the thin piece of paper back and forth as he spoke.

Nelson took the cablegram again and looked at it briefly before shrugging to emphasize how commonsensical it was. "It's only a problem, sir, if you don't send back a body like you've been ordered to do."

Harlan blinked and rubbed his eyes. "Yeah, that's the problem all right," he said. "I can see that. It's the solution that I'm having some trouble with."

Nelson smiled again. "Yes, sir. So send them a body."

Captain Wayne Harlan stared at his corporal. "I don't follow. What do you mean? Send them a body? That's the problem, isn't it? Where do we find this guy's body?"

Corporal Nelson summoned all of his enlisted-man skills and patiently replied, "With all due respect, Captain, you're commander of the largest military identification unit in Europe. I'd think that finding a body is not an insurmountable problem for a man of your considerable talents." He paused. "Give the word, sir."

Harlan slowly stood up. He was intimidated by this junior NCO and standing up at least allowed him to physically dominate the discussion even if he was outmatched mentally. He ran his hand over his chin, feeling the emerging stubble and realizing that he'd forgotten to shave this morning. "Our job is to recover, identify, and return missing American soldiers. What you're suggesting is, is . . ."

"Pragmatic, sir. I believe that's the word you're searching for."

"I'm not sure that's what many would call it, Corporal."

Corporal Nelson smiled and handed the cablegram back to his captain. "Understood, sir. In that case, does the Captain have anything else?"

Wayne Harlan said all that he needed to for the record. From that point onward, the conversation had never taken place. "So, tell me, Corporal Nelson. I'm interested in how you define *pragmatic*?"

"Me, sir? Well, I guess I see it like this; we lost a great many men in this theater. Many will never be found no matter what we do, and many of the ones that are found will never be identified. That is just a sad fact of war. The way I see it, in the end, it's sort of like a lottery, sir. Some folks will get their answers, and some won't. That's also a fact."

Harlan took the cablegram back from his aide and read the strips of words again. "And this, this—James S. B. Jordan, Junior—he'll be one of the lottery winners?"

"Technically, his father would, but that's your call, sir. That's why the War Department saw to put a man like you in charge; to make those difficult decisions. The way I see it, it's like pancakes and syrup. They never come out even in the end, do they? No matter how hard a man like you works, it'll never be a perfect world. There will always be more families than bodies to send home. Somebody has to play God, sir. I can't think of anyone better for that role than you."

Wayne Harlan walked to his window and looked out. It was preferable to maintaining eye contact with his aide. It also allowed him to rest his forehead on the cool glass and ease the pulse of his headache. "But why Jordan?"

"Why not, is the better question. The Jordan family has taken the matter up with some very important people. It seems like they deserve to get their son back as much as anyone. Maybe even more so."

"Even if it's not their son?"

"With all due respect, sir, that's the point. It's your call. You have, if I may say so, the power to make it their son with the stroke of your pen."

Harlan let his head throb against the smooth glass for a long minute before he turned around. "We don't even know where this guy was killed. The records—"

"I'll take care of the records, sir."

"What about the scientists? They can be hard to control. If they find out . . ."

"You worry about officer things, sir, and let me deal with the administrative matters. That's what I'm good at."

"But, where do we get a body, Corporal? Let's assume . . . I mean, if we were to . . ." he paused while he sought for the proper word.

"Identify James Jordan? That really shouldn't be a problem, sir. As you'll recall, Lieutenant Smith and Tech Sergeant Ludlow were quite successful in their search in Metz a few months ago, sir. Quite successful. And I don't believe those bodies have yet to find a home."

EPILOGUE

Fort Smith, Arkansas

Friday, January 9

A few phone calls had taken care of it. A few calls and way too many forms. McKelvey's jurisdiction didn't officially extend to foreign POWs, but no one really challenged the issue. In the end, a federal magistrate concurred that there was sufficient circumstantial and physical evidence to establish a presumptive identification, and a uniformed escort from the Army Casualty office in Washington, D.C.—a young staff sergeant whose excited complexion resembled a newly shaved cat—had flown to Hawaii and signed for the skeletal remains of Obergefreiter Dieter Ketel. He would escort the remains, with full military honors, to the U.S. Air Force base in Ramstein, Germany, where they would be signed over to German military officials for burial. All things considered, very few questions had been asked, and no one—not even the German authorities—seemed particularly interested in where Herr Ketel's remains had been for the last sixty-five years. That would probably change as the national newspapers sniffed out the story, but for the present the local media were still fixated on Levine's role in foiling a local kidnapping, and Ketel's story was a footnote.

Special Agent Michael Levine went to Maryland for a week of convalescence leave with his family before returning to his small, interior office in Memphis. A few co-workers nodded a quiet recognition in the hall that he had been away and was now back, a few congratulated him on his recent case, a couple acknowledged the rumors of a possible promotion, but most didn't. Most hadn't even noticed that he had been gone and even fewer cared one way or the other. Their indifference didn't bother him. He settled in and spent the first half of a day deleting large blocks of emails and filling out his most recent expense voucher. After lunch he rebooted his computer. While he waited, he looked at the photograph of his wife and daughters on his desk and thought about what needed to be done.

When the computer was ready he began typing his resignation.

In Fort Smith, Kel kissed Mary Louise and put her on the airplane with their two sons. They had delayed their departure almost a week so that both Kel and his wife could give depositions in a coroner's inquest into the death of Dennis Viktor. Now they needed to get home to Hawaii so that their boys could start school. The original plan had been to all fly home together, but a few hours before they were scheduled to leave, Kel received a call from Les Neep asking if he could represent the CILHI at a budget meeting at the Pentagon. The meeting would undoubtedly be a waste of time, but it did offer another couple of day's respite from Colonel Botch-It. So, instead of returning home, he'd agreed to rent a car and drive to Tulsa to catch a late-night flight to Dallas and then to Atlanta and then on to National Airport. Before leaving town, however, he stopped by his mother's house.

"Mary Louise and the boys get off all right?" his mother asked him as he took off his coat and draped it over the back of a chair. She was sitting near the window in the living room reading another old Erle Stanley Gardner novel.

"Yes, ma'am. Sure did. About an hour or so ago," he answered. "Her folks said to tell you *hey*. They want you to be sure to call them if you need anythin'."

"They're nice folk," she replied. "You got lucky when you married that girl. Speakin' of which, when does your family get home?"

Kel looked at his watch and calculated. "They should be home in about . . . oh, about eleven hours from now; give or take. D.S. is goin' to pick them up at the airport."

"Mercy," Anne McKelvey replied, closing her book and marking the page with a thumb. "I surely don't see how y'all do it; makin' that long, old trip, and all."

"Don't have much choice, Mother. Not if we want to have Christmas here with our families. It's not like there's much of a short-cut to Hawaii." He picked up the morning newspaper from the sofa and sat down, absentmindedly scanning the front page. After a moment he sighed and tossed the paper aside.

"You're still sighin'."

"Tired, I guess," Kel replied.

His mother laughed. "Can't imagine why. I guess almost gettin' yourself killed can be taxin'."

"Yes, ma'am. It can at that."

"Probably shouldn't do that again."

"No ma'am; no plans to."

"Now that you've figured out your Chaffee man was a German, how about that other case of yours? Haven't heard you mention it recently. You get it all figured out?"

"Other case?"

"The one that you said was misidentified."

"James Jordan? I'm afraid he's still a mystery," Kel said and shrugged.

His mother straightened the blanket over her knees and set the book aside. "So what's goin' to happen to him?"

Kel laughed. "Hell, mom—"

"Robert."

"Sorry. Well, the answer to that is, who knows? All we know is that the skeleton out at Chaffee wasn't him, and the skeleton that's buried over in California isn't him either."

"So, do you plan on diggin' up that poor boy in California?"

"The misidentified one? No, ma'am. It'd take a court order, and I'm not sure what the point of it would be. We don't have a clue who he is. As it is, he's at least buried in hallowed ground—for now—even if it's with the wrong tombstone. Unless we get some leads, all we'd end up doin' is puttin' him in a damn . . . ahh, puttin' him in a cardboard box on a shelf in the lab."

"Robert, you really need to mind your language. You have impressionable sons now."

"Yes, ma'am."

"I mean it."

"I know you do. I'm tryin'. Anyhow . . ."

"So, if that California boy isn't in California, where you reckon he is?"

"You mean Jordan? That's the problem. I don't reckon, Mom; I flat out don't know. I suspect he's out buried in the middle of nowhere. Unmarked and forgotten, likely."

"That's pretty sad."

"Yes, ma'am. That's a fact."

"And you say he worked for Fist?"

Kel leaned forward and started to stand up but changed his mind and remained seated. "General Wiggins? Yes, ma'am. Sort of, from what we can piece together, anyhow. The records are pretty slim."

She was quiet for a moment. "Your father worked for Fist Wiggins. Did you know that?"

Kel squinted. "No shi—I mean, no, I didn't. General Wiggins? You mean durin' the war? I never could get Dad to talk about the war, other than him gettin' to meet you."

Anne McKelvey slowly stood up and walked over to a dresser that stood in the hallway adjoining the living room. She spoke as she walked. "Yes. He worked for him for a half year or better."

"I thought Dad was in Africa and Italy."

"He was, but I'm talkin' about later; late in the war, after he came home wounded. He was assigned out to Camp Chaffee while he healed up." She'd pulled a wooden frame from the dresser drawer and returned with it to the sofa. "I dug this out the other night. You might as well have it, you bein' in the army and all."

"I'm not *in* the army, Mom, I *work for* the army," Kel answered as he took the frame from his mother. "Big difference."

His mother simply shrugged away the distinction.

"I don't recall ever seein' this," Kel said as he looked up briefly. "Are you sayin' this is Fist Wiggins?"

Anne McKelvey nodded.

The portrait photograph in the frame showed a smiling M. Fritz Wiggins, Jr., an American flag behind his shoulder and a Medal of Honor suspended around his neck by a light-blue ribbon. Kel looked at the handwritten inscription. "I'll be damn—I mean, I'll be. Will you look at that? Autographed and everythin'. So Dad was, what? His aide?"

"He was. For a short while anyway. You're right about that, he didn't talk much about the war. Too many things that he didn't like to remember, I guess. I can't tell you how many times I've rescued that photo from the trash," Anne McKelvey answered. She tugged the blanket over her knees again and resumed reading her book.

"The general must have known Dad pretty well."

His mother's face registered some confusion.

Kel turned the photograph so that his mother could see it. He tapped on the handwritten inscription with his index finger. "Here," Kel replied, "Here, where he wrote, *To my loyal aide, Captain Mac.*"

ACKNOWLEDGMENTS

This story is not intended to be the end of the McKelvey series, but rather was intended to tie up some loose ends from the first two books: *One Drop of Blood* and KIA. I began drafting it a few years ago after I read a somewhat forgotten account of a German prisoner who had been murdered by fellow prisoners at an equally forgotten POW camp in Tonkawa, Oklahoma. I grew up hearing stories of German POWs being held just outside of my home town of Fort Smith, Arkansas, and it pricked my interest. A little digging through the newspaper archives in the Fort Smith city library revealed that the murder at Tonkawa was not an isolated event; another German POW, Hans Geller, had met a similar fate at Fort Chaffee. Today, the land where Fort Chaffee and its POW compound once stood is being developed by the state and the municipalities of Barling and Fort Smith, and construction is now a commonplace occurrence, even if finding skeletons is not. From those facts, a story germinated.

Parts of the plot were discussed with Bob Mann years ago. Bob might just be the second-best forensic anthropologist in the world, and he didn't require me to write that in exchange for giving me the photograph of the skull used on the cover. Written versions of this tale were read, and commented upon, by two excellent writers in their own rights: Marilyn London and Sarah Wagner. I'm sure they both think that I ignored all of their good suggestions. Of course, my long-suffering wife had to wade through the thickest of thicket. Tragically, she sustained a rather severe retinal sprain from rolling her eyes too much, all the while *"blessing my heart,"* in that half-reproach-half-pity sort of way that southern women come to master as small girls. I have to admit that she had us worried—it was touch and go for a while—but she has a strong support group and, with their help and prayers, she now is on the mend; just in time to start reading a new manuscript.

Finally, just to reiterate: This is a work of fiction. Other than the historical events noted in the beginning, the people, businesses, places, events, locales, and incidents described in this shaggy dog tale are either the products of my imagination or are used in a fictitious manner, and any resemblance to actual persons, living or dead, or actual events is purely coincidental. In other words, they exist only in my head, where they talk and argue and play out their lives way too loudly and constantly. I hope this book sells well enough to allow me to finally buy the necessary meds to make them go away.

Turn The Page For A Preview Of:

Their Feet Run To Evil

A Big Ray Elmore Novel

Thomas D. Holland

"For their feet run to evil, and make haste to shed blood."

Proverbs 1:16

Prologue

Locust County, Arkansas

August 3, 1931

Opal Alice should have known better. She'd been told. Her mother knew better and had warned her before she put her on the train from Chicago to Memphis and from there by Greyhound bus to her uncle's house in the Arkansas delta. She was to spend the summer.

She should have known better.

Twelve days earlier, fifteen-year-old Opal Alice Turner left her uncle's farm house with two of her cousins and seventeen cents in their collective pockets. They'd walked two and a half miles to Jim Neel's Drug store where they drank cherry fountain cokes at the plank table out back and purchased inch-and-a-half-diameter cinnamon jaw breakers before tight-roping down the Chicago-Rock Island Railroad tracks past the sluggish oxbow slue known as McKelvey Lake. It was there that Opal Alice first saw him.

He was fourteen and gristled-up with youth and testosterone; already a broom-handle wide at the shoulders. He looked as if he was ready to crow. He was also white.

For all the walls that existed in Locust County, whites and Coloreds mixed freely at the swimming hole. It was as if skins were shed along with garments in the heat. And for a girl as precocious— her local kin called her brazen—as Opal Alice, he was nothing short of a sharp-edged dare tossed into the deep end of the pool; the ripples ever widening—until they encountered something immovable.

She'd giggled when he cannonballed off the yellow-clay cut-bank into turbid green water. Her cousins had told her to hush, which only made her giggle louder and more openly. Defiantly. She'd made eye contact with him when he surfaced and locked onto her gaze, not averting her amber-colored eyes the way she should have; the way the other Colored girls from the area would have. She was city-bred and anxious to prove it to her cousins and all their country-mouse friends. She didn't miss an opportunity to remind them that she was from the broad-shouldered city of Chicago.

It was as much her brashness, this strange girl's taunt, as it was her beauty that made his body thrum in a manner that he hadn't felt before, and he began to swim around her in ever-tightening circles. Like an alligator gar with the scent of crappie.

She should have known better.

And now she was dead.

Chapter 1

Split Tree, Arkansas

Friday, July 12, 1957

"Some folks can be immensely improved upon by a good beatin'," I said. I could have elaborated I suppose, but that about summed up the situation, and I didn't really feel that much useful was to be gained by further explanation. It was an expression my father had used frequently, to great effect, and as I grew older I was becoming more and more impressed with its wholesale validity.

Curtis Jim LaBelle, Jr., looked up at me from the piece of paper he was reading. His glasses were on the end of his nose, and he looked over the thick, plastic frame with a pair of sad, watery brown eyes that would have fit better into the face of a black-and-tan hound than a hard-bitten peckerwood from eastern Arkansas. His thin sandy hair was brushed straight back and fixed with a bay-rum oil. It smelled vaguely like molasses, and in the late summer he would attract an occasional sweat bee if he stood in the sun for too long without moving. He'd been wearing his short-brimmed Stetson earlier, and the sweatband had left a faint red impression on his forehead as if the top of his head had previously been removed and replaced with no worse for the ordeal than a pale-pink surgical scar. "That all you got to say?" he responded. "Shit, Ray, good thing the town council don't pay you to give speeches. You're poor wife and boys would starve."

Curtis Jim LaBelle is an adequate man and an acceptable policeman. Not perfect by any method of figuring, but probably about as good as you could expect to find within a 100-mile radius of where we sat, certainly for the money that the town can afford to pay. He was a few years ahead of me in school, and I've always just assumed that he's a couple of years older than I am, maybe forty-three, possibly forty-four; he always brushes the matter of his age aside with a joke about being weaned while Jesus was still wearing short pants, and over the years I've known him, I've slowly come to the conclusion that maybe he doesn't know his own age with anything approaching the accuracy most white folks take for granted. His momma died bringing him into this world, and his widowed daddy raised him alone on a ten-acre spit-and-pea-gravel farm south of town—at least when he wasn't slicked up on the corn mash he made in a shack out behind his house. It was located about seven miles past the dump, near an old silted-in ox-bow slough that used to breed fevers from late April through the first hard frost. It's gone now, the farm, that is. In late 1941, the Army Air Corps, looking for a location for a practice airfield, took advantage of the lack of any meaningful topography and the abundance of baked floodplain clay and bought the LaBelle place for pennies to nothing. They laid out a lopsided lazy-X of runway in the same field where the two LaBelle's used to bust a gut coaxing heat-stunted cotton from the hard pan and then commenced landing bi-winged training aircraft from sun up to sun down. From what I recall of the LaBelle's place, a lopsided runway was a notable improvement, and I am reasonably certain that Curtis Jim wouldn't bother to muster much of a disagreement if you put the matter to him in polite company.

Best as I recall, his daddy, Curtis Jim Senior, bounced from job to job after the farm was sold. He was a bit touched in the head by then, and he ended up working at the federal cotton compress up in West Helena, where he managed to get hisself crushed in the machinery in 1943 while his son was away down in Louisiana serving with the Coast Guard. The newspaper story described his dismemberment in some degree of colorful detail and even included the comment that he'd ruined over six-thousand-and-fifty pounds of long-staple upland lint. Even put a price on the ruined cotton. When Curtis Junior returned to Split Tree in 1945, there was nothing here for him but his name and his lack of imagination as to where else to go. No more family. No more farm. He'd served some as the Coast Guard liaison with New Orleans police department and learned the lingo of law enforcement, if not something of the procedure, and in a world of limited options, that was enough to decide his future for him. He's been a sworn police officer for the town of Split Tree ever since.

Now, my other officer, Tillman Sparks, is no longer my other officer. He succumbed last fall to what Doc Begley, our coroner, called a faulty mitral valve. Stove up dead in the front seat of the town's best police cruiser two days after Thanksgiving. To make matters worse, he ran the car into a tree by the town's water tank and bent the bumper into a shiny chrome horseshoe that still hasn't been fixed and probably won't for a while given my current operating budget. That's the car I drive now. I'm a small-town police chief and not a medical doctor, so I won't dispute the cause and manner of his death, but I do know that Tillman drank more than a Christian man should, and if it hadn't been a sticky heart valve, it likely would have been a liver wormed out like an old stumpwood fencepost. His position remains vacant, and, most likely will remain so for the foreseeable future; much like the condition of my car's bumper. Money's tight, and the town of Split Tree, Arkansas, is doing its best just to continue justifying the ink used to draw its spot on the map. Besides, two policemen and a part-time secretary are more than adequate to maintain order, and if the chickens do riot, or if a couple-three cows find themselves tipped over on Senior Day, then there's always the Locust County Sheriff's office and the highway patrol to provide back up.

I heard Curtis Jim shift in his chair. Despite keeping my eyes fixed on an old mulberry tree outside my office window, I could sense that he was watching me, and when I finally glanced in his direction, I saw that he was still looking at me over the top of his glasses, as if the act of staring could coax some elaboration out of me. I took a sip of my Grape Nehi, it was flat and room temperature and tasted more like thin grape jelly than soda pop, and reached across the desk for the report that he was so anxious to hand me. "When'd it happen?" I asked as I returned my gaze to the tree outside. A couple of Negro boys were pointing to a squirrel nest in its branches, just beyond their reach. They each held a four-foot stick, and I suspect they meant the squirrel a bad day.

"Last Tuesday night. Says he came home from a meeting and parked in his driveway. When he came out the next day all his tires was flat. He swears the Hudson boys did it. Cut the valve stems."

"Meetin', huh? I can guess." I looked at him as I lit a cigarette. In the sunshine Carl Trimble could pass for respectable, provided you didn't look too close. He was a prominent businessman and an officer in a good many civic groups and organizations. I also knew that one of the organizations that he belonged to met by torchlight once a month in a secluded clearing down by the river. Fact of the matter, I'd known the man the whole of my life and for as long as I can remember, I've thought of him as something best scraped off the bottom of your shoe with a long stick.

Curtis Jim shrugged and smiled. "That ain't none of your matter, boss. What is your matter is that he wants to know what you're plannin' to do about it—about his tires." He absent-mindedly reached down and pulled his pant leg up, scratching a cluster of what I assumed were chigger bites around his ankle. It was that time a year if you wandered into the wrong patch of weeds.

I tossed the report onto a stack near the edge of my desk. I put enough wrist into it that its momentum carried it over the edge and directly into the trashcan. I wish I'd done it intentionally. I pretended I had. "Carl Trimble's a piece of shit. Always has been." I took a deep draw on my cigarette and held it in my lungs for a long time before letting it wisp out slowly through my nose. It added to the thin blue lens of smoke that undulated across the room at shoulder height.

"No argument, boss. None what-so-damn-ever. Unfortunately, while we might make that distinction, the law don't." He paused, "What you want me to do?" As he waited for a response, he wiggled his fingers at me to indicate that I should toss my pack of Luckies to him.

I could feel my jaw tightening at the thought of Carl Trimble, and I had to will it to relax. I waited a good thirty seconds before I answered. "Well, partner, I'd say we've done it. He filed a complaint; you wrote up a report." I nodded at the trash can. "And I just filed it.

I suspect that's about ten minutes more attention than he deserves." I closed my eyes and took a deep breath calculated to keep me buoyant amid the dark mood that I felt myself sinking into. My hip was hurting and getting worse by the minute. Sometimes I swear I can almost feel the sixteen individual screws that the doctors at the navy hospital used to reconstruct my thighbone with. I twisted in my seat and felt and heard a muffled pop as something unforgiving readjusted. I flipped the pack of Lucky Strikes toward Curtis Jim. "I'll talk to the Hudson boys. And their daddy." I sighed. "What else you got?"

He paused scratching while he lit a cigarette and took a puff, enjoying the initial rush of nicotine. He exhaled, blowing the smoke up and away, adding to the lens. "That's about it. Half-dozen complaints about that Rainmaker shootin' off fireworks at night. Somethin' ate up one of Tom Bell's goats last Friday. He's all up in arms about it, but I suspect it was probably one of his own dogs. Last time I was out there, I counted about a damn dozen of them redbone hounds of his. Sons-of-bitches will eat anythin' that don't eat them first."

I continued looking out of the window.

"Ahhh, what else?" Curtis Jim continued. "Oh, Ed Milligan says someone's been hangin' dead blackbirds on his wife's clothesline next to her big ol' brassieres."

I nodded and turned to face him. "That it?"

Curtis Jim screwed his forehead into a knot as he picked up a report. "Well, there's this," he said as he tossed the sheet of paper across the desk. The air caught underneath it, and it started to drift, wafting like a fat autumn sweetgum leaf. I speared it to the brown desk blotter with my palm.

"What's this one?" I asked.

"Probably nothin'. In the sheriff's jurisdiction actually, but I reckon you might be interested in it. Colored woman east of town says her daughter's been missin' for a couple-three days."

Made in the USA
Monee, IL
13 December 2020